FIGHTING ATTRACTION

SARAH CASTILLE

sourcebooks
casablanca

Published by Sourcebooks Casablanca, an imprint of Sourcebooks, Inc.
P.O. Box 4410, Naperville, Illinois 60567-4410
(630) 961-3900
Fax: (630) 961-2168
www.sourcebooks.com

Library of Congress Cataloging-in-Publication Data

Names: Castille, Sarah, author.
Title: Fighting attraction / Sarah Castille.
Description: Naperville, Illinois : Sourcebooks Casablanca, [2017]
Identifiers: LCCN 2016046136 (trade paperback : alk. paper)
Subjects: | GSAFD: Erotic fiction. | Love stories.
Classification: LCC PR9199.4.C38596 F54 2017 | DDC 813/.6—dc23 LC record available at https://lccn.loc.gov/2016046136

Printed and bound in the United States of America.
VP 10 9 8 7 6 5 4 3 2 1

For Bunny, because we should all have someone to cuddle at night

1

I like the bad boys

PENNY

"Rampage!"

"Rampage!"

"Rampage!"

All heads turn as Jack "Rampage" Caldwell enters Miller Stadium in San Francisco for his debut professional MMA fight. Through the shouts and cheers of the near-capacity crowd, I can hear the voices of the Redemption fighters, come to cheer on the most popular member of the team.

Situated in Oakland, Redemption is the premier MMA training facility in Southern California, and Rampage is our newest professional star. Although not an MMA fighter, I work out at Redemption and tag along to all the social events because all my friends there and the Redemption fighters are some of the best, and hottest, guys I know.

"He's loving this." Amanda, my boss and good friend, holds her phone up to snap a picture. "Look at him smile."

Oh, I'm looking. Rampage used to be a super heavyweight fighter, but after a mysterious health scare, he lost a lot of weight and dropped down to the heavyweight class. After going pro and signing with the Mega Extreme Fighting Championship (MEFC) promotion, Rampage got a makeover. His new management team convinced him to crop his thick blond hair and do away with his trademark yellow happy face tank top, although they couldn't do anything about the jagged scar across his throat and the skull-and-crossbones tattoos covering his arms like sleeves. I thought he was hot when I first met him at the gym two years ago, but now he is drop-dead gorgeous.

A shiver runs down my spine as I drink him in. At six feet two inches, with an incredible reach, he is the tallest fighter on the card tonight. His body is almost too perfect, from the massive shoulders to the toned pecs, and from his narrow waist to his slim hips. When he fought as a super heavyweight, he had a lot less definition, but now I count at least eight ridges on his abs, and the mouthwatering V of his obliques is an invitation not to be ignored.

His opponent, Jerry "Juice Can" Jones, is going to be kissing the mats tonight.

"Isn't this the part where you jump on a chair, wave, and scream yourself hoarse? We don't want our front-row seats to go to waste." Amanda brushes back her long, golden curls. "Or does Rampage not warrant the full Penny Worthington treatment?"

An attorney with her own firm in the Lower Haight district of San Francisco, Amanda does sarcasm almost too well. Her fiancé, Jake, a.k.a. Renegade, also a fighter on the Redemption team, just laughs her off. I don't have his thick skin or his ability to cajole her back to good humor when she's annoyed, so I usually fall back on my British stiff upper lip.

"I've matured since the death metal concert incident." I huff and shoot her what I hope is a scathing look. A few years ago, we went to see my favorite band, the Slugs, in concert, and I jumped on the stage and did a little dirty dancing with Vetch Retch, the lead singer. Vetch and I had a couple of dates, and then things went bad, as they always do for me when it comes to men. "I'm not as excitable anymore. In fact, I think I'm…"

My voice trails off when Rampage makes an unexpected detour that will take him right past our seats. Heart pounding, I jump to my feet, scream his name, and pump my fist in the air.

Adrenaline shoots through me, and I get the rush I've been craving all day. My heart beats a little faster, my vision becomes a little clearer, my smile grows a little wider, and all my stress fades away.

"I don't think he heard you," Amanda says. "Maybe it's your British accent. Can you shout in American?" She's all sarcasm tonight. Just to spite her, I scream his name again.

Rampage pauses in front of us, and his gaze lingers on me. His deep-set eyes are sable-brown flecked with gold. He has a strong jaw, wide cheekbones, and a perfectly shaped mouth. The tat on his left arm, a tumble of grimacing skulls and roses, and the faint scars running down the sides of his face only add to his appeal.

I've never been this close to him before a fight, and although he is the same old Rampage—Redemption's gossip king, everyone's best friend, and all-around nice guy—there is something different about him tonight, a darkness, as if he let his mask slip and set the real Rampage free.

My breath catches in my throat as he stares at me. I know that darkness—understand it—because beneath my pearls, pastels, and pretty clothes, I hide darkness, too.

He startles, and then his face smooths over and he gives me the old Rampage grin. "Pen!"

We high-five, my small, pale hand smacking against his massive palm. With a nod for Amanda, he turns away and heads up the stairs to the cage, leaving me with a sore hand, a faint smile, and a perfect view of his tight ass.

"He likes you." Amanda gives me a nudge. "He's always looking at you when you're at the gym."

"That's because we're friends, and he probably can't believe he has a friend as out of shape as me. Check out my total lack of tone." I hold out my arm and flex my nonexistent bicep. "Plus, although he's hot, he's too nice for me. I like a little dark and dirty. I need a bad boy who can rein in my wild side because I can get a little bit out of control."

Amanda snorts a laugh. "Just a little?"

"A teensy bit."

Inside the cage, Rampage slips off his robe and prepares for his fight. He stretches, flexing his arms, rocking up on his toes, curling and uncurling his gloved hands. At a signal from the referee, he touches gloves with Juice Can and immediately moves in with a jab.

I've never been to a professional MMA fight, and the

atmosphere in the stadium is electric. Cameras swing over the cage, flashing close-ups on the big screens for the audience live-streaming the event. Lights flash. The crowd cheers. A woman in a gold bikini holds up a sign that says "I love Rampage," and the ring girls shake and shimmy for the cameras.

Rampage throws a few more punches and slams Juice Can to the canvas like he was flipping a burger at the Redemption summer picnic. Wow. Just wow. Juice Can is supposed to be unbeatable. His last opponent couldn't get him down on the mat once during their bout. Rampage has him kissing the canvas in less than thirty seconds.

Juice Can tries to get up, but Rampage pins him down. Desire pools in my belly. I imagine I am Juice Can, laid out on the floor with Rampage hot, hard, and heavy on top of me, holding me immobile. I give myself a shake. Except for a few disastrous blind dates orchestrated by my bestie, Cora, and a couple of Tinder hookups that never made it past lunch, I've been off the dating circuit since the spectacular media circus that accompanied the end of my relationship with Vetch. Clearly, it's time for me to get my feet properly wet, but the last place I should be fishing is in the Redemption pond.

Juice Can gives up on trying to get Rampage into submission and rockets to his feet. He lands a couple of shots from the outside, but Rampage doesn't seem to notice. Juice Can throws a kick. Big mistake. Although Rampage is a heavy, muscular man, he is surprisingly light on his feet. He dodges the blow and delivers a return kick that almost takes off Juice Can's head. Stunned and desperate, Juice Can shoots in for a takedown.

Rampage sweeps his legs and then follows him down to the mat with shot after shot to the head.

"Take him down," I scream. Although I have resigned myself to friendship, I am not unmoved by the sight of Rampage's powerful body quivering with each blow he delivers or the way he dominates the fight and commands the cage. So unlike the Rampage I know outside the gym. "Knock the bastard out."

"Bloodthirsty tonight, aren't you?" Amanda laughs, but she enjoys a good fight, too. Her fiancé, Renegade, has been moving quickly up the amateur ranks, and she is his number one fan. "But Rampage is too nice. He'll do what it takes to win, but never more than that."

Juice Can taps three times, indicating he gives up. Rampage looks up, sweat glistening on his body, blood trickling from the side of his mouth. Our gazes lock, and in that moment I see power and I see pain. And beneath it all, I see darkness.

Rampage helps Juice Can to his feet. He grins when the referee holds up his hand in a victory salute. Juice Can slams open the cage door as the crowd chants Rampage's name. I jump back up on my chair and cheer for Rampage as Juice Can storms by.

"Fucking cunt." Juice Can kicks the leg of my chair, and I lose my balance, falling into Amanda before I crash to the ground.

"Penny!" Amanda shrieks. Stunned, and praying my fall wasn't caught on TV, I scramble to sit.

I hear a roar, the bang of the cage door, and feet pounding on the concrete floor. A warm, strong hand clasps my arm. Rampage crouches beside me, his face a mask of worry. "Pen? You okay?"

"Fine. I'm fine." I try to wave him away.

"She's British," Amanda says. "*Fine* could mean anything from 'I'm having a heart attack' to 'I'm bleeding to death' to 'I have a paper cut.'"

"I'm good." I put my face between my legs more to hide my embarrassment than anything else. "Please just go. I don't want to cause a fuss."

"I think she's okay." Amanda gives him a reassuring pat on the arm. "I'll get Makayla to check her over before we come to the bar tonight."

Makayla is Amanda's best friend. She is fun and easygoing and pretty much the only person on the planet who can manage the fearsomeness that is Torment, the owner of Redemption. She is also a paramedic and in charge of first aid at the gym.

Rampage gently lifts my head, cups my jaw in his broad palm. "What happened?"

"It was my fault." I lean into the warmth of his hand. "I shouldn't have been up on my chair, and I especially shouldn't have screamed your name when Juice Can passed by. I was taking the piss. He called me a 'fucking cunt' and kicked the leg of my chair, although I don't think he meant to knock me over. That was probably just me being uncoordinated, as usual, or maybe he hit the chair harder than he meant to…" I trail off when Rampage's face morphs from friendly to fierce in a heartbeat. "Rampage?"

With a growl, he jumps up and runs along the edge of the cage. Juice Can is making his way down the aisle to the locker rooms. Rampage shouts. Juice Can turns. Rampage rushes him, knocking him to the ground in the aisle between rows of seats. Excitement ripples through the crowd. Images of Rampage pounding on Juice Can flash on the big screens. Spectators scatter. This is Rampage as I have never seen him before. No holding back. No being a gentleman. No Mr. Nice Guy. He is full-on out of control. A warrior in full battle frenzy.

"Oh God. Someone stop him." I look around for the rest of the Redemption team, and Amanda gasps.

"You're on TV."

I look up, and there I am, twenty feet high and fifteen feet wide, sitting on the floor with my skirt hiked up, my knickers on show, my cheek bruised, and my hair in disarray. *Bloody hell.* Everything I hate about myself is magnified for the whole world to see, from my extra rolls to my chubby cheeks and from my overly generous pasty thighs to the plain white knickers that scream "She doesn't have a boyfriend." The camera pans from me to Rampage and back to me as if the TV crew is trying to figure out why the hell Rampage would risk his career for someone like me when there are a dozen scantily clad toned and tanned ring girls waiting outside his changing room door.

"Kill me now," I whisper.

"The camera is back on Rampage." Amanda helps me to my feet. "Time for a quick escape."

"Is Rampage okay?" I look back over my shoulder, but the crowd is in my way.

"The Redemption team will look after him." She tugs on my arm. "Come on. Let's get you out of here and go see Makayla."

"We don't need to bother her just because I fell off a chair."

I grab my bag and we quickly make our way toward the exit. As a rule, I try to avoid medical professionals, and I'm not about to risk anyone finding out my secret for a few bumps and bruises.

"If you're hurt, I could start a lawsuit for you." Amanda grins. "We didn't do so bad when we sued Vetch Retch."

I force a smile as we walk toward the exit, although inwardly I cringe. Filing a personal injury civil lawsuit against the Slugs' front man after he was found guilty of criminal assault wasn't something I was keen to do, but because he was a public figure and I wanted to make sure no one else went through what I did, I accepted Amanda's offer to drag his sorry ass through court. Just as she predicted, he couldn't handle the negative press. We settled the case out of court and I used the money to buy a little house in Mission Bay, one of San Francisco's newest neighborhoods.

"I think I'll skip the party tonight. I'll never be able to show my face in public again." I make a move toward the side door, but Amanda tugs on my sleeve.

"No way," she says. "If people think it doesn't affect you, then they won't think twice about it. And once we get a few drinks into you, I promise you won't care."

"You're not the one who flashed her knickers for the world to see." But I know it's no use. Once Amanda gets something in her head, there's no changing her mind.

"Hey, guys. Got room for one more?" Jimmy "Blade Saw" Sanchez, a bodybuilder and member of the Redemption team, joins us at the door. Darkly handsome, with the worst relationship luck of anyone I have ever met, Blade Saw is a nice guy, a good friend, and one of the first people I met when I joined the gym.

Amanda's face brightens. "I didn't think you were coming tonight."

"I had a family dinner, but it got cancelled." Blade Saw cracks a smile. "And I gotta be there to celebrate Rampage's big win. I had fifty dollars riding on him winning the fight, and I have to collect."

Damn. How can I let Cora down? I promised I would try to set her up with Blade Saw, and this is the perfect opportunity.

"You're in luck," Amanda says. "We have one extra seat on the direct express to party central. You can keep Penny company in the back while Renegade complains about my driving."

I glance back at the screen where Rampage's fight and my knickers are already on replay. Can I handle more humiliation? And what price will I have to pay when I get home tonight?

2

Who wants a beating?

PENNY

SCORE, A POPULAR LOCAL SPORTS BAR IN CHINATOWN, IS PACKED when we arrive. With ten television screens, good brew on tap, decent pub food, and long, communal tables, it has been the Redemption team's go-to place ever since they were kicked out of their last go-to place for causing too many fights. The exposed brick walls are covered in Oakland decor—Raiders, A's, and Warriors stuff is everywhere—and the delicious scent of chicken wings and beer fills my head.

I spot Cora over by the bar and make my way through the crowd to join her. Despite the short notice, she looks effortlessly put-together in a floaty pink top, fitted paisley blazer, and tight jeans tucked inside a pair of worn cowboy boots. Her thick, blond hair is tied up in a loose ponytail, and her mother's big cameo dangles on a slim gold chain, perfectly finishing off her outfit.

"I only texted you an hour ago," I complain. "And you said you were in class. How did you get home, change, get fabulous, and make it here before me?"

"Desperation." She toasts me with her empty glass. "Plus, I've never met the boys from Redemption, and after hearing all about the mysterious Jimmy 'Blade Saw' Sanchez, I didn't want to waste any time." Cora fell hard for one of her professors during first term, and they had a heated affair until she discovered he was married. With kids. And one on the way. Cora wasn't having any of that crap and sent the bastard packing, but her heart is still a bit bruised, and this is the first time in a long time she's been interested in meeting someone new.

She frowns, taking in the scrape on my forehead, the bruise on my cheek, and the bandage on my finger. "What happened to you?"

"Just a little accident. After Rampage's fight, I got knocked over by his opponent as he stormed out of the stadium. I fell off my chair, and my knickers were live-streamed around the world while Rampage beat up the guy in the aisle."

"Oh, honey." Cora makes a good show of concern for all of three seconds before she laughs in a good-natured bestie kind of way. "Why am I not surprised? You always seem to attract the wrong kind of attention. I hope you were wearing sexy underwear."

Trust Cora to drill right down to what is most important, my health and happiness clearly not being as important as the pattern on my knickers.

"Since I don't have a boyfriend and no hope of ever finding someone who's into overly excitable, clumsy, curvy British girls who like frilly pastels, death metal, and whiskey, I was going for comfort, not seduction," I say dryly. "Plus, it's that time of the month. My knickers are two sizes too big, plain white, and have very little elastic left. Every month I'm amazed they don't fall down."

"People have all sorts of kinks," she assures me. "No doubt there is a man out there who is thinking right now that he has just found his soul mate."

"You think he wants to sleep with my knickers?"

"I've heard worse." She flags the bartender for a refill and follows me to the long table at the center of the bar where the Redemption team has gathered. Blade Saw and Amanda are chatting with Obsidian at the far end of the table. With a movie narrator voice, a drop-dead gorgeous body, and deliciously dark skin, Obsidian always attracts attention whenever we go out. Amanda and Obsidian had a brief fling before she and Renegade got serious, but that's a secret I would never share. Renegade is as possessive and protective as they come.

We find a couple of empty chairs across from Obsidian and Blade Saw, now engaged in a heated argument about whether their favorite professional fighter, Slayer, is coming back from retirement. Cora's gaze flicks from Blade Saw to Obsidian and back to Blade Saw.

"Which one is for me?" she whispers.

I watch her pretending not to look at Blade Saw and laugh. "The one you can't take your eyes off. He's into mechanical stuff, so you two have lots in common."

Until she started her degree in mechanical engineering at San Francisco State University, Cora had never been west of the Mississippi. She introduced me to sweet tea and grits with sausage gravy. She also introduced me to really bad science fiction movies, something for which I have never forgiven her.

"If he doesn't do it for you, there are other options." I wave my hand vaguely over the table. Cora scans the motley crowd of Redemption fighters, some chugging their beer, others arguing over the last of the chicken wings, and, of course, Doctor Death, a blue-eyed, blond-haired Adonis and Redemption's own man whore, trying to charm one of the waitresses into his bed. "Or maybe not."

"How's Pen tonight?" Rampage appears out of nowhere and gives my ponytail a tug. Sometimes I forget he's from Tennessee, but his slightly gruff, soft twangy accent always sends a delicious shiver down my spine.

"Throat's a little sore from screaming myself hoarse after your win, falling off my chair, and being subjected to worldwide humiliation. But otherwise good."

His smile fades, and he crouches beside my chair. "How are you really?"

I shrug, discomfited by his attention and his quiet intensity. Until he went pro, Rampage was just one of the guys I knew at Redemption. We chatted at social events and fights, exchanged numerous high fives and fist bumps, and had the occasional dance at bars. But now that he's gone pro, he's a star. Now he works for MEFC, one of the biggest MMA promotions in the world. He has a manager and an agent, PR and marketing people, lawyers and doctors, coaches and fitness consultants. He has sponsors who give him clothes, bags, and bottles and splash his face all over the Internet. Yes, I think he's hot, but hot sports stars like him don't go for curvy, broken girls like me.

"I'm okay."

"Your cheek is bruised." He strokes a thick finger over my cheek. "And you've got a cut on your forehead."

"Um." His gentleness takes my breath away. This is Rampage. King of the cage. "Yes. But they don't hurt."

His mouth tightens, and I worry for a moment I've done something wrong. Not that I'm afraid of Rampage. He isn't like the fighters who are aggressive both in and out of the cage. He goes in; he fights; he shakes hands; and once the fight is done, he usually buys his opponent a drink. A nicer guy you couldn't hope to meet. Too nice for a girl like me.

Rampage's gaze drifts down my body, and I squirm in my seat, wishing I had dressed up a bit more for the bar instead of wearing my usual pastel tank top, cream sweater, pearls, kitten heels, and floral-patterned skirt. Amanda says I dress the way she always imagined British women dressed for tea in the fifties, but I shop at the same stores as her. I just make different choices.

"What's this?" He lifts my hand, glares at the bandage on my finger.

"It was just a bit sore."

"Sore?" He holds my hand gently in his palm and strokes my bandaged finger. "Christ. I was too easy on him. I should have broken more than his nose."

"You broke his nose?" My voice rises with concern. "Is MEFC going to kick you out?"

Rampage drops my hand, and I feel instantly bereft. "Nah. I'll probably just get off with a warning. Juice Can made the mistake of bumping into the wife of one of the California State Athletic Commission's officers before I got to him. It's not the first time he's pulled a stunt like that. Looks like he'll be suspended, and they'll cut me some slack 'cause my manager, James, told them you were my girlfriend."

"Girlfriend?" I force a laugh. "Well, if it helps you out of a bind, I'm happy to play along. Just don't expect me to kiss you or anything."

My attempt at humor falls flat. Rampage studies me for a long moment and looks away. "No, of course not."

Desperate to move past the awkward moment, I introduce Cora to Rampage, Blade Saw, and Obsidian. She dazzles them with her smile.

"Why don't you use their real names?" she asks when the waitress comes to take their orders.

"I dunno. At the gym, Torment has a ring-name-only rule for the fighters who have earned one. I suppose it's a way of acknowledging their hard work. But if you hang around the gym enough and always use those names, you forget what their real names are. Or in the case of Obsidian, you don't even know and after a while it becomes too embarrassing to ask. When we're all together like this, we all use ring names. I don't even think about it anymore."

Rampage stands and excuses himself. "Gotta do the rounds, ladies. I'll catch up with you later."

A tiny frown crinkles Cora's perfect brow. "The rounds?"

"He's Rampage. Even though this party is for him, he'll make his way around the table, talking to everyone, getting the gossip, making sure everyone's glass is filled and there's enough food. He'll ask about their girlfriends, boyfriends, mothers, aunts, and kids. He knows who just got a new job, who lost a job, who got divorced, and who just bought a new car. He'll shake hands, pat backs, and kiss cheeks, but not in a slimy politician kind of way. He's genuinely interested in everyone at Redemption, and he's just that kind of guy."

Cora watches Rampage flag down a waitress to fill Amanda's glass. "A perfect Southern gentleman, and that accent…"

"He really is." A smile tugs at the corners of my mouth. "At least until he gets into the cage."

"You like him." She tears her gaze away from Rampage. "Why didn't you tell me about him?"

"Because he's just a friend. We fist-bump. He tugs my ponytail and calls me 'Pen.' Sometimes we compete in submission dummy tossing at the gym, although I get a handicap because the dummies weigh about eighty pounds. We play drinking games together, which I always lose, and we gossip about people at the gym. I've been trying to find him a girlfriend, but he doesn't like any of my choices."

"Maybe he's already found her." She gives me a nudge, and I look up to see Rampage watching me from the other side of the table.

"Still alive," I say to him. "It takes more than a fall from a chair to really hurt me."

"Don't like the idea of you being hurt in any way, darlin'."

Darlin'. He's never called me *darlin'* before. And in that accent… My mouth waters as I conjure up all sorts of naughty things Rampage and I might do together as he whispers Southern-style *darlin's* in my ear in that soft Tennessee twang.

"That's because you don't know me very well. I like pain."

"You don't strike me as a masochist." A curious expression crosses his face—part thoughtful, part longing—but it passes so quickly, I wonder if I saw it.

"I'm not." Horrified at the truth I never meant to share, I hold up my injured hand and wiggle my bandaged finger to make my admission seem like a joke, although it's not. Pain is part of me—an inescapable component of my life. "See. Doesn't hurt. I'm thinking I should take up MMA seriously instead of watching everyone while I work out. I can take a beating and be ready for another go the next day."

I press my lips together to shut myself up. Damn. I don't know what's wrong with me tonight.

"Who wants a beating?" Doctor Death pulls up a chair and squeezes into the tiny space between Cora and me. Redemption's man whore didn't get his reputation by ignoring a new and very pretty face, and Cora won a few beauty pageants before she gave up the stage to become an engineer.

"Now, here's your masochist," I say to Rampage, relieved to have a diversion, even if the diversion already has a hand on my thigh. "He wants to be hurt. Otherwise his hand would be on the table and not on a place it shouldn't be."

Rampage's face creases in a scowl, and I knock Doctor Death's hand away.

"Penny. Darling." Seemingly unfazed by my rejection,

Doctor Death pecks me on the cheek. "Introduce me to your friend, and please tell me she's joining the gym. We need more beautiful women to brighten the place up."

"Cora Montgomery, meet Doctor Donald Drake, otherwise known as Doctor Death. He is one of California's foremost heart surgeons, an MMA fighter, and ring doctor at Redemption. Doctor Death, meet Cora. She's doing her degree in mechanical engineering at SF State."

Doctor Death's eyes widen. "I'm definitely sitting on the right side of the table. I don't know which of you to sleep with first."

"Don't mind him," I say to Cora. "If you tell him to stop, he'll stop. Basically, he's oversexed, an incorrigible flirt, but harmless."

An hour later, after the fighters at the table have discussed the fight to death, Cora and I head to the bar for a change of scenery and discreet conversation.

"What did you think of Blade Saw?" I lean against the worn wooden counter and try to catch the bartender's eye.

"He's all sorts of hot. Very sweet. Funny. I like how dedicated he is to the sport." She smiles at the bartender. He winks and gestures that he'll be right over. Sigh.

"What about you?" she asks. "I can't believe you've been hanging around so many gorgeous men and you haven't asked any of them out. Rampage is really into you."

"The guys at Redemption are friends, almost like brothers." I try the smile-at-the-bartender routine and get a cold stare in return. "I want a bit of danger. A thrill. I want someone who lives on the edge."

"You want another man who's going to beat you like Vetch Retch? That's the kind of thrill you want?" Cora bristles, now in full-on protective mode. Even when I've had too much to drink and I'm making an ass of myself, Cora has my back. When she found out Vetch hit me on one of our dates, I had to physically restrain her from going after him. She only backed down after Amanda's private investigator, Ray, also known as "the Predator" at Redemption, dragged Vetch into an alley to teach him a lesson that involved more than one broken bone.

"Go out with the nice guy." She gestures to Rampage, who is playing darts with Blade Saw at the back of the bar. "We'll double-date."

"How about you go out with the nice guy and invite me to your wedding?"

"How about we get a couple of Mai Tais and head over to the pool table where we can have a game while watching your Redemption friends bend over to pick up fallen darts?"

"Is no an option?" I glance over at the dartboard and catch a glimpse of Rampage's beautiful, tight ass outlined in blue denim.

Cora follows my gaze and laughs. "Definitely not."

After we get our drinks, we head over to the pool table. Cora strikes up a conversation with Rick, a thin dude with long, dark hair, and his ponytailed friend, Jim, who is wearing a "Bassists Go Down" T-shirt beneath a leather vest, cut to show off his two full sleeves of tats. We chat with them a bit and they invite us to join them.

I never played pool until I came to America, but after my first game with Cora, I was hooked. We went out every weekend, and I practiced until I had blisters on my fingers. Although I can now hold my own at a table, I'm nowhere near as good as Cora, who learned how to play when she was young and never misses an opportunity for a hustle.

"I noticed you when you walked in," Jim says as I lean over to rack the balls. "All sweet and sexy. I'll bet underneath those girly clothes, you're a wildcat inside. How about we make the game more interesting?" He discreetly waggles a small cellophane envelope of white powder with a happy face sticker on it beneath his jacket.

"How about I just ride the high from our win?"

"Don't be so uptight, sexy girl." Jim comes up behind me when I turn back to the table. "Our place is just around the corner. We can all go there after the game, have a little fun…" He leans closer, his breath hot on the back of my neck. "You look like you could use a little excitement."

My breath catches in my throat. Jim is the kind of guy I usually go for—a little bad, a little dangerous—and if Cora comes with me, I won't have to worry about something going wrong. But there's something about him that makes me uneasy, and when I think about being alone with him, my heart pounds, and not in a good way.

"Who's going to break?" I step back, but Jim doesn't step with me. Instead, he plasters himself against my back, winds one arm around my middle, and grinds his crotch into my ass.

"Stop it. We just want to play pool." I try to pull away, but he tightens his grip.

"You being a tease?" he murmurs in my ear. "Bending over

the table showing off those sweet tits, wiggling that beautiful ass until I'm so fucking hard I can't…"

And then he's gone.

Rampage shoves Jim face-first into the wall, his hand around Jim's neck. On the other side of the table, Blade Saw grabs Rick's collar, keeping him out of the fight.

"You got a problem with the word *no*?"

"It's okay." I put my hand on Rampage's massive tatted forearm. "I had it under control."

"Got real tired of watching him trying to get under your skirt." Rampage shakes my hand away. "This is the kind of fucker who's gonna take advantage. He's gonna hurt you. Sweet girl like you needs to be with someone decent. I don't know why you keep going after the trash. Makes me worry about the nights you go out when I'm not around."

"Ouch." I step away, swallow past the lump in my throat.

"I'm telling you like it is because I'm your friend." He drops his voice so only I can hear. "Friends watch out for friends. And right now this fucker is going for a walk, and you're not going with him." He grabs the back of Jim's shirt with his free hand and frog-marches him out of the bar. Blade Saw gives Rick a shove and follows them out.

"So you're just friends?" Cora raises a quizzical eyebrow.

"Yeah," I say. "Just friends."

3

Go home, Pen

PENNY

BETWEEN THE HUMILIATION OF FRIDAY, THE ALCOHOL, AND A late-night party with Cora's university friends on Saturday night, I get very little sleep over the weekend and arrive at Amanda's office on Monday morning in a very bad mood.

"So, how was the fight on Friday?"

Ray "the Predator" Black, Amanda's private investigator, Redemption fighter, and permanent resident on Amanda's client couch, peers over his newspaper as I walk into the office. He's the only person I know who reads an actual physical newspaper. He's also the only person I know who would beat up a celebrity in a dark alley to avenge me and pretend it wasn't him. Although he's now married, he is very protective of me in an overbearing-brother kind of way.

"Fine." I'm not interested in talking. I am interested in coffee, and lots of it. Ray and I have an unspoken understanding that whoever gets to the office first has to make the coffee, and if he's shirked his duty today, I'm going to kill him.

"I heard Rampage won his fight and you were on TV," he says casually, although Ray is not a casual man. Rumor has it that he used to be in the CIA, and from some of the things that happened when he first hooked up with his wife, Sia, I suspect the rumors are true. "I also heard that Rampage beat up Juice Can 'cause he knocked you over, and some dude in Score who was hitting on you," he continues.

Damn. Gossip at Redemption spreads faster than it did at secondary school. "If you know everything, why are you asking me?" I grab the coffeepot and fill my cup. Everyone thinks that because I'm British, I drink tea, but I've been a coffee drinker since I left home at the age of seventeen.

"I like to get my information from the source."

I add a little cream and sugar and take my first sip. My tension eases a tiny bit as the warm, bittersweet liquid slides over my tongue. This is definitely going to be a three- or four-coffee day. "Your source confirms the information you already have, except you missed the bit about me having the bar situation under control and being irritated that Rampage interfered. Maybe I wanted to go home with the guy. Maybe he was the one and I lost my chance. Maybe I learned something hanging around the gym and could have knocked him flat with one hand tied behind my back. Can I get to work now?"

Ray snorts a laugh. "If Rampage stepped in, then the guy was no good."

"Maybe I like the no-good guys."

"Yeah. Picked that up when you walked in here with a busted-up face after a night out with Vetch Retch. Not going to let it happen again. Rampage feels the same."

My next sip of coffee scalds my tongue, and I try to not choke on the burning liquid. "How do you know how he feels?"

"I know."

I heave an exasperated sigh. "Well then, why does he care? He's a big sports star now, a pro fighter. I'm sure he has other things to think about than Penny the legal assistant who drags her ass to Redemption three times a week for a workout so she can enjoy the occasional piece of cake, or three."

Ray crosses his feet and leans back on the couch. "We got each other's backs at Redemption. Everyone cares."

Everyone. Disappointment worms its way into my chest, and I quickly change the subject before I give myself away. "Shoes." I point to his feet, and he swings his feet down with an irritated groan.

"They're clean."

"They're on your feet, so they're not clean." I take another sip of coffee, and the cobwebs start to clear from my head. "Although Amanda tolerates your bad behavior at the office, I have a feeling Sia might have something to say about it. And, if this was my office, your feet would be staying on the floor."

Ray's face softens at the mention of his wife, Sia, the owner of the tattoo parlor in the massive warehouse that houses Redemption. "She's eased up on me since Sam was born," he says. "As long as I pull my weight."

"Which you're doing by lounging on Amanda's couch and reading the paper?"

"I was reading about the fight." He turns the paper around and shows me a grainy picture of Rampage in the cage.

"I'd never been to a professional MMA fight before." I top up my coffee and add more cream. "It was very different from the amateurs and those underground events you like to go to. Very glitzy and very public. You could see every drop of sweat, every grimace... I couldn't do something like that. I'm a shy, retiring type of person."

Ray barks a laugh. "You try to make people think that, with those frilly clothes, but there's a lot more to you than you let on. Cotton candy girls don't like death metal, Pen. They don't jump up on stage at a concert and go fucking crazy with the front man. They listen to their friend when he warns them the guy's no good..."

My lips press together, and I shoot Ray a warning look. He knows better than to go there. I haven't dated anyone since Vetch, and Ray knows it. Ray also knows what happened in the alley behind Vetch's hotel shortly after I walked into the office covered in bruises, although he has never talked about it. No one hurts people Ray cares about, and although we're just friends, he cares about me.

"Cotton candy girls." I huff as I walk into my office, a cozy room just off the reception area, with big windows overlooking the street. "That doesn't even make sense."

"Shy and retiring," Ray mutters behind me. "That doesn't add up."

Amanda goes straight into a client meeting when she arrives, and I help her associates, Jill and Dana, get her documents ready for her court hearing in the afternoon. When she comes into my office to collect her boxes a few hours later, all dressed up in her new dove-gray suit, I feel a little stab of jealousy. My mom wore a suit every day for her job as a marketing executive. I used to dress up in her clothes and carry a briefcase around the house, dreaming of the day I'd go to work in a suit, too. But it was never meant to be. Now, I'm on the outside looking in, watching someone else live my dream.

"Did the process server show up yet?" Amanda loads files into her briefcase. "We need to serve papers on Club Sin tonight. It took me longer than I thought to draft the claim because the tenant hasn't breached any terms of the lease, but I promised Gerry Turner we would get his lawsuit started before he leaves for vacation tomorrow. He wants that sex club out of his building as soon as possible."

"I just got a call that the process server is running late," I say. "I was planning run some errands after work and it's on my way home. I don't mind dropping them off. That way we can be sure they get served tonight." Amanda's new client, Gerry, is a real estate magnate who owns almost an entire city block in the South of Market (SoMa) District as well as other properties in the city that he leases out at exorbitant rates. Although he could get Club Sin to vacate the premises with proper notice under its lease or by waiting for the lease term to expire, he doesn't want to wait because he's had an offer from a developer who wants to tear down the building and turn the block into a shopping center. The deal is time sensitive and worth a lot of money, and Gerry is getting desperate.

"They don't open until eight tonight..." Amanda's voice trails off, but she looks so hopeful that I can't let her down.

"No problem. I was planning to be down there for a few hours. Plus, I've never been to a sex club before, and I'm curious to see what goes on inside a place with a name like Club Sin."

Ray offers to drive Amanda to court, and I leave our receptionist, Mari, to close the office while I head downtown. I run my errands and browse the racks at Nordstrom, lingering over the suits for so long I'm sure I've attracted the attention of the store's undercover detectives. Just after eight, I head over to SoMa and park a few blocks away from the club.

My phone GPS leads me to a massive brown four-story brick building that goes back half a city block. All the ground-floor tenants have Going Out of Business signs in their windows, but I can't find a door or a sign for Club Sin. After my second walk up and down the street, I spot a woman dressed in a black corset, skirt, and thigh-high boots. I follow her down the alley to a gray metal door. When she slides a card through a reader on the wall, I kick it into gear and catch her before she enters the building.

"Is this Club Sin?"

She startles and frowns. "Why do you want to know?"

I show her the envelope with the company name on it. "I have to give this to Damien Stone."

"Come on in." She motions me forward. "I'll let Master Damien know you're here."

Master Damien. A thrill of excitement shoots through me. Although I've heard about BDSM clubs, I never thought about actually visiting one. Except for Vetch, I've led a pretty conservative life as far as sex and relationships go.

My pulse kicks up a notch, and I follow the woman down the brightly lit stairwell and into a spacious reception area decorated with framed pictures of people suspended from the ceiling, attached to giant wooden crosses, shackled to tables, and hanging from what look to be giant swings. Despite the photos, which are at once terrifying and titillating, the foyer is tastefully decorated in red and gold, with sparkly tiled floors, gilt mirrors, and a large red velvet couch. A crystal chandelier twinkles above the ornate gold reception desk.

My guide introduces me to the receptionist, Kitty, and excuses herself to find Master Damien. I catch the clink of glassware, the murmur of voices, and the distinctive sound of a scream as she exits the reception area through a heavy wooden door.

"It's early, so it's still quiet," Kitty says. "I don't think Master Damien is busy, so you won't have to wait long." She smooths her hand over her electric blue corset, heavily embroidered and trimmed with black lace that barely covers the crescents of her breasts. I've never seen anything more beautiful in my life.

Ten minutes pass. Twenty. Forty. More people enter the club, usually in groups of two or three. Despite the wide variety of clothing—some people are dressed like the woman from the alley, some in leather, and some in normal street clothes—I feel overly conspicuous in my pink miniskirt, white cashmere sweater, and kitten heels.

After an hour, Kitty takes pity on me and sends a text to someone inside. "If he's in the middle of a scene, you might have a long wait." She gives me an apologetic smile. "I've been a member here for five years, and I've never once seen Master Damien allow an interruption. That's him in most of the photographs."

I glance up at the pictures where people are being teased and tortured, spanked and whipped, and yet it is not pain on their faces but pleasure. Erotic pleasure. My hand drifts to my thighs, scarred after years of abuse. I get relief from my pain and, in that release, pleasure.

Seized with an almost-desperate longing to go inside, I pull out my purse. "Could I go in and look for him? Or just wait inside? I'll pay the entrance fee."

"Members only." She points to a sign on the wall. "Even if I let you into the lounge, Master Damien won't be there. We have a separate play area exclusively for members who are concerned about privacy. That's where Master Damien will be. Except for Master Jack, he's the most sought-after Dom in the club, which is why he's always so busy." She hesitates, shrugs. "He knows you're here. It's all about control with the Doms. He'll come when he thinks the time is right."

Control? Or does he just not want to be served? Clearly, forcing the issue isn't going to work. But patience always wins out in the end.

"Could you let him know that I plan to wait here until closing?" I settle back on the couch. "You could also pass on the message that if he doesn't come out, then we'll get an order for substituted service. If he's big into control, he might not like that because it means he might lose control of the proceedings because he might not get notice of court dates or of any further applications we file."

Kitty gives a nervous laugh. "That's not the kind of message Master Damien is going to like to hear. If I don't come back, or if I come back and I don't sit down, you'll know what he thought about it."

After she leaves, I pace around the reception area, fiddling with the ring I wear on a chain around my neck. Although there are no good memories associated with the ring, I can't bear to part with it, but sometimes it really weighs me down.

Finally, Kitty returns, her face flushed. "He says if you sign a waiver, you can go in."

My pulse kicks up a notch when she hands me the document. "Where's the pen?"

"You should read it first."

"I've seen lots of liability waivers," I tell her. "And I'm not planning to stay, so there is little risk of anything happening to me. I'm in, and then I'm out."

"It's not that kind of waiver."

With a sigh, I sit and read over the short document in which I am asked to confirm that I am over the age of eighteen, agree to all activities that take place in the club, hold the owner and attendees harmless from damages or injuries, and agree that anything I hear or see will be kept confidential, including the identity of club members. No cell phones or recording devices are allowed. Violation of the agreement or the club rules will result in legal and/or civil action or punishment as the owner sees fit.

"Punishment?" My hand hovers over the signature line. "What do they mean by *punishment*?"

Kitty turns around to show me the bright red backs of her thighs. I can just make out actual handprints on her skin.

"Oh. My. God." I stare at her in shock after she turns back around. "He did that to you because of my message?"

"He did it because I left the reception desk unattended without permission." A smile spreads across her face. "Isn't it hot? Most of the submissives here would die to get a spanking from Master Damien."

A thrill of fear runs through me, but when I make a move to the door, she hands me another document. "You need to read and sign this, too."

"Seriously?" I take the papers. "I'm only going to be in there for five minutes. Four if I walk fast."

Kitty laughs. "He thinks you'll be longer than that."

Five minutes later, I follow Kitty into the belly of the beast. My heart pounds wildly as I step through the door, only to thud to a stop when I see nothing more than a fancy bar—long sweeping counter, shelves full of bottles, leather chairs, a few tables, televisions in the corners... But wait. Is that a man on a leash?

The surroundings may be ordinary, but the people are not. I see everything from nudity to corsets, from leather straps to lace, and from rubber to chains.

"Master Damien doesn't allow any play in this area," she says. "It's just for relaxing."

"Sure," I say, although how relaxed can a person be kneeling on the floor in a collar and leash?

She nods to two burly bouncers, and they open a steel door at the side of the bar. "These are the private fetish and play rooms." Kitty gestures me into the hallway. "Don't forget that the waiver you signed means you can't tell anyone what or who you see in here."

I glance down at her still-pink thighs and swallow hard. "Yeah, I got that message."

Wide and spacious, with shiny black marble tiles, deep purple–painted walls, ornate sconces, and wrought-iron chandeliers, the hallway is at once sensual and frightening. We pass several closed doors and a few with windows, curtains open to reveal rooms containing everything from padded benches to cages.

"Watch yourself here." Kitty draws me to one side. "This is the whipping alcove for longer implements, like single tails."

I startle at the crack of a whip and glance into the alcove, dimly lit and painted a deep red. A woman in red lingerie is bound face-first to a large wooden cross. Behind her a tall, muscular man with short, dark hair raises his whip. He is wearing leather pants and a black T-shirt. From the back, he is breathtaking. Broad shoulders narrow to slim hips, a tight toned ass, and muscular thighs.

Something niggles at the back of my mind, and I pause as he cracks the whip, the motion both smooth and powerful, his lats bunching and flexing as he lets it glide, the tip brushing over the woman's exposed buttocks. She screams and arches her back, her hands straining against her restraints.

"Did I give you permission to scream?" His deep, rich, commanding voice sends a familiar tingle down my spine.

"No, sir."

"That's Master Jack," Kitty whispers. "He's a sadist. He'll only play with the most experienced submissives, and even then, he's very selective." She tugs on my arm, but I can't move. Whether it's the scene or the man, I don't know, but I cannot tear myself away.

Master Jack strikes the woman again. Light glints off the tats on his left arm, but I can't make out the designs. The woman arches against the cross, and I cringe at the red welts covering her back, although I see no blood. The whip cracks again, and she gasps, her legs giving out until she is held up solely by the restraints.

"Yellow," she says, her voice hoarse.

"We have a safety system," Kitty explains. "Red means stop. Yellow means slow down or she's not sure she can take anymore. Green means go."

Master Jack carefully replaces the whip on the rack on the wall and walks across the floor to the woman on the cross. His leather pants creak with every stride of his long legs, and his boots thump on the floor. He is all raw power and lean grace and so achingly familiar I shake off Kitty's insistent tug. I have to see his face.

After a brief conversation with the woman, he turns, and his gaze locks on me.

Rampage.

My hand flies to my mouth, but I can't suppress a gasp. How can Redemption's gossip king, all-around good guy, everyone's best friend, professional athlete, and the epitome of chivalry be here, whipping a woman until she screams?

His eyes narrow and harden, and then he turns away as if he doesn't know me. He retrieves the whip and strikes the woman again.

"We have to go," Kitty insists. "Master Damien doesn't like to be kept waiting."

Still in shock, I follow her to an office at the end of the hallway. A dark-haired man wearing a sleek Italian suit and crisp white shirt open at the neck greets us from behind his desk. Power radiates from him, and he fills the ornately decorated room with the force of his presence alone.

"Are you Damien Stone?" Still reeling from my encounter with Rampage, I barely register Kitty backing out the open door.

"I am." He holds out his hand. "I believe you have something for me."

I hand him the envelope and pull out my cell phone to make a note of the time.

"Cell phones aren't allowed in the club." He rips open the envelope. "You agreed to that when you signed the waiver."

"I was just noting the time. We need it for the affidavit of service." I hold up the phone for him to see, and he gives me a cold, hard stare.

"You also agreed to be punished if you broke the rules, which you just have done."

My blood chills, and I take a quick glance behind me to make sure the door is still open. Although Kitty has disappeared, the hallway is empty, and my escape route is clear. "I wasn't taking pictures or recording anything."

"There are no qualifications to the rule." He skims the

documents and tosses them on his desk. "And since you seem determined to put me out of business, I see no reason to exercise any leniency."

"Whoa." I take a step back and then another, my hands flying up in a defensive position. "First of all, I'm not a lawyer or the claimant in the case. I'm just serving the documents. And second, I haven't done anything wrong. I didn't agree to be punished for doing my job."

Damien rounds on me, moving so quickly I stumble in my haste to retreat. "You did agree. Now, I'm wondering how best to teach you a lesson."

"If you touch me, I'll scream."

Amusement glints in his eyes, and he reaches for my hair, tangling my ponytail around his hand before he yanks, forcing my head back. "Scream, then. I love the sound."

Maybe he thinks I'm one of those women who don't like to cause a scene, a woman who's afraid of the adrenaline rush, a woman who can't take a bit of pain. Boy, has he pegged me wrong.

I scream. Just like I screamed in delight when Vetch Retch picked me out of the crowd and pulled me onstage; like I screamed in horror when I caught the love of my life in bed with another woman; like I screamed with joy when Rampage won his fight.

Footsteps ring out in the hall behind me.

"What the fuck?" Rampage storms into the office, chest heaving, a scowl on his handsome face. "Christ, Damien. What are you doing?"

For a moment, I am stunned into silence. He is breathtaking. And not just because he is wearing tight leathers, snug in all the right places, and a form-fitting T-shirt that shows off every ripple of his abs. He is beautiful in his darkness, glorious in his anger, and my body trembles when he catches my gaze.

Master Damien tightens his grip on my hair. "She signed the agreement. She broke the rules. She threatened to scream if I touched her. You know I can't resist a challenge."

"Let her go."

Electricity crackles in the air between them. Although the two are evenly matched in presence, Rampage is taller by at least two inches, broader, and more muscular. And, seriously, does Master Damien really think he can compete with a professional MMA fighter in his prime?

Still, Master Damien is clearly not a man to be pushed around. With a jerk of his chin he directs Rampage's attention to the papers on his desk. "She served the club. Gerry Turner made his move. He's trying to shut us down."

"Fucking bastard."

"My thoughts exactly." Master Damien gives my hair a tug. "I thought I'd take out my frustrations on this little rule breaker."

"Then you're no better than Turner." Rampage lifts an eyebrow in warning. "I'll deal with her."

"She waited four hours to come in." Master Damien finally releases me, and I rub my head. "You'd better give her a taste of what she wants."

Rampage's gaze flicks over me, and he clasps my hand. "Come." He stalks out of the room, half leading, half dragging me behind him. The hallway becomes a blur of light and color until he pushes open a side door and leads me into a small parking lot behind the building.

"You signed the waiver?" he asks, releasing me so abruptly I stumble back.

"Yes, but…"

"Then you understand you don't talk about anything you saw here." His lips press together, and he fixes me with a glare. "And if you even think about it, what Master Damien was going to do is nothing compared to what I will do."

My mouth opens and closes again, and my brain is unable to reconcile this fierce, angry, threatening man with the Rampage I know who has only ever been violent in the ring or with people who have wronged someone he cares about.

"I'm sorry. I didn't know you were here. Amanda needed someone to serve the documents."

"Amanda." He rakes his hand through his hair and shakes his head. "Christ. I didn't know she was involved."

"I won't tell her about you." I pull out my phone and hold it up. "I just recorded the time of service. That's all that goes in the affidavit. Time, address, and confirmation of identity. Nothing else."

Rampage heaves a sigh. "Where are you parked? I'll walk you to your car. It's too late for you to be walking around here alone at night."

He walks silently beside me down the road. I have so many questions about the club and what he does and what goes on and what he was doing with that woman, and isn't he worried someone will find out and destroy his professional career? But mostly I want to know if I can become a member and if he will do that with me. However, his grim demeanor dissuades me from saying anything more than "This is my car" when we reach the parking lot.

"I'm sorry," I say again as I unlock the door.

"Stop saying that."

"Sorry—" I cut myself off when he glares. "It's a British thing. Tea and apologies are part of our DNA. If someone knocks you down in the street, you say sorry for getting in his or her way. And anytime anything happens—death, war, marriage, babies—we have tea." I give a little shrug and continue to babble. "Well, except for me because I like coffee. I don't suppose…"

"Go home, Pen."

I can't tell from his tone whether it's pity he feels for me, disgust, or anger. But I do know something is broken between us. I feel like I've just lost a friend.

So I go home. And then I take out my little box of razor blades and cut myself until all my pain goes away.

Why are you looking at me like that?

RAMPAGE

UNTIL YESTERDAY, MY LIFE WAS STABLE. I HAD MADE IT IN THE MMA world, finally going pro after years of training. Blade Saw and I had finally turned a profit in our distillery business. My sometime play partner, Sylvia, had finally accepted that our relationship was never going to extend outside Club Sin despite that one hot night we had together after a party. I had a room at the club where I could indulge my kink without any risk of public exposure. And I had resigned myself to being forever alienated from my family.

Now, everything has gone to hell.

And all because of Penny.

Shifting on the weight bench in the middle of Redemption, I press the bar straight up above my chest. Blade Saw, my spotter, makes approving noises behind me, while around us people grunt, groan, run, jump, punch, kick, row, strike, and grapple in the twenty-five-thousand-square-foot warehouse that Torment built from the shell of a packing crate factory. When I first joined Redemption, we had a few mats, a makeshift fight ring, and a rack of free weights. Now we have a cardio area with three long rows of equipment, a sea of weight machines, benches and free weights, rowing machines, and stretching mats. The walls have been painted bright shades of blue, red, and green, and over in the practice area, grapple dummies line the walls like an army of soldiers. After I accepted MEFC's offer to go pro, I could have trained at any gym in the country. But Redemption is my home.

I try to focus on the bar, on the burn in my arms, on the drumroll of speed bags and the whirr of the cardio machines, the clank of weights, the scents of sweat and vinyl mats, and the murmur of voices, but all I can think about is her.

Damn Damien for letting her into the club. Although he had no way of knowing we knew each other, he could have just met her in reception instead of telling Kitty to bring her to his office. What the hell was he thinking? And Penny. Christ. Just the thought of her at Club Sin makes my stomach twist in a knot. I can't imagine anyone less suited to a BDSM club, or anyone I would have wanted less to discover my secret. Penny is the antithesis of Club Sin. She is sweetness and light, delicate and feminine, soft and pretty. Definitely not the girl for me. Been there. Done that. Got my heart ripped out to prove it. Learned the hard way what happens when darkness meets light.

"Whoa, buddy." Blade Saw grips the bar, catching it as my arms shake. "You've never had trouble with that weight before. What's up?"

"Nothing." I sit up, run my hand through my hair. If there's one thing I've learned over the years, it's how to hide what I feel and who I am. Even Blade Saw, my best friend and business partner, doesn't know about Club Sin.

"Maybe you should've taken a day off after the big fight." He racks the bar for me and pulls off the weights. "You could have gotten lucky last night. That ring girl who was falling all over you after the fight was at Score asking about you."

"Not my type," I mutter.

"What about Penny?" He adds lighter weights to the bar, and we change positions. "The way you went after that bastard over at the pool table, I thought you were finally gonna make your move."

"What do you mean 'finally'?" I lift the bar off the rack and hold it while Blade Saw lies on the bench and adjusts his grip.

He looks up at me and grins. "Everyone knows you've got a thing for her. That's why we all stay away."

"I don't have a fucking thing for her." I purposely drop the weight a few seconds before he's ready, and he grunts in annoyance. "She's a friend."

"Sure. You risked your career beating on Juice Can in the middle of the stadium after a professional fight 'cause she's a friend."

"You want that bar on your fucking throat?" I don't know what the hell is wrong with Blade Saw. Usually he's the most laid-back member of the team, always chill, never rocking the boat, never prying into a dude's business…

He pushes the bar up, his arms shaking with the effort. "So."

He locks and lowers, straining against the weight. "If you're not interested in Penny, I'm gonna ask her out."

Jesus fucking Christ. Not going to happen. I can't have her, and it's not fair of me to stand in the way, but Blade Saw and Penny?

"Her friend Cora was checking you out." I try a diversion tactic instead of breaking my best friend's arm.

"Seriously?" Blade sits up on the bench. "She was hot, and my family would love to see me with a Southern girl."

As did mine. And now Avery is part of the family. Just not with me.

"I didn't think she'd go for a guy who only had a business degree," he continues. "She's super smart. She's getting a master's in engineering."

"You're not a moron." I pat him on the back. "I wouldn't have gone into the distillery business with you if you were."

"Gee, thanks."

His gaze flicks over to the workout area where Fuzzy, a cop by day and MMA coach by night, is teaching his Punch or Perish class that I'm doing my best not to watch because Penny and Cora are there. So far, I've only looked over every thirty seconds or so, preparing myself in case Penny gets it into her head to talk to me about last night.

"Maybe they'd be interested in a threesome," he muses. "I could have them both."

Don't hit him. Don't hit him. Don't hit him.

I hit him.

"What the fuck?" Blade Saw jumps up, holding his jaw. Fucking pansy. It was only a light jab.

"Slipped."

His face twists into a scowl. "You think I don't know you, but I do. What's the worst that can happen? You ask her out and she says no. You move on. Look at me. I fell for Sandy. Got dumped. Got back together with her. Got dumped. Fell for Jess. Got dumped. Not much of my heart left, but I'm still standing and taking shit from you."

"I'm not good for her," I say honestly. "She's sweet and innocent. She looks like she stepped out of one of those romance movies where they run through fields of flowers. She needs a good guy, a nice guy. Not someone like me."

Blade Saw snorts a laugh and wipes himself down with a towel. "Are we talking about the same Penny? The girl who jumped on stage and rocked it with the death metal front man or who goes crazy on the dance floor whenever we're at a bar? The girl who tore the head off one of the submission dummies and made it through Fuzzy's beginner classes in record time? You've got selective vision, my friend. There's a lot more to her than sweetness and light."

And there's more to me than even my best friend knows. We all have our secrets. But some are more dangerous than others, and there's no way I could ever involve Penny in the dark side of my life.

—◆—

After working out with Blade Saw, I meet my coach, Andy, to go over the schedule for next week. It took me a while to get used to the fact that going pro is not a solo event. In addition to MEFC, I now have a team behind me, including my manager

James, my agent, a fitness trainer, a public relations consultant, and a nutritionist. Torment is also part of my team as a coach. They handle all the details so I can focus on training for the next fight.

We spend a few hours going over some new moves and practicing technique before I finally hit the shower, then head out the door.

"Rampage."

Although I've managed to avoid Penny all evening, my hopes of a clean escape are dashed when I hear the tap of heels on the floor behind me. Damn Penny and her sexy little shoes. Most men love women in stilettos, and at Club Sin, the rule is the higher the better. But Penny, in those fucking little heels with the sides cut out, drives me insane.

Everything about Penny drives me insane. From her silky brown hair to her creamy complexion, and from her soft curves to her feminine clothes. If I wasn't who I was, with the secret she now knows, I would have asked her out the first day she stepped foot in Redemption. But girls like Penny don't belong with sadists like me. I learned that lesson the hard way.

"Can I talk to you?" She runs up behind me, catching my arm as I push open the door.

"No."

"Please. Just for a minute." She follows me out into the dark parking lot, panting as she struggles to keep up.

"No."

"Why are you acting like this?" Penny tugs on my arm, forcing me to stop. "You've been avoiding me all night. You won't even look at me. I'm not going to say anything. We're friends, and friends don't do that to each other."

Maybe not, but in my experience friendship ends when shame begins. Although it's been years since I've told my secret to anyone outside Club Sin, the sense of shame still lingers. Yes, I've accepted I have needs that are considered unconventional, and I've found a community that embraces the world of kink, but I still can't stop seeing myself as my family sees me—a disappointment, a failure, and a freak.

Or, as Avery put it before she married my younger brother Beau on what was supposed to be our wedding day, a monster.

"We're not friends." I turn to face her and almost drown in her deep blue eyes. "We're acquaintances. And, yes, obviously it's a concern given that I've just gone pro and I've already had reporters digging into my background."

"This isn't about you," she says as I turn to walk away. "It's about me. I want to become a member of Club Sin. I want what you did."

Jesus Christ. Penny at Club Sin? "You have no fucking idea what goes on there."

Her lush lips press tight together. "I was there. I blooming well know what goes on."

Despite my irritation, I have to fight back a smile. Although she's clearly angry, her attempt at swearing in that clipped British accent is sexy as hell.

"It's not a fucking game." My fist curls around the handle of my bag, and my family ring bites into my finger. I should have taken it off when the family disowned me, but it was the one thing I couldn't leave behind when I walked away. Now the heavy silver band bearing the Caldwell family crest is a burden I carry to remind me of what I could have had and who I could have been if I wasn't so fucked up.

"I know it's not a game." Her shoulders sag, and she twists the ring she wears on a chain around her neck. I've always wanted to know why she wears that damn ring. It's a man's ring, thick and heavy and too big for her delicate fingers. Did she have a man? I know she doesn't have one now. Although she can never be mine, I've kept tabs on her through Ray, watched out for her when she's been out with the team, and at night, when I'm alone…

"It's not a silly little fantasy, like you read in books." My heart thuds in my chest as I try another tactic to dissuade her. "You want that; you want to try it out; you want what you read in books or see in the movies, there are plenty of places in San Francisco you can go."

Even in the dim light, I can see her anger rise. Her cheeks heat, her lips press into a thin line, and her eyes narrow.

"Don't be so condescending," she snaps. "I know about the other clubs. I spent all night researching them when I was supposed to be sleeping and all day reading about BDSM when I was supposed to be working. I want to try it, and I don't want to go anywhere else."

Don't engage. Don't engage. But I can't help myself because she is beautiful in her fury. She's beautiful all the time. She's the most beautiful woman I've ever met and never fucked. "Why?"

"Because you're there." She twists the ring again, and her

voice drops. "That means it has to be a good place, a safe place. I trust you."

I give a bitter laugh. "Trust me? You don't know me. Until yesterday you thought I was someone else."

"We're all someone else." Her face tightens, and her voice takes on a pleading tone. "I felt something click when I walked into the club. I felt like I'd found something I didn't know I was looking for. I need to explore it. Can't you understand that?"

Although I won't admit it, I do understand because I felt the same way when I first walked into Club Sin. For years I'd thought there was something wrong with me because I got pleasure from other people's pain. Only when I'd hit rock bottom did I start searching the Internet only to discover there were others like me and places where I could go to find people who wanted the pain I wanted to give. I met Damien in a chat room, and he invited me to his club. My life changed the minute I walked in the door. It clicked, just like Penny said.

"All else aside," I say, trying to rationalize it all away, "you have a conflict. You can't be a member of a club you are trying to shut down."

Penny leans against her car, a bright-red Ford Mustang convertible that always makes me smile. She doesn't often let her wild child free, but when she bought that car, she did it in style.

"I thought about that, but because I signed all those documents before I served the papers, technically I was a member first, so I don't think it would be a problem."

Christ. Does she have an answer for everything? I play my final card, although I feel like a bastard doing it. "There's an application and a screening process, and I'll tell you right now, you won't make it through. I'll make sure of it."

Penny jerks back as if I slapped her, and even I am shocked at the vehemence in my tone. But it's bad enough she saw me at my worst, doing the one thing I crave and hating myself for it. I can't stomach the thought of her seeing me at the club again or, worse, seeing her on the other end of the whip.

"This is a free country, Jackson Caldwell." Her body trembles, her eyes fiery in the night, her words touching my soul. "You can't stop me..." She trails off, her anger fading beneath a puzzled frown. "What? Why are you looking at me like that?"

"I've never heard you say my name."

"Oh." She deflates, and her cheeks redden. "Well, I'm not allowed to use your real name at the gym, and no one seems to use real names when the team is out together, so I never really had a chance."

"Say it again." I don't know what the fuck I'm doing, but I like hearing my name on her lips, her British accent turning something ordinary into a sensual feast of rounded vowels and soft consonants.

"Jackson," she says softly, nibbling on her bottom lip. "Jackson Caldwell."

I reach out and tuck a strand of hair behind her ear, trailing my fingers over her high cheekbone and the graceful line of her jaw. Just once I would like to see her hair down from that ponytail, the chestnut strands spreading across her back, her beautiful face framed in silky softness. "You don't belong at Club Sin, Pen. What you're looking for isn't there."

My words break the spell between us, and she pulls away. "You have no idea what I'm looking for. You don't even know who I am." She unlocks her vehicle, opens the door. "I'm going back to Club Sin. And if you won't help me, I'll find someone who will."

5

Get your hands off her

REDEMPTION OR SIN? REDEMPTION OR SIN?

After spending the day trying to work while researching BDSM clubs on my phone and not thinking about Rampage… no, *Jack* and his incredibly hot body, or the way his muscles bulge when he lifts weights, or the curious warmth I felt when he called me darlin' with that soft Southern twang, I get in my car after work on Wednesday and drive toward the Golden Gate Bridge.

Do I go to Redemption for a workout, or do I go to Club Sin and ask Master Damien for an application form? Is Jack right that I don't belong? Will I get hurt? Do I want to go back because of him? Or am I doing it for me?

My pulse kicks up a notch when I approach the turnoff. Left for Sin. Straight on for Redemption. Fear gets the better of me, and I choose Redemption, but just as I signal to change lanes, a white van cuts me off, and I am forced to take the overpass into the city. I might have chosen Redemption, but it seems like Sin has chosen me.

Half an hour later, I walk into Club Sin, letting out a relieved sigh when I see Kitty at the front desk. She is wearing a spectacular flame-red corset trimmed in gold, her blond hair piled high on her head.

"Look who's here." She grins. "The only woman who has ever made Master Damien lose control. After you gave him those papers, he went crazy. We had to lock him in his office until he calmed down."

"I'm not here on business today." I fiddle with the chain around my neck. "I… What do I need to do to become a member of the club?"

"Master Damien said you'd be back." She reaches into the desk. "He left an envelope with the application forms for you."

"He said I'd be back?" I take the envelope from her, glance up at the camera above her desk. "How did he know?"

"He's a psychologist. And he's very good at reading people. I guess he saw something in you when you were here."

I'm not sure if that is good or bad or if he saw something I don't want anyone to see, but now that I'm on this path, I'm not going to let anything or anyone turn me away.

Determined to get the application process done with tonight, I open the envelope and settle down on the red velvet couch. The first few forms are easy—medical history, contact information, and a brief description of my sexual history, work, and fitness. But I hesitate when I come to the ten-page questionnaire that requires me to answer *yes*, *no*, or *maybe* to a long list of activities, half of which I don't even recognize.

"If you need help, let me know." Kitty tugs on the front laces of her corset until her breasts look like they are going to explode over the top. "There was a lot of stuff I didn't understand when I first came to the club, and it can be intimidating."

Frightening is more like it. Fisting? DP? A spreader bar? Mummification? Suspension? My imagination works overtime, and I finally enlist Kitty's help with the unfamiliar terms. I quickly decide I'm not into humiliation, service, exhibitionism, or any of the more extreme BDSM practices. I'm good with bondage, whipping, spanking, clamping, and all impact or sensation play. I'm willing to be controlled but not tortured. Hurt but not harmed. Everything else gets a question mark.

After I'm done, Kitty whisks the package off to Master Damien, and I fidget for five minutes, pacing the room, looking at the photographs with new eyes, imagining those leather cuffs around my wrists and that crop slicing across my thighs.

Kitty gives me a smile when she returns. "He has some time free, so he's going through it now. Do you want to wait?"

"Of course I want." I want it so bad, my mouth waters at the thought of going inside.

An hour of fidgeting with my ring, chatting with Kitty, and staring at the pictures on the wall later, Kitty leads me back to Master Damien's office. We travel along the same hallway, although this time the alcove is empty. No Jack in sight.

Master Damien waves me in. I close the door and take a seat in the giant black leather chair in front of his desk. His office has a sensual, masculine feel, with red ochre–painted walls, heavy wood, dark leather furnishings, and lights so dim I can barely make out his face.

"I've read your paperwork." Master Damien's chair creaks as he leans back. "Usually we would do background checks to verify the information, but I've already spoken to Master Jack about you, and he assures me you are who you say you are."

"You talked to him about me?"

"He expressed a concern about your interest in the club." His cold, searching gaze bores into me, and even if I'd thought about outing Jack, I wouldn't do it now.

Leaning forward, I say in earnest, "I would never tell anyone what I saw. Even if I hadn't signed those documents. I told him that."

"And I believe you." He drums his fingers on his desk, as if deep in thought. "But we do have a problem, and that is a conflict of interest. Perception is everything. It looks bad for you. It looks bad for your law firm. It looks bad for me."

I have a sick feeling that maybe this isn't going to be as easy as signing on the dotted line. But damned if I'm going to back down when I've finally found something else that might take away my pain. "It looks bad if I'm doing something wrong. But I'm not. As far as I understand it, nothing I do or say can change the facts of the case. And as for perception, I can keep a secret."

Master Damien rounds his desk and leans against the edge, arms folded across his chest. "There are other clubs."

"But Jack is here. I know him, and I trust him. I'm not saying I want to do a scene with him, but the fact that he picked this club tells me it's a place where I can explore this side of myself and be safe." And if Amanda succeeds in shutting down the club—which I know she will do—Club Sin is my best chance at flirting with the dark side without falling too deep.

"Ah… Master Jack." He smiles. Lots of teeth. Like the wolf probably smiled at Little Red Riding Hood when he met her in the forest. All predator. No man.

"He asked me to send you on your way if you showed up again," he continues. "He's a good friend and a regular client. I'm afraid I have to abide by his wishes."

Bloody hell. I stand and sigh. "Why didn't you just tell me that up front instead of making me fill out all the forms?"

"Curiosity." Master Damien follows me to the door. "I hope this won't deter you from trying another club."

"Honestly, I don't think I would be able to work up the nerve again or go somewhere I don't know anyone. Please reconsider." I pull open the door, look back over my shoulder with my most plaintive look. Master Damien is studying me, his head tilted to the side.

"Well… I can't see that anyone would be harmed if we did a scene together, just to give you a taste of what you're looking for. Maybe then you won't feel as hesitant to try another club."

Scene with Master Damien? "I…uh…"

He closes the distance between us. "You want to be hurt, don't you, love?" He cups my jaw in his warm palm and strokes his thumb over my cheek. "You want pain."

I swallow a few times, willing the tears back. I've never told anyone about the release I get from hurting myself, the relief

I get through pain. And yet the shame and embarrassment at what I have to do to cope with my emotional tension freeze my tongue, and all I can do is nod.

"Do you want to play with me, Penny?"

My heart gives a little flutter. When I imagined myself in the club, it was Jack behind me, Jack on the other end of the whip, Jack making me scream. But he doesn't want me to be here, and if I can't have him, at least I can find out if this is really what I want. Now or never. A once-in-a-lifetime opportunity.

Redemption or Sin?

Sin.

"Yes." My voice comes out in a whisper.

"Excellent. My room is free tonight. Last-minute cancellation." Master Damien pushes open the door to a small room adjacent to his office. With its pristine white walls and stainless steel equipment, it has a cold, clinical feel, much like a doctor's office.

"What is this place?"

"My personal playroom." Master Damien pulls a wide padded bench away from the wall and positions it in the center of the room. "I was all set to do a doctor–patient scene tonight with one of our regular submissives, but she couldn't make it." He pats the bench, clearly wanting me to join him.

"Um…" I scramble for a reason to delay the scene. "Should I take off my clothes?"

He undoes the leather straps on the four corners of the bench. "Do you want to take off your clothes?"

I bite my lip so hard I'm surprised it doesn't bleed. "I'm not really comfortable going starkers."

"Totally up to you. I can work with whatever you want to give me."

"Well, then you get me with the skirt and blouse I wore to work." Taking a deep breath, I join him at the bench.

"Up here." Master Damien helps me onto the wide padded bench, positioning me on all fours, my knees and elbows on two ledges and my body resting on what feels like the padded top of a sawhorse. I feel like a jockey, urging a horse on to the finish line, and if I didn't have my skirt covering my ass, I would feel uncomfortably exposed.

"Good girl." He gives my ass a gentle pat, and I fight back the urge to whinny.

"Um, thank you." When in doubt and feeling deeply humiliated while crawling onto a spanking bench, always be polite.

"I'm going to restrain you now." Master Damien gestures to the leather straps at the front and back of the bench. "Do you remember our safe words from the application form?"

"Red for stop. Yellow for slow down. Green for go." I swallow hard, clench my fists. "I'm not going to ask you to stop."

A grin splits his face, and he chuckles. "If I had a dollar for every time I heard that, I'd be able to buy this building outright, and no one would be trying to kick us out." He slides a leather strap around my ankle and buckles it tight. "Of course, no one ever says things like that to Master Jack. They go to him because they know he'll take them right to the edge, that point where they will beg him to stop." He cuffs my second ankle, and a violent tremble runs through my body.

"Shh." Master Damien buckles a strap around my wrist, and

my heart pounds in my chest. This is it. One more strap, and I won't be able to get away. I check out the room, hoping to distract myself from the panic building inside me, but the shiny silver racks holding an assortment of ropes, handcuffs, whips, chains, crops, and paddles do little to assuage my concerns.

I take a deep breath, inhale the scent of vinyl, and whimper.

"Relax." Master Damien fastens the last strap and tugs out my ponytail holder, massaging my scalp as my hair spreads across my back. My tension eases a tiny bit, and I turn my head just as someone pounds on the door.

"Damien!" Jack's deep voice with its rough edge is unmistakable. "I know she's in there. Kitty told me. Open the fucking door."

I suck in a sharp breath and jerk against the restraints. "Let me up."

"It's okay." Master Damien strokes a soothing hand down my back. "He's not coming in. We have rules about interrupting a scene."

"Obviously, you don't know him very well."

Bang. Bang. Bang. The door shakes with the force of Jack's blows. A part of me thrills at the thought that he cares enough to cause a scene, but another part wonders if he's angry because I disregarded his wishes and he thinks that I will out him to his friends.

"Damien! I'll break the fucking door down if you don't open it right this fucking minute."

Master Damien's lips quirk, amused. "It's interesting how you can know someone for years and still discover new facets to their character."

"He can do it," I warn Damien. "He broke down the door to the women's changing room at Redemption when the locking mechanism jammed and people were trapped inside. I also saw him break down a door at a bar when some bloke…" I trail off when a heavy thud makes all the whips and chains shake on their racks.

"Don't you fucking touch her."

"How badly do you want this, Pen? If I tell him to go, he'll have to go."

I drop my head to the bench and sigh. "He seems very agitated. I think it would probably be best if you released me so I can try to soothe the savage beast."

Master Damien releases my restraints as Jack continues his vicious assault, but before I can get off the bench, the door splinters and slams open.

Boom. I look up to see Jack glowering in the doorway, dressed in a delicious pair of worn jeans and a black T-shirt that clings to his muscular body.

"Jesus fucking Christ." He stalks into the room, his face a mask of fury. "What the fuck are you doing here?"

"You're interfering with my scene, Master Jack." Master Damien's voice tightens in warning, and he presses a firm hand against my back, keeping me down on the bench.

A growl curls up Jack's throat, and darkness crosses his face. "Get your hands off her."

"Jack." I slide off the bench and stand between him and Master Damien. I've never called him Jack before, but he doesn't seem to notice. "I want to be here. I want to do this."

Danger rolls off him as he closes the distance between us, his gaze firmly on Damien, his six-pack rippling as he moves. "I told you this wasn't a fucking game. Damien knows better."

I have watched enough fights to know what happens next, and although Master Damien is a formidable man, he has no chance against Jack in full battle frenzy.

"No." I wrap my arms around Jack's waist, press myself against him, my temper beginning to fray. Who does he think he is, rampaging in here and telling me what to do? Enraging an angry fighter is never a good move, but with my emotions and nerves shot, I don't give a damn. "You're out of line."

Jack stiffens, and I look up only to see his eyes narrow. "I told you not to come here."

"I heard you. I didn't listen."

His eyes darken almost to black, but the golden specks still shine bright. "You. Here. It's not right."

"Maybe. But that's what I'm trying to figure out. That's why I came here. And if you have a problem with Damien helping me out, then why don't you take over?"

Jack's heart thunders in his chest, beating so hard I can feel it beneath his ribs. His arms tighten around me, and the world fades away until I feel only his warm hands on my back, his strong arms around me, his powerful body pressed against mine.

"No." His head dips down. I think—no, I hope—maybe he'll kiss me, but instead he rests his forehead against mine and closes his eyes, as if he is fighting for the same calm that has eluded me since he barged into the room.

"Please," I whisper. "I want to try it. Just once. And I want it to be with you. I feel safe with you."

"You are safer away from me." His voice is strained. "People come to me because they want me to hurt them. They don't come to learn, except about how much they can take." Lines of pain fan out from his eyes, and his voice becomes bitter, laced with the same self-hatred I feel when I drag the razor blade over my thighs, and yet curiously softened by the drawn-out vowels. "I don't want to enjoy hurting you. I can't."

His words are meant to push me away, and yet his arms are still tight around me, tighter than before.

"I'm not afraid of you, Jack. It's my choice. I choose you."

6

I didn't come here for sex

RAMPAGE

WHAT THE FUCK AM I DOING?

I strip off my jeans in the Club Sin changing room and try to clear my head for the scene with Penny, but my body won't relax, and my stomach is tied in knots. How can I give her what she wants when it is the one thing that has kept me away from her since we met? Especially now when I'm on edge and barely in control.

Damien will never forgive me for intruding on his scene and threatening him in front of Penny. Even though I'm a silent partner in the business, providing the financing without bearing any of the legal or managerial responsibility for running the club, he is well within his rights to kick me out. He should have kicked me out instead of so graciously relinquishing control of the scene to me. Why the fuck did he do that? And the damned smirk on his face as he led Penny to my private playroom…

Despite his reputation, Penny is safe with him. Safer than with me. Once she sees me as I really am, she'll see her trust was misplaced, as was her friendship.

But, damn, friendship was the last thing I was thinking when she pressed herself up against me, her soft body curving into mine, the light, floral scent of her perfume filling my head, a year of fantasies coalescing into a burning need that completely overwhelmed me.

I tug on my leather pants and pull a black cotton T-shirt over my head—a uniform of sorts that allows me to compartmentalize what happens here from the rest of my life. Except right now the rest of my life is waiting in room six for the bite of my whip.

My cock hardens, solid as steel, pulsing with need. All I have to do is walk out that door to live out my deepest, darkest fantasy and my greatest fear. Craving takes hold of me, and I pull off my family ring and slam the locker door. I will have her. And then I will lose her and suffer a lifetime of regret.

My boots thud on the marble floor as I make my way down the hallway. Damien spared no expense when he set up Club Sin in a bid to make it unlike any other BDSM club on the West Coast. From the marble tiles to the wooden furnishings and from the exotic lighting to the high-end equipment, he has created an environment that is decadent and sensual, intimidating and yet welcoming.

"Master Jack!" Sylvia makes her way toward me, her blue eyes warm and bright. A masochist and my sometime play partner, Sylvia struggled to accept that I wasn't interested in having a relationship despite the night we spent together. Still, I'm partly to blame. I had never fucked any of the women I played with at the club, and after I broke my rule for her, she jumped to the wrong conclusion. Even after I explained that I didn't get involved with anyone—in or out of the club—she didn't give up, and I had to end our play sessions for good because I didn't want to lead her on. Since then she's never missed an opportunity to let me know she'd like to go back to how things used to be—sometime play partners, casual friends.

"Sylvia." I frown, reminding her that shouting at a Dom in the corridor is an invitation to punishment. Which is probably why she did it.

"Room three is free tonight." She bows her head, and her thick, blond hair falls in waves over her cheeks. Slim and pretty, Sylvia has high, small breasts and an athletic build. Although she has more stamina than many of the other masochists in the club and is always in demand, physically she doesn't do anything for me. I'm a big man, and I like a woman with curves. Full breasts, softly rounded hips, and an ass that I can hold on to are what I look for in a woman—or what I would look for if I were a normal man who could have a normal relationship.

"I thought I made it clear that we weren't playing together anymore."

She nibbles her bottom lip, and her shoulders drop. "I just thought…you've seemed really tense the last few days. I just wanted to help."

"You can help by finding someone else to play with so you're not always looking to me." I'm being harsh, but right now, all I want is Penny, and every minute I delay is another minute she might change her mind. "Master Damien is free," I offer. "He had a rare cancellation. Tell him I sent you to see him."

Her face brightens. Damien isn't a sadist, but he is a Master Dom and highly sought after in the club. "Thank you, sir."

"Have a good night." I wait until she's gone and push open the door to room six, forcing my gaze away from the couch where Penny sits, to make sure everything is in order. Damien and I created a playroom that looks like an upscale hotel. Modern and austere and decorated in black and white with red accents, with polished concrete floors and a beamed wooden ceiling, the room contains a small wet bar, a four-poster bed, and a bathroom with a shower. A padded table affixed to a cage sits on a thick red carpet, dominating the center of the room, and beside it is a black wooden St. Andrew's Cross. Suspension equipment, pulleys, and ropes adorn the ceiling, and red accent lights highlight photographs of BDSM play around the walls.

There is no comfort in this room. There is no peace. There is pain, and there is pleasure. Mutual gratification and nothing more.

Except for the initial design, I've never thought much about the room, but when my gaze drops to Penny, wearing a pink blouse, her flowery skirt spread over her knees, a faint blush on her creamy skin, I am struck with the incongruity of the scene. She is a rose among thorns, a flower in the desert, beauty with the beast. If I could take her to another room, I would.

"Stand up."

She stands. Right away, she stands. Without hesitation and

despite the abruptness of my tone. She stands, and the Dominant in me growls with approval.

Fuck, she's beautiful. Curved where a woman should be curved, toned from all the workouts she does at the gym, sweetly self-conscious. And, if she was honest in the paperwork I reviewed while she waited, hiding a secret that I want to uncover.

"Look at me." She meets my gaze, her posture almost defiant, as if she knows I still want to send her away. Her courage and the curious vulnerability that shows in her eyes intrigue me. She needs something, but it shames her. She wants something badly enough to come to the club and yet she can't voice what it is.

Maybe it is that hidden contradiction that first drew me to her at the gym. Still, I never encouraged a relationship, never treated her as anything more than a friend, simply because I have nothing to offer a woman besides what I can give them in this room.

Pain.

Pain of every kind—whether it is the lash of my whip, the sting of my paddle, the burn of fire or wax, the stab of a violet wand, or simply the smack of my palm on bare flesh. I take my pleasure through their pain.

"What are you looking for?"

"I want to be hurt." She twists the ring around her neck. Fuck. I hate that ring and her attachment to it. If she's in this room, I want her to think only of me and not the man who gave it to her—a man who touched her and wasn't me.

"What kind of hurt?" I reach around her neck and undo the clasp of the chain that holds the ring.

After a brief, tense pause, she says, "Physical pain."

"There are all kinds of physical pain." I place the chain and ring on a table beside the couch and watch her gaze linger on it. Wanting her full attention, I twist my hand in her hair, forcing her head back, bringing her gaze to mine. Her eyes widen, and she sucks in a sharp breath. I feel her fear as a throb in my groin, a delicious burn in my chest.

"There can be as much pain in withholding an orgasm as there is in whipping. Withdrawal of sensory stimulation can hurt as much as the sting of a cane. I can hurt you in every way you can imagine and then many you've never even considered. What are you looking for exactly?" I step in closer, invading her space, but with her hair firmly wrapped around my fist, she cannot retreat.

Her breathing hitches, and her cheeks flush with arousal. She may not be naturally submissive, but submission arouses her.

"I don't know." She shrugs. "I knew this kind of club existed, but I never thought about it in relation to me. I thought it was all about kinky sex. But when I saw you in that alcove the night I came to serve the documents…it wasn't about sex. There was more. She was getting pleasure from the pain. You gave her…"

"Release."

"Yes." She lets out a breath. "That's what I want."

Christ. She's almost too good to be true. Can she really need what I have to give?

"Do you need pain to get off?"

She struggles against my grip, trying to look away, and then she bites her lip so hard blood beads on the surface. Arousal surges though me, so fierce my body shakes. That blood is *my* blood. Her pain is mine to give.

"I don't know. I've never been with anyone who didn't... I mean, sex and pain have always gone together for me. But that's not why I came here. I wasn't thinking I fancied a shag and this was the place to get it."

"I understand, Pen." I don't come to Club Sin for sex either, preferring to wait until my partners have gone home before I seek my release. The risks of mixing sex with BDSM play became abundantly clear after my one night with Sylvia, and I will not make that mistake again.

"Master Damien said you've only got one night here," I continue. "We need to discuss what we're going to do."

She sucks in a sharp breath. "What are we going to do?"

"I want your clothes off. Everything except your bra and panties. I can restrain you, spank you, and use a soft flogger. I don't think you're ready for anything else." I lift her chin up with my finger, directing her gaze to me. "You do what I say, when I say it, without question. You trust me to look after you and make sure you aren't pushed past your limits."

She trembles, cheeks flushing. "Everything you said is okay, but I want to leave my skirt on. I'll do my best to follow your directions, but you'll have to forgive me if I slip up because, to be honest, I'm not good with being bossed around."

Don't I know it. Which is why this will be so much fun. "No skirt. I need full access, and your clothes will get in the way."

Penny's mouth opens and closes again, and she fists the edge of her skirt. Clearly, there is more to her reluctance than just being shy or insecure about her body, but aside from the practical issues, clothing serves to hide the things we need to expose to embrace the core of our being.

Hands trembling, she slowly undoes the buttons on her blouse. Unable to look away, I follow her fingers as the fabric parts to reveal soft, creamy breasts nestled in a froth of pink lace. *Christ*. I can't remember the last time I was with a woman who wore pink. Usually, the women who grace my playroom are of a type—hard-core submissives covered in tats who wear black latex or leather, red or black bras and thongs, and black stilettos or boots. Penny's skin is pale and unmarked. Soft.

I suppress a shudder of desire, and my mouth waters in anticipation of leaving my mark on that perfect skin.

Penny toes off her shoes and tosses her blouse on the couch. Her hands drop to her skirt, and she fumbles with the waistband. "I don't think I can do it," she whispers. "And it's not that I'm trying to be difficult. I just…can't."

"I'll help you." With my hand on her lower back, I guide her to the center of the room where a pair of cuffs dangles from a beam across the ceiling. I make a quick adjustment for her height and glide my hands up her body, bringing her arms over her head. I've never touched Penny in anything other than a friendly way, although I've imagined how she might feel countless times. Usually only pain arouses me, but her soft curves and the slight tremble of her body send my thoughts in a direction I'm not prepared for them to go.

"You have your safe words. Use them if you need to." I wrap a leather cuff around her slender wrist and buckle it tight. I give her a moment to adjust before I attach the second cuff. When she is secure, I pull on the chain, drawing her hands up just enough to stretch her past the point of comfort.

She swallows hard, and I gently stroke her cheek. "Anything too tight?"

"I'm okay."

I come up behind her, cup her breasts in my hands. Her nipples are hard and peaked beneath her lacy bra. Although I'm tempted to stroke her pussy, test her wetness, my main goal is to lower her inhibitions enough to remove her skirt without having her retreat.

"This excites you." I gently pinch her nipples through her bra, and she bites back a moan.

"No. It's about the pain. Not sex."

"There's a profound connection between sex and pain." I smooth my hands down her rib cage and over her stomach. She is warm, despite the slight chill in the room, her skin so soft I want to touch her all over. When she dips her head to watch my hands, her hair drops over her shoulders, leaving her neck exposed, vulnerable, and I struggle with an inexplicable urge to kiss her nape. "Sex and pain stimulate the release of similar chemicals and hormones in the body," I continue. "The endorphins that are released in stressful situations or painful experiences are often perceived as pleasurable because they give a form of release."

She freezes, her body stiffening, and I wonder for a moment if I've scared her. "A release?"

"Yes." I undo the button on the back of her skirt and pull

down the zipper. She's wearing pink lace panties that match her bra, and my arousal kicks up another notch. "But it can be achieved in many ways. Some people just come here for the sensual experience and then go home and relieve the sexual tension with a partner or on their own." With slow, gentle movements, I ease her skirt down over her hips. Penny's breaths come in short pants, and her teeth chatter.

"I can't do this."

"You don't have to. I'm doing it for you." I release the skirt, and it hits the floor with a soft thud.

She shakes so violently the chains rattle overhead. I wrap my arms around her, pull her back into my chest.

"Relax." I brush my lips over her ear, inhale the light scent of her perfume. "What happens here stays here."

She relaxes slightly into my body, her ass a warm weight against my cock. I glide my hand over the curve of her hip, trail my fingers down her thigh.

Soft skin gives way to raised ridges, slick and smooth.

I steel myself not to react, but my voice catches in my throat. "Ah, Pen. That's how you let the pain out, isn't it?" I draw my finger along what feels to be the worst of the scars. "You do it yourself."

7

Maybe I'm too close

PENNY

Oh God. He knows. Or if he doesn't know, he will as soon as he stands in front of me. In some ways it was actually easier with Master Damien. I didn't know him that well. There was little chance I would be bumping into him at the gym or partying with him on the weekends. I wouldn't have to see him working out or talking with my friends. And even if he saw the scars on my legs, there would be no risk of him telling anyone I knew.

Over the years, I've become adept at hiding my scars: avoiding pools and beaches, or swimming in wet suits, sex with the lights out, no showers or baths with my boyfriends, and pleading modesty whenever people expected me to bare what I couldn't stand for anyone else to see.

Jack walks around and crouches in front of me. My body flushes with embarrassment, not just because he can see my scars but because I have been pulled out of the fantasy, of the arousal he made me feel, of the momentary illusion of safety I had in his arms. Now, I'm hanging from the ceiling in a cold, impersonal room, with Jack, my friend from the gym, in front of me, his face level with my pussy, his eyes on the scars no one except my ex-boyfriend, Adam, has ever seen before. Adam who thought I was broken. Adam who shattered my heart.

"How long?" He traces a thick finger over one of the long silvery lines on my thigh.

"Since I was thirteen." My throat tightens. Will he end this? Tell me I can't have what I want because I'm too badly damaged for anyone to touch?

He gently turns me side to side, inspecting every inch of my scarred skin.

"When was the last time?"

I press my lips together and look away.

"Answer me or we're done. And I want the truth."

Emotion wells up in my chest, and I swallow past the lump in my throat. "Last week."

"Here." He presses hard on the most recent welt, and I wince. "Yes."

"Have you seen a therapist?" He stands in front of me, arms folded over his massive chest, studying me intently.

"Yes. But not for a few years. There wasn't much more she could do. Part of it is just how I am, and part is…daddy issues." I give a laugh, trying to shrug off years of my father's controlling and abusive behavior and my desperate attempts to please a man who never wanted me.

"If you're looking for help…"

God. Can this get any worse? "I'm not looking for help," I bite out. "I don't need help. I need pain. I saw you with that woman, and I thought maybe you could do that for me."

He is silent for so long I give up hope. Suddenly, I'm done with this whole thing. "Just let me down."

"Not yet," he says, his voice rough. "I'm going to give you what you want."

He walks around me. Touching. A brush of his hand through my hair. Fingers feathering over my jaw. A stroke of his palm over my ass. My body tenses, ready for a blow, a slap, a strike. But it never comes. Instead, his soft touches arouse me, make me hot. Wet. And my cheeks burn, knowing he can see what he does to me.

"You are beautiful." He cups my breasts, squeezes and strokes just enough to feed my desire but not enough to hurt. Everything south of my belly button tightens, and I let out a soft moan.

Jack lifts an eyebrow. "That's not the sound I like to hear." He pinches my nipples so hard my eyes water, and I jerk in the restraints. And then his warm hands are back, soothing the pain away. "Give me your pain, darlin'." He pinches my nipples again, giving them a cruel twist that makes me cry out. I'm on a roller coaster of sensation, one moment rocking with pleasure, the next moment writhing in pain. Blood rushes down to my core, and I can feel my pulse throb between my legs. I am wet. So wet. I can't remember the last time I was this aroused. So desperately needing to come.

His callused, rough fingers run down my body and over my hips. He cups my ass, his fingers sliding over my knickers, and then he releases me to explore my curves again. I try to anticipate his touch, swaying toward his hands.

"Don't move."

I freeze in place. Is this how to get more of what I want? Maybe if I move, he'll punish me. I lean toward him again, and he lifts his hands.

"What did I say?"

I hear none of his soothing, Southern drawl in the cold, sharp tone of his voice. Sweat beads on my forehead, and my heart pounds against my ribs.

"You told me not to move."

A sensual smile curves his lips, and he crosses the room to the black couch by the wall. "In this room, you do what I tell you to do. You have no control here. You can't ask, coax, or force me to do anything. You take what I give you, when and how I want to give it. And right now, I want to give you nothing." He settles on the couch, and flips through a magazine that was lying on the table, leaving me suspended, aroused, and alone.

"Ramp…Master Jack?"

"No talking unless you want to spend the rest of the night like that," he says without looking up.

Nipples aching, pussy throbbing, I twist in the restraints. My muscles burn, and my shoulders protest my confinement. Frustrated and overwhelmed by the combination of physical pain and unfulfilled desire, I whimper.

Jack doesn't even look up from his magazine. "I've seen your scars. You can take a lot more than that."

I take in a deep breath and then another, using the tricks I've learned to get through the pain of the blade. But unspent arousal is a different beast. It is an ache that spreads through my body, getting worse with every passing minute because every time I move I am reminded that I am half naked and chained to the ceiling and my only source of relief is sitting five feet away.

Seeking a distraction, I glance around the room, but it only serves to worsen the situation. This room is about pain and sex and nothing else. White walls, gray floors, red carpet, black furniture, racks of whips and crops and equipment I can't understand but all of which I know I want to try. A cold, ultramodern hotel room for the discerning sadist in one's life.

After an interminable amount of time, Rampage places his magazine on the table and walks toward me. I tremble, trying desperately not to move as he scans me with his hooded gaze.

"How do you feel?"

Not the question I was expecting, and I can hardly tell him I'm desperate to come after insisting this had nothing to do with sex. "Uncomfortable. My muscles are…sore."

He gives me a half smile. "That's all?" He stares pointedly at my breasts, my erect nipples, visible through my bra, giving my arousal away.

"That's all," I say.

"Perfect." He reaches for the cuffs, and I look up at him, confused.

"You said we were going to do a scene."

"We just did."

My breath leaves me in a rush. "But…this isn't the kind of hurting I was looking for."

"But you do hurt." A statement. Not a question. His fingers glide up my inner thigh, and I feel a rush of heat between my legs that serves only to increase the ache in my pussy.

"Yes, it hurts."

He steps closer, so close I can feel the heat from his body as his finger stops its upward journey at the edge of my knickers. "Where does it hurt? Tell me."

My brain does a disconnect. Rampage. Jack. My high-fiving, fist-bumping gym buddy. This dangerously sensual Dom. I open my mouth, and only a whimper comes out.

Without warning, Jack shoves my knickers aside and slicks his finger through my slit. "Does it hurt here?"

Shocked at his unexpected, intimate touch, I jerk against the restraints.

His Southern accent returns, husky and soothing. "Yes, it does. Poor Pen." He presses his thick finger into my entrance, and I almost choke on the sensation.

"Christ. You're soaked," he murmurs. "I would love to fuck you right now. I'd tie you up on my table, spread you out, and fuck you till you scream."

Electricity sheets across my skin, as I struggle to reconcile this man with the fist-bumping Rampage I know. "This isn't supposed to be about sex." I've never really enjoyed sex. Never been with a man who was interested in my pleasure. I've always been a means for getting someone else off, nothing more.

"But it is." He pushes two fingers deep inside me. "At least it is for you."

I groan and he adds a third finger, stretching me to the edge of pain. His thumb circles my clit, and I am caught in a maelstrom of emotion, a storm of need.

"That's it," he whispers. "Give it to me. Give me every dirty, indecent thought you've ever had, every dark craving, every sick fantasy. I can make them all come true." His voice rumbles, raw and rough, thick with desire. "Give me your pain."

My hands clench into fists. My head falls back. A low rolling ache builds inside me. I am coiled tight, tight…

He pulls his fingers away.

"No." I gasp as the sudden loss of sensation cuts through me like a knife.

"We're done." He presses his fingers to his mouth and licks his lips. "That's as close as I will ever get to tasting you."

"Please." I am so wound up, so desperate to come, I am not above begging.

"You wanted to hurt," he says. "That's as much as I can hurt you. Don't touch yourself when you go home. No fingers. No vibrators. No men. Don't get yourself off." He pinches my nipple, and the throb in my pussy turns to a sharp, fierce ache.

"It hurts."

"I know it does, darlin'. That's the point."

My gaze drops below his belt to the thick erection pressing against his fly. My pain arouses him. At least I know this isn't easy for him either.

He releases the restraints and rubs my arms to restore

the circulation. I tremble beneath his touch, lost in a sea of unmet desire.

"Let's get you dressed." He picks up my clothes and helps me dress, his fingers making quick work of the buttons on my blouse. When I'm fully clothed, he clasps my chain around my neck, then twists my hair into a ponytail and wraps the elastic around it with practiced efficiency.

My stomach knots at the thought of all the women he's dressed and undressed in this room, the ponytails he's fixed, the dirty things he's said. But I have no right to feel jealous. He made me no promises. Told me no lies. I had my one night, my one chance.

I just never expected to want another, and especially not with him.

***

After a sleepless night of trying to keep my promise, I give in to my burning need for release and hit the shower with my vibrator in hand. After I've relieved enough tension to feel almost human again, I get dressed, feed my cat, Clarice, and drive to the office, arriving only a minute before Ray walks in the door.

"What happened to you?" he demands the moment he sees me.

Oh God. Do I look like I spent a night in sleepless sexual frustration and a morning having multiple orgasms in the shower?

"Nothing." I turn on the coffeepot and give myself a mental check—skirt, shoes, top, bra—nothing outwardly amiss. "Why?"

Ray shrugs. "You've never been early before, especially on a Thursday when you're revving up for the weekend." He tosses his jacket on the coatrack and stretches out on the couch. People

might think he's lazy, but Ray gets up at four a.m. every morning, goes for a run, lifts weights, showers, and makes breakfast,
all before normal people, including his wife, Sia, roll out of bed.

"I couldn't sleep, so I thought I'd get an early start on the day.
And I'm not a car, Ray. I don't rev."

"You have a date?"

"No, I did not have a date. Not that it's any of your business." Usually I just let Ray's nosy questions wash over me, but
today, his interest grates.

"You need to go on a date." He folds his arms behind his
head. "It's been a long time. You're letting that fucking Vetch
Retch ruin your life."

Still unsettled over my encounter last night, I spin around and
glare. "There are so many things wrong with that statement, I
don't know where to begin. First, you are married with a kid,
so you're not in a position to give me dating advice. Second,
you're a guy. If I need dating advice, I'll ask a woman. Third,
and FYI, I have been on dates since Vetch; I just haven't shared
them with you. Fourth, no, I am not letting him ruin my life.
I've just become more cautious about who I go out with. And
finally, *long time* is a relative term."

Ray studies me, his dark eyes boring into my soul. "Who?"

"Who what?"

"Who did you go out with and not tell me about?"

Mercifully, the coffeepot beeps, and I pour two cups and then
add two creams and two sugars to each of them. "If I didn't tell
you, I might have a reason."

Ray bolts up off the couch. "Why? Did someone hurt you?

Someone hurts you, and I'll rip off his balls and stuff them down his throat."

"That's sweet in an unnecessarily overprotective coworker kind of way." I hand him his coffee and wrap my hands around my own cup, letting out a sigh as the warmth seeps into my perpetually cold hands. "Are you this bad with Sia? I mean, we're just friends, and you almost wound up in jail for me."

"It's worse." Ray tenses when the front door closes, and frowns at the wall separating the outer hallway from the reception area as if he can't tell from the click of heels on the wooden floor who has just come in. "She has to threaten me before we go anywhere 'cause I want to beat up every fucking guy who looks at her. If I didn't have Redemption to blow off some steam, I'd probably be divorced already."

"Who's getting divorced?" Amanda joins us in the reception area, looking stunning in a fitted, dark gray suit and pearl silk blouse.

"No one," I say. "Ray's having protectiveness issues with the women in his life."

"We gotta get Penny hitched." He sips his coffee and resumes his position, stretched full-out on the couch. "I can't handle looking after two women, especially since Sam was born. I feel like I gotta be on alert all the time."

Amanda's lips quirk in a smile as she jumps on the "get Penny hitched" bandwagon. "Penny's looking for a bit of wild, a badass type like Vetch Retch but without the abusive tendencies. You know anyone?"

"What?" I stare at Amanda, aghast. "I don't need—"

"Yeah, I know lots of guys like that." Ray whips out his phone and scrolls through his address book, muttering to himself. "Stan? No. He's in a Thai jail. Rick? No, he's hiding in Panama. Steve? Missing a couple of screws. Arn? Still in rehab. Mike? No. He thinks he's the reincarnation of Johnny Cash."

"Hello." I wave my free hand in Ray's face. "I'm happy with things the way they are, thank you very much. I don't need a man."

"You need a man, and you need him bad," Ray says. "I'm a man. I know these things."

"How about you take those psychic skills into the field and leave the guy stuff to me." Amanda pulls a file from her briefcase. "I've got a dude here who says he can't walk after my client broadsided his car, but his neighbors have seen him doing yard work."

Ray takes the file and flips through it. Although we run an almost-paperless office, he insists on hard-copy briefing documents that he shreds as soon as he dictates his report. I like to tease him about kicking it old school, but I suspect his antipathy toward electronic communications has something to do with the rumors about his involvement with the CIA.

"How 'bout something challenging?" he says with a groan. "Like hunting down an escaped con, or retrieving missile launch codes from a billionaire black-market arms dealer, or spying on the president?"

"How about a video of Mr. Paul Williams cleaning his gutters before three o'clock this afternoon?" Amanda gestures to the door.

"Man can't even finish his morning coffee." Ray downs the rest of his coffee in one gulp and jumps to his feet.

"Man loves PI work even though he pretends he doesn't," I say as he heads out the door.

He looks back over his shoulder and gives me a rare smile. He's one of the best PIs in the city, and although he is in high demand, he is never too busy for Amanda, and he never misses a morning coffee with me.

Midafternoon, I bring Ray's report to Amanda for her approval. "Ray caught the guy climbing a tree, fixing his roof, chopping wood, and chasing his dog around the yard. If you're happy with his report, he can sign a statement in the morning, or I can bring it to Redemption after work. I'm taking a jiu-jitsu class tonight, and I'll see him there."

Amanda laughs. "Yeah, he'd love that. Mixing business and pleasure. No need to harass him. Tomorrow's fine."

I just mixed business and pleasure in the worst possible way, and yet all I can think about is spending another night with Jack at Club Sin. I feel a stab of guilt about going behind her back, but it was just one night, and I haven't disclosed any secrets or compromised the case. I just don't know how I'll deal with seeing Jack at the gym, knowing just what he can give me but never will.

As if she can read my thoughts, Amanda says, "It looks like we might be able to evict Club Sin by Monday. I just went through the commercial tenancy agreement, and I think I've found a loophole. It might be easier to evict them than I initially thought. I'm going to keep it under my hat and bring it up at the hearing on Monday."

"What will they do?" I toe the floor, trying to hide my disappointment. "The whole place has been renovated to accommodate all their special equipment. I can't imagine it's going to be easy to relocate that quickly."

Amanda shrugs. "Not our problem. They took a risk leasing the space instead of buying property outright, although I feel for them because they negotiated a long-term lease with a view to making that investment pay off. If Gerry didn't want them out so badly, they could have been there for at least another ten years."

"That's great." I force a smile. "He must be pleased."

She doesn't return my smile. "He is pleased, but I'll be glad when the case is over, to be honest." She doodles on a piece of paper in front of her. "Something about Gerry doesn't sit right with me. He's too insistent on getting them out fast, too blasé about the legal ramifications of what he's trying to do, and totally unconcerned about the tenants in the building. I know it's all business, but one of the reasons I left my old firm was to get away from cold corporate clients like him, and now I feel like I'm falling into that trap again."

Maybe because she's still flying a corporate brand. Amanda worked at one of the biggest law firms in the city before starting up on her own. Although she added her own quirky touches to her new office, outwardly it's still got a big law firm feel—from her stationery to her website, and from her signage to her logo. Over the last year I've come up with a few different ideas for logos and branding, but I've never shown them to her. I figure when she wants a change, she'll hire professionals.

She doesn't need her legal assistant telling her how to brand her business.

"Anything else you need?"

"Could you prepare a draft notice of eviction so it's ready for Monday?" Amanda turns back to her desk. "I'll bring it to the hearing so we don't have any more issues with service."

"No problem." A part of me is relieved that the club will be shut down. Although I feel bad for Kitty, Master Damien, and Jack, the temptation is almost too much for me to bear. If the club stayed open, I don't think I could stay away.

One taste wasn't enough.

One night with Jack has ruined me forever.

8

Prepare to be punished

PENNY

After work, I head to Redemption. With all the beginner-level fitness classes under my belt, I was up for a new challenge, and the class coordinator, Fuzzy, suggested I try Brazilian jiu-jitsu, which is one of the key martial arts used in MMA fighting. Blade Saw and Shilla the Killa, Redemption's top female amateur fighter, are teaching tonight, and the dojo is packed with people wearing gis and belts in a variety of colors.

I change into my gi and join the other white belts at the front of the class. Fuzzy suggested jiu-jitsu because it's a good sport for smaller people who want to fight larger opponents, and from a quick assessment of the room behind me, I'm the smallest person here.

"Sorry I'm late." Cora slips into the space beside me, her eyes fixed on Blade Saw. After watching her and Blade Saw dance around each other at Score, both afraid to take that next step,

I suggested she come to class with me to watch him in action. Blade Saw really comes into his own when he's teaching a class.

Shilla leads us through a warm-up unlike any I've ever done before. We do tumbling, army crawls, bear crawls, and cartwheels. We jump, lunge, crawl, roll, and do push-ups at specific intervals. By the time Blade Saw partners us for our first lesson, I'm ready to call it a night.

"I think this was a bad idea," Cora pants as we go to the beginner section to learn new techniques. "The drowned rat look isn't particularly flattering. I can't really get my sexy on when I'm beet-red and covered in sweat."

Blade Saw decides to partner everyone up to practice passing the guard. He shouts at everyone to get in line, grabs Cora for the demo, and sends me across the room to Rampage, who must have sneaked in when Shilla had us hauling ass across the mat.

Heart pounding, I make my way across the dojo. What do I say to a man who chained me to the ceiling of his playroom and aroused me to the point of pain?

Rampage tracks me with his gaze as I skirt around the people getting into position on the mat. He is breathtaking in his crisp white gi, a worn black belt tied tight around his narrow waist. Some of the fighters wear T-shirts under their gis, but I am not so lucky. As I slow to a stop in front of him, I am forced to endure the visual feast of his truly magnificent chest.

Burn, cheeks, burn. "Um…hi."

"Pen." His voice is laced with amusement, thick with his Southern drawl.

"Blade Saw said you needed a partner." I amaze myself at

my ability to form a coherent sentence without collapsing in a puddle on the floor.

"So he sent me a white belt? Did I do something to piss him off?"

My cheeks heat, and I look up, only to fall into the warmth of his gaze. "No one else is free."

A smile tugs at his lips. "I'm just messing with you, darlin'."

My insides turn to mush, and I dip my head so he can't see just how red my cheeks can get.

Rampage lies on his mat, propping himself up on his elbows in a semi-recline. His gaze sweeps over me as I get in position on my knees in front of him. He's got guard, which means he has to make me submit, and I have the goal of passing guard to a dominant position and holding it for three seconds. The irony isn't lost on me, but I don't laugh because his eyes suddenly darken almost to black.

"You ready?"

Boy, am I ever. "Yes." I try to play it cool, like I wasn't shackled to the ceiling of his BDSM playroom in my bra and knickers last night, stroked into a frenzy, and ordered not to touch myself. Like that was going to happen.

"You understand the drill?" He licks his lips, like a predator about to feast. "When one of us succeeds in our goal, we stop, and the loser goes back to the end of the line. The winner stays out and takes guard on the next person in line."

"You have to make me submit." I toy with the ends of my very white belt. "Maybe I should just go to the end of the line now. You didn't seem to have any trouble with that last night."

"Come here and say that," he murmurs, patting his belt. "I'll give you the advantage of full mount."

My mouth goes dry as I crawl up his body and seat myself over his belt, my knees spread uncomfortably wide on either side of his hips in a fully dominant position. Something hard and smooth presses against the juncture of my thighs, and I pray he is wearing a cup because the urge to rock against that delicious hardness is almost overwhelming.

Rampage's corded neck tightens when he swallows. "Move up. Your knees should be under my arms."

I shuffle up, and he grabs my hips and drags me forward until my knees are on either side of his chest and I can feel the heat of his breath on a place where heat should not be felt in the middle of a packed Brazilian jiu-jitsu class.

"I think maybe I'm too close."

He heaves in a breath, his eyes glittering as he grips the inside edges of my gi. "Not close enough." With a hard yank, he pulls me down until I am lying flat on his body, my breasts against his chest, my hips against his cup, my hands braced on either side of his head.

"Full mount is where you want to be when you're grappling a bigger, stronger opponent." His words whisper over me, his lips so close to mine I only have to drop a few inches to have a little taste.

"You can use the strength and power of your own body and the force of gravity to your advantage." He pulls me right down, wraps his free hand around me, shifts his hips and rolls. Before I can catch my breath, I'm flat on my back and Rampage is on top of me.

"This is where you don't want to be, as a smaller grappler," he says. "How are you going to get out of this?"

The question isn't so much how am I going to get out of it but do I want to get out of it? And with Rampage's hard, muscular body on top of me, his legs between my thighs, his hardness pressed tight against my hips, I'm not sure I do.

Rampage stills, and his eyes widen.

Bugger. Did I say that out loud?

"I'm not sure I want you to either." His breath is warm against my ear. "But if you don't move, we'll both get kicked out of class. So, what are you going to do?"

"Um…overhook an arm, bridge and roll, then get on top into the closed guard?"

Rampage drops his weight, stealing my breath. "Won't work against a larger opponent. You need to blast through my hips and use a bit of strength to overturn me. Strength you don't have. Your best bet is to escape back to half guard."

"Okay." I wiggle just the tiniest bit against him, seeking more of that delicious pressure against my clit. With my vibrator on high, I was able to take the edge off this morning, but with Rampage on top of me, I'm wound up all over again.

A low growl rumbles in his throat. "You'd better be wiggling 'cause you're moving into half guard," he warns. "Now straighten up and make your transition."

"This is as straight as I get," I mutter. "I'm a woman. Women have curves. I happen to have a curve in my back, and it wants to stay that way."

"I can feel your curves. Every one of them. And it's making

it fucking hard to concentrate. Make your move 'cause if you don't do it soon, I'll have to go out and get a cup."

I suck in a sharp breath. "You aren't wearing a cup?"

"No."

Don't move. Don't move.

I can't help it. I move. Or more accurately, I grind.

Wham. Rampage transitions into half guard and flips me onto my front. While I try to get my knees under me, he straddles me and grabs my hips in his huge hands. Heat surges through my body, and I groan quietly in my throat. "What are we doing?"

"Hips up," he barks. "Ass down."

"They're connected," I point out. "Where the hips go, the ass follows."

Shilla snorts a laugh and drops to the floor beside me. "Like this." She stretches her body out into a perfectly smooth, flat, plank position, holding it with one hand. On her knuckles. Then she rolls to show me what Rampage wants me to do.

"If my body was one solid sheet of muscle, I could do that." I tense my muscles, try to force myself into a position my body is not meant to go. "However, I have a weakness for chocolate biscuits, lazy Sundays on a blanket in the park, scones with clotted cream, and chicken tikka with thick, white naan bread slathered in butter. Unfortunately, it lowers my middle center of gravity."

Rampage's hands slide over my stomach, his touch firm, arousing my whole body with the promise of what those fingers could do if they drifted just a little lower. My mind goes hazy with desire and I can't tell if I'm flying or if my hands and feet are still on the floor. I don't care about jiu-jitsu transitions. I don't care that Shilla is watching us with curious eyes or that we're supposed to be doing a group drill. I don't care if the whole class is watching us. All I care about is feeling connected to Rampage and wanting this moment to last forever.

He lifts me right off the floor, as if I weigh nothing, and pulls me against his broad chest, my ass against his hips, feet barely touching the mat, his hands firm around my body. My stomach clenches. My heart pounds. He leans down until his mouth is so close to my ear, I can feel the heat of his breath.

"I told you not to touch yourself last night," he whispers.

Oh God, how did he know? A flush of adrenaline tingles through my body, followed by a thrill of fear. "What are you going to do about it?"

His hands tighten on my hips, fingers digging into my flesh. "I'll show you tomorrow night. I want you to come back to the club."

His words awaken my darkest desires and a fierce longing to know just how far he will take me. But Amanda…the lawsuit… "I was only allowed one night. Is there another club?"

"I'll deal with Damien. I can't go anywhere else."

Anticipation crackles in the air between us, and I feel like we've come to the edge of a cliff. Do we turn back, or do we jump? What if one more night isn't enough?

"We shouldn't."

"No, we shouldn't." He strokes one finger over my hip, and my breath rushes from me in a wave of white-hot heat.

"Friday," I say softly.

He spins me around, sweeps out my legs, and carries me to the ground. We land in reverse of the position we started in. Me on my back. Rampage straddling my hips in the dominant position.

"Friday." A slow, sensual smile spreads across his face. "Prepare to be punished."

Maybe I shouldn't have told you

RAMPAGE

Friday night. Fight night. Except tonight the fight won't be in a cage. And it damn well won't be professional.

"You fucking bastard." I stalk into Damien's office at Club Sin and slam the door.

"The usual greeting is *hello*." He leans back in his leather chair and folds his arms. Defensive. And well he should be. I wanted to have it out with him on Wednesday night, but he slipped out of the club when I was with Penny, and I've been stewing for the last two days.

"You had no right giving Pen a membership to the club, and especially not to the private members' area." I am tempted to smash my fist through one of the freshly plastered walls, but I hold back, knowing the worst is still to come.

"Last I heard, this was my club," Damien says. "She went through the same process as everyone else, albeit a little bit faster. She has a need, and I think this is the place where she can fulfill it."

Maybe if I hadn't been putting so much energy into keeping my desire at bay, I would have seen what he saw in Penny. Or maybe I did, and that's why I pushed her away.

"You wouldn't have a club if not for your very silent silent partner," I spit out. My thumb flicks over my ring, twisting it around my finger. I wish I could just get rid of the damned thing. Accept who I am and move on with my life.

Damien winces ever so slightly at the low blow. His ego is still bruised after having to come to me for financial assistance when the club was in the red. I was happy to help out to keep the club afloat, and I've never once held it over his head, never interfered with the running of the club, never asked to be named on any documents. It was a gentlemen's agreement, and where I'm from, that's as good as any legal document— sometimes better.

"We agreed you wouldn't get involved with how I run the club." Damien pushes himself up from the desk and walks over to the wet bar in the corner. He pours two shots of scotch and hands me a glass. If Penny wasn't coming in tonight, I would be tempted to finish the bottle, but heavy drinking and play sessions don't mix.

"I wouldn't have felt the need to get involved if you hadn't brought in someone I know. She goes to my gym, hangs out with my friends, and she works for the landlord's attorney, who is the fiancée of one of my close friends. I can't think of a bigger conflict of interest." I throw back the drink and let the bitter liquid slide over my tongue. I'm not partial to scotch. My family built an empire on bourbon, and I'm a bourbon man through and through.

Damien sips his drink, savoring the taste. "Something clicked for her when she came in. How could I turn her away? She might never have had the courage to try somewhere else. She's not here to feed a kink, Jack. There's something else driving her."

Sometimes his psychology background is as much a hindrance as a help, and right now I'm putting it in the hindrance category. He's as close to the truth as he'll get without asking her directly, and I'm not about to tell. That's Penny's secret, and one I'm sure she didn't want me to know.

Just as I didn't want her to know mine. How can a Southern gentleman, born and bred to respect and protect women, want to hurt them? That's the question even Damien could not answer for me. That's the question Avery screamed at me when she found out about my kink and left me; the question that was on the mind of every member of my family when she married my brother Beau the day she was supposed to marry me.

"You set me up." I take the bottle from Damien and pour myself another shot. "You knew I'd find out you had her in your playroom."

Damien shrugs. "You're giving me a lot of credit. Maybe I like pretty, innocent English girls who dress like they're on their way to a picnic with the queen. Maybe I wanted to see that soft, creamy skin redden under my palms."

"Fuck off."

"Protective." He swirls his drink. "Big sign of attachment. If you wanted her so bad, why didn't you ever ask her out?"

"Because I can't have a fucking normal relationship." I thud my glass on the bar counter. "Especially with someone like her—all sweet and innocent, soft and pretty. Why would she want to be with someone who gets off on giving her pain?"

He raises an eyebrow, dabs at the liquid that splashed out of my glass with a napkin. "Ask any of the masochists."

"She's not a masochist."

He cocks his head to the side in his goddamn "I'm a fucking psychologist" pose. "What is she, then?"

Hurting. Beautiful. Brave. Funny. Determined.

Broken.

Pain gives her release, but I suspect she never realized it could give her pleasure, too.

Sighing into the silence, Damien answers his own question. "She's not what you thought."

"Is that how you justify what you've done?" My voice rises in pitch, and I slam the glass on the counter again.

Unfazed by my uncharacteristic outburst, Damien shrugs. "I did nothing more than introduce someone to the lifestyle. I take it from this visit that you enjoyed your time with her."

Enjoy? I can't even find a word to express the maelstrom of emotion that has consumed me since I had Penny in my playroom. I never intended to take her that far. I just wanted to get her the hell away from Damien, and then I thought I'd give her a taste of what she thought she wanted. I never expected her to respond to me the way she did, to be so willing, so brave, and so open to my touch.

And the scars…

Fuck.

My sweet, sexy Penny has a dark side. Just like me.

Damien studies me and grins. The bastard fucking grins. "She's coming back, isn't she?"

"Fuck off."

He chuckles. "You invited her."

"Shut the fuck up."

"You just spent five minutes giving me shit for letting her in, and now you're pissed off because I'm pointing out an inconsistency in your behavior. You're lucky I'm such a good friend or you'd be looking for new play space."

I fold my arms and glare. He's right. But I wouldn't have been tempted to ask her back if he hadn't invited her in the first place.

"She's the kind of girl you could actually take back to Tennessee," Damien says casually. "She's as close to being Southern as a non-Southerner can be."

"There is no going back," I spit out. "I was fucking disowned. Beau got everything. The family distillery business, Avery…" I swallow the bitterness clogging my throat. More than anything, I wish I could take back the night I shared the darkest part of my soul with Avery. I didn't want any secrets in our marriage. It never occurred to me that love had limits, and although I assured her I would never hurt her or do anything she didn't want, my kink was a limit for her.

Bad enough she walked away only a week before our

wedding. Worse—that she told my family my secret and married Beau on what was supposed to be our wedding day, leaving me to wonder just how long she'd loved him and if what we'd had together was real.

I let out a frustrated breath, knowing the frustration is directed as much at myself as at Damien. If not for my kink, I'd be in Tennessee, running the business I'd been groomed to run alongside my dad, married to the prettiest girl in the county, probably with a couple of kids and a house… Instead, I'm sitting in a sex club with a Master Dominant, on my way to hurt the first woman who has made me feel anything except self-loathing and regret since the day Avery broke off our engagement.

A woman who discovered my secret and came back for more.

Maybe if I give her what she wants, I'll get her out of my system. I'm pretty damn sure she'll never come back. Which is a good thing. I have nothing to offer but pain. Nothing to gain from a relationship but betrayal and heartache.

Damien lifts a quizzical eyebrow. "So, should I add her to your client list?"

"No. After tonight, she won't be back."

"I don't think Penny is the kind of woman who is easily dissuaded from going after something she wants. She was delightful on my spanking bench. I'd like to see her there again." He licks his lips, and I wonder if he's got a death wish he wants to come true tonight.

"She's mine."

"Only tonight," he says. "After that, it's ladies' choice."

Tension curls in the air between us. Cool and calm, Damien

tips his head back and finishes his drink. "Enjoy your evening. Because if you don't, I will."

———∿∿∿———

PENNY

"Back again?" Kitty smiles when I walk into the reception area of Club Sin. Tonight, her corset is black, trimmed in red velvet, the bodice cut in a heart shape that dips low, highlighting her ample cleavage. There are bruises on her upper arms shaped suspiciously like fingers. She sees me staring at them, and her eyes soften.

"Aren't they hot?" she says. "I played with Master Sean last night. He knows I like a little visual reminder of our evenings together. And check this out."

Before I can protest, she stands and turns around. Her corset drops low enough to cover her garter belt and the tops of her buttocks, but the rest of her ass and her thighs are bared, giving me a good view of her welts and bruises. Although I have no problem hurting myself, her injuries make me feel queasy inside.

"Are you okay?" I suck in my lips. "I mean, doesn't it hurt to sit?"

"Sitting's a bitch," she says. "But Master Sean made me promise not to stand at reception tonight unless it was necessary. He always seems to know when I break the rules, and then he punishes me."

"That wasn't punishment?" Is this what's in store for me? Is this really what I want?

Kitty laughs. "That was a whip. A crop or single tail would be punishment. Then there would be no question of me being able to sit all night."

Panic looms in the pit of my stomach, but I fight for control. I didn't come all this way just to chicken out at the prospect of a little pain. "Are all the Doms like that?"

She takes her seat again, gritting her teeth as she settles on the chair. "The Doms here are all fantastic. Very professional. Very serious. But they also know how to have fun. That's why we're one of the top clubs in the city and why the membership fee is so high. If I didn't have this as a second job, I would never be able to afford to play here."

"I didn't pay," I blurt out, ashamed to be freeloading.

"Master Damien took care of your membership fee."

"I'll need…to talk to him about that." I twist my dress in my hand. "I can't let him pay for me."

"There is no talking to him. He does what he wants to do." Kitty laughs. "And he's given instructions not to be disturbed all evening. He's in a meeting with his attorney."

"His attorney?" My breaths come in short pants. Does he know what Amanda has planned? Is that why they're meeting on a Friday night?

"Maybe I shouldn't have told you." Kitty grimaces. "I'm always getting punished for talking too much."

Punished. I am suddenly reminded why I've come to the club tonight. "Um…I'm meeting Master Jack. Where should I go?"

"Are you sure it's Master Jack you're meeting? He only scenes with the most experienced submissives and the die-hard masochists."

"And me, it seems." I smooth my hands down over my stretchy little white dress, the only thing in my closet remotely close to the fetish wear I saw when I visited the club. Black would have been better, but I don't own anything darker than eggshell blue.

"If you need someone when you get out…" Her voice trails off. "To talk to. Or if you need someone to call you a cab or take you to the hospital, just let me know."

Hospital? "You're scaring me, Kitty."

"You should be scared. Even I wouldn't play with Master Jack, and I like it rough." She pushes the buzzer, and the door to the club opens. "Room six. It's the one with all the scratches on the door."

"Yeah. I know."

Heart pounding, I walk along the corridor to room six. All the doors to the other rooms are closed, and the hallway is eerily silent. My heels echo on the polished tile, and I slow my pace to check out the framed, lighted photos on the walls of people bound in intricately tied rope. Everything I've seen so far speaks of an incredible attention to detail. Class rather than crass. I feel another twinge of regret that I will have some part in shutting it all down.

The door to room six is open. I step inside and find a note taped to one of the glass display cases: "Clothes off. Underwear on. Kneel on rug."

Kneel? I'm not so sure about kneeling to anyone, but if this is the game I need to play, I'll give it a try. After closing the door, I slip off my dress and shoes and put them in the white locker at the side of the room along with my purse. My pony-tail brushes over my shoulders, and I adjust the straps of my new mint-green lace bra, at once relieved and disappointed he doesn't want me naked.

My knees hit the soft red carpet, and I take a few deep breaths as I look around the room. The bench with the cage beneath it has been pushed over to the wall, but I can still see the indenta-tions in the area rug around me. I can't imagine agreeing to be put into a cage. After spending the better part of my child-hood being locked in my room as punishment for even the most minor disobedience, I haven't been able to handle closed-in spaces. And yet I could never have imagined being here either.

Stripped down, on my knees, my scars bared for all to see.

10

Do you want me to stop?

PENNY

"EYES ON THE FLOOR."

I startle at the sound of Jack's voice. So caught up in my thoughts, I didn't hear the door open or notice him enter the room. My eyes drop right away, and I pull at the carpet with my fingers, at a loss for something to do with my hands.

Jack's footsteps echo on the polished concrete, and I wince when the door slams, catch my breath when the bolt slides into place. I am a mess of nervous anticipation, desperate to raise my head to see his face.

"Hands on your lap. I like the area rug the way it is."

Grimacing, I place my hands on my lap in what feels like a very submissive position. Except I'm not submissive, and I have no secret desire to give up my power. I'm just here for the pain. I drop my hands to my sides and look up, only to see Jack leaning against the wall watching me. He is dressed head to toe in black, his leather pants encasing legs that are thick with muscle, his short-sleeved T-shirt stretched tight over powerful muscles, emblazoned with an ad for a local distillery.

He lifts an eyebrow at my all-too-obvious perusal of his mouth-watering body. "You're not very good at following directions."

My body heats at the unmistakable note of warning in his tone, but I owe it to him, and to me, to explain. "Not if they go against the grain."

"And the grain is?"

"I'm not submissive, and I have no desire to be submissive. I didn't really think about it the other night, but if that's what you need, if that's what needs to happen, I don't know if this will work for me."

Jack cocks his head to the side and studies me. "You're kneeling."

"Your couch isn't really that comfy," I point out. "So the kneeling wasn't really a hardship."

A reluctant smile spreads across his face. "It's not meant for comfort. Nothing in this room is about comfort. People don't come here to be hugged and cuddled."

"So why the bed?" I gesture to the four-poster bed in the corner, the posts and beams surrounding it embedded with D-rings and chains.

"Master Damien insisted," he says. "He rents the room out for private parties when I'm not around. I've never used it."

"A virgin bed."

This time he laughs out loud. "I suppose it is."

I work the carpet again between my fingers. The pile is soft and thick, unexpectedly luxurious compared to the austerity of the room. "So what do we do now that you know I'm not submissive and I'm not comfortable sitting with my hands on my lap staring at the floor like a good little girl?"

"We don't get hung up on labels." Jack walks across the room and drags the giant padded bench from against the wall, identical to the one Master Damien used on Wednesday night. "But I am going to restrain you on this bench and spank you for disobeying my rules. How does that sound?"

I nibble on my bottom lip. "You're asking me? I thought you were the Dom and what you say goes. Isn't that how it works?"

He lifts the heavy bench easily and places it on the carpet in front of me, his delicious biceps bulging with the effort. "You have all the power is how it works," he says. "How much you want to give up to me is entirely up to you. I'll never take anything from you that you don't want to give. If you want to trust me to take you as far as I think you can go, then you can. Or we can set limits before we begin. And you can always stop the scene with your safe word."

His words speak to the fear deep inside me—the loss of power, the loss of control, the futility of trying to please someone who could never be pleased, of obeying all the rules only to be punished anyway out of spite, of looking for love where no love could be found.

"I set out all my limits in the questionnaire. Except for the hard-core stuff, permanent injury, or scarring, I'm up for anything."

Jack gestures me over to the bench. He seems guarded tonight, not the chill, friendly Jack I know from the gym and yet not quite the cold, distant Dom he was the last time we were here. It is almost like he's not sure what mask to wear.

"One knee on each ledge, body across the center." He pats the padded sides of the bench, and I take up the required position, shifting to accommodate my breasts and the almost-uncomfortable spread of my thighs. I feel less exposed on the bench than I did chained to his ceiling, and yet the way it forces my legs apart makes me feel curiously vulnerable.

"I just want you to hurt me."

His face tightens, the Dom mask slipping into place. "I will."

I lay my head down, and watch him select cuffs from the rack on the wall. My heart is thudding so hard I can hear the vibration through the bench.

"Really hurt me. I can take a lot."

"In this room, Pen, I'm in charge." His voice drops to a warning tone. "I make the decisions. I decide how much you get and how much you can take." He buckles one cuff around my wrist and affixes it to the nearest D-clip. After testing for movement, he restrains my other wrist, clipping the cuff to the side of the bench.

"I'm not a masochist, though." I don't know why I can't stop talking, but my mouth just keeps going. "I don't get off on the pain."

"Apparently you do, or I wouldn't be punishing you."

His words hang heavy in the air. I've never derived any sexual pleasure from cutting myself, but I do get a rush that gives me release from the emotional pressure that builds up inside me when life throws its curve balls. But it was different with Jack. Although I didn't get release, the feelings I had from our encounter were most definitely sexual. Very sexual. Very intense.

"I think the getting off part has more to do with you than the pain." The words fall out before I can catch them, and I squeeze my eyes shut as if blocking out the sight of him could erase my faux pas.

An awkward silence fills the room. Jack turns away and takes another set of cuffs from the rack. From my vantage point on the bench, I can see his shoulders stiffen and his fingers tighten around the stiff leather until his knuckles turn white. Have I overstepped? Whatever I've done, it's had some kind of effect on him because for a long moment he doesn't turn around.

"Do you get pleasure from this?" I ask to cover my embarrassment.

He releases a long breath and turns around. "The pain aspect, yes."

A shiver runs down my spine. "Do you need it, the way I need to…" My voice trails off. I've never discussed my cutting with anyone except my therapist. Adam, my ex, didn't give a damn about my cutting so long as I cooked and cleaned, did as I was told, and made myself available in his bed for his sexual pleasure and on the other side of his fists as an outlet for his anger. Only once did he bring it up, and that was when he threw me out, telling me I was sick and twisted and no one would ever want a broken girl like me. But here, in this room designed for pain, with a man who already knows the secret

I've kept for so long, I feel free. Even more, I don't feel judged. "Cut myself?" I finish.

He hesitates, the cuffs in his hand. "No. It's more like a craving. I could give it up if I had to." Regret crosses his face, but it disappears so quickly I wonder if I saw it.

"I couldn't give up coffee."

"That's an addiction," he says dryly. "Not a craving."

"So you're not addicted to tying curvy British girls to your spanking bench and giving them a sound beating?"

I look up and see that Jack has turned away again, but the rise and fall of his shoulders betray his laughter. Why does he feel the need to hide his emotions from me? I know Jack. He has a great sense of humor, and he especially enjoys British wit. How many times did we kick back in the lounge at Redemption watching reruns of *Blackadder* or the British version of *The Office*? Or practicing swear words in each other's accents? I've never laughed so hard as when I heard *bollocks* in his Southern twang.

"I'm going to have to gag you if you keep this up." He clears his throat and walks over to the rack of terrifying implements on the wall.

"I'm ruining the mood, aren't I? I suppose this is supposed to be very serious and scary. I shouldn't be mouthing off while I'm tied half-naked to a spanking bench. But this is why I…"

My words trail off when Jack holds up a gag with a ball in the center. I suck in a sharp breath, and he smiles.

"Now that's the look I like to see. Fear."

Fear is right. No way is he sticking that ball in my mouth. "Don't put that on me…please," I whisper.

"No more talking. I'm not your friend in here, Pen."

But he is, because we've just had the kind of conversation we used to have, albeit about a topic I never imagined we would discuss. It was easy, fun. And yet something more. If we weren't friends, I wouldn't trust him enough to be here, or to bare my secrets and my body. If we weren't friends, he wouldn't call me Pen before he spanked me.

He places the gag on the table in front of me and slides a soft, padded cuff around my thigh.

I wince, and he freezes.

"Did you disobey me about the cutting, too? When I told you not to touch yourself the other night, I meant all kinds of touch."

Embarrassed, I look away. "No, but the last time I went kind of deep, and it hasn't healed. And the skin is all kinds of sensitive with all the scarring." I shock myself with my ability to talk about this secret part of me so openly, but this club, this room, and this man I think of as a friend all seem designed to lower my inhibitions. Differences are celebrated here. Judgments suspended. Needs and desires, no matter how far off the beaten track, can be met and fulfilled. I feel relaxed here in a way I've never felt before. At home in a place that's not going to exist in two more days.

Jack squats down in front of the bench and lifts my head with a finger under my chin so I meet his gaze. "I want you to make me a promise. A real promise. Not because I ordered it or because it is part of the scene, but because it is a promise you want to give a friend. The next time you feel like cutting yourself, you call me. No matter what time of day or where I am or what I'm doing, you call me and we'll come here and I'll give you what you need."

"What do I need?"

He makes his way to the back of the bench and, without warning, strikes me with the full force of his hand. "This."

Pain sheets across my left ass cheek, setting my skin on fire. My limbs jerk against the restraints, and my inability to move sends adrenaline coursing through me, making the pain more intense.

His hand smacks my ass again, and the burning sensation floods my mind, pushing out every thought except how to get away from his hand. I struggle furiously against the restraints, and my clit rubs against the bench, sending confusing signals of pleasure mixing with the pain.

"You're very quiet. Makes me think I'm not working hard enough." He grips my neck with one hand, holding me still, and swats again, this time so hard my breath leaves me in a rush.

"Why are you being spanked?" He hits me again, and my eyes fill with tears.

"Because I want you to hurt me."

"No."

Another blast of heat explodes across my skin, and my body jerks forward on the bench. Blood roars in my ears. My breath comes in short pants, and sweat beads on my brow. In the back of my mind, I know he's waiting for an answer, but I can't think for the pressure building up behind my clit that is somehow connected to the pain.

I freeze, shame heating my cheeks. I can't come on the bench while Jack is spanking me. It's not right. It doesn't make sense. And he's…my friend.

He strikes again, four blows in quick succession, two on each burning cheek. Fire sizzles straight to my clit, and I am awash in sensation: the cool wood against my thighs, the soft padding beneath my forehead, the firm press of the pad against my body, the burn of the skin on my ass, the slight pinch of the cuffs, and the pressure of the bench holding my legs apart. I squirm, unable to stop myself from seeking more friction where I need it the most.

"Don't you dare come," he barks.

Humiliation floods me with heat almost as intense as my burning ass. My breath catches in my throat, and I press my forehead to the cool bench and moan in frustration. "I'm sorry." I don't know what else to say. Every time he touches me, I turn into a raging horny beast, and that's not why either of us is here.

"Nothing to be sorry about." Still holding me firmly with one hand on my neck, he strokes down my back with a firm, knowing touch. Not sexual—thank God—but assessing. When he reaches my stinging ass, I wince.

"Nicely warmed up," he says. But his voice cracks the tiniest bit.

Every muscle in my body tenses at once. *That was the warm-up?*

"You didn't give me that promise I asked for." His next blow sends me jerking forward so hard the small bit of friction from my knickers sliding on the bench is almost too much to bear. My breasts are aching and swollen, the nipples hard and peaked beneath my bra.

"I promise."

"What do you promise?" The next few blows come in rapid succession, and I struggle to tell him what he wants to hear, but it's so damn hard with my ass on fire and every muscle in my body tensed as I fight the urgent, desperate need to come.

"To call you if I feel the need to cut myself."

"Good girl." He gently removes my ponytail holder, and my hair sheets down my back. His breath catches in his throat ever so softly, but before I can turn to look at him, he twists my hair in his fist and yanks my head back.

"You're right," he says, musing. "Your back does like to arch. And it brings your ass up all ready to be spanked again, just like it did in the gym. I wanted to spank the sass right out of you the other day, but I thought about how much more fun it would be to do it here, where I could make you scream." He jerks my head back so hard tears come to my eyes. "Do you like to be spanked?"

"Yes," I whisper. But only by him.

Jack leans down and brushes his lips over my ear in an intimate caress.

"I can't hear you, darlin'."

"Yes."

Jack gives a satisfied grunt in his throat and smacks my ass over and over, hard and fast with no discernible pattern. I try to breathe through the pain, try not to cry as the blows continue, but I can't help myself. Tears run down my face, and I cry in earnest. My brain fuzzes, and I feel a rush of pleasure. Suddenly, I'm floating, free of pain and the guilt and shame I carry with me every day, free of feelings of unworthiness that weigh me down. I am…just me.

———∿∿∿———

RAMPAGE

Sweat beads on my forehead, and I smack Penny's perfect ass again. She whimpers but doesn't scream. I suspect she has a high pain tolerance after what she's done to herself, and I ramp up the intensity, hitting her harder with the next blow. I still can't believe this is real, my perfect English rose strapped to my table, begging for my hand. Her lacy green thong covers the top part of her ass, an attempt at modesty that serves only to heighten my desire, and with her creamy skin now pink, marked by my hand, I'm painfully hard, my cock straining against my leathers.

Sex and pain. I was taught that hitting girls was not only wrong but also morally reprehensible and against everything we stood for in the South. So when I was thirteen or fourteen years old and started having thoughts that involved inflicting pain but were somehow mixed up with sex, I was appalled at myself. I suppressed those thoughts and urges and tried to be normal. I dated. I fumbled. I had my first sexual encounter with a sweet blond Southern belle named Daisy. But around the time I was seventeen, those thoughts and urges came back, more intense, more disconcerting, and I thought I was twisted, broken. Desperate, I searched the Internet for answers and finally stumbled on BDSM. That's when I realized there was a different kind of normal and I wasn't alone.

Still, I've never been able to fully accept my kink or get rid of the self-loathing, the incongruity of an upbringing that is fundamentally incompatible with my need to blend sex and pain. Avery didn't help. Although I knew sadism wasn't socially acceptable, I wasn't prepared for her disgust or revulsion. I didn't expect to be judged by the woman I loved and who claimed to love me. I never even touched her. She condemned me on my words alone. Rejected me. Betrayed me. Broke my fucking heart. Ruined me for women forever.

Or so I thought.

Penny moans softly, and I strike her ass again. Sweet and soft, she shares Avery's fragile beauty, and yet she is not destroyed by my touch. Her body responds to every blow, absorbing the pain. She whimpers but doesn't scream. Moans but doesn't sob. She is aroused even though she didn't expect it, and her embarrassment at her body's natural response only fuels my fire. I feel a rush with every strike, like I'm high. My senses magnify. I can smell her arousal and the fragrance of her perfume. I can feel the softness of her skin beneath my palm. I can sense when she needs me to continue and when she needs to catch her breath. I could push her to come with one well-placed blow, but I know that would send her over the edge. She wasn't ready for this connection, but then neither was I.

I raise my hand to strike again, pulling back when she goes limp on the bench. Awareness swamps me in a rush, clearing the haze from my mind. "Pen? You with me?"

My heart skips a beat when she doesn't respond, and I walk

around to the front of the bench. Her head is turned to the side, resting on the flat surface, eyes closed, cheeks streaked with tears.

"Pen?"

She draws in a shuddering breath. "Tickety-boo."

"What?"

"Crackin'," she mumbles.

"Since I don't have my British–American dictionary handy, I'm going to guess you've had enough."

She opens her eyes and frowns. "Don't be daft."

I undo the clips holding her wrists and ankles to the bench. Her hands are cold, her limbs soft. She mumbles British swear words as I lift her and carry her to the couch.

Lust rages through me as I hold her in my arms, and I wrap an aftercare blanket around her, as much to keep her warm as to curb my desire to take the scene one step too far. Her pain fulfills me, soothes the dark passenger who rides my heart, yet for the first time, pain isn't enough. I want something else— something to fill the longing that burns in my soul.

"I think we went too far. That's my fault. You were so damn responsive. So brave. So strong." I stroke her hair as she snuggles into my chest, knowing this intimate moment won't last. A scene that intense requires some form of release—either emotional or physical—and Penny has had neither.

"Easy peasy," she murmurs.

I cradle her in my arms. Her curves sink into my body, her ass resting on my painfully erect cock. I never fuck my play partners after a scene, preferring to take my release by my own hand. But right now, if she wanted me, I'd rip those panties off her and take her right here.

She shudders, and I pull her closer, tuck her head beneath my chin, and tighten my arms around her. She fits perfectly into my body, as if she were made for me.

"Oh God." She stiffens suddenly, thrashes against me, struggling to get out of the blanket as her mind and body become one again. Her ass grinds against my cock, and I can barely breathe with the effort of holding myself back.

"Shh." I tighten the edges of the blanket, trapping her hands, and drop my voice to the low, commanding tone she responded to the other day. "Be still. You're okay."

"I need to go." Her body trembles, and she chews on her bottom lip, squirms on my lap.

"When I think you're ready."

"No," she snaps. "Now. I have to go now. You don't understand." Her cheeks flush crimson, and as she struggles, the blanket falls away, giving me a clear view of her taut, hard nipples, straining beneath her bra.

"I do understand." I rest my hand on her quivering stomach, stroke my finger along the lacy edge of her panties. She needs to come, and although I will have to wait for my physical release, I can give Penny hers.

She tenses, caught between need and fear. I slip one finger beneath the elastic and stroke over her mound.

"Yes?"

She turns her head, looks away. "Yes," she whispers.

I glide a finger over her mound and through the slick folds

of her pussy. "You're so wet. So fucking wet. I never thought a spanking would arouse you this much."

She grabs my shirt, moans in frustration. I push two fingers into her tight, wet heat and pump. Once. Twice. I press my palm against her clit, and she comes apart with a scream, back arching, body rigid. Her first scream for me, and I drink it in, taking my pleasure from her erotic pain.

I thrust my fingers deeper, dragging out her orgasm, watching her totally let go. She is beautiful. Wild. Breathtaking. But she doesn't belong to me.

When her body goes limp, I withdraw my hand, pull her up against me, and rest her cheek against my chest. For a long time, we sit in silence. My cock is still painfully hard despite the lack of stimulation. Just being near Penny, it seems, is enough to keep me fully aroused.

Finally, her muscles tense, and she pushes away. "Can I go now?"

"You need water. Some chocolate." I reach across her to the table where I keep snacks to replenish my subs after the scenes.

"I'm good," she says stiffly. "Really. I just…I'm knackered. I need to go."

"Look at me." I cup her jaw and tilt her head back. Her eyes dart to mine and then away.

"You don't need to be embarrassed around me," I say softly. "There is little I haven't seen in here. Less I haven't done. Although I have to admit I've never pushed anyone the way I pushed you, never had anyone respond so beautifully to the pain I gave them."

"I have to go." She pushes hard against my chest and wriggles out of my arms. I don't know what to say to soothe her or assuage her fears without letting my Dom loose again, and that would scare her away for good. I don't know how to make her stay, simply because I've never wanted anyone to stay before.

"You're not ready. We should talk about the scene," I say, folding the blanket as she crosses the floor toward the locker.

Penny pulls open the door, turns away as she gets dressed. "I don't want to talk. Please. Jack. It's over. No more."

I feel a curious tightening in my chest, and I cross the floor toward her. "You need to sit down for a few minutes. You aren't thinking straight."

"Don't tell me what I need," she snaps. "You have no idea. I needed pain. You gave me—" Her voice cracks, breaks, and she shakes her head.

Pleasure? Release? What did I give her that has triggered this storm?

"Good-bye, Jack." She slings her purse over her shoulder, and I follow her to the door.

"I'll ask Kitty to call a taxi. Let me do that for you."

Her shoulders drop, and she sighs. "Okay."

I head over to the table to grab my phone. By the time I turn, she is gone.

What if we weren't friends?

PENNY

MONDAY MORNING I TRY TO BURY MYSELF IN MY WORK WHILE Amanda is in court, but every five minutes I'm on my phone looking things up. First I search spanking and how long the bruises last. I am relieved to discover my two days of tenderness is normal. Next I search for articles on people getting aroused by spanking. Many people. So, still normal. How about people who get an emotional release through spanking so they don't feel the urge to cut themselves for the first time in years? A few. How curious. Now I'm on a roll. I search for blogs about people getting so aroused when they are spanked by their friend that he has to get them off right there and then and they die of humiliation. A few. Except those bloggers don't seem to be humiliated and are keen to repeat the experience. Me? Not so much.

I don't know what to think. I don't know what to feel. And the only person I can talk to about it is the one person who confuses me. Is this just part of what happens in the club, or is it more? I can't imagine doing anything I've done with Jack in the club with anyone else. My kink experiences are intimately tied with him. I like him. I trust him. He's my friend, but now he's more. At least to me.

Amanda walks into my office, and I quickly tuck away my phone. Not that she can see it from the doorway, but sometimes she likes to sit and chat, and I'm not sure what she would think about my interest in spanking.

"Gerry's here," she says. "Can you meet us in the conference room? The hearing didn't go well, and he's unhappy, to put it mildly. I want at least three of us there."

"What happened?" I grab my notepad and pen from my desk and follow her out into the reception area. Amanda isn't usually concerned about being alone with male clients. She once had to defend herself from an attorney who became obsessed with her, and she did a bang-up job, giving him a solid beating using some of the techniques she learned at Redemption.

"I don't know." She grabs a tray while Jill pours four cups of coffee. "Damien Stone showed up with his attorney and half a dozen affidavits that made the judge turn down our application. It was like they knew exactly what I had planned to do and spent the weekend collecting the evidence to refute my arguments."

"How could he know?" My forehead creases in a frown. "The only people you shared your plan with were Gerry, Jill, and me. Gerry isn't about to let the cat out of the bag on his own case, and you know we wouldn't talk."

Or did I?

Things got pretty foggy for a while there when I was at Club Sin two nights ago, and what I do remember I don't want to remember—restrained on the spanking bench, Jack's hand on my ass, fire, pain, and arousal so fierce I thought I would die if I couldn't come. I remember mumbled words as he took me off the bench. I remember being snuggled in his arms. And then it all went away, and suddenly I was a raging, horny beast begging him to make me come. Oh God.

"You okay?"

Amanda's voice pulls me off the humiliation roundabout, and I am wrenched back into the moment. My pulse kicks up a notch. Did I say anything to him about the case when I was on the bench, floating on the pleasure train?

"Penny?"

"Sure. Yeah. Just…knackered today. And the hearing. Wow. What are we going to do?"

"We have to calm Gerry down first," she says. "Then we'll come up with a new plan."

We file into the bright, airy boardroom with its cream leather chairs, polished oak table, and sea green carpet. With his blue-black hair, thick features, cruel slash of a mouth, and dark Armani suit, Gerry looks more mafia than real estate magnate, and he shares a similar disdain for the law. I had a bad feeling about him when he first walked in the door, and now that we're up close and personal, my bad feeling gets worse. Gerry nods at Amanda and openly leers at Jill as she hands out the coffee. His dark gaze rakes over me from head to toe and zooms in on my chest. I lift my notebook, blocking his view as I sit beside

Amanda. From the corner of my eye, I can see her lip curl, and I know she feels as disgusted as I do.

"There were really only a few ways around the lease provisions." Amanda forestalls Gerry, who has just opened his mouth, no doubt to rant at us. "They must have prepared for all the possibilities over the weekend so they were ready for us this afternoon. It's a setback but not a disaster. I'm confident we can still get them out without having to wait the duration of the notice period. I mentioned before that mediation was an option—"

"I got a plan." Gerry gives us the kind of smile that sharks give before they chomp off your leg—all teeth. "A lot of high-profile people go to the club using a hidden entrance. Under the terms of the lease, I have access to the property to make improvements for security. I'm thinking of putting cameras on all the doors and then sending the tapes to Stone. I'll tell him to get out or I'll make them public and let the world see all the fucking celebrities who got a dirty secret."

"That's not the kind of mediation I was thinking about," Amanda says calmly. When Gerry first came to us, she'd pushed for mediation to avoid the high costs of litigation in a case ill-suited to the courts, but Gerry wouldn't hear of it. He'd already talked to Damien Stone, he said, and they hadn't been able to come to an agreement. So why waste time with more talking?

"Blackmail is illegal," she continues. "I can't condone it as a course of action, and if you were to tell me that it was something you planned to do or had done, I would be forced to withdraw as your attorney. We do have other options available to us, however, and I'm happy to discuss them. Mediation would be much faster."

Gerry's face tightens, and he pushes back his chair. "I need them out of that building now. I've got plans for that property, and I won't let Stone and his fucking sex club get in my way. He was supposed to give in as soon as he got served with the papers. I never expected him to hire a fucking lawyer and go through with the damn court case." He slams his fist on the table and stands so quickly his chair topples over. "You didn't do your fucking job. You were supposed to scare him off."

"I'm a lawyer, not an enforcer," she says as he storms out the door. "If there are any legal avenues you want to pursue, just give me a call."

"He's a real piece of work," I say after Jill follows Gerry out to make sure he doesn't cause any trouble. "Do you think he really will try to blackmail Stone?"

"I wouldn't put it past him." Amanda sighs. "I've been fighting him to keep everything legal ever since I took him on as a client. Personally, I don't like trying to kick the club out early when there are notice provisions in the lease that would give them time to wind up the business, but I'll still do my best for my client. I almost wish he'd do something illegal so I have an excuse to drop him. I only agreed to take the case as a favor to one of the guys at the gym because Gerry's a distant relation. You know how it goes."

Not having many relatives and none in the U.S., I don't know how it goes, but I nod and smile anyway and take a sip of my now-cold and bitter coffee.

"You'd better type up a note of our meeting so we have on record that I advised him against blackmail and explained that it's illegal," Amanda says. "The last thing we need is to be dragged through the mud with him. I can't afford to have the firm's reputation tarnished when we're just starting out."

Guilt spears me in the chest. I have to tell Amanda. She's not just my boss, she's my friend, and I wouldn't want to do anything to hurt her or compromise her business. "Should we…warn the club about what he might do? I mean, if there are people there who don't want to be outed, they should probably know."

Amanda pushes back her chair. "Morally, yes. Legally, no. He gave that information to us in confidence and under attorney–client privilege. He didn't tell us outright that's what he was going to do, so there is no crime for me to report. And I can't call up Stone's attorney to warn him about something that might just be an emotional reaction to what happened in court today because it could have a significant financial impact on Stone's business. Basically, that means unless we have evidence or a serious reason to believe he would carry out his threat, we can't say anything to anyone." She moves to leave, and I hold out my hand.

"I need to tell you something." Bile rises in my throat, and I twist the ring on its chain. "I went back to the club after I served the documents. I'd never seen anything like it, and I was curious, and I figured it was my only chance to check it out because I thought we would win in court today and they would be evicted. I didn't say anything about the case or tip anyone off, but now I'm worried I've compromised you somehow, especially after what happened today, and hurting you in any way is the last thing I would ever do. I'm so sorry."

Amanda falls back in her chair and lets out a long breath. "Thank you for telling me. I trust you implicitly, Penny. I don't believe for a second you would have discussed the case. Still, it would be better if you don't go back while this case is going on. Appearances matter, and we don't want to give Gerry any ammunition when it comes time to pay the bill."

"Of course, I won't." I am both gutted and relieved, but mostly I am thankful I haven't compromised Amanda or, worse, lost my job. But what about Jack?

"Anything else?" She gathers up her papers, and we push in our chairs. "You still look worried."

"I know someone whose career could be damaged if he was caught on camera—"

Amanda cuts me off with a shake of her head. "I wish I didn't have to put you in this position, but you can't say anything. If he's a friend or someone you care about, do what you can to keep him away from the club until the lawsuit is resolved, but you can't tell him why."

A friend or someone I care about.

Jack is both. And now I have to keep a secret that could destroy his career.

—⁓—

Cora meets me at the Redemption snack bar after I get out of my meeting with Amanda. We are taking another jiu-jitsu class, and I am both hoping and dreading that Jack will be there.

"I'm going to set up a double date for us on Thursday night," she announces.

Since I can guess who my half of the double date might be, and since it is someone who spanked me, finger-fucked me, and then watched me run away with my proverbial tail between my legs, I am not overly enthusiastic about the idea.

"I'm busy. You and Blade Saw go out and have fun."

"You have to come." Cora grabs my arm, pulls me away from the counter. "I can't be alone with Blade Saw. When we were rolling on the mats in jiu-jitsu class, I drooled every time he talked to me. It was too much. He has an amazing body, and he was lying on top of me, and then I was lying on him, and then my head was locked between his legs… I don't know how people who do the sport aren't horny all the time."

"You have to pick the right partner," I say. "If you partner with someone who hasn't washed his cup or had a shower since Sunday, you aren't thinking of anything except getting the beast off you." I shake her off and order a blueberry acai wheatgrass shake, although what I really want is the big fat cinnamon bun with extra cream cheese frosting that I saw in the coffee shop across from Amanda's office this morning. However, while tied to the spanking bench with my bare ass in the air, I had an epiphany of sorts and decided to follow a slightly lower-calorie eating regime.

"I only want Blade Saw." She sighs. "I've never met anyone like him. The guys I hang out with are all about their brains, not their bodies. They're pale, skinny, and hunched. Most of them have bad eyesight from staring at a computer for too long.

They game all night long, and watch *The Big Bang Theory* for the science. They kiss like droids, and they get so excited about having a live woman in their bed, it's over before it begins, if you know what I mean."

"I get the picture." I take the shake from the cashier and gag on the healthy taste. Maybe if I pretend it's ice cream…

"On the other hand," she continues, "I understand them. I like *The Big Bang Theory*. I love gaming all night long. Maybe I'm not cut out for an alpha male. Maybe I kiss like a droid, and he can sense that with his alpha senses."

"Oh, honey. I'm pretty sure he likes you. He didn't spend that much time with anyone else in class last week. I think he's just gun-shy because he's had a lot of really bad relationships. He's always on the wrong end of a love triangle."

"Does that mean you'll come on the double date?" She gives me the big-eyed, pathetic puppy dog look that she uses when we're kicking back and watching TV and she wants to watch shows with aliens and spaceships.

"Fine. I'll come on the date if you put this shake out of its misery. I can't drink something this healthy."

Cora snatches it from my hand. "I thought you were into Jack. The two of you were pretty much going at it on the mats during the last class."

My cheeks heat, and I give an indignant sniff. "We were not 'going at it.' He was teaching me some moves."

"I wish Blade Saw would teach me those moves."

We sit at the nearest table, and Cora sips the shake while I dream of soft, warm buns and cream cheese frosting. I take a quick glance around to make sure we won't be overheard. "Those moves were moving things too fast."

"You slept with him!" Her face lights up.

"No. Close. But before it got too out of control, I cut and ran."

She claps her hand over her mouth. "You cut and ran? Poor guy."

Annoyed, I frown. "What do you mean 'poor guy'? It was getting too serious too fast. I didn't want him to get any ideas."

"He already had ideas," Cora says. "I'll bet if you'd been alone with him in class, his ideas would have included stripping off your clothes and doing you right there on the mats. You clearly weren't paying attention, but a couple of the guys went over to break you two up 'cause you were supposed to be doing a drill, and he growled them away."

"Well, now I've growled him away. So going out with him is going to be awkward."

Cora makes a sad puppy dog face and I cave, like I always do. I can't resist that face. "Fine. I'll do it for you so you can have your own hot MMA fighter in your bed who I'm pretty sure doesn't kiss like a droid."

And I'll be able to make sure he doesn't go to the club that night. One down. Countless nights to go.

Unfortunately for Cora, Blade Saw isn't teaching jiu-jitsu tonight. Instead, we get blond-haired, blue-eyed Renegade, Amanda's fiancée, who is chill and laid-back unless he's in the cage or another male is breathing in Amanda's direction or we're in class and I'm trying to avoid touching my sore ass to the mats. We also get his assistant and matching blond beauty, Redemption's own man whore, Doctor Death.

"Ladies." Doctor Death kneels in front of me on the mat. "I'll show you a trick for breaking the triangle submission. Penny, prepare to be mounted."

"I'll bet you say that to all your women." I drop my legs so he can straddle my hips in full mount, while Cora drools beside me. If I didn't know Doctor Death so well, I would be drooling, too. He's soap-opera-doctor handsome, he's in great shape, and he has a Ken-doll smile.

"I do say that to all my women." He settles his weight and leans forward. "And some men. I don't discriminate."

Cora chokes back a laugh while I roll up into position for putting Doctor Death in a triangle choke submission, which entails tucking his head between my legs.

"This is good," he says. "I can do a lot from down here. It makes me think we should go out sometime and play this game for real."

I hook my leg around his neck and grab his arm, pulling him forward. "I can't go out with you," I say, huffing with the effort of holding him in place. "I know you too well. I wouldn't be able to take you seriously. If you tried to kiss me, I'd probably laugh and damage your fragile ego."

He twists to the side, easily loosening my grip, and I make a mental note to remember that escape trick next time I'm caught in a triangle submission when out with friends.

"I have a very robust ego, and as long as your lips are in the right place, I don't care what they are doing. Now, stop trying to submit me, and submit me."

"I know that movie," Cora says with delight. "He's a geek."

"Damn it, Cora. I'm a doctor, not a geek." He and Cora share a laugh at their private geek jokes while I untwist myself from his grasp.

After we've practiced our submissions, Renegade lines the class up along the wall. "Rampage is joining us today to show us the gogoplata submission that he used to win his last fight. He only just volunteered to help at the start of class, so he's not wearing his gi. Go easy on him."

An excited murmur fills the dojo, mingled with laughter, but this time, mercifully, there are no screams when he gestures to the corner where Jack—I can't think of him as Rampage after what we did together in the club—is waiting. Usually, he would smile at the class and make a joke, but today he is all scowls. He seems particularly irritated with Doctor Death from the way he's trying to burn a hole through him with his eyes.

Renegade clears his throat. "Who wants to volunteer to be Rampage's partner for the demo?"

Silence. No one wants to be his bitch, especially when he looks like he's about to eat someone for lunch.

"Doctor Death," Jack barks. "On the mat."

If I was a suspicious kind of person, I might think that he picked Doctor Death for a reason related to the scowl on his face and not because Doctor Death needs some practice with the gogoplata submission, but since I'm not, I assume he picked him at random.

"Go go gadget," Cora whispers.

Doctor Death grins at her and drops into a low crouch, facing Jack.

At a signal from Renegade, now standing beside me, he rushes Jack, who pretends to go down. Doctor Death grabs him around the middle. Jack mumbles something to him, and Doctor Death freezes and shoots a panicked glance at me. He tries to pull away, but it's too late. Seconds later, his head is trapped under Jack's foot, and he's locked up in a pretzel twist on the ground.

Renegade explains the submission and the different ways to escape. Doctor Death taps out, but Jack doesn't release him. Doctor Death taps again, flails. Renegade looks over and frowns.

"Let him go."

With a lazy stretch, Jack releases Doctor Death, lifting one massive leg, then the other, until Doctor Death collapses on all fours on the mat.

Jack gives a satisfied snort and joins Renegade, Cora, and me, his chest puffed out like he just won a fight.

"What the fuck was that about?" Renegade says quietly to Jack.

"Message."

"What message?"

Jack's gaze flicks to me and then away. "The usual message he gets when he's out of fucking line. Same message you gave him when he was messing with Amanda."

Cora jabs me indiscreetly in the side, and I shoot her a dirty look. "Friends," I whisper. "We're just friends."

Renegade sends us back to our sections to practice the new submission. Jack comes over to our newbie section and watches Cora and me struggle with the move. His thick, broad fingers tap against his thigh, and a rush of longing runs over me as I imagine what those fingers did two nights ago.

God, this is ridiculous. This is Rampage. Redemption's mascot. Everybody's best friend. And a professional athlete. So he has a dark side. That doesn't mean anything will change between us. He's still a nice guy, except he's a sadist who spanked me so hard I came on his hand.

"Did you watch what I did?"

My body pulses at the sound of his voice, and I force my eyes up, over his thick, muscular thighs, the fight shorts hanging low on his hips, the bulge of his cup, the chiseled abs, broad chest… Oh, and there's his ridiculously handsome face. "Yes."

He gives a cocky smile, his eyes glittering. "Then you know you'll need to lie back on the mat."

"Okay." I drop to sitting and suck in a sharp breath as my poor abused ass hits the mat.

Jack studies me for a long moment and then he bends down and presses his lips to my ear. "Does it hurt to sit, darlin'?"

My breath leaves me in a rush, and my pulse throbs between my thighs. "Ah. Yes."

"Good." His voice is low, rough, and sends an erotic shiver down my spine. "Stay like that. I'll help Cora first."

Breathe, Penny. Breathe. I inhale deeply and let it out slowly, like we do in yoga class. Is he playing mind games with me, or was that just an innocent "sit on the ass I bruised up the other night and remember every stroke of my hand while I help your friend"? My mind swirls with the possibilities while my insides clench, but there is no way for me to tell what he's thinking, and if I don't shut it down, I will twist myself up imagining things that might not be there.

He lies on the mat and coaches Cora through the move. I try not to notice the way his muscles bulge, his aura of pure, raw strength, and the ease with which he moves despite his size. After he sends Cora to practice with Doctor Death, he kneels in front of me, his eyes missing nothing. "How are you doing?"

"Good, thanks." My voice rises in pitch, belying my cheerful words. I let my eyes drift down his powerful chest and arms. Until he went pro, he always wore a yellow tank top with a happy face on it. Now he wears his sponsor shirts advertising everything from gear to power bars to sports drinks. Although I understand the business, part of me misses the old days when he was just another guy in the gym and not on his way to becoming a star.

"If you'd stayed, I would have looked after you," he whispers.

"I…you…did…look after me." I lie on my back and part my legs so he can get in position. His massive forearms harden and clench beside me, the way they must have done when he spanked me on Friday night.

He cocks one dark eyebrow, amused. "You were embarrassed."

"That wasn't why I was there."

"You were so fucking sexy." He grabs my wrists and pins my hands to the mat above my head.

My blood rushes hot through my veins. "What?"

"Sexy." He leans over me, makes a deep humming noise in the back of his throat. "I want you to come back."

Adrenaline surges through my body. Jack thinks I'm sexy. He thought spanking me was sexy, making me come was sexy. "Tonight?" I try to keep the panic from my voice. "Don't you have to train?"

He gives me a quizzical look. "You think I go there every day? It's pretty intense, Pen. I go on Saturday because Sunday is my day off training, and only sometimes during the week, usually if someone makes a specific request."

"Do you…have any specific requests this week?"

A smile tugs at his lips. "Tomorrow night. But if you want…"

My stomach tightens, and I'm not sure if it's the thought of him with another woman in his playroom or because I need to keep him away from the club. "No." My hands fly up in a warding gesture, and his smile fades.

"I scared you."

"You didn't scare me. I just felt awkward because we're friends and it…went somewhere I wasn't expecting. I'm sorry."

He studies me intently, like he's searching for lies. "What if we weren't friends?"

"I don't think I could have done that with someone I don't know," I say honestly. "That night with Master Damien, I didn't really understand what it was all about. I still don't, but I'm pretty sure I need some kind of emotional connection—trust."

Jack drops his weight, and I am deliciously enveloped in hot, hard, musky male.

"If I kissed you now," he says softly, "we wouldn't be friends."

My brain fuzzes over. "What would we be?"

He dips his head down. His breath is warm on my cheek, his body hot and heavy on mine. "Not friends."

Confused, aroused, desperately wanting to close that inch between us and press my lips against his, I whisper, "Oh."

He shakes his head, frowns. "That wouldn't be good."

What? He wants to kiss me and then he doesn't? He seems as confused as I am.

"Not sure I know that submission, but I'm willing to learn." Renegade squats down beside us, a grin splitting his face. "Class is over, folks. You might want to take it outside. Torment is teaching next, and he's not as forgiving about sexing it up in class as I am."

Jack releases my hands and helps me up as Renegade makes a discreet exit. Blinking, I stare at the empty room, and heat flushes my cheeks. God. I was so far gone I missed the end of class. And now we're fodder for the Redemption gossip mill. For nothing.

"I've got to go meet up with my coach," Jack says. "I'm training all day tomorrow, usually cool down around six with a run. You want to come for a run after work?"

Run with Jack? Like on a date? At the very least, though, it will keep him away from the club. "Okay." I smile brightly. "Tomorrow. We'll go for a run. And afterward, you can take me to the hospital because I have a feeling your idea of an easy cooldown is going to be like running a marathon for me."

"I'll tell Blade Saw to meet us at six. I always run with him." Blade Saw? Bam. My heart crashes into my stomach. Stupid. Stupid. Stupid. Not a date. I scramble for a way to hide my misunderstanding.

"I'll ask Cora to come, too. She loves to run."

Jack smiles. "Maybe we can get the whole team out and then head over to the Protein Palace for a shake when we're done."

He holds up his fist, and we bump. Just like old times. Just like we were before the night he chained me to his ceiling.

"Great," I say with feigned enthusiasm. "I'll see you tomorrow, then. Group run. Looking forward to it."

Not.

12

You're a funny girl

PENNY

"I HATE RUNNING."

Cora wheezes out her words as we jog along the pavement, the rhythmic thud of our feet matching the frantic pounding of my surprisingly still-beating heart. Ahead of us, Blade Saw and Jack haven't even broken a sweat, although we've been running for at least thirty minutes in the evening heat. We are running the Bay Trail, which is one of the most beautiful places to be during any dry day. Not that I'm paying much attention to the scenery as I struggle for breath while trying to navigate around the other runners, dogs, bikers, and kids.

"You wanted a double date," I huff. "I got one for you." I gesture vaguely around. "Baby blue skies, water, boats, amazing views of the coast…what more could you want? I think it goes for five hundred miles, so you'll have lots of time to spend with him."

Cora glares. At least I think she glares, but her face is covered in sweat, and I'm not sure if she's angry or crying. "I was thinking of having a few drinks, listening to a band, going to a club, maybe going for a walk along Pier 39, holding hands in the dark…"

"This is what you get when you're with an MMA fighter." I stumble and just catch myself from falling. "They work. They train. They hang out at the Protein Palace and down a couple of shakes. Occasionally they'll socialize at a bar."

"Doctor Death goes out a lot." Her cheeks flush, and she looks away. "He was at Comic-Con, WonderCon, the Anime Expo, and the Star Trek Convention."

"I thought you wanted a fighter, not a geek."

Cora shrugs. "He's both, and he's kinda cute. We were having a good time trading *Star Trek* quotes at the gym. Blade Saw barely looked at me when I met him and Jack outside."

"Doctor Death will sleep with anything that moves," I warn her. "And he won't be back for more. He's a noncommittal kind of guy."

"You okay back there?" Jack does a little spin, sprints past us, and then doubles back to catch up.

"Yeah," I pant. "Blooming marvelous. And you?"

His eyes glisten, amused. "We can stop if you want."

I wipe the sweat off my face with the back of my hand, no longer concerned about appearances since there is no part of me that is now not totally soaked. "I don't need to stop, but Cora might need to stop. She tires easily. Do you need to stop, Cora? You don't have to feel bad if you do."

Of course, Cora's still annoyed that I dragged her into running, so she's not on board the "save Penny from making a fool of herself" train. She shakes her head. "I could do the entire five hundred miles, I feel so good."

"You both look tired." Jack jogs backward beside me, as confident in his stride as I am when I can see. "Maybe we should have turned back with the others and gone for a beer."

We definitely should have gone back with the other fighters who started the run with us but sensibly turned around after twenty minutes, but how could I when he asked me if I wanted to continue on? Of course, my plan to impress him with my fitness quickly gave way to a plan not to fall flat on my face when I realized he'd considered the group part of the run a warm-up.

"Are you trying to make me feel bad?"

Jack frowns. "Of course not."

"Then stop dancing around and stop asking me if I want to quit. Just go run with Blade Saw. Silently. Maybe a bit slower. You could also try to sweat a bit and pant so I feel like you're exerting yourself in some way and not out for a casual stroll."

Jack chuckles and falls into step beside me. "It isn't a competition."

"Then you shouldn't have asked me to come," I snap. "I have a competitiveness problem. I'll keep running until I fall or you stop or I win."

"She's not lying," Cora says. "Sometimes she's a danger to herself."

"What?" My head snaps to the side, and I stumble, try to catch myself, and land on one knee, hands scraping across the pavement. Before I have even a moment to wallow in my misery, Jack wraps his arms around my waist and lifts me off the ground.

Bleeding, exhausted, drenched in sweat, and humiliated yet again, I don't even put up a fight.

After making sure I'm okay, Cora races ahead to catch up to Blade Saw. Jack carries me to a secluded bench under the trees and kneels in front of me to inspect my injuries. "You scraped your knee pretty bad."

"I like the skinned look," I say. "It's different. It screams 'total lack of coordination' with a dash of 'lack of class.'"

"Let me see your hands." He grabs my hands and turns them palm up, frowning at the scrapes. "I'll take you back to Redemption. Doctor Death is working tonight. He can fix you up."

"I'm sure he'll be delighted to fix me up," I mutter.

Jack pulls out his phone and bashes his finger on the screen. "Not anymore."

"What do you mean 'not anymore'?"

He plasters a stiff smile on his face and gives instructions to someone—I hope an anonymous stranger—to come and pick us up. "I mean," he says after he puts down the phone, "I told him I'd rip his balls off and shove them down his throat if he went anywhere near you."

"Why?"

"Why?" He gives me a curious look. "Because I don't want him touching you. That's why."

"I've been friends with Doctor Death for a long time. You never threatened to rip off his balls before."

"You weren't mine before," he says.

With nothing left to lose, I lay it on the line. "You feel possessive because you spanked me?"

Jack sits beside me on the bench, scrubs his hands over his face. "You don't hold anything back, do you?"

"I'm sorry." My shoulders sag, and I mentally add another failure to my day. "I shouldn't have said anything."

"I like it. It's refreshing." He leans back, casually drapes his arm over the back of the bench. "I can't talk about the club with anyone, especially now that I've gone pro. No one knows— not my close friends, not my agent or my manager, James, not even the team at Redemption. My family disowned me when they found out about my kink. They are very old school, very Southern, very concerned about their reputation. That kind of scandal could bring down everything my family has built over the generations."

"What did they build?" Although I've been hanging around with the Redemption team for almost two years, I know very little about Jack.

"Bourbon." He pulls out his phone and shows me the website of one of the country's top bourbon companies. "That's us. Them. They've been in the business for more than one hundred and fifty years."

His fingers brush over mine as he hands me the phone, sending a zing of electricity straight to my core. "It was supposed to be my business, handed down from father to eldest son. I was involved as soon as I could walk. My dad took me to work with him every day."

"What happened?"

"I got engaged to a girl who used my kink as an excuse to break off our engagement and marry my brother, Beau. She told my family, and they disowned me. Beau got my position in the company as well as my girl." He gives me the sordid details about Avery, and I wish my hands weren't bleeding so I could hunt her down and punch her in the face.

"Oh God, Jack. That's awful. I'm so sorry."

"Learned my lesson. Love isn't worth the pain."

"You're right about that," I say quietly. "My dad hated me for being born because he never wanted me. My mom lied about being on birth control so she could have a baby. It didn't matter how hard I tried, nothing I did made him happy. Nothing could make him love me. My mom kind of faded away under all his physical abuse, and by the time he started abusing me, she wasn't in a position to help. He drove a wedge between my sister and me, played us off each other. I think that's why I'm so competitive. I was glad to leave England. Glad to leave them behind. The only thing I regret is that I didn't get to finish law school. I had just started when I had to leave."

"Jesus Christ." He pulls me against him. "He hit you?"

"Yeah, he did." My chest tightens when I think about those horrible years. "But that's all in the past. I have a new life here."

"Yeah, me too." He sighs, and his fingers tighten on my hip. "I came out here, got a job with a local distillery since that's all I knew. I took up MMA and met Blade Saw at Redemption. His family is in the liquor business, too. We bought a small distillery together, and it's been doing pretty well. We keep it quiet though. If word got out around Redemption that we made booze…"

"You keep a lot of secrets." I hand him his phone and he tucks it away.

"So do you."

More than he knows. My fingers close around my wrist, hiding the scar that changed my life, the cry for help that no one else could hear.

Homicide Hank's white van comes barreling down the street and Jack squeezes my uninjured knee in a totally nonsexual, buddy-buddy kind of way. "Let's go. We'll get you fixed up, and you'll be ready for another run tomorrow."

"Great. A second long run in two days, here I come."

Jack snorts a laugh. "You're funny, Pen."

Ah, the kiss of death. "Thanks."

"And sweet." He waves Homicide Hank over to the curb in front of us.

"Innocent," he continues, half to himself. "Quirky, sexy, strong, brave, and a bit naive."

"I'm my very own romantic comedy."

Although right now, I wonder if I'm a tragedy instead.

—◇—

Jack growls when Doctor Death runs his hand up my leg in the Redemption first aid room. A real, honest-to-goodness growl like something out of a movie.

"I need some space to examine the patient," Doctor Death says when Jack leans over to watch, almost knocking me off the examination table. "As you may have noticed, the first aid room is meant to accommodate only the patient and medical personnel."

"Don't hurt her."

"Then don't get in my way."

Jack's head jerks up, and he gives Doctor Death a menacing stare. What the hell is wrong with him? Twenty minutes ago he was all about being friends, and now I'm worried Doctor Death might not make it out of here alive.

"She hurt her hands and her knee." Jack slides an arm around my waist, pulling me against him. "No examination required. Your fingers shouldn't be anywhere north of her thigh."

"He's a doctor," I say. "I'm sure he's seen plenty of what lies north of my thigh."

Wrong thing to say. Jack's muscles tense, and for a moment I think he is going to explode. I backtrack quickly because I do need some medical attention and I sense an imminent threat to Doctor Death's life. "I mean that in the generic sense, as in other women's thighs but not mine."

Doctor Death, with the worst possible timing, decides this is the moment to examine the area in question.

Bam. Jack bats Doctor Death's hand off my leg. "Below the fucking knee. How many fucking times do I have to tell you?"

"Call off the guard dog." Doctor Death shoots me an exasperated glance. "Or better yet, tie him up outside and give him a chew toy."

I look up at Jack, and he brushes a loose strand of hair behind my ear. Damn, he's gorgeous. And furious. So unlike the Jack we usually see at the gym. I always wanted a protective boyfriend, someone who would have stood up to my father and told him it wasn't okay to hit your daughter. Instead, I wound up with Adam, who turned out to be exactly the same.

Doctor Death cleans the scrapes on my hands and covers the worst of the cuts with tiny bandages. I try not to cry out when he dabs stinging lotion on my knee, but I do suck in a breath.

"You hurt her." Jack grabs a fistful of Doctor Death's shirt and I slap at his hand until he releases him.

"Stop it. You're acting crazy. It's not that bad. I've had worse." I glance down at my thighs, still covered by my gym pants, which I've pushed above my knees. Curious how the pain from Doctor Death's treatment does nothing for me either sexually, like the pain Jack gave me, or emotionally, like the pain I give myself.

Doctor Death picks up his tweezers. "Between Torment, Renegade, the Predator, and you all acting like a bunch of testosterone-laced cavemen around your women, it's a wonder I can even do my job."

"She's not my woman," Jack says. "She's a friend."

I don't even try to keep up. One day I'm his friend. The next he says "you're mine." And now I'm a friend again.

"Yeah. I'm getting that message." Doctor Death picks at a piece of gravel in my knee, and I break out in a sweat. "Loud and clear."

"Hold my hand." Jack pries open my fingers and wraps his warm palm around mine, careful not to press on the bandages. "Squeeze when it hurts," he demands.

"I don't want to hurt you." I hiss in a breath when Doctor Death digs into my knee again.

His lifts a challenging eyebrow. "Try."

So I squeeze. I clench his hand so hard I'm surprised I don't break any bones as Doctor Death works all the little pieces of gravel out of my knee, alternating with squirts of the stinging disinfectant. Finally, I give up the challenge and sag against Jack's body. He puts one arm around me and tucks me into his side, as he curses Doctor Death under his breath. He is warm and solid. In the circle of his arm I feel like nothing can hurt me, and despite the pain, I wish I could stay here forever.

"All done," Doctor Death says ten minutes later. He tapes big white bandages over my knees. "Come back if you see any signs of infection. Your knees will feel stiff for a few days as the skin heals. Palms won't be so bad."

"Thanks very much." I give Jack a nudge, and he mumbles something that I think is meant to express gratitude, albeit couched in filthy language about Doctor Death's man whore ways and all the things that might happen to him if he touches me again.

"Gonna take you home," Jack says as I limp out of the first aid office.

"It's okay, I've got my car."

"Then I'll drive you home and come back in a cab." He clears a path down the hallway with the fierceness of his scowl.

"You don't have to," I say. "I'm fine. Really. You didn't even need to stay with me. None of this is your fault. It's just me pushing myself too hard and then paying the price by falling on my face in front of the hottest guy in Redemption."

"Hottest?" He pulls to a stop, his eyes glittering, amused.

Did I just say that? Well, there's no taking it back.

"Yes." I watch him, waiting to see what he'll do. His gaze

drifts to my lips, and electricity sparks in the air between us, the same energy I felt in the club. I lean closer, tilt my head back just the tiniest bit. His chest heaves, and his scent fills me—soap and sweat, masculine and raw.

"Let's get going," he says.

Disappointment floods me, and my cheeks flame. I'm about to turn away when I feel his fingers under my chin. Gritting my teeth, I force myself to meet his gaze, surprised to see his soft smile. "I'm driving," he says.

"Okay."

He bends down, brushes his lips over my cheek, sending a rush of heat through my body that shimmies up my spine. "When we get there, I'm coming inside."

Every part of me tingles, and when he pulls away, I can barely breathe. "Okay."

"Pen?"

"Yes?" I whisper.

"I need your keys."

13

Please. Please. Please.

PENNY

Jack drives like he fights. Full on. High intensity. Steamrolling anything that gets in his way. Good thing I've got a car that has a bit of punch. My Mustang is my absolute pride and joy.

"This is a fucking sweet ride." He weaves in and out of traffic so fast the world becomes a blur. Or maybe that's because my hair is whipping in my face. No way could Jack fit in my car with the top up, so we're kicking it cold style.

"You're the only person I've allowed to drive it." I grip the padded armrest as he takes a sharp turn. "I bought it with money my grandfather left me when he passed. He would have loved it. He was a big car collector. Every weekend he would take me for a ride in a different car. My dad hated him. He was furious when he found out Grandpa left everything to me. He got Mom to contest the will, but the judge threw the whole thing out of court. I would never have been able to move to America with-out that money. He took care of me, even when he was gone."

"Sounds like my kinda guy." He turns into Rockridge, and I direct him to a quiet street off Claremont Avenue and up to a small Southwestern-style duplex, brightly painted in cream and ochre.

Jack parks in my little garage and then follows me outside and up the steps, where my giant ball of white fluff, Clarice, is waiting impatiently.

"Didn't think you were a cat person," he says.

"I didn't think I was either because I wasn't allowed to have a pet growing up, but then I met Clarice." I bend down to give her a pat. "I found her on my driveway just after I moved in. She'd been abused and abandoned and looked like she'd had a rough time on the street. She's got a bit of a temper, and she gets annoyed when I'm late, so watch yourself."

Clarice arches and hisses when Jack reaches for her, and he backs off while I open the door.

"Oh, and she doesn't like men," I add.

"Yeah, picked that up." Jack waits for Clarice to saunter into the house before he steps inside. "I always had dogs," he says. "We had a lot of land, so they had lots of room to run. Wanted a dog when I came to California, but I didn't think it was fair when I was living in an apartment. One day, I'm gonna have a house with a big yard, and then I'll get my dogs. Big ones. But good with kids."

"You want kids?" I close the door, and Clarice rubs up against me and purrs.

"I used to. Thought about it a lot when I was with Avery. Now I don't think I'd be able to make that kind of commitment to someone."

"She burned you really bad, didn't she?" I reach around him to hang up my gym bag, bringing us so close I get heated all over again.

"Yeah, she did."

Jack follows me into the kitchen. Clarice noses her dish, and I avoid the awkward silence by chastising her for her bad behavior. I feed her and turn to see Jack leaning against the door, watching me.

"You help everyone." His face softens. "Serve documents for Amanda, save an ornery cat, fix Cora and Blade Saw up, help out the newbies in jiu-jitsu class by giving them tips. Who helps you?"

"I don't need help." I turn away, avoiding his scrutiny. "I learned early on to look after myself. But I like to help out people when I can because I know what it's like to need help and have no one there to give it."

"Everyone needs help." His gaze drops to my thighs, and I cringe inside. He thinks I need help to stop the cutting. Is that why he's here? He thinks I'm going to hurt myself tonight?

"I totally lucked out with this place." I lead him into the living room as an excuse to change the topic. "They had just renovated, and I was driving by when they were putting out the for-sale sign. I had a bit of money left over from my grandpa's estate, and the money from the lawsuit against Vetch Retch, so I took it on the spot."

I love my little place with its small corner kitchen, dark wood cabinets, white granite counters, and polished wood floors. A small dining table surrounded by four red plastic chairs takes up the space by the window. The rest of the open-plan area is dominated by a giant gray sectional that I have positioned in front of the television and decorated with accent cushions and a thick, red rug.

"The red is very you." He gestures to the bright red lights hanging in the kitchen, which match the three cherry-red chairs at the counter.

"Yeah. The red sold me. I like color."

We talk about the gym and his training and his move into professional life while I make coffee, and then I turn on the television and excuse myself to take a quick shower, which proves to be a challenge because of the bandages. I slip into shorts and a T-shirt, comb my fingers through my damp hair, and join Jack on the couch.

"What are we watching?"

"Soccer." He reaches past me for the remote, and his arm brushes against mine. I look up to see him staring at me, his eyes taking in every detail of my face, the damp tendrils of my hair, the V of my shirt...

"You clean up nice."

"You mean I look better when I'm not soaked in sweat and covered in gravel, dirt, and blood?" I want to touch him, feel him against me. I want to curl into his body like I did in the first aid room and feel safe all over again.

"I mean you're a beautiful woman." He strokes his fingers along my jaw, caressing my cheek. My eyes flutter closed, and

I lean into the warmth of his palm. I don't remember the last time I felt like this, like I'm alive, like I can be myself because he already knows my secret.

"So beautiful," he whispers.

I melt into his touch, the deep, low rumble of his voice, and his hot, hard body on the couch beside me.

He brushes the damp hair away from my face and dips his head, brushing his cheek against mine. His breath is warm on my ear, his five-o'clock shadow rough on my skin. I inch toward him, leaning up for more.

"Beautiful lips." His mouth brushes against mine, and he slides his tongue between the seam of my lips. I open for him, and he kisses me. Soft and sweet. Slow and gentle. So unlike the man from the club or the fighter from Redemption. This is Jack as I have never seen him before. He tastes of coffee and desire, and I want to drink him down.

He sweeps my mouth, kisses me deeper, his hands cupping my face, holding me still. I slide my hands around his neck, burning, floating, desperate to be free.

"Beautiful face," he murmurs.

I press myself closer, grip his massive shoulders. His hand drifts down to my waist, slips beneath the hem of my T-shirt. His warm touch on my bare skin sends my pulse skyrocketing, and I moan.

He lowers me to the cushions, follows me down, never breaking the kiss. His body is deliciously hot and hard above me. I feel connected to him, protected, like we are one person, not two.

"You're so fucking soft," he breathes. "So sweet." He presses a kiss to my neck as his hands move over my body. I wrap my arms around his neck, pull him down for more. I want his full weight on top of me. I want to feel crushed, smothered, enveloped in hot, musky male.

Jack groans. His hips press into my stomach, his erection a delicious friction between my thighs. I part my legs wider, grind against him, seeking the delicious sensation of rough denim on my throbbing clit.

"Shh. Slow down. I want to enjoy you." He trails kisses down my neck, over my throat. Shifting to the side, he cups and squeezes my breasts through my bra, his touch solid and strong. I writhe and wriggle, unable to stay still. He is driving me crazy with his touches, making me so wet it's all I can do not to rip off his clothes and make him give me what I want.

His eyes darken, and he shoves my shirt up over my head, baring me to his heated gaze. "Ah, Pen."

My hands find his back and smooth over his muscles, feeling them ripple beneath his shirt as he slides one bra strap over my shoulder. His breathing is heavy, his gaze intense as his head dips down to press a soft kiss to my bare skin.

He slides the other strap off, slowly, gently, carefully unwrapping me as if he is teasing himself. I arch my back, offer my breasts for the pleasure of his mouth. Beyond rational thought, I am lost in sensation, a seething, yearning mass of want.

Jack traces his finger along the edge of my bra, leaving a burning trail across my skin. With painful slowness, he eases the cups down, releasing my breasts from their restraint. I gasp when my burning skin comes into contact with the cool air, and my nipples bead so hard they ache.

I want his mouth on me, his lips, and his heat. But he doesn't oblige. Instead, he traces a finger around my nipple. Around and around until I tangle my hands in his soft hair and pull him down to my breast. "Please."

"You're making it very difficult to go slow." He feathers hot kisses across the curve of one breast, moving down to draw my left nipple between his teeth. I moan as he licks and sucks, nips and bites, while his other hand squeezes and caresses my right breast. My thighs fall open, inviting, and he lowers his hand to my leg and traces his finger slowly along the sensitive skin of my inner thigh.

I have never known lust like this, want so fierce I burn, and need so intense I ache. He is a master of manipulation, a purveyor of pleasure. He knows just where to touch and how hard. He knows how to drive me up and take me down, when I can't take any more and when it isn't enough. I try not to think about where he gained all that knowledge, the countless women he's been with, the things he has done to them in his room at the club. I pretend I am the only one he has caressed into a haze of lust, the only one he wants.

I open my eyes to see him watching me, assessing my reaction to his touch. I feel at once stripped bare and treasured by the intensity of his focus. He moves to my other breast, pulling down my bra cup, teasing and torturing my nipple with his mouth. He trails his fingers up my thigh and then cups the curve of my sex, over my shorts. I let out a guttural moan and in seconds he's on top of me, as if I've broken his self-control. He kisses me hard, rough, grinds his hips against me as he presses me into the couch. I reach for him, and he grabs my wrists with one hand and pins them over my head. He pushes my shorts and knickers aside and strokes a thick finger along my labia while he sucks and bites my nipple until I am writhing and groaning beneath him.

"Please," I moan. "Please. Please. Please."

"Tell me what you want." He buries his face in my neck, bites down on the sensitive skin at the top of my shoulder.

"Sex. I want to have sex. I want you inside me. Now. Take off my clothes."

His hand tightens on my wrists so hard it hurts. "I don't have normal sex," he growls. "If I take off your clothes, I'm going to hurt you. I need your pain, darlin'. It gives me pleasure."

My heart skips a beat. "You want to spank me?"

He twists my nipple between his thumb and forefinger, making me gasp. "I want to do more than spank you. I want to tease you until you need to come so bad it hurts. I want to hear you scream and cry. I want your tears. I want to hurt you so bad you never feel the need to hurt yourself. And I want to give you so much pleasure you can't form a coherent thought."

My brain fuzzes with both fear and desire. "You can't do it like this?"

Jack's phone vibrates on the coffee table, and he hisses in a breath.

"I need you," I whisper, rubbing my body against him. But the incessant vibrating of the phone has broken the spell. He pushes himself up and grabs the phone.

"Jack here," he says, holding the phone to his ear. He walks toward the bedroom, and I sink into the couch.

He wants to hurt me. Not just in the club but here. Am I just going back down the road I was on before? Opening myself up to being abused again? How do I draw the line when I couldn't draw it before? I thought Adam was my savior, and he turned out to be as bad as my dad. And yet I feel a connection with Jack that I've never felt with anyone before. We both find pleasure through pain; we both have suffered betrayal and loss. The only risk is if I fall so deep I can't find my way out.

Jack returns a few minutes later and sits on the edge of the couch. He sighs and scrubs his hand over his face. By the time he speaks, I already know what he's going to say.

"I can't do this."

Hope shatters inside me. My dad was right. Adam was right. No wonder they didn't want me. I am worthless. No good. Damaged. So damaged I can't even give a sadist my pain.

"I'm sorry," I say, pulling on my shirt. "I shouldn't have pushed."

Jack frowns. "Don't be sorry. It has nothing to do with you. It's me. I'm fucked up. It's why I don't date. It's why I don't have relationships. I keep everything strictly in the club."

"I get it."

My stomach twists in knots, and I stare at the floor, unable to meet his gaze. "Thanks for looking after me tonight."

Silence weighs heavy in the air between us, but still he doesn't leave. Finally I look up and I am startled at the softness in his face, the longing and regret. He really does think it's him, and for some strange reason, it makes me want him all over again.

"I think you should go."

He winces like I hurt him, but I need to be alone, and for some reason he isn't taking the hint. Maybe because he senses we can't be friends after this. We went too far, revealed too much, and now… We both feel the pain.

"I guess I'll see you at the gym." He pulls open the door and looks back over his shoulder, questioning.

"See you at the gym."

And then he disappears into the night.

My stomach floods with dread when I wake up the next morning feeling numb. After Jack left, I did everything I could think of to ease the pressure. I took a bath, ate a tub of ice cream, and watched some bad telly. But it wasn't enough to deal with the stress of being rejected all over again.

Worthless, no-good piece of shit. The monsters start chanting before I get out of bed, always in my father's voice, their words— his words—pounding into my brain with the same rhythm as his fists when he decided to punish me yet again for being born. Of course Jack didn't want me. Why did I think he would?

My gaze flicks to my nightstand where I keep my blade case—six shiny razor blades, cleaned and sterilized, a surgical scalpel, cotton to mop up the blood, and disinfectant to clean the area before and after the big event. I could call in sick and cut myself this morning, which would give me almost the full day to treat the wounds and recover, but if the monsters have only just started chanting now, it is going to get a lot worse, and I don't want to have to cut twice.

Heaving myself out of bed, I pull on yesterday's pale blue chiffon skirt from the floor and pair it with a sleeveless white tank from the laundry bin. I add a white sweater and finger-comb my hair before tying it back in a ponytail. A quick look in the mirror reveals a disheveled, exhausted, rumpled version of myself in all my dull, pale, curvy glory. But I don't have the energy to fix myself up. The monsters are howling, and I need to get to work to drown out the noise.

I show up at the office a few minutes early and thankfully before Ray arrives. After putting on the coffee, I head to my office and close the door. The building is quiet, and I lay my head on my desk and try to find the courage to make it through the day, even though I have learned that courage is overrated.

When I turned seventeen, I met Adam. He made me feel loved and gave me the courage to stand up to my dad. But when I did, my dad said he never wanted to see me again. He told me he never wanted me and never loved me. He said that I was a worthless, no-good piece of shit and that I had made his life a living hell. Despite his hatred, I had always nurtured the tiniest hope that I could make him proud. That was the moment I knew I never would.

I had failed. Just as I always fail.

"Penny? You in here?" Ray pushes open the door, and I jerk up, rustle the papers on my desk, pretend to be busy although my computer is off and I have no pen.

"Coffee's on," I say, forcing a smile.

Ray stares at me. He's dressed in dark jeans and a dark hoodie, which means he'll be out on surveillance all day. This is a good thing. Ray is far too astute, and he has a way of seeing things people don't want him to see. Like right now, he's scowling, which means he knows something's up and he's not going to leave until he finds out what it is. Too bad I have practiced deception for years.

"What's wrong?"

"Nothing." I turn on my computer, pull open my desk drawer, and hunt for a pen.

"Don't give me that bullshit. You look like you just went a coupla rounds in the ring with Torment. You sick or something?"

There is only one way to put a man like Ray off a line of questioning, and right now I'm sinking so fast I don't give a damn if I'm betraying all of womankind. "It's that time of the month."

"Whoa." Ray's hands fly up, and he backs up a step, as if I've just told him I have a communicable disease. "Right. Okay, then. Yeah. So, I'm gonna be out of the office until around four this afternoon. Maybe all day. You…uh…look after yourself. See you later." His footsteps echo in reception, and I breathe a sigh of relief when I hear the door slam.

Nothing. Works. Better.

Amanda keeps me busy for the rest of the day. I try to focus on the work and not on the taunting of the monsters in my head, but they shriek and yell every time I do something wrong. I drop a pen, stumble on a crack, miss a button, drop my papers, and all the time they chant that I'm worthless and no good and no one could ever love me.

Cora stops by for lunch so we can talk about the double date she has planned for tomorrow night. I tell her I'm too busy for anything—lunch, the gym, the double date. From the way her lips purse, I know she doesn't believe me, but good friend that she is, she doesn't make a fuss.

By the time I get home at the end of the day, my head is pounding, and I am desperate to feel something, anything except the emptiness inside me. I stumble to my bedroom and pull out my kit.

Release is at hand.

14

I never claimed to be a gentleman

RAMPAGE

THURSDAY AFTERNOON AFTER TRAINING, I STOP CORA ON HER
way out of jiu-jitsu class. I haven't seen Penny at the gym since
Tuesday night when I broke every rule I made to keep me sane
after Avery left me—no relationships, no intimacy, no vanilla
anything. And yet I couldn't stop myself. I had to touch her, kiss
her, and when she let me know what she wanted, I lost control.
Walking away wasn't easy, but it was the right decision. For
both of us. So why hasn't she been at the gym?

"Have you seen Pen?" I draw Cora to the side under
Blade Saw's watchful gaze. I've never seen two people dance
around each other the way they've been doing for the past
two weeks.

"I saw her yesterday. She said she was too busy with work
to come to the gym." She narrows her eyes in what I assume is
meant to be an admonishing way but just makes her look cute.

I don't know what the hell is holding Blade Saw back, but if he doesn't make his move soon, he's going to miss out. He's not the only fighter at Redemption who's noticed Cora.

"Okay. Thanks."

Cora gives an exasperated sigh. "She's not really busy."

Puzzled, I frown. "I thought you just said she was."

"You're not paying attention. There's a big difference between what she says and how she is."

"How is she?"

Her brow creases in a worried frown. "She has a hard time dealing with stress. She gets all strung out like she is now, and then she shuts me out. I worry about her when she gets like this. She won't answer my calls; she doesn't come to the gym; sometimes she doesn't even make it to work. I can always see it coming, but she won't talk to me about it, so I don't know how to help."

"What happened?" My stomach clenches, and something niggles at the back of my mind, a conversation Penny and I had about her need for pain as an emotional release.

"I don't know," Cora says. "I thought maybe you did. She's had one bad relationship after another, one guy beating on her after another. I thought, finally, she's met a guy who's going to treat her right, who's not going to hurt her… Maybe she's found someone she can talk to, someone who can take away her pain."

"That's not me, Cora."

"No," she says softly. "I guess not."

—⁓—

PENNY

Cora calls me for the fifth time today as if she knows what I did last night and is determined to ensure it doesn't happen again.

"Cora, I'm working."

"Well, I'm not. I saw Rampage yesterday at the gym. And I've been thinking, since things seem to be a bit rocky with Rampage, you should get some no-strings, no-heartbreak loving, Doctor Death style."

"He was flirting with you, not me."

Cora makes a tsk-tsk sound into the phone. "You told me Doctor Death would sleep with anything that moves. And he was flirting with you, too. In fact, I don't think he knows how to talk to a woman without flirting. It's Friday, and you need to get out tonight. Blade Saw is up for it, and I'm hoping to get him drunk enough that he'll come home with me and show me some MMA skills in bed."

Someone knocks on the door, and I put down the phone. Amanda doesn't have a problem with me taking the odd personal call because I don't do it very often.

"I'm on my way to the Bar Association dinner with Jill and Dana," Amanda says when I open the door. "I sent Mari home early, and Ray is out on surveillance. You can go whenever you want. Just be sure to lock up for me."

"No problem. Have fun tonight."

I pick up the phone and lean against my desk, waving to everyone as they leave. "I thought you said you hadn't dated many guys, so I'm not sure where the dating advice is coming from."

Cora laughs. "I wasn't a nun. But the guys I was with were overexcitable types. All I had to do was smile and they'd be whipping off their pants, 'cause when you're spending most of your day sitting in front of a computer having virtual sex with aliens, you don't waste time when you're offered the real thing."

"I couldn't sleep with Doctor Death, Cora. He's a friend. He's so outrageous he makes me laugh. I wouldn't be able to take it seriously."

"Jack was a friend, too. You were getting serious with him."

My heart squeezes in my chest. Yeah, I was getting serious, but he shut it down pretty fast. And now that I've dealt with the stress and emotional pressure in the usual way, I'm resigned to move on. Story of my life.

"Not anymore." Although I have been keeping tabs on him at the gym through mutual friends, to make sure he's not cutting out of training early to go to the club.

"Well, he was asking about you," Cora says. "And this is perfect. If he is on the fence, then seeing you with Doctor Death could tip the balance. And if not, at least you'll have a good time."

"Are you meeting Blade Saw at the gym?"

"Eight o'clock," she says. "Right after Fuzzy's Punch or Perish class that you forced me to join with you. I already asked Doctor Death if he wanted to come out with us, and he said yes. Actually, he thought at first I was inviting him for a threesome with me and Blade Saw, but he got over his disappointment when I told him you were our fourth."

I hear the front doorbell tinkle and I head into reception to check out the visitor. "Okay, I'll…"

"You'll what?" Cora says.

"I'll call you back. Jack is here."

She sucks in a sharp breath. "I'll see you at class tonight. I can hardly wait to hear all about it."

I end the call and swallow past the lump in my throat. It's only been three days, and yet it feels like I haven't seen Jack in forever. He's wearing a white T-shirt that clings to his taut, muscle-ridged abdomen, and worn jeans that ride low on his narrow hips.

"What are you doing here?"

He pins me with a direct stare, his eyes fierce and hard. I feel like he's trying to see into my soul, but my heart is pounding so hard I'm not sure enough oxygen is getting to my brain to make any sense of what's going on.

"Jack?"

His gaze rakes over my body, lingering on my thighs as if he can see beneath my skirt. He tenses, and his eyes narrow. If I didn't know X-ray vision was impossible, I would swear he knows I broke my promise.

"Are you alone?"

"Yes." My pulse kicks up a notch. "Everyone's out for the rest of the afternoon and I was about to close up and go."

He takes a step toward me, and the hair on the back of my neck stands on end.

"Lock the door."

A thrill of fear shoots through me, and sweat beads on my forehead. What if he knows? Or suspects? What will he do?

"Now." His deep, commanding Dom voice ripples through

me, fanning the flames of my desire. Do I trust Jack enough to lock myself in the office with him, especially when I know what is coming? Do I trust myself?

I brush past him and lock the front door.

"Your office," he snaps after I return. "Now."

I jump at his sharp tone and scramble out of his way as he brushes past me and through my office door, a lithe and powerful animal herding its prey.

"What's going on?"

"Stand in front of the desk." He gestures to the big oak desk Amanda and I refinished when we first moved into the building.

Puzzled, I do as he asks, my breath catching in my throat when he closes and locks my office door behind him.

"Jack?"

He gives me his back as he draws the curtains at the side of my office. "Don't move."

A sting of disappointment hits me in the chest. Has he come to reject me all over again? Does he want to make sure I understand there is nothing between us? It shouldn't bother me because I got the message the other night. I'm nothing. Nothing special. Nothing extraordinary. Not worth his time, especially since he's on the cusp of fame. I'm just his pal. Plain old quirky Pen. But he doesn't have to be so cold.

Worthless, no-good piece of shit.

No. No. No. My fingers tighten on the lip of the desk. I haven't even started to heal from last night.

Jack leans against the door across from me, thick arms folded over his massive chest. "Lift your skirt."

Shock steals my breath away, and all I can do is stare. "What?"

"You heard me. Lift your skirt. Now."

Bang. Bang. Bang. My heart thuds frantically against my ribs. Adrenaline pounds through my veins, and I feel a rush of heat between my legs. He knows. I can see it in his eyes, hear it in his voice…

"Why?" I whisper, stalling. And why is this turning me on?

"You know why," he snaps. "You didn't keep your promise."

I smooth my hands over my cream skirt, silky underneath with a cotton macramé overlay, pressing it tight against my thighs. "It doesn't matter if I kept it or not. We're not in the club. There's nothing between us. You made that clear the other night."

"I fucked up the other night." He shifts his stance. "I'm not good for you, Pen. You need to be with someone normal. A nice guy who's going to treat you right and doesn't want to hurt you."

My hand fists on my thigh. "I don't like nice guys. They don't understand me. They're too gentle. My life is about pain. Emotional and physical pain. It's what I know, what I understand, what I need."

"So you hurt yourself?"

"I didn't—"

He cuts me off with a scowl. "Don't lie to me." He pauses, and his voice takes on a deeper, cutting edge. "Show me."

My mouth goes dry at his abrupt command, and I fiddle with the edge of my skirt, at once indignant that he would try to boss me around and aroused that he did.

"What if I did?" I say defiantly. "There's nothing you can do about it."

His corded throat tightens when he swallows, and he fixes me with a level stare. "I'll give you what you need."

All the air leaves my lungs in a rush, and I feel a disconcerting wetness between my thighs. "You wouldn't dare. I'm at work."

"Try me."

Electricity sparks in the air between us, and a curious mix of fear and arousal courses through my veins. Stiffening my spine, I curl my fingers under the edge of my skirt and draw it slowly, painfully slowly up my thighs. Jack stills. His eyes flick down and then back up again. He licks his lips, and his eyes darken.

I have awakened the beast.

RAMPAGE

She stares at me. Defiant. Beautiful. But beneath her challenge I can feel her need—a need for pain, a need the sadist in me cannot ignore.

A man doesn't hurt a woman. Not where I come from. But when I found BDSM, I learned that there are many people who take pleasure in pain, whether it is to heighten their arousal or to fill an emotional need. Although I have accepted my kink, I still haven't been able to free myself of the judgment that goes with it. I can't forget the horror on Avery's face or the disappointment of my family when I told them it was not something that could be "cured." I am the antithesis of who I was raised to be, and yet Penny calls to the deepest, darkest side of me and I cannot resist.

Hand trembling, she tugs her skirt up another inch, baring the soft, creamy skin of her thigh. With her lips pressed tight together, her eyes locked on mine, she is a reflection of the maelstrom of emotions storming through my body—fear and longing, anger and arousal, beauty and the beast.

I drop my gaze, mouth watering in anticipation of the moment we both know is coming. When I saw the flicker of guilt, I knew she had broken her promise. And when I saw her need, I couldn't walk away.

Damn, she is tempting. I lick my lips, remembering her taste, her scent, her sweet arousal, the way she moaned when I touched her. Pink and pretty on the outside, tough and resilient on the inside. She is aroused now, her cheeks flushed, body trembling. Sex and pain. They may never have connected for her before, but they sure as hell have now.

"Higher." Awakened by her need, the Dominant in me demands obedience.

Her cheeks flush and desire heats her eyes as she lifts her skirt. It pleases me. Not just because she accepts my dominance, but because it means I can give her what she needs and she won't put up a fight.

One more inch, and I see the edge of a bandage. I narrow my eyes, let her see my disapproval as I unbuckle my belt. My cock throbs painfully against my fly. I am hard. So fucking hard I can barely think straight. I grit my teeth. Force back my arousal. This is about her. My needs will have to wait.

With one last tug, she bares her thigh, locks her challenging gaze on me. My stomach knots when I see the long white bandage. I did that. I pushed her over the edge. And now I have to fix my mistake. I yank my belt off and double it in my fist.

"You broke your promise."

"What are you going to do about it?" Her trembling hands belie the defiance in her tone.

"I'm going to hurt you, darlin', so the next time you think about hurting yourself, you'll remember to call me first." I walk up to her, so close I can feel the heat of her body. "I want you facedown over the desk. Lift your skirt, and then reach up and hold on to the edge."

Her cheeks flush and she bites her lip, indecision clear on her face. I can almost hear the frantic beat of her heart, but I can sense her arousal, too. Part of me is almost tempted to take her in my arms and soothe her, feel her softness against me, but I closed myself off to those feelings long ago and shifted my focus to the darkness inside me. Her need aligns so perfectly with mine. I want to punish her. I need her pain.

She stares up at me, an edge of uncertainty in her eyes, but courage too, passion, and desire.

With a jagged breath, she turns and leans over the desk.

Ah. Beautiful submission.

She reaches back and flips up her skirt, baring her lovely ass for me. Her panties are white, lacy, three inches at the top and a string nestled between her plump cheeks. Pure. Innocent. Fitting for her punishment by my hand.

A hand that shouldn't be wearing the damn family ring. I

slip it off and stuff it in my pocket, feeling at once unburdened and relieved.

"Hold on." I position myself behind her, wrap one hand around her neck to hold her still, and kick her legs apart. "Ten strikes with my belt for breaking your promise. Do you agree?"

"Yes," she whispers.

"I want you to count them off. Do you remember your safe word?"

"I can use a safe word?" She struggles to look back, and I hold her down.

"You always have a safe word when you're with me," I assure her.

I can feel the tension ease from her body as she lets out a breath. "Can I choose something else since we're not at the club?"

"Anything that means something to you, so it's easy to remember."

Her trembling arouses me. Her fear, a balm for my soul.

"*Redemption,*" she says. "It's my…happy place. I know it's stupid."

My stomach churns as guilt drips like acid inside me. She didn't come to Redemption this week because of me. "It's not stupid at all. It's been a special place for me since the day I joined, when it was just the shell of a warehouse with a couple of mats and a few guys who had a dream."

A dream that came true for me. A dream that could easily die if anyone discovered my secret.

I smooth my hand over Penny's perfect ass and raise my arm to strike. "Ready?"

"Yes."

My belt cracks across her ass, and she gasps, her body going rigid beneath my hand. A red line wells up on her perfect, creamy skin, and adrenaline floods through my veins, rushing straight for my cock.

"One," she chokes out.

I crack my belt against her soft skin again, and she whimpers and arches her back. "Two."

The next three blows I do hard and fast, careful never to hit the same spot twice. Her muscles are rock hard beneath my palm, her knuckles white around the edge of the table.

"Breathe through it, Pen. Breathe." I give her a few seconds to catch her breath, and then I whip the belt along the sensitive tops of her thighs, first one, then the other. "This is the pain I want you to remember," I tell her. "When you need release, this is the pain I want you to crave. Pain I will give you."

She sobs, her body shaking as she counts the blows. Sweat beads on my brow, trickles down my back. My body thrums with need, hunger, and pleasure. She is everything I have ever wanted and never imagined I could have. She is the flower I shouldn't pick because I know I will destroy her.

"Shh. Almost done." I tighten my hand around her neck, assuring her that I am here, that I won't let her go, but I won't stop until the punishment is done. Her ass is red, hot, and streaked with the lines from my belt. Fiercely beautiful.

I crack my belt across her ass three more times, giving her a moment between each blow. When the last one is done, I drop the belt and pull her up, turning her so I can cradle her in my arms.

Penny sobs against my shirt, her hands clenched against my chest. I stroke her hair, murmur assurances, tell her how proud I am, how well she did, how I hope she learned her lesson. My need to provide comfort is as great as her need to receive it. Something about Penny triggers my most basic protective instincts. Outwardly she doesn't seem vulnerable, with her sassy mouth and her cheerful warmth, and yet beneath those smiles lies a woman who needs what I can give her.

She sighs, her breaths deepening, her hands loosening their grip. She feels so soft in my arms, so right. How long has it been since I held a woman this way? Held something beautiful in my arms?

"We need to put something on your skin." I brush a kiss over her hair.

"There's salve in the first aid box." She straightens her clothing, and opens the door, returning a few moments later with a tube of cream.

"Back in position." I close and lock the door behind me.

Penny leans over the desk and flips up her skirt, wincing as I rub the cream into her skin. My fingers drift down between her legs, and she lets out a tortured moan that I feel in every inch of my rock-hard cock.

I push aside her panties and slick a finger through her folds. "You're so wet. You liked your punishment."

She parts her legs and whispers, "More."

"More what?" I spread her moisture up and around her clit,

rubbing my finger gently beside the swollen nub beneath the soaked lace. "Tell me what you need."

"I need…you." She looks back over her shoulder, bites her lip. "Was that enough? Do you need…more?"

I like how she blushes when she tells me what she needs. Her darkness touched with erotic innocence. "Yeah, darlin', I do."

"I can take it," she says quickly.

"I know you can."

And then I rip her panties away.

―――

PENNY

Jack spins me around and positions me on top of the desk, leaning me back on my elbows, my burning ass on the cold, hard wood, heels on the edge. With rough hands, he spreads me wide, and I shiver, my sex damp and throbbing with anticipation.

His fingers trace a lazy path up the soft skin of my inner thighs, fingertips brushing over my mons, so light I catch my breath, silently willing him to give me more.

"I like that you're bare." He dips his head. Blows a warm breath over my clit, ripping a groan from my throat.

"I like it, too." Although I had never thought about waxing down there until Amanda told me about the day she took Makayla to get waxed. She said Makayla cursed and screamed but later declared it was worth the pain. Once I heard that, I decided to try it for myself, although hiding my scars was a bit of a challenge. Still, the release I got from the pain kept me going for an extra few weeks, and it made me feel sexy on the outside when I was feeling ugly on the inside.

"Easily accessible." Jack strokes a thick finger through my slit and pushes it fast and deep inside me.

"Ahh." The press of his finger against my swollen tissue creates an erotic burn that sends tingles through my body. I struggle against the exquisite intrusion, and he slaps my thigh hard, adding fresh pain to the fire.

"Don't move."

My pussy clenches around his finger, and I rock my hips to move him deeper. He pulls out, tilting his head to look at me.

"Please, Jack."

"You're not ready." He adds a second finger, watching me carefully as he pushes deep inside, sending waves of pleasure through me. I am so wet, so hot, so close to the edge I could come if he just picks up the pace. But I don't want to. I want him inside me. I want a connection, not just a climax.

Jack pumps his fingers slowly in and out of me, alternating strokes with a brush of his thumb over my clit. My pussy throbs, swells, aches for more. I spread my legs wider, inviting. He hums his approval, but he keeps his steady rhythm. Thrusting. Striking. Rubbing. My body coils, tightens, and I lift my hips, uncaring whether I am asking for pain or pleasure.

"Now?"

"No."

He withdraws, leaving me bereft. I pant for breath as he shoves down his jeans and boxers to his knees, freeing his cock from its restraint. Jack is a big man, and he has a cock to match.

Thick, hard, and heavy, it bounces gently in my direction. I reach for him, and he slaps my hand away.

"You do that, I won't last," he says, his voice rough and raw. He sheaths himself with a condom from his pocket and shoves my skirt up over my hips. "Do you want this?"

"Yes." I am so wet, so desperate to come that I will take anything he has to give me.

Jack swirls the head of his cock over my labia, dipping into my wetness. He brushes the swollen head over my clit, and my body shakes.

"Do you need to come?"

"God, yes."

"Beg."

"What?" I groan, poised on the edge of climax, my breasts swollen and aching, my pussy wet and throbbing, my brain fuzzed with lust.

"I want to hear you beg for my cock."

"Please," I whisper. "Give it to me."

He slides his thick shaft all the way in, and I moan at the exquisite sensation. So hard. So thick. So deliciously hot. I rock my hips, angle myself for more.

He presses deeper, filling me, stretching me. I welcome the burn, swallow the erotic pain.

"You're so slick, so tight," he murmurs. "I'm gonna fuck you hard, and I'm going to hold your ass when I do because it's going to hurt and I want to hear you scream for me. Bury your head in my shoulder so no one hears you. Use your safe word if you need to."

Just the thought of pain so intense I might need my safe word sends a tremor up my spine, but he doesn't give me a chance to think. His hands slide under my ass, and he lifts me against him as his fingers dig into my burning skin.

My eyes water from the pain, and I gasp, wrap my legs around him, throw myself forward, and bury my face in his shoulder. He smells of sweat and cologne and sex and sin. He smells of Jack, and I missed him.

"Yes." He lifts me and slams me down over his cock until he is sheathed completely inside me. I moan, wrap my arms around his shoulders, and hang on for the ride.

"Good girl." He pulls out and hammers into me, lifting me as if I weigh nothing. His hips piston back and forth. My nipples pebble beneath my bra. Sweat beads on my brow. Pain and pleasure blend into pure sensation.

Jack slides his hand between us, his fingers circling my clit. My muscles tense, and a violent climax rips through me, tearing a scream from my throat as my pussy clenches around his thick cock. He hammers into me, drawing out my orgasm, and then his arms tighten around me and he groans as he comes in hard, long, heated jerks.

He holds me against him until our breaths slow and our hearts stop pounding. Jack lowers me to sit on the edge of the desk and runs his hand up and down my back, through my hair, the whisper of a caress over my ass. Dazed, I look up at him, and he kisses me softly.

"Why didn't you come to me?" he murmurs.

I relax against him, floating in a sea of calm. "I didn't think you wanted to see me, and I didn't know you could make me feel…like this."

"Next time, call or text or just show up at my door or Redemption. I'll give you my address. Promise me. Promise me and mean it."

"I promise." I rest my head against his chest.

"I want you to do something else for me." He helps me down, and I lower my skirt and lean against my desk, watching as he disposes of the condom. He is still erect, still hard, and still glorious in his masculinity.

"What?"

"I want you to see a therapist."

My blood chills, and I push away, letting my hair fall over my face to hide my burning cheeks. For a moment I felt normal. I should have known it wouldn't last.

"Pen. Look at me." His voice drops to that deep, commanding tone that makes me melt inside.

"Been there," I say. "Done that. Dissected my entire childhood. I am who I am. I'm not going to change." I grab my ruined knickers from the floor and ball them in my fist. "I've accepted this about me. I don't think you can say the same about you."

He flinches and I know I've hit the mark. "We're not talking about me. And maybe you didn't see the right person." He pulls up his clothes and buttons his fly, then threads his belt back around his waist.

"I'm not going to let you make me feel like I need help," I snap. "I'm not suicidal. I'm not going to hurt anyone. This is my form of release like going to the club is yours. Are we really that different, Jack? We both need pain—you need to give it; I need to take it."

The front bell tinkles. Shoes thud across the wooden floor. Only someone with a key could be out in reception, and I have a sick feeling I know who it is. I brush past Jack and unlock the door. "I'll see you at Redemption."

If I thought he would let me so easily dismiss him, I am sorely mistaken. Something has changed between us, and I'm not sure what. He walks past me and reaches for the door. Then he turns, his expression soft and a touch wounded. "I'll come by later tonight, and we can talk. I've got to meet some sponsors over dinner."

"I've got plans tonight. I'm meeting Cora, Blade Saw, and… Doctor Death after Fuzzy's class."

His face tightens. "Don't even think about it."

"*He* doesn't think there's anything wrong with me." I flinch at the unmistakable warning in my tone, but now I'm hurting inside, and I want him to hurt, too.

"Damn it, Pen—"

"Penny?" Ray's voice echoes through the door. I reach around Jack and pull it open, abruptly ending our conversation.

Ray startles when he sees Jack in the doorway. "What are you…?"

"Ray." Jack gives him a nod, and Ray watches him walk out the door.

Ray's gaze flicks to me, and he lifts a questioning eyebrow. I thought there was only one way to put a man like Ray off an impending interrogation. But now I know another.

"We fucked on my desk," I say.

And I close my door.

I promise I won't attack you

PENNY

WHEN I GET TO REDEMPTION, I'M IN A BAD MOOD. I OPENED myself up to a man I thought understood me, only to discover he doesn't understand me at all. I'm broken, damaged, and unfixable. And no amount of therapy is going to change that.

Worthless. No good…

With the monsters clawing inside me, I need to do something to relieve the pressure, and I need to do it fast, or, promise or no promise, I won't be able to stop myself from cutting tonight. I briefly consider calling Jack and asking him for another round of mind-blowing, ass-bruising sex. But all that would do is reinforce in his mind just how broken I really am.

I change into my workout clothes, wincing at every touch of my tender skin, and walk through the gym to the fitness area where Fuzzy holds Punch or Perish. The warehouse hums with the buzz of cardio equipment, the rattle of speed bags, and the grunts and groans of fighters grappling on the mats and straining with the free weights. On a mission, I stand front and center of the group. I missed class yesterday and nothing pisses Fuzzy off more than people who miss class, except people who miss class and then show up without an excuse and don't even make an effort to hide.

"What are you doing?" Cora whispers, coming up behind me. "He's going to eat you alive."

"I feel like being tortured today," I tell her. "It'll make for an easy class for the rest of you."

Fuzzy's eyes narrow when he sees me, and he walks right up to me and leans into my face. "Thanks for joining us."

"You're welcome." My words drip sarcasm. But I want him angry. I want him to punish me. I want to feel pain.

"Were you sick or injured?" He runs a hand over his dark hair, closely shaved and bristly. Broad, thick, and heavily muscled, with rigid standards and high expectations of everyone around him, Fuzzy is the cop no criminal wants to meet and the instructor no one wants to piss off. Except me.

"Neither. I just didn't feel like coming."

The class draws in a collective breath and Fuzzy's jaw tightens. "So you let down the team."

"It's a class. Not a team."

Behind me, Cora gasps. I look over my shoulder and give the class an apologetic shrug. We are sort of a team, having bonded over Fuzzy's verbal abuse and his penchant for working us until we throw up.

"Fifty push-ups on your knuckles for disrespecting your

instructor." He points to the mat. "Then you catch up with the rest of the class."

"Seriously? Don't you think the knuckle push-up thing is getting old?"

Cora moans quietly behind me. Fuzzy tips his head to the side and strokes his chin.

"You're right. It is getting old. And since I was planning to get everyone into the ring today for a few practice rounds, how about we start with you? But instead of partnering with one of your non-teammates, you can partner with Shilla the Killa."

"No!" Cora shrieks. "She'll be killed."

"She'll suffer," Fuzz says. "But she won't die."

Ten minutes later I climb into the practice ring. Shilla nods her head. All my classmates are gathered around, and a few fighters drift over to see what's going on.

"If you stay in the ring for the full three minutes, you're off the hook," Fuzzy says. "Shilla's going to give you a one-minute handicap, so that's two minutes you have to stay on your feet. Try to remember the techniques we've practiced in class, your positioning, and footwork. If you tap out or if she knocks you out, then you're my bitch forever."

"Thanks for the pep talk." I pump my arms like Shilla, although I have no idea why she's doing that crazy move. Cora leans in and grabs my arm.

"You don't have to do this. He can't force you to fight or do push-ups on your knuckles. It's not the army. Tell him where to go, and we'll ditch him and go for a drink while we wait for the guys."

"I want to fight."

Shilla jumps up and down on her toes, and I follow suit, except she has very little in the way of breasts, and I'm in serious danger of knocking myself out before we even get started.

"You don't know how to fight like this," Cora wails.

"Despite being a mean SOB, Fuzzy is a good teacher," I assure her. "I've picked up a lot in his classes. And don't forget, I'm a white belt in Brazilian jiu-jitsu."

Fuzzy crosses the ring to talk to Shilla, and I clench and unclench my fists like I've seen some fighters do. We have attracted a considerable crowd, but the one person I do want to see isn't among them.

"Climb the ropes." Homicide Hank, a lean, wiry, red-haired fighter, leans against the ropes beside me. When Redemption was an underground fight club, he made a name for himself by climbing the ropes, screaming, and throwing himself on his opponents. Now that Redemption is licensed and regulated with a couple of pros in the gym, he has had to exercise more restraint in the ring and limit himself to unsanctioned fights. But since this is just for Fuzzy and I have no hope in hell of making it out alive, I give his suggestion serious consideration before finally turning it down.

"It wouldn't give me much of an advantage," I say. "But your screaming trick might work."

"Bring it from the diaphragm." He sucks in a sharp breath, ready to scream, and I hold up my hand. "I don't want to ruin the element of surprise."

Fuzzy blows his whistle to start the fight, and I take a page from Homicide's book and run, screaming, directly at Shilla.

Bam. She sweeps my leg out from under me, and I go down hard.

Dazed but undefeated, I draw in a deep breath of disinfectant-scented mat and then jump up, ready for more.

Bam. I'm down again, having missed her standing beside me with her irritating sweeping foot at the ready. I glance over at the clock. Twenty seconds have passed. Only one hundred seconds to go.

Fuzzy calls a time-out and ushers Shilla to the corner, giving me a moment to breathe. Obviously, a direct assault is not the way to go. What can I do that she won't expect?

I drop into the fight stance Fuzzy taught us. She's known as a striker, so if I can get her on the ground, I can use the jiu-jitsu moves I practiced with Jack. All I have to do is sweep her leg before she sweeps mine. Shilla moves toward me. I sweep.

Bam. She catches me with a right hook because I forgot to protect my face. Now that's the kind of pain I was looking for. Haze-inducing, gut-wrenching, knock-the-breath-out-of-me pain. I lie on the mat to catch my breath. Now, only seventy-five seconds to go.

Cora calls another time-out and helps me to my corner. Shilla hasn't even broken a sweat. She lounges on the other side of the practice ring, talking to Homicide Hank, who seems displeased that she's beating me up in the ring.

"You're not going to make it." Cora holds an ice pack to my cheek and hands me a bottle of water. "This is utterly ridiculous. I sent one of the guys from the class to tell Torment. He'll put a stop to it."

"I can take more," I tell her. "She pulled that punch. And I would rather be pulverized by Shilla than become Fuzzy's lifetime bitch."

Fuzzy blows his whistle to start the fight again. Shilla disarms me with a smile.

"I'm impressed you lasted this long," she says, circling like a predator around wounded prey. "You're tougher than you look in your frills and pastels and kitten heels."

"It's a disguise," I say honestly. "Pretty on the outside to hide the ugly on the inside."

She cocks her head to the side, considering. "We all have a bit of ugly inside."

"Not as much as me." I take advantage of her distraction by lunging forward. I try to sweep her front leg again, but she is ready for my amateur attempt and rushes me, her shoulder in my stomach as she takes me to the ground. I go down hard, and my tender ass protests the violent thud before my head snaps back and hits the mat.

"Jesus fucking Christ. What the fucking hell is going on?"

From my comfy position on the mat, I see Jack climb through the ropes. Fuzzy steps in front of him and warns him not to interfere with the fight. Jack grabs him by the collar and shakes him like he's a rag doll and not a two-hundred-pound police officer and top MMA coach.

"Get out, Rampage," Shilla says, standing in front of me. "I'm just playing with her. Fuzzy wanted me to scare her a bit."

His head snaps in her direction, and he pushes Fuzzy aside. Shilla and Jack are very close friends, so I am shocked when he reaches for her, clearly intending to have her join Fuzzy on the mat.

But wait. Torment is in the ring, and although Shilla is a top-ranked female fighter, Torment is…well…Torment. He is the man, the boss, the king. Once an amateur underground heavyweight champ, Torment turned down offers to go pro but still trains every day. He runs Redemption with a tight fist, and he has a very low tolerance for anyone who breaks the rules.

"Stand down," he orders.

Chests heave, biceps flex. Testosterone laces the air between them. For a moment I think Jack will back down, but then his fist flies up, and he takes a swing at Torment.

A fighter challenging Torment is a once-in-a-lifetime event. Punch bags slow. Treadmills stop. Weights are racked. Everyone rushes over for the big event. Cora and Homicide Hank help me out of the ring.

Torment lands a ferocious right hand. Jack tags him back. Torment lands a good uppercut in a clinch and then drives forward, looking for a takedown, but Jack evades, only to take an elbow in the face. He lands a big right punch to the head and goes in for another takedown, just as Renegade arrives with Doctor Death.

"Enough." Renegade, Torment's oldest friend and once his underground fight promoter, is the only man who can get him to back down. Torment and Jack step away from each other, chests heaving, bodies covered in sweat.

"How are you feeling, Pen?" Doctor Death kneels beside me.

"Fine. It was just a little bump."

Thump. Thump. Thump. I look up just as Jack yanks Doctor Death to his feet. "Don't touch her. Where's Doc?"

Torment's girlfriend, Makayla, known as Doc at the gym, is the head of first aid at Redemption and is usually around when she's not working as a paramedic.

"She's at home," Torment says, coming up behind him. "She's three months pregnant, so I don't approve of her leaving the house."

Someone in the crowd snorts a laugh. Others join in. Doc is about the only person who is not cowed by Torment's controlling and dominating personality, and she is not the kind of woman who would let anyone tell her what to do.

"How's that working out for you?" Shilla says to him.

"I have a few bruises, but it's nothing I can't handle." Torment turns his scowl on Jack. "What the hell has gotten into you?"

"Fuck off." He looks down at me, and a pained expression crosses his face. "I'll take Pen to the hospital."

"Seriously? I don't need to go to the hospital. My head barely touched the mat."

"You shouldn't move her until I've checked her over," Doctor Death unhelpfully says with a naughty smirk on his face. "She might have a concussion."

"A concussion?" Jack spins around. "Shilla! What the fuck?"

The gym stills, chatter quiets, nobody moves. Except for fights, Jack has never once raised his voice in the gym. He has never lost his temper, never pushed anyone or fought anyone except in the ring, or acted like anything other than a Southern gentleman. He has never lost control, and his behavior tonight is shocking, even to me.

"Jack." Although I'm supposed to use his ring name in the gym, I suspect his real name is the only way to get through. "He's winding you up. I'm okay. Really. And there's no one to blame. I chose to step into the ring."

He squats down beside me and squeezes my hand. "You're okay?"

"Yes."

"I'm taking you home." He helps me up and turns me around, inspecting me for injuries as everyone drifts away now that the drama is done.

"Actually, I have plans tonight with Cora, Blade Saw, and… um…Doctor Death."

"Cancel them."

I step back, putting some distance between us. "Why? So I can spend the evening with someone who thinks I'm broken?"

"So you can spend the evening with someone who cares," he says quietly. "Someone who can't stand the thought of you being hurt, and lost it when he saw you lying on the mat." He reaches for me and pulls me close. "Someone who might be lacking in tact."

"People are going to get ideas," I murmur into his chest. "Especially if they hear you grovel like that."

"Good."

"Good?" I look up and study his face.

"We're friends, Pen. Nothing wrong with that."

⁓

RAMPAGE

Penny doesn't talk on the drive home. At first I figure she's shaken up after the fight, but every so often I catch her scowling at me, so I figure I've done something wrong. Not that she's about to tell me what it is.

By the time we arrive at her house, I have twenty messages on my phone. Everyone wants to know what's going on. What happened to me? Why did I lose it in the gym? Are Penny and I together? Do I have a will? Because Torment will never forgive me.

Once inside, Penny feeds Clarice and goes to take a shower. I throw myself on the couch and try to figure out what kind of damage control I'm going to have to do to fix things at the gym. I let my mask slip tonight. Now I have to convince everybody that what they saw wasn't real.

"I'm knackered, so I'm going to bed," Penny announces from the hallway. She's wearing an oversized T-shirt with a "Mind the Gap" logo on the front. Given the girly clothes she wears every day, I would have expected her to wear something frilly and feminine to bed, but the way the T-shirt drapes over her softly rounded breasts and skirts the tops of her thighs is more erotic than the finest lingerie.

"Come here." I pat the seat beside me.

She gives me a wary look. "Why?"

"So we can talk." I lean forward, elbows on my knees, my hands dangling down so I am not tempted to push myself up and take her in my arms. Given her cold, stiff demeanor, I'd probably get a slap for my efforts.

"You made me a promise, darlin'. You said you'd come to me if you felt a need to hurt yourself. You picked that fight with Fuzzy knowing how it would end."

Guilt flickers across her face, followed by defensive anger. "So what if I did?"

"I could have given you what you needed, but without the harm."

She bends down and picks up Clarice, holding the cat against her chest. "As a friend?"

"Yes."

Her bottom lip quivers. "A friendship where you spank me and whip me and fuck me but we aren't together in a way anyone understands?"

"I can't give you anything else. I can't give you normal. I'm not going to change. I've been this way as long as I can remember, and there's nothing I can point to as a trigger, nothing that needs to be cured."

"I don't want normal." She puts Clarice down and gives her a pat. "I want pain because that's the only way I can get emotional release. I just never realized there might be other ways of getting that release that involve pleasure, too."

And I never realized it would be possible to share my kink with someone who not only wants what I have to give, but needs it, too, although I'm pretty sure she wouldn't be able to tolerate the kind of pain I give the hard-core masochists at Club Sin.

"I like who you are," she says softly. "The real Jack you revealed at the gym tonight; the Jack from the club; and the Jack who's my friend. I like your kind of normal."

I like who she is too, but what happens when she gets the help she needs and realizes there is a life beyond pain—a life I can't share?

"What's going to happen if I leave tonight?"

She tugs at the hem of her shirt, twists her lips to the side. "I don't know. I can still feel the need; it's like an itch under my skin. Maybe you could stay…"

"I'll stick around for a bit."

I follow her into the bedroom and stretch out on the covers. Her room is decorated in bold primary colors, a decided contrast to the pastels she always wears. Is this the real her? For a man who wears a mask, I am supremely incapable of seeing through hers.

"You can get under the covers," she says, lying on the bed beside me. "I promise I won't attack you. I'm a quiet sleeper. I don't moan or talk or thrash around. I won't even steal the covers."

I turn on my side, prop my head up on my elbow. "I've never slept in a bed with a woman, Pen. Not even Avery. She wanted to wait until we were married. When I said I don't do relationships, I meant I don't do intimacy in any form. I have sex. I scene at the club. But that's it. I don't want to lead anyone on. I don't want anyone to have expectations that I can't fulfill." She turns to face me, and I can't help but smooth my hand over her arm, in and out of the dip of her waist, and over the curve of her hip. Her shirt rides up, exposing the lacy edge of her panties. My cock hardens, and I grit my teeth and roll to my back.

"You can turn off the light." She gestures to the light beside me. "I only need it when I'm alone."

My stomach clenches at the thought of all the other times she hasn't been alone, other men who have shared her bed, held her while she slept, made love to her like normal men do.

I turn out the light. Fold my arms behind my head. Stare at the darkened ceiling. Try not to think about the beautiful woman lying beside me.

Penny rests her hand against my chest, snuggles against me. I've never had a woman snuggle with me before, but then I've never let anyone get as close as she is right now. At the club or in the few private encounters I have had, I've kept my submissives at arm's length. We do our scene. I endure the aftercare. I send them home. There are no cuddles, no nights spent in each other's arms, no lazy weekend mornings in bed. Even that crazy night with Sylvia, when I gave in to my longing for a connection beyond pain, I didn't stay a minute longer than I had to.

But this is Penny. And I feel something for her—the kind of emotional connection I never thought I would feel again.

And it fucking scares me.

16

It's the dirty things you say

PENNY

WHEN I OPEN MY EYES, I AM SURROUNDED IN WARMTH. JACK'S scent fills my head. His arms are around me, his clothed body curled around mine. His warm breath tickles the back of my neck. His chest rises and falls. The room is dark and quiet. Peaceful.

I stroke his forearm, so strong and thick. He is one of the biggest fighters at Redemption, and one of the strongest. He is scared of nothing and no one. He makes me feel safe.

Slowly, so as not to wake him, I turn in his arms. My eyes trace the planes and angles of his face and search out the scars barely visible in the darkness. I wonder what it must be like to be so strong, inside and out, to never be afraid.

Gently, I rest my hand on his chest. I can feel the steady beat of his heart, the heat of his body. I run my hand over his pecs and down, lightly tracing over the ripples of his abs beneath his shirt, stopping just above his belt.

My pussy clenches at the memory of this belt in his hand. The crack of leather on my ass. The fierce sting that sizzled into pleasure. Even now I am still tender. How many women has he whipped with this belt? How many begged him to make them come?

"None."

I look up. His eyes are open, lids heavy with sleep. "Only use I've ever had for this belt is holding up my pants."

"How did you know what I was thinking?" I trace my finger along the edge of his belt, my palm brushing over the bulge in his jeans.

"Your fingers talk." He reaches for my hand, brings it to his lips, kisses my fingers one by one. "Curious fingers. Naughty fingers."

I scoot closer to him, so close our noses almost touch. "How naughty?"

He growls, a low rumble deep in his chest. "Very naughty. Fingers going where fingers aren't allowed to go."

Cocooned in the darkness, surrounded in his heat, safe in his arms, I feel brave tonight. I ease my free hand down between us and cup the heavy length of his erection through his jeans. He groans, nuzzles my neck, his five-o'clock shadow an erotic burn on my sensitive skin. His fingers dig into my hip so hard I catch my breath. "Do you want to play, naughty girl?"

Moisture seeps between my thighs, dampening my knickers. "Yes," I breathe. "I want to play."

In one swift move, he pushes himself up and tears the blanket off my body. I shiver as cool air brushes over my heated skin.

"Hmm." His sensual gaze rakes over me, and he licks his lips like I'm a tasty treat. "Do you have any toys?"

My cheeks heat, and I suck in my lips, inexplicably embarrassed at having to reveal something so personal when I'm about to get naked and have rough sex with the man of my dreams. "Nightstand beside the bed."

Jack chuckles and pulls open the drawer. "Quite the collection," he says, rummaging through my assortment of sex toys. "I don't know which one to use first."

"Don't talk. Just...take something."

He assumes an innocent look. "Why can't I talk? Don't you think we should discuss your sex toy addiction? Although there are a few classic items missing and nothing for anal play."

"Jack!"

"I love it when you blush. It makes me want to introduce you to all sorts of naughty things." He pulls out my rabbit and holds it up in the beam of moonlight filtering through the curtains. "We can get up to all sorts of trouble with this."

My mouth goes dry when he kneels on the bed in front of me and unbuckles his belt. He yanks it from the loops and doubles it in his palm.

"Not again," I whisper.

His face softens, and he leans over, reaching for my hands. "Not again. You wouldn't be able to take it. I have something else in mind." He lifts my hands over my head and binds them together with his belt, twisting it around the wrought iron headboard to hold me fast.

"What's your safe word?" he asks as he tests my bonds,

tightening the belt so I am stretched to the point of discomfort but not pain.

"*Redemption.*"

"Good girl." He reaches under my shirt and slides my knickers over my hips. After tossing them on the floor, he grabs the rabbit and flicks the switch. "It lights up," he says in delight when it glows purple. "Is that in case it gets lost? Or maybe to help me find my way?"

"You're killing me," I groan. "I ordered it online because it was on sale. I didn't know it glowed until I turned it on the first time. It gave me quite a fright."

He's laughing so hard he has to brace himself on the bed. I like seeing him laugh. It reminds me that he is still Rampage, my friend from the gym, the man who can cheer anyone up.

"I can imagine," he says, finally. And then his face smooths, and he turns off the vibrator and holds it to my lips. "I didn't see any lube. Lick."

I wrinkle my nose at the scent of plastic and the disinfectant soap I use for washing up. "Um…actually, I don't think I need to do that. I'm pretty wet."

"I didn't ask." His voice carries a low, warning note that makes my core tighten.

Tentatively, I touch my tongue to the cool, smooth plastic, swallow down the taste of soap.

With a grunt of disapproval, Jack presses the head of the vibrator between my lips, forcing me to take more into my mouth. "Let's see a bit more enthusiasm."

Drawing in a deep breath, I swirl my tongue over the softly

rounded head, lick up and down the plastic shaft. Jack watches me intently, his gaze never leaving my mouth as I work to lubricate the entire surface.

"Good girl." He pulls the vibrator away. "Now spread your legs for me."

I part my legs, and he frowns. "Wider."

"They don't go wider."

"I need you open and available to me, darlin'. Do I need to tie your ankles to the corners of the bed?"

A moan escapes my lips. Everything he says makes my pussy throb. I never imagined I could get aroused just from words and the tone of a voice.

Jack leans over and presses his lips to my ear. "Are you moaning because you like the idea of being totally restrained or being open to me? Vulnerable. At my mercy?"

"It's the things you say," I whisper. "They make me so hot I ache inside. Especially when you say *darlin'* with that soft Tennessee twang. It makes me wet."

His eyes shoot wide, and a flicker of darkness dances within them. "You shouldn't have told me that. I'll never use your real name again."

"It's not just that word. It's…well, most of them. Your accent makes everything sound sexy. Before I ever saw you at the club, I used to imagine you talking dirty to me with that Southern drawl."

"Now, that's interesting, 'cause I used to imagine you talking dirty to me in that prim and proper British accent." His warm hands glide over my calves, tickle the back of my knees, caress the inside of my thighs. My legs fall open wider, and desire blooms hot inside me.

"What did I say when you imagined me?" I ask.

He gives a satisfied smile and glides the vibrator through my labia. "You begged me to fuck your wet cunt." With one broad hand across my hips, holding me still, he slides the vibrator inside me, rocking it gently as it pulses against my sensitive tissue. I curl my fingers around the belt, tensing as he presses the vibrator in further, my mouth watering in anticipation of the moment those rabbit ears dance over my clit.

"Aah!" My cry makes him chuckle, and he turns it down a notch.

"Beg. Use your dirty words."

I drop my head to the pillow as the ache grows inside me. "Please, Jack. Fuck my…cunt."

"That's a start." He turns up the speed on the vibe and presses the external attachment against my clit. I jerk against the restraints, every muscle taut, and my body on the edge of release.

He turns it down again, and I let out a guttural groan.

"I also imagined you swearing at me," he says. "Let it out. Let me know how you feel when I take you to the edge and don't let you come. Give me your pain, your frustration. Nothing as sexy as a beautiful girl who talks like the Queen of England giving me her dirty mouth." He flicks the switch, and the vibrator hums to life again, buzzing against my clit, the unrelenting waves making my muscles clench. My clit engorges, throbs, and I draw in a deep breath as my body coils tight, ready to spring.

But before I can go over, he moves the vibe, rocking the rabbit ears from side to side over my clit, just enough to keep me on edge but not enough to come. The ache for release slides into pain, and I dig my heels into the bed and rock my hips up for more.

"Down." Jack slaps the side of my thigh so hard it takes my breath away.

"Bloody hell," I mutter. "I need to come."

A smile tugs at Jack's lips. "You can do better than that."

He turns the vibrator off, and I let my frustration go. "Miserable git. Bellend. Tosser. Pillock. Bastard. Wanker. Twat."

Jack roars with laughter. "When I imagined you dirty talking, I never thought it would all be directed at me."

"I need to come, you arse." I groan and drop my legs to the bed.

"You want to come." His voice is hoarse, rough, and his erection strains against the fly of his jeans. "You need something else."

I look down and meet his firm gaze. "What do I need?"

"You need pain, beautiful girl. And I'm going to give it to you."

He draws the vibe out and then presses it back in, just enough to tease but not enough to satisfy. The rabbit ears dance over my clit, and every time I near my peak, he moves them somewhere else. I curse him using every American swear word I know, and then I pull out the all the British swear words I can remember. But he keeps it up until my labia are swollen, and every thrust and lick of the vibrator sends electricity shooting through my veins, burning away every thought in my head except the desperate, gut-wrenching need to come.

A sob rips from my throat. Jack drops the vibrator and tears open his jeans, making quick work of discarding them on the floor. Unable to speak, a breath away from orgasm, I tremble as he sheaths himself with a condom from his pocket. How can I feel so much pain and so much pleasure at once?

Without a word, he flips me over. My hands twist the belt and it tightens around my wrists. Jack grabs my hips, pulling my ass upward as my upper body falls to the bed, my weight on my elbows and forearms. He kicks my legs apart with his knee and yanks me back on his huge, hard cock.

Ah God. So good. I whimper as he pushes deep inside.

"Let me hear you." He hammers into me with long, deep strokes that rip my breath from my lungs. "I want to hear you scream."

My heart pounds. Blood rushes through my veins. My nipples pinch hard with desire, and sweat beads on my flesh. Fire consumes me, possesses me, fanning the flames of need.

Jack reaches over my hip. His thumb grazes my slick flesh, whispering over my throbbing clit. "Are you ready to pay for your pleasure? Are you going to give me your pain?"

"Yes. Please. Yes."

"Brace yourself." He slaps my mound, right over my clit.

I am undone.

Pleasure ripples out from my center all the way to my fingers and toes. Jack circles my clit with his finger, dragging out my

orgasm until I cannot think or breathe for the exquisite clenching of my pussy.

With a low groan he grabs my hips, his fingers digging into
my tender flesh, and pounds into me so hard the bed thuds
against the wall. Finally he climaxes, his cock jerking deep inside
me, pulsing against my sensitive inner walls.

Jack collapses over my back, taking his weight on his hands. He
presses a soft kiss to my neck, rests his forehead in my hair. Sighs.

"Jack? You okay?"

He releases the restraints and pulls me up to my knees, set-
tling me back against his body as he rubs my wrists to restore
my circulation. "Fucks with my head, wanting to hurt you and
protect you at the same time."

"I trust you, Jack. I know you would never go too far."

"Means a lot to me, you saying that." He tightens his arms
around me.

"Does that mean you'll stay the night?" I check the clock.
"It's three a.m. No point going all the way home when there's
a nice soft bed right here."

"I gotta be at the gym at six a.m. on Saturdays, and I have
to pick up my gear first." He eases away and grabs his jeans as
he goes to dispose of the condom, leaving me bereft. I pull my
T-shirt down and slide back under the covers. Jack returns fully
clothed, and stands in the doorway. Although he's not far from
the bed, it feels like he's miles away.

"You busy later?" he says, finally. "Maybe we can hook up
for lunch."

"Third Saturday in the month I always go to Ambleside, it's a seniors' home in Alameda. I play some bingo, a little backgam-mon, hang with my friend Rose…"

"Seniors' home? You got grandparents here?"

I tuck the covers tight around me. "No, but I got to know the director when she brought a couple of the residents to one of Amanda's legal aid clinics to get their wills done. Rose was one of them. She was found on the street with a big bag stuffed with cash. No ID. No family. And she doesn't talk. She seemed so sad. I went to visit the next week and I brought Clarice with me. The director said that was the first time she saw Rose smile. I've been going every month to see her and spend time with some of the other residents who don't have family or friends."

He stares at me for a long moment, and then his face softens, warms. "Fuck me," he says softly. He unbuckles his belt, strips off his jeans.

Hope flares in my chest. "What are you doing?"

"Got a few hours, and I want to spend it lying beside the prettiest fucking girl I ever laid eyes on, who's so busy giving out caring she doesn't get any for herself." He throws back the covers and slides into bed beside me.

Warmth blooms inside me. I snuggle up against him, rest my head against his chest.

"Are you sure you won't go up in flames when the sun comes up?" I tease. "Or break out in a rash because you're in a girl's bed? Or—"

"Maybe I didn't whip you enough in the office," he muses, his hand gently caressing my still-tender behind.

"I'm suddenly feeling very sleepy and not really in the mood for all this talking." I lean up and nuzzle his neck. "I'm glad you're staying, even if it is only for a few hours."

"Yeah, me too."

I drift off to sleep; the only thing ruining this perfect moment is Jack's taut, tense body beneath me.

—⁓—

Clarice and I arrive at Ambleside Meadows just before noon.

Julie, the executive director, greets me at the door of the Shaker-style building decorated in cream, mauve, and sage. Thin and wiry, with short blond hair and so much energy she puts even the MMA fighters to shame, Julie is one of the most caring people I've ever met. Ambleside is her dream—a retirement home with a difference. Every weekend, she invites people from the community to share their talents with the retirees, who can then share their experience in turn. They learn from each other, and as a result, her residents are happier and more engaged in the community. "We've got a full house today," she says. "Chess player, opera singer, accountant, actor, a pastry chef…"

"And me and my cat." I put down my kitty travel carrier, and Clarice meows in protest.

"Our marketing genius." Julie beams and waves her hand at the Ambleside logo on the door that I designed for them the first year I started visiting.

When Julie first brought her residents to see Amanda about getting wills drafted, she mentioned that Ambleside might be reverting to an ordinary care home at the end of the year. Although her residents loved the community involvement program, she had been unable to attract enough volunteers to make it viable or enough residents who were willing to pay the higher fee for the service, given the stiff competition in the area.

The first time I walked in the door, I knew why. No branding, no logo, nothing to catch the eye, capture the imagination, or differentiate them from other care homes. In my free time, I sketched a few things for Julie and put her in touch with another one of Amanda's clients in a marketing firm. Six months later, they had a waiting list, not just of residents but also of people in the community who were interested in helping out.

"I thought she was a legal assistant," says a deep voice behind me, soft with a Southern twang.

I spin around, startled when I see Jack behind me. "What are you doing here? How did you find me?"

"You gave me the name. Wasn't hard to track down." Jack leans down and presses a kiss to my forehead. "I do three hours on, three hours off on Saturdays. Thought I'd spend my three hours off seeing what you get up to when I'm not around."

A thrill of joy runs through my body. He came all this way for me. For the briefest of moments I feel something I've never felt before—wanted, worthy, and insanely happy.

A smile splits Julie's face. "You have a boyfriend? Why didn't you tell me?"

My joy wavers a little, and I glance over at Jack, still uncertain where we stand. "We're just…uh…friends," I stammer. "This is Jack. He's a professional MMA fighter. I think some of the guys here might enjoy talking to him."

"Are you kidding me?" Julie's voice rises in pitch. "I'm going to make an announcement right now."

"I hope you don't mind." I look up at Jack's amused face after Julie races away. "I know a couple of the guys here used to be boxers, and I think a few of the residents used to be professional athletes, too."

"Not at all. There's nothing I like better than sharing fight stories, except spending time with you." He pulls me against him, brushes his lips over mine. "Didn't like leaving you this morning, all soft and sleepy, cuddled against me."

"Didn't like waking up alone." I run my tongue over the seam of his lips, and he opens for me with a groan. "But seeing you here kind of makes up for it. This is better than Christmas morning."

"You keep doing that, you're gonna get an unexpected present," he murmurs.

"Is it a big present?" I press myself against him, rub my hip against the bulge in his jeans.

Jack chuckles. "They don't get bigger."

"I'm glad one of us doesn't have problems with his ego." I wrap my arms around his neck and pull him down for a proper kiss. If this is the kind of friendship he wants, then I'll take it, even if I can sense heartbreak ahead.

"So what's this about you being a marketing genius?" He pulls away just enough to talk, and I lean against him, soak in the delicious heat of his body. He's rocking a short-sleeved button-down black shirt over his worn jeans, but then with a body like his, everything he wears looks hot.

"Just a hobby. My mom was a marketing executive, and I like doodling designs. Sometimes I see a sign or a product and I think I could come up with something catchier or more compelling.

I don't have any training. It's just something I do for fun. I did the logo you see on the door…"

"It's really good," he says, studying the design. "You've got a lot of talent. You ever think of running with that?"

Clarice meows for my attention, and I bend down and open the cage door to let her out. "I'm not good enough to take it anywhere. Plus, I'd have to go back to school, and I have to work to pay the rent. It's more of a hobby."

"MMA was a hobby for me, and then it became something more." He tucks a rogue strand of hair behind my ear when I stand. "If you love something, it doesn't seem like work when you're learning the ropes. In the beginning, the distillery was paying the bills. Now, it's gonna be the other way around."

"Not everyone is lucky enough to find a talent and make it into a career."

"It's not about luck," he says. "It's about going after what you want and not letting anything stand in your way."

Julie returns and picks up Clarice to give her a cuddle. "We're all set. I'm going to steal Jack away for a chat with some of the guys and you and Clarice can visit with Rose."

"Why did you name her Clarice?" Jack gives her a tentative pat and gets an unexpected purr in return.

"Heroine of my favorite movie. She was beautiful, brave, strong, and determined. No matter how bad it got, she didn't give up. Clarice went through a lot before I found her. I thought she'd earned her name."

"She's not the only one who went through a lot and came out strong."

I look up at him to protest but stop at the soft expression on his face.

Julie coughs loudly, and I bite back a smile.

"I'll come and find you after I'm done talking with Rose."

Jack frowns. "I thought you said Rose couldn't talk."

I slide my hand into his and give it a squeeze. "Sometimes actions speak louder than words."

—⁓—

RAMPAGE

Torment sends one of his minions to drag me to his office as soon as I walk into Redemption after returning from Ambleside. I knew it was coming. No one breaks the rules and lives to tell the tale. Not even me, and I'm one of the founding members of the gym.

I stalk ahead of the young kid who was unlucky enough to be in Torment's line of sight when he heard I was back from my break, and my good mood fades. Meeting the seniors at Ambleside was an unexpected pleasure. All professional athletes back in the day, they had some great stories to tell, and damned if they didn't have a few tips that I plan to implement in the cage. But seeing Penny so happy was the greatest pleasure of all. She expects so little that even the smallest gesture means so much, and it is hard not to be drawn by someone who gives so willingly of herself.

I don't bother knocking when we reach Torment's office. Instead, I go on the offensive and push open his frosted glass door.

"Sit." He gestures to the black leather chair in front of his massive cherry wood desk. Torment, being Torment, never does anything by halves.

Bristling, I sit only because I know I'm in the wrong.

"Never seen you lose it like you did last night." No pleasantries. Torment never beats around the bush. "You broke one of our fundamental rules about fighting in the gym."

"The rule is that fighting isn't allowed outside of the practice ring," I counter. "We were in the ring."

Torment's eyes narrow. "Don't play technicalities with me. You know damn well what the rule means and the purpose behind it. You wrote it."

"It won't happen again."

"Penny is a member of the gym," he says. "She's here a couple of times a week. How can you guarantee you aren't going to flip out again if she gets hurt?"

Goddamn bastard thinks he knows everything. "There's nothing between us."

Torment snorts a laugh. "We all start out telling ourselves that, but at some point you start seeing what everyone else sees. I ripped through the gym when I caught Makayla playing strip poker with you losers. Renegade almost broke Doctor Death's neck when he was putting the moves on Amanda. The Predator risked his job and his life to avenge Sia. We protect our friends, but we only lose control when it comes to the women we care about."

"You're wrong." I push myself to my feet, uncomfortable with where this conversation is headed and the reminder that I am breaking one of my cardinal rules about getting involved.

"Yeah?" Torment grins. "Where did you spend the night after you took her home?"

"Fuck off."

He holds up his hands in a pacifying gesture. "I'm happy for you. All these years I've known you, I've never seen you with a woman in any way other than friendship."

"Christ. Just let it go." Fucking bastard is trying to get under my skin in the worst possible way.

"What does she think?" Torment scrawls something on a piece of paper and slides it over the desk.

"It doesn't matter what she thinks. It is what it is. Friendship."

"Are you sure about that?" He gives me a smug smile when I pick up the piece of paper. "From what I've seen, Penny's a very determined woman. When she wants something, she gives it 110 percent effort. No one works harder in the classes. No one has ever challenged Fuzzy the way she does. She had next to no experience, and yet she stepped into the ring with Shilla because there was something she wanted from that encounter and she wasn't afraid to go after it. She's got more courage than most of the guys who walk in here and tell me they want to be fighters. Hell, if she wanted to become a fighter, I'd train her myself."

The thought of Torment going anywhere near Penny has me crushing the paper in my hand. I know everything that goes on at Redemption, and Torment is number one on the single ladies' fantasy list of whom they want to sleep with at the gym. I trust Torment. He's one of my closest friends. He is head over heels in love with Makayla, and he isn't the kind of man who would ever stray. And yet the thought of him training Penny, being with her every day, touching her, drives me out of my fucking mind.

"I wouldn't allow her to fight. It's too fucking dangerous." I slam my hand against the wall. "Christ. Just the thought of her in the ring makes me fucking crazy."

Torment chuckles. "Welcome to the club."

"What club?"

"The club where you fight the inevitable and lose."

Fed up with Torment and his insinuations, I grab the door handle. "I'm outta here."

"Don't lose that piece of paper," Torment calls out. "You'll need it tonight."

"What is it?" Pausing in the doorway, I smooth the paper and frown at the number written on it in blue pen.

"The number of drinks you'll have to buy for the team at Score tonight to atone for your sins," he says. "Plus one."

"Plus one?"

Torment gives me an irritating bastard smile. "You want to keep your membership at Redemption, I expect to see Penny there. Just try not to cause any trouble."

17

Goddamn. Bastard. Touching. My. Girl.

PENNY

"We're rocking this sports bar."

Cora turns away from the sea of big-screen TVs and checks out the crowd. She's wearing a black-and-red dress with vinyl strips angling across her breasts and running down the front, with knee-high black leather boots. She says it's a sci-fi thing, although it looks more peace sign than alien to me. She hasn't said anything about how things are going with Blade Saw, but when I called her up after getting Jack's text about coming out tonight, she was more than happy to join us.

"You're rocking. I'm normal." Well, sort of normal. I'm wearing a dove-gray, curve-hugging dress with a naughty heart-shaped cutout in the front that exposes the crescents of my breasts. Cora convinced me to ditch the girly frills, pastels, and flowers tonight, but she couldn't get me to wear black. Gray is as far outside my color spectrum as I get.

One of three sports bars in Chinatown and the go-to place for MMA fighters in town, Score is packed tonight with pumped, cut, testosterone-filled fighters all ready to shout at the game on the televisions and battle it out in drunken arm-wrestling matches that often devolve into alley fights. From rank amateurs to seasoned pros, everyone comes to Score, not just for its fabulous sports-themed drinks and vast selection of international beer, but for the gossip, the ring girls, and the chance to see and be seen.

A DJ spins music from a small stage, and fight posters are plastered all over the walls. I head over to the Redemption corner where Doctor Death, Torment, Makayla, and Blade Saw have snagged a couple of highboy tables and an entire tray of vodka shots that are disappearing at lightning speed.

Blade Saw nods at Cora but doesn't go over to greet her. She grabs a drink from the tray, and we join Doctor Death and Makayla.

If Torment hadn't told us Makayla was three months pregnant, I never would have guessed. Even dressed up in a tight black dress and heels, she looks exactly the same: small and curvy with fantastic, thick auburn hair and big hazel eyes.

"Cora, what's going on with you and Blade Saw?" she whispers.

"Nothing." Cora downs her shot and leans across Doctor Death to get another, her breasts brushing over his arm, which appears to be on purpose. I catch Blade Saw watching them from another table, his face cold and hard.

"You sure you want to play this game?" I say softly. "Blade Saw's a pretty chill guy. It takes a lot to rile him, but once he's there, he's really there. I've seen him punch holes in walls and break the windshield of a car."

"I'm tired of the whole 'let's just see where it takes us' thing," she says. "Maybe he just needs a little kick, and if that doesn't work, I'm up for a no-strings night of fun with someone who gets all my geek jokes but doesn't play the geek game."

Doctor Death whispers something to Cora, and she laughs. I have to admit he seems to be a better match for her than Blade Saw. They are both easygoing, slightly quirky, and academically inclined. But Blade Saw is a good guy, fiercely loyal, totally honest and up-front. Mashed potatoes to Doctor Death's couscous.

What about Jack and me? Do we go together? Aside from our kinks and the fact we both work out at Redemption, we don't have much in common. He's from a high-society family in Tennessee, and I'm from a working-class family in Leeds. He's on his way to becoming a big MMA star, and I'm a legal assistant. He doesn't do relationships, and I still secretly dream of finding someone to love me who makes me feel safe. He's breathtakingly gorgeous, and I'm...well, me. But he did stay over last night, and I still feel warm fuzzies when I think about him coming to Ambleside.

Torment joins our table, and I frown at the green froth in his glass. "What is that?"

"Spinach shake." He holds it up like he's won a prize. "Makayla isn't drinking while she's pregnant, so I asked the bartender to whip up something healthy for her."

"I asked for something yummy," she says, her voice sharp with warning.

"You need vitamins." Torment offers the glass and Makayla shakes her head.

"That doesn't even look close to being edible. I need one of their creamy chocolate ice cream cocktails but without the booze, and a big plate of fries or I might collapse from starvation."

Torment's lips press into a thin line. "If you'd just stayed at home like I told you—"

Makayla cuts him off with a glare. "I'm pregnant. I don't have a fatal disease. Pregnant women lead normal lives. They go to work, they go out with their friends, they exercise, occasionally eat junk food, go to the bar to have a good time, drink creamy drinks, and eat fried food. So get over your overprotective self and go get me something unhealthy to eat."

We all hold our breaths, waiting for the inevitable explosion. No one tells Torment what to do.

"You want ketchup with that?" he asks.

Makayla's lips quiver with a smile. "Lots of ketchup." She leans over to kiss Torment on the cheek, but he cups her neck, turning her toward him as he pulls her in for a real kiss, hard and hungry, full of love and passion.

Cora and I sigh.

"Ah. True love." Doctor Death moves to the side as Torment brushes past. "I gave up on that concept a long time ago. Too many women want me, and it would be inconsiderate not to share myself around. It's all about public service and sacrificing for womankind." He holds out a hand to Cora and then one to me. "Ladies. Care for a drink and a dance? Afterward, maybe we can go back to my place and I'll bathe you in chocolate and show you what a good licker I am."

Laughter bubbles up in my chest, but since Jack isn't here yet, we're out of vodka shots, and the DJ is pretty good, I follow him and Cora to the bar.

"What are you having?" He waves to the bartender, and she drops what she's doing and makes her way toward us. Doctor Death has that effect on women.

"Long Island iced teas," Cora offers. "To start."

I shoot her a worried glance. Cora started two shots ago, and she can get drunk on half a glass of wine. She doesn't hold her liquor well.

Fifteen minutes and another round of drinks later, we are up on the raised dance floor, dancing to the Kongos' "Come with Me Now." I keep my distance from Doctor Death's octopus hands because I know Jack is on his way, but Cora succumbs to his charms. They gyrate to the music as he whispers in her ear. I dance beside them, and yet all I can think about is Jack—his hands on my body, his lips in my ear, his shadowy figure at the bar beside Blade Saw, watching me.

Wait. Jack?

Our eyes meet, and his gaze heats every inch of my skin, blazing a trail straight down to my core. He lifts his beer, takes a slow sip. Blade Saw says something to him, but Jack's eyes never leave mine. A thrill of excitement shoots down my spine, and I let myself go, dancing just for him.

"Blade Saw and Jack are watching," I warn Cora.

"I know." She reaches behind her and puts her arms around

Doctor Death's neck. He gives a delighted rumble, and they sway to the music. His hands run up and down her curves. His lips press into her hair. Blade Saw grows more agitated over by the bar, shifting his weight, his hand clenching around his glass.

"Cora..." But it's too late. Blade Saw breaks away from the bar and steamrolls through the crowd, pushing people aside as he hurtles toward the dance floor. In one smooth move, he leaps up on the riser, grabs Doctor Death, and throws him to the floor. Doctor Death hits a table on his way down. Drinks spill. Angry customers jump up. One goes after Doctor Death, and the other goes after Blade Saw. Redemption fighters swarm in to protect them. I grab Cora's hand and pull her away.

"Down here." I pull her down the back hallway, past the restrooms, and out into the alley. As the door swings closed behind us, I hear shouts and yells, the crack of tables, and the sound of breaking glass. Looks like the Redemption team will have to find a new watering hole. Again.

"What the hell were you doing?" I dig around in my purse for my phone, breathing through my mouth when the first scent of stale piss hits me. "I warned you about him. And it was clear from the moment we walked in that he's into you in a big way."

"He just nodded." She wipes away a tear. "He didn't even say hi. I'm not desperate. I'm smart and fairly attractive, although maybe lacking in a few social skills. I'm worth more than a guy who says he just wants to see how things go, who kisses me one day after a run, fools around with me for a bit, and then tells me the next day we should just be friends and hang out."

"I think he cares about you so much that it scares him." I send a quick text to Jack to let him know we're okay and then one to Makayla to make sure she got out. "I told you he's had a rough time with women. Everyone he cares about leaves him. After that much heartbreak, it's not easy for him to dive in again."

Maybe it's the same for Jack, but he was burned in a worse way—outed and shamed for who he was by someone he cared deeply about. Despite what he might think, what we have when we're together isn't just friendship, and it's not just play like he does at the club. At least not for me.

"Pen!" Jack jogs down the alley toward us. He has a cut across his cheek, and his left eye is swollen. Without slowing his stride, he wraps his arms around me and his momentum carries us into the side of the building with a thud.

"I didn't know where the fuck you were." He holds me tight, his chest heaving. "Cora, Torment is waiting out front with Makayla. They can give you a ride home."

"What about the fight?" I say into his chest. He smells of whiskey and the faintest trace of cologne.

"Torment stopped it and paid off the bar owner so he didn't call the police, but we had to agree to leave."

"Is Blade Saw okay?" Cora straightens her dress. "Maybe I should go find him instead."

Jack frowns. "Probably better if you go with Torment and Makayla. Blade Saw needs a bit of time to cool off, and Makayla needs someone to run interference. Torment has decided she's never going to leave the house again."

After Cora is safely out of the alley, Jack's eyes harden. "What the fuck were you doing?"

Puzzled, I shrug. "Dancing."

"Yeah, I saw how you were dancing," he growls.

It takes me a minute to get my head around what he's saying, and when I do, my anger flares. "Seriously? I don't play those kinds of games. I wasn't trying to make you jealous, and I wasn't trying to pick up other guys, although I should have since you keep telling everyone we're just friends. I like you, Jack. I like spending time with you. I know you had a rough time, but I had a rough time, too, and it's doing my head in trying to understand what we have together, because frankly, I don't have sex with my friends. I trust you in a way I haven't trusted anyone else before. I thought you trusted me, too. I want to be more than just your friend, and more than just a play partner, but if—"

He pushes me against the cold brick wall and cuts me off with a kiss that I feel deep in my soul.

"I thought I'd lose my fucking mind when the fight broke out," he murmurs against my lips. "I beat on half a dozen guys looking for you. You are more than just a friend to me. It just took me a long time to see it."

Warm shivers run down my spine. I press my hand against his chest, feel his heart beat steady beneath my palm. His T-shirt is soft over hard muscle, cool over his heated body. His jeans ride low on his hips. He makes me feel bold, beautiful, and just a little bit wild. "I like that you came looking for me."

"I went a bit crazy." He pulls me close, his arm around my waist. "Got wound up when I saw you dancing with Doctor Death, and then when I couldn't find you…"

"How wound up?" I slide my hand down to the belt he used to whip me in the office and then lower to the bulge in his jeans.

"Fuck." He groans. "Don't—"

I cup his groin and grind my palm over his erection, rock hard beneath his jeans. I've never been sexually aggressive, always letting my partner take the lead, but knowing Jack wants me gives me a sense of power I've never felt before—a power that sets my wild side free.

"Is this for me?" I whisper. "Did you like watching me dance?"

"Every fucking dude in the entire bar liked watching you dance," he growls. "They were all watching you, wanting you, wanting what's mine." His hand slides down my thigh, and he teases the edge of my dress, slowly lifting.

"And yet here I am. Outside. With you." I lean up, press a kiss to his firm, hard lips.

"Damn right you're with me." He returns my kiss, soft at first, then hungrier, his tongue delving into my mouth, leaving no inch untouched. He feathers kisses along my jaw, nibbles my ear, sucks at the pulse hammering wildly at the base of my neck.

I part my legs, rock against his thigh. "I want you. Here. Now."

"So fucking sexy, my girl wanting me so bad." He pushes up my dress and slides one finger along the lacy edge of my knickers. "You sure about this? Someone might come down the alley looking for us."

"I know." I wrap my arms around his neck, arch my back so my taut nipples rub against his chest.

Jack slides my knickers off, helping me balance as I step out of them. He shoves them in the purse I unwittingly dropped on the ground when he first found me and slicks a thick finger along my slit. "You're so wet, so hot."

"For you," I murmur. "I thought about you fucking me when I danced. I thought about the sexy bruises on my wrists, your cock driving into my pussy, your head between my legs."

"Christ. My girl talking dirty with her fancy accent. Drives me fucking wild." Jack lets out a low groan and pushes a finger inside me. "You'd better have been thinking about me on that dance floor. You're fucking mine."

"Yours." The word is sweet on my lips.

He twists a hand through my hair, tugs my hair back. "No one touches you. No one except me." His cock, rock hard beneath his jeans, presses into the side of my hip. His finger pumps in and out, and I draw in a deep breath, inhaling the fetid scent of the alley. Dirty and dangerous. The kind of place a girl who wears kitten heels, floaty florals, and pearls shouldn't go with the kind of man she shouldn't be with—a man who can make her deepest, darkest fantasies come true.

Unable to wait another minute, I undo Jack's belt and rip open his fly. He jerks back and slides his finger away as I shove his boxers down and free his cock from its restraint.

"Be gentle with me, Pen."

"Says the sadist." I wrap my hand around his erection, squeeze him tight, rub my thumb over the bead of moisture at the tip. His cock throbs in my hand, huge and heavy, a promise of what is to come.

His eyes darken with sensual pleasure. "Fuck, that feels good."

I hold his gaze as I stroke him. Seeing the desire in his eyes only makes the thought of sexing it up in the alley all the more appealing. "I like that you're hard for me."

"I'm always fucking hard for you." He rocks his hips, thrusting into my hand. "I wake up hard for you. I'm hard for you in the shower. And when I walked into the bar—" His breath hitches, and he lifts my leg, spreading me in front of him. Bracing myself against the wall, I hook my knee around his hip and rub the head of his cock through my soaking slit. He is hot, his soft skin a contrast to the hardness underneath.

His hands tighten on my hips, digging into my flesh so hard my eyes water. "You keep that up," he growls, "and this will be over before it begins."

"Please tell me you have protection." I tilt my hips and rock against the length of his cock.

Jack reaches into his back pocket and pulls out a condom. I stroke him hard, base to tip as he tears the package open, ripping a groan from his throat.

"Touch yourself while I put it on." His voice drops to a low, husky rasp. "Fingers on either side of your clit, but not on top."

After releasing him, I slide two fingers along either side of my swollen clit, spreading my wetness around, aching for the touch that will set me free. "You're mean."

"Like you can't believe." He rolls the condom on and lifts my other leg, securing me against the wall. I wrap my legs around his hips, but before I can put my arms around his shoulders, he grabs my wrists and slams my hands up over my head. The rough brick scrapes my skin, but I can endure the pain.

"Fuck me, Jack. Fuck me like you wanted to fuck me when I was dancing. Hurt me if you need to."

"Christ. Nothing as sexy as those words coming from your sweet lips." He pushes in with one long, deep thrust that takes my breath away. A feral light burns in his eyes, and my world narrows to the filthy, dirty alley, the dark, dangerous man who sets me on fire, and the burning, almost-desperate need to come.

With each wild pump of his hips, he slams me against the brick wall. I give myself over to the power of his thrusts, the delicious slide of his huge, hard cock inside me, the ferocity with which he seeks to claim me, the intensity of his gaze, and his strong arms holding me safe. This is Jack—the fighter, the man, the sadist—all in one.

"Scream for me, darlin'."

My climax comes in a rush of white-hot heat. I scream into his shoulder to muffle the sound. I scream from the pleasure and the pain. But mostly, I scream because he needs to hear me scream.

"Jesus Christ. Fuck. I'm gonna come." He yanks me down, pushing in deep, and he climaxes with a low guttural groan.

Finally, he stills, releases my hands. He wraps his arms around me, pulling me against him, and draws in a shuddering breath. "What the fuck do you do to me?" he murmurs. His cock pulses inside me, and I squeeze my inner muscles, delighted when he moans. I've never had sex outside before, never thought I would enjoy getting down and dirty in an alley, never been so aroused I already want more.

"Hopefully the same thing you do to me." I press a soft kiss to his cheek, and he pulls out, setting me on my feet as he rolls off the condom.

I bend to pick up my purse and dismiss the idea of putting on my knickers when I feel how damp they are.

Jack studies me as I rise, then spins me around. "I hurt you." He runs a hand over the exposed skin on my back at the top of my dress. "You're bleeding."

"Hopefully I'll have some bruises on my hips, too." I turn and smile. "Collateral damage from having sex with a sadist."

"You're fucking bleeding, Pen."

I put a hand to his chest, feel his heart pound against his ribs. "It's okay."

"It's not okay." He looks down, examines my wrists, which are also scraped and sore. "I lost control. That doesn't happen in the club. Every mark I leave on my play partners is deliberate. I make sure it's done in a safe and controlled way. But this—"

"I'm not your play partner, Jack. I'm not your submissive. I'm just me. And I'm fine with a few cuts and bruises."

A pained expression crosses his face, and we stare at each other for what seems to be an eternity. I can't even imagine what is going through his head, but the reminder that he sees other women at the club—plays with them—unsettles me. Although I'm pretty certain he hasn't been back since Gerry made his threat about the cameras, I don't really know. And I also don't know if I could deal with him playing with women at the club if he's sleeping with me. But what if I'm not enough for him? How can I ask him to give up what he needs when I know just how difficult it can be?

"Come." He clasps my hand. "I'll take you home and look after those cuts."

"You don't have to."

"Yes, I do. Not just because I'm the one who hurt you, but also so I won't forget why we can never do this again."

"Jack." I stumble after him as he stalks down the alley. "You're overreacting."

"Fuck, Pen." He stops suddenly and spins to face me. "Don't you fucking understand? I got off on hurting you like that, on taking my kink out of the club. There are no rules outside the club, no limits, nothing to stop me from going too far."

"This will stop you." I press my hand to his chest where his heart pounds frantically against his ribs. "I will stop you. My safe word, *Redemption*, will stop you."

"There's nothing there." He tears my hand away from his heart. "If that's what you're looking for, I've got nothing to give."

18

Do I taste like whiskey?

RAMPAGE

Sunday morning, I meet with my agent and my manager, James, at Redemption. We go over some new sponsorship opportunities, upcoming fights, and changes to the contract requested by MEFC. Far from being upset about the fight at Score last night, they want to feed the rumor mill about my hidden temper. Apparently, the one thing that might hold back my career is my reputation for being a nice guy, so a few broken noses in a bar fight is good for my image.

If they knew the real me, they wouldn't be concerned. Nice guys don't hurt the people they care about; they don't want to make their women scream.

After the meeting is over, I go over the training schedule for next week with Andy, Torment, and my fitness trainers. I asked Torment to stay on my team as a coach after I signed with

MEFC. He's still one of the best fighters I know, a great teacher, and one of the few people I really trust.

He also knows me well enough to see that I'm wound up tight and irritable as hell. After patching Penny up last night, I went home and tried to work out my frustration on my punching bag. But two hours and ten bloody knuckles didn't do a goddamned thing, and after a morning of meetings, I feel like I'm going to explode.

"You wanna take a break and go a few rounds in the cage?" Torment asks when we're done.

"Fuck yeah." Torment is the man. He just gets it. He knows I'm losing the fucking plot dealing with all that admin on my training day off, especially when my mind is somewhere else.

We meet in the practice cage after a quick change. Twenty-eight feet in diameter with a six-foot-tall chain-link fence and a thick padded floor, the practice cage is Torment's favorite place to work out his stress.

Not one to waste time, Torment plants a fist in my fucking face only seconds after I close the cage door, and the fight is on.

"Good night?" He throws a big high kick, and I step aside.

"Started off okay. Then it turned to shit."

He laughs. "You broke two noses in Score last night trying to find your girl."

"That was the good part." I bull forward and hit the fence with Torment in a clinch. I muscle him to the ground momentarily, but he bounces up after his knee hits, and we break.

"You might want to take it down a notch, or you'll scare her away." He throws a body kick and then a kick to the head that misses me only because I stumble back. "I almost lost Makayla that night Misery kidnapped her," he says. "Some women can't handle too much violence."

I snort a laugh. "Violence isn't a problem for Pen." I throw an easy sidekick, and he makes me pay over the top, landing two long rights to my shoulder when I leave myself open.

"Fuck, you're not pulling any punches."

"You left yourself exposed." He drops back, bounces around. "You do that, prepare for some pain. But vulnerability gives you strength. It builds confidence, lets you see your true self. Not only that, it builds trust. If your opponent thinks you're vulnerable, he'll come closer, open up. Then you can decide whether to push for the win or retreat."

Is this a fight lesson or a fucking life lesson? With Torment, you never know. I spring, landing back-to-back right kicks that force Torment back to the center of the cage. Before I can gloat, he rushes me, landing a right, then a left. The barrage is on. He throws a body kick followed by a spinning kick, and I counter with a solid one-two. We pummel each other for almost ten minutes, letting off steam, until Renegade stops the fight to remind us there are others waiting for the cage.

I limp out the door, holding my ribs, my only satisfaction the fact that Torment is suffering behind me.

I wipe myself down with a towel, gritting my teeth against the pain in my shoulder.

"You get hurt?" Torment grabs his water bottle, showing no sign of injury in the least.

"Fuck yeah. You're a bastard for not pulling your punches when I left myself open."

"You gonna die from it?"

"No."

"Good man." He slaps me on the shoulder right where it hurts and I hiss in a breath.

"By the way," he says, his lips tipping up at the corners, "that lesson was free."

───∿∿∿───

PENNY

After his meetings at Redemption, Jack picks me up and drives us down to the docks in Mission Bay. He refuses to tell me where we're going or why, and I feel a little trepidation when he parks his SUV outside a red brick warehouse within a stone's throw of the water. The pier is dark, quiet, and totally empty. Water laps softly against pilings, and the odd sea lion barks in the distance. I exit the vehicle and draw in a breath of crisp ocean air.

"What is this place?"

"You'll see." Jack pulls a set of keys from his pocket and leads me up to a huge double door, the window portion heavily barred as is the portico above. A discreet gold plaque affixed to the wall reads *Kilkeelan Distillery*.

"Is this yours?" I hesitate when he pushes open the door, afraid to walk into the dark.

A smile tugs at his lips. "Mine and Jimmy's." He reaches

around and flicks on the lights to reveal a huge room with exposed brick walls, iron beams, and painted pipes. A long, narrow glass-topped bar takes up one side of the room, and behind it are glass shelves filled with liquor bottles. Small tables surrounded by bar stools dot the Plexiglas floor through which I can see a vast room filled with oak barrels, stills, machinery, and tools.

"This is amazing."

"This is just the tasting room." He locks the door behind us. "We run tours on the weekends and hire the room out for parties. We're an independent craft distiller—spirits only. We produce nearly a dozen spirits, including a number of small-batch whiskeys that won medals in the San Francisco Spirits Competition. We're doing an absinthe this year and an autumn moonshine."

"You run this and train to fight?" I walk over to the far wall and check out all the framed awards: New York International Spirits Competition, Wizards of Whiskey, and dozens more.

Jack pulls a bottle off the shelf behind the counter. "I enjoy the business, it pays the bills, and it's what I was raised and trained to do." He pours two glasses of amber liquid, and I join him at the bar.

"What's below us?"

"Stills, fermentation tanks, barrel storage, and the bottling line. The big machines are the heating equipment."

He seems suddenly shy, and I give him an encouraging smile. "I would love to see it all. You're a very complicated man. Every time I think I have you figured out, you show me something new."

"I've never brought anyone here except for business." He pushes the glass toward me. "This was our first product to win an award. It's a single-grain, double-barrel whiskey. It's sweet and creamy on the palate with hints of butterscotch, honey, peppercorn, and Christmas pudding notes on the nose."

I take a sip, expecting the usual bitterness of whiskey, but the smooth finish pleasantly surprises me. "I have to admit I don't taste all those things, but it's very good, and I'm not even a whiskey drinker."

Jack beams and pulls out another bottle. "Try this one. It was aged in bourbon barrels and then Spanish sherry casks."

He tells me about the distillery and how it runs as I sample everything from gin to absinthe, with water and crackers to wash out my mouth between sips. When I've tasted everything he wants me to taste, he takes me downstairs to show me the rows and rows of oak barrels, gleaming copper machinery, and crates of bottles all waiting to be shipped. Scents of oak grain, sawdust, and liquor thicken the warm air. I ease myself up on a wooden table in the center of the packing room as I drink it all in. "I can't believe you've never brought anyone here."

Jack sits beside me, his long legs easily reaching the floor. "I've never met anyone I wanted to share it with. I wasn't kidding when I said I haven't had a serious relationship since Avery. I've had hook-ups, but mostly I've kept my encounters to the club." He fiddles with his ring, and his expression softens. "Wait here. I'm going to grab a blanket."

He returns a few minutes later and we spread the blanket

over the table and lie side by side staring up at the tasting room through the Plexiglas ceiling.

"I hope you don't do this when there are people upstairs," I tease. "They might get a fright looking down to see you staring up at them. The women might think you're trying to see up their skirts."

"If you'd walked in when I was down here, I would definitely have tried to look up your skirt." He pulls me closer, presses a kiss to my forehead.

"I might not have succumbed to your charms if I caught you looking up my skirt. You would have been added to my no-good men collection."

He stiffens beside me. "Anyone I need to beat up?"

"Well, Ray already took care of Vetch Retch, not that he will ever admit to it."

Jack brushes his thumb along my jaw, turning my head toward him, his expression serious. "Who else?"

"Do you really want to know? I thought guys didn't like to know that kind of stuff."

"We don't like to know about the guys you liked. Bastards like Vetch Retch are fair game." His eyes narrow, and he tenses as if preparing to battle imaginary foes.

"Well, there was Adam. I met him when I was fifteen and living at home..." As if he can sense my trepidation, Jack threads his fingers through mine, giving me the strength to go on.

"I thought he loved me." My voice wavers, but Jack has shared this special part of himself with me, and I want to share everything with him. But more than that, I want to know if he'll accept me when he finds out my cutting isn't the worst of my secrets. "He encouraged me to stand up to my dad when I turned sixteen, but it didn't turn out well. My father threw me out of the house. Adam let me move in with him, and I stayed with him for four years. I thought he was my savior, and when he started hitting me, I thought I deserved it. But part of me couldn't forgive him for hurting me, so I would cut myself, and he would pretend not to know."

"Jesus Christ." Jack pulls me on top of him so I am lying on his hot, hard body with his strong arms tight around me. "You had one hell of a rough time."

"It got worse. When I caught him in bed with another woman, he told me he never loved me. He said that I was too broken and fucked up to love. He took the ring I'd given him and threw it at me. Told me to get out. I wanted to die." Taking a deep breath, I hold up my hand. "I slit my wrist that night. My sister found me and bandaged it up. I left England shortly after that to start a new life away from Adam and my family."

Jack takes my wrist in his warm, broad hand. Slowly, gently, he brings it to his mouth. Softly, tenderly, he kisses the scar.

"Do you hate me?" I whisper. "Some people would think what I did was a sin."

"No, darlin'. I'll save my hating for the bastard who caused you so much pain." He hugs me so tight I can barely breathe, but it is the only place in the world I want to be.

"Thank you for sharing this special place with me." I push up and give him a kiss. Longing flickers across his face so fast I wonder if I saw it.

"I want to share something else with you." His hand slips under my shirt, and he flicks the catch on my bra. "Something I haven't shared before."

A tremor of desire runs through me and I smile. "What is it?"

He kisses me and eases me off his warmth and onto my back on the table. "Me."

"I thought I knew all your secrets," I tease. "There's more?"

"Do you trust me?" He rolls off the table and pulls me to sit.

"Yes." I say it without hesitation. "I trust you."

"Take off your clothes. Lie down on the blanket. Arms over your head. Legs spread."

I frown at his determined expression, but I do what he says. He disappears for a few moments and returns with a few lengths of soft cloth. Without speaking, he ties my wrists and ankles to the outer edges of the table.

"You would make a nice display for our clients." He points to the Plexiglas ceiling above me.

"Jack!" Uneasiness nips at my stomach. "What are you going to do?"

"I want to love you without the pain." He leans over and kisses me lightly. "Close your eyes."

My pulse kicks up a notch when he ties the blindfold around my eyes, but before I can panic, Jack presses his lips to my ear. "I want you to feel what I see. I want you to know that you are worth so much more than you got from the people in your life. You are strong. You are brave. You are worth loving. You are the kind of woman that deserves to have a man on his knees." His hands press against my inner thighs, and I feel his breath teasing my pussy, his tongue flicking lightly over my clit.

My hands clench around the ties as he runs his hands over me.

"Hang on." He slides his tongue up one side of my clit and down the other, until my tissues feel swollen and tight.

"Jack." I groan at the erotic sensation.

"Shh." His fingers curl around my hips, his thumbs opening my labia, exposing my clit to the firm stroke of his tongue. Pressure builds inside me, and my thighs tremble.

"So sweet," he says. "But I'm getting carried away."

He touches me all over, a gentle caress on my neck, a squeeze on my breasts, and a stroke over my stomach. I moan, and he draws my nipple into my mouth, biting and sucking until I arch up on the table.

"Did you like my whiskey?" He sucks the other nipple until it peaks.

"Yes. It was delicious."

"Like you." He blows a soft breath over my clit and gives it a little lick that shoots me right to the edge in a heartbeat.

"Do I taste like whiskey?"

He chuckles and then I feel a splash of cold liquid on my breast, followed by the warm slide of his tongue. "You do now."

His lips press against mine. Cool, sweet liquid follows into my mouth. I choke at first, and swallow. He kisses me again, dripping whiskey into my mouth, and licks it from my lips.

"I could get drunk on you." Whiskey splashes into the hollow at the base of my throat, trickles down my neck. He follows it with his mouth, sucking and lapping, leaving no inch of my skin untouched.

My hips come up off the table, and I whimper. I am wet, throbbing, my core pulsing with a delicious ache.

With a rough press of his hand over my hips, he pushes me back down. "Do I have to tie your hips down, too?"

"No. I just… I can't take it anymore. I need to come."

Droplets fall on my taut nipples, slide down my breasts in an erotic caress. "I've only just started. I'm a big man." He chuckles softly. "It takes a lot to get me drunk." He licks the liquid away, warming my skin with his tongue.

"How about you make me come and then you get drunk?"

He alternates drops of cool whiskey and warm kisses down my chest and my stomach. I hold my breath when his chin grazes my mound. And then he's gone.

I whimper, and he kisses the inside of my thigh.

"I'm getting closer," he murmurs.

"Closer to being drunk?" I would part my legs wider, tilt my hips higher, open myself more, but I am tied to the table in the position he wants me to be in, and the knowledge I can't move only adds to my arousal.

"Closer to giving you what you want." He pulls me open and pours a stream of cool whiskey over my clit.

My brain fuzzes with the sensation, trying to find a climax in the wave. "More."

"How about this?" He laps up the whiskey, flicking his tongue over my clit, through my labia, and along the insides of my thighs. It feels so good, and yet it makes me shake with need. My breasts are swollen and aching, my pussy throbbing. I am outside my body, and I need him in. It is pure erotic torture, and I want it to go on, and I want it to end.

"Do you need me?" he whispers.

"Yes."

"Do you want me?"

"God, Jack. Yes. Yes, I want you. Now. Don't make me wait anymore."

"You're ready." He pushes his fingers in as deep as they can go and uses his other hand to spread me wide. "Now, hold on." He puts his tongue to my clit, and I am lost in a blaze of white-hot heat. He strokes and sucks, pushing his fingers in and drawing them out. He presses his teeth to my sensitive nub and adds a third finger, filling me, until I can't tell pleasure from pain. I writhe on the table, so close to orgasm and yet not close enough.

"Please."

"I like it when you beg." He rips off my blindfold. "Watch yourself come. See how everyone sees you. See how beautiful you are." I blink to clear my vision. He has changed the lights and the Plexiglas is a mirror, showing me flushed and sweaty, my lips swollen and my lids heavy with lust.

"Beautiful." He sucks my clit between his teeth, and the ache in my pussy swells and bursts, consuming me in a tidal wave of stars. My back arches, my head thuds against the table. Jack presses one hand over my hips, holding me down as he continues to pound his fingers inside me. My orgasm rolls and rolls, never stopping, never slowing, and I cry out his name as all my tension and emotion leave me in a rush.

"Jack!"

———~~~———

RAMPAGE

My name on her lips does me in.

I shove down my clothes and sheath myself, my cock so hard and tight even the slide of latex is a painful pleasure. Penny is languid on the table, beautiful in her release. I undo her restraints, drop my knee to the blanket-clad table, and move over her. "Are you ready for me, beautiful girl?"

"Yes." She wraps her arms around my neck, presses her lips to mine. Her kiss is sweet, her lips warm and soft, trusting and giving. Our eyes meet, linger, and I lose myself in the deep blue sea. I rock against her, teasing her clit hard again. When I feel her tremble, I slide in, gritting my teeth to hold myself back. She is so hot, so tight, so wet, and her body molds to mine. She is perfect for me. Perfectly made. A perfect fit. A perfect match.

Her pussy quivers, and I thrust in and out, inch by inch, each time a little deeper but not deep enough, each time a little harder but not hard enough.

"Jack," she whispers. "Please, Jack. Please."

Her skin flushes, and her breaths come in short pants. I pick up the pace, hammering into her as I sweep my thumb over her clit. Her pussy tightens around me like a velvet glove, and she climaxes, her little nails digging into my shoulders, her heels digging into my ass, her voice raw and rough, groaning in my ear. I thrust one more time. Pleasure shoots down my spine and erupts through my cock in long, hot jerks.

I collapse over Penny, drop my head to her chest. For the first time, I don't feel the familiar bite of self-loathing. I have never felt such pleasure without pain. Although that need is still part of me, for Penny, I can push it away.

"Thank you." She strokes her hand down my back, her breath warm against my cheek.

"For what?"

"For showing me this side of you. I didn't think you could have sex without some element of pain."

"Neither did I," I say honestly. "I would be a happy man if I could make love to you like this every day." I roll to my back and gather her in my arms, cradling her soft body against me.

Penny pulls back and studies me, worry creasing her brow. "Happy, but not fulfilled."

"Happy is enough for me," I assure her. "Pain is a craving. Not a need. And from what you just told me, I think you've had enough pain in your life."

Far from being reassured, Penny's frown deepens, and she pushes herself to sit. "If you don't feed the craving, it becomes a need. I know that better than anyone."

I'm not sure where she's going with this. I am willing to change for her, to do what I promised Avery I would do, to suppress the part of me that destroyed my life for a chance at normal with her. "What are you saying?"

She twists her hair around her finger, and her face softens. "I'm saying I enjoyed making love, but I also enjoyed what we did in the alley and what we did at the club and when you used your belt. You don't have to give that up for me."

Emotion wells up in my throat, bittersweet. Penny could never give me what I get at Club Sin. She needs pain for emotional release, but she doesn't enjoy it the way the masochists at the club do; she couldn't tolerate the level of pain that gives me a total emotional release. And I couldn't hurt her that way.

"Means a lot to me, your saying that." I stroke a finger along the curve of her jaw. "But I don't think you really understand what goes on during a hard session at the club—the level of pain involved—and I don't want you to. I want you, just the way you are, doing things the way we do them. That means exclusive, darlin'. I'm not the kind of man who shares."

I'm also not the kind of man who can find true release without pain.

But for Penny, I'm willing to try.

19

You were very angry

Monday morning, after staying up half the night fretting over Jack's decision to give up the club for me, I make the mistake of trying to sneak past Ray.

"Stop right there," he barks from behind his newspaper. "I see you, Pen. We got things to discuss."

"Amanda's in court this morning." I keep walking, looking straight ahead. "I have to get her stuff ready."

"She just called to say the hearing has been postponed, so we got lots of time to talk." He folds his newspaper and swings his legs off the couch. "Friday. Things were happening in this office that made me concerned."

"Well, since they aren't your concern, you don't need to be concerned. Is the coffee ready?"

"Don't try to change the subject," he growls. "All I care about is making sure you're being treated right, and the way you looked when Jack walked out of your office on Friday made me think that's not the case."

I head over to the coffeepot and pour a cup, trying to figure out how to get Ray to back down. Even if I tell him to stuff it, he's not going to let this one go. "You know Jack. He's a good guy."

"You never really know anybody, Pen." He picks up his cup and sighs. "I love Sia, but I won't even pretend to know what goes on in that head of hers sometimes. Why does leaving the toilet seat up mean I don't care? Is it such a hardship to put it down? And she does act like her mother sometimes. Doesn't mean I don't love her. I'm just pointing out a similarity of behavior."

Now he's making me worried all over again. How well do I know Jack? I never considered that his needs would go beyond our previous rough encounters. But it makes sense. A little spanking and a couple of wallops with a belt don't even come close to what he did with that woman on the St. Andrew's Cross the first time I saw him at Club Sin. I can get the same release with him as I do with my blade, but I can't do the same for him.

Or can I?

"Ray?"

He stops mid-rant and lifts an eyebrow. "Yeah?"

"I'm seeing him."

Ray rolls his eyes. "Yeah. I got that when you told me you fucked on your desk."

"You were supposed to think I was lying."

"Pen, you can't lie for shit. You're like Pinocchio except

your eyes get big instead of your nose. You got a good heart and a good soul and not an ounce of deceit in your body."

If only he knew. And now I feel guilty for deceiving him about being deceitful. The whole thing makes my head spin. "Don't get your knickers in a twist. Maybe it won't last. He has issues. I have issues…"

Ray snorts a laugh. "That's called a relationship."

"I don't know if this is a relationship, to be honest." I sit beside Ray on the big blue couch. With the rest of the office decorated in cream and sage, the couch doesn't fit in with Amanda's decor. But it's like that with everything at her firm. Her new, relaxed look is tainted with dark blue, monograms, and big-city style. Even her logo is pure corporate conservative, like she just can't totally let go of her past. Someday I'm going to show her the designs I drew for her office, a fresh new look that would attract the kind of clients she really wants.

"Does a relationship mean you get crazy jealous when you think of him with someone else?" I ask Ray, the most possessive and protective man I know. "Or that you'll do the thing that frightens you the most so you can be the one who gives him what he needs?" I have no idea why I'm asking Ray for advice, but Cora is wrapped up in Blade Saw and Amanda is a good friend of Jack's.

Ray folds his hands behind his head and leans back on the couch. "Pretty much."

"That's it? Pretty much?"

Ray frowns. "You asked a question. I gave you an answer. What else do you want?"

"I don't know…" I open my hands and shrug. "Maybe a bit more detail, real-life examples, some discussion…"

"That's what girls do," Ray says. "You want to talk it to death and overthink things, you talk to a girl. You want an answer, you come to me."

"So, you don't think I'm stupid for planning to do something that scares me, basically to keep him away from other women?"

"I almost killed a man for touching Sia, so I'm the wrong person to ask." He yawns and stretches like he just told me what he ate for dinner last night and not that he almost committed a homicide.

"Okay then. That's good." I pick up my cup and take a sip of rapidly cooling coffee. "So, next time he needs something, I'll make sure he comes to me. It makes sense because we're…you know…a couple… I think." And because I need to keep him away from the club, although now I don't know if I'm doing it for me or for him.

Ray snorts a laugh. "Oh, you're a couple, all right. Word has gone around Redemption that you're off-limits. Anyone touches you and…" He slams his fist into his palm. "Boom. They're dead."

"You're beginning to scare me, Ray."

"Just beginning?"

My phone buzzes and I paw through the junk in my purse, trying to find it. "Okay. You always scared me. But you got a bit more scary after you and Sia got together."

"Love makes you crazy. That's all I can say."

I find the phone and frown when the screen shows an unknown caller. But the voice, when I answer, is well known to me.

"Babe? It's Adam."

—∿∿—

RAMPAGE

Monday afternoon, after wasting a morning in meetings, I try to lose myself in training as I prepare for a charity fundraiser match tomorrow. There are lots of fighters in the lower levels of the professional circuit, and it takes a combination of skill and profile to rise to the top.

I start with skipping rope, followed by shadowboxing drills, speed work, sparring, Muay Thai clinching, and circuit training. I spend an hour on weights and take a break for lunch, pounding back as much protein as my body can handle. Then I'm back in the gym with Andy for new techniques, drills, and sparring. By six o'clock I have pushed myself until my muscles are burning, but the knot of tension I have been fighting for the last three weeks is still there.

Before I met Penny, I would have been tempted to call Sylvia or a willing masochist to help me work off the tension with a good, hard session at the club. But I made a promise to Pen, and when I think about going to the club, it is Penny I imagine in my playroom. Penny I want on my cross. Penny I want in my arms after the scene is done. Penny who so sweetly offered herself to me even though she has no idea what a bastard I can be.

After a quick shower between training sessions, I change into my gi and slam my locker closed just as my phone starts to ring. My hand wavers. Renegade is teaching an advanced class tonight, and I need to work on my ground game. Still, since most of my friends are at the gym or know I'm here, there aren't many people who would call at this time. Curious, I pull open the locker and catch Damien's name on the screen on the last ring.

"Damien. What's up?"

"Gerry, that fucking bastard, has got a bunch of contractors here. They say they've got a work order to come inside, but they won't let me see it. Under the lease, Gerry's allowed in for emergency repairs, but I haven't reported any problems. I called my attorney, but he's out of town. His law firm is trying to find someone else to take a look at the file, but I'm not convinced they'll be able to stop these guys. You got some time to come down and play muscle for me?"

"I'm on my way."

Fuck. What kind of game is Amanda playing? This kind of crap is crossing the line. Is Penny part of this? Is that why she didn't want me to go to the club? Because she knew about this plan?

Fuming, I throw on one of my MEFC T-shirts and a pair of jeans and drive down to Club Sin. Damien is standing at the front door, munching on an apple fritter. A couple of guys in safety vests and hard hats lean against their work vans drinking designer coffee across the street. It's a standoff, San Francisco style.

"Thanks for coming." Damien claps me on the back. "The

junior lawyer called a few minutes ago. This is fucking bullshit. Gerry can't get me out legally, so now he's playing games."

"What's the work order for?"

"Not sure."

I glance across the road. One of the construction guys is wearing a T-shirt with the name of a rival MMA promotion splashed across the front. Now that I have a bit of star power, maybe I should use it.

"I've got an idea." I make my way across the street and nod at the guy in the MMA shirt. He's a short dude, crew cut, not much in the way of muscle. "What's going on?"

He gives me a wary look. "Just waiting for our boss. We got a work order to go into that building, but the owner won't let us in." He looks at my T-shirt and nods. "You into MMA?"

"I fight for MEFC."

"No way." His face changes from indifferent to interested, and he studies my face. "Fuck. You're Rampage! Holy shit." He calls his buddies over, and ten minutes later I'm signing stuff for them—lunch bags, hats, T-shirts, and one guy's boot. I pose for a few pictures while we talk about my last fight. In between, I find out that Gerry plans to demolish the building in a few weeks, and their work order is to measure things up, knock a few holes in the walls, and report on the stability for the demolition experts.

"I called for muscle. Not the fucking Friendly Giant," Damien mutters when I rejoin him at the door. He holds up his phone. "I'm on the phone with the junior lawyer. She's looking at the lease right now to see if Gerry has a right of entry."

"Tell her the work order is for a site survey for an upcoming demolition in a few weeks."

Damien's face turns three shades of red. "Fucking hell. It will take me months to find a new place and get it outfitted for all the equipment. That's why I negotiated such a long notice provision in the lease. He'll put me out of business." He repeats my information to the lawyer. After a few minutes he nods and ends the call.

"He has no right to come in on that basis. Thank fuck you found out what the work order was for. The lawyer says it was an underhanded way of trying to get around the lease provisions. Gerry's lawyer should be disbarred for pulling this crap."

"Yeah. It's not right." I twist my lips to the side. I've known Amanda a long time, and I can't believe she would condone something like this. She's always been strictly above board. One of the most ethical lawyers I know.

I hear the screech of tires, and Penny's little Mustang zips around the corner at full tilt. She pulls up to the curb in a loading zone and runs down the street toward me, her heels clacking on the pavement, her floaty skirt flying indecently high in the breeze, her breasts bouncing beneath her light blouse. "Jack!"

One of the workers across the street wolf-whistles. Another makes a lewd comment. My head snaps to the side, and I am a hairbreadth from pounding on my new friends when she throws herself into my arms. "Don't go in."

"What are you doing here?" I hold her by the shoulders, still uncertain about her role in this mess.

She brushes her hair back from her face, takes a deep breath. "I needed to talk to you, so I went down to the gym. Andy said you told him you had an emergency in the SoMa District. I texted, but you didn't answer, and I was worried you might be coming to the club, so I thought I'd just check."

I feel a tightness in my chest, and I study her flushed face. "Is that really why you're here, or did you know about this?" I gesture to the workers across the street. "Did you come to make sure Amanda's plan went smoothly?"

"What?" She stares at me, her brow creasing in a frown. "I don't know what's going on. I came because of you."

"You don't know about Gerry trying to get into the building on false pretenses?"

There is no feigning the shock in her face, but even if she isn't here because of Gerry, I can't believe she would leave work just because she was afraid I would come to the club without her. Avery couldn't look at me after I told her about my kink. How could I have found a woman who not only accepts me for who I am but wants to share my darkness, too?

She makes a quick call, and returns a few minutes later. "Amanda is calling Gerry now to tell him to send the contractors away." She sucks in her lips, hesitates. "She's pretty annoyed."

"You said you were looking for me at Redemption."

"Oh." Her shoulders sag. "Adam, my ex, called me this morning. He got his shit together and now he's studying for a psychology degree. He's in LA on some internship program and he called my parents and tracked me down. He thought…" Her voice hitches. "…that I'd make a good field study."

My upper lip curls in disgust. "A field study?"

"Yeah." She gives a resigned sigh. "I guess I fit a type: abusive

childhood leading to self-harm, recreating the abusive relationships as I try, and fail, to find the love I didn't get at home—he
didn't even see the irony in that one—self-harm as emotional
release, blah, blah, blah… I can't remember everything he said,
but basically, he wants to study me because I'm broken. I told
him to take a hike."

"Jesus Christ. You're not broken, Pen. You are perfect, just
the way you are." I wrap my arms around her and hold her tight.
I don't care that Damien is watching from the doorway or that
the workers are taking pictures with their phones. She's hurting,
and she needs me, and there is nothing I want more than to take
away her pain. "You got an address for that bastard?"

"Yeah." She looks up, a smile ghosting her lips. "But I'm not
giving it to you because I have a feeling I won't like what you're
planning to do."

No matter. Ray is the best PI in the city. Once I tell him the
bastard who hurt Penny is in the country, he'll track him down.
Then we can pay a visit to him together.

"Jack?" She pulls me back to the moment, and I study her
sweet face. If I were a better man, I would let her go, find
someone who won't hurt her in any way, and continue as I was
before she walked into my club and showed me her pain.

But I am not that man.

I am a selfish man. I have found a woman who lights my life,
and I cannot let her go.

"What happened to my muscle?" Damien shouts.

"Is that why you're here?" Hope flares in her eyes. "Because
of the contractors? Not because you were going inside?"

"Damien called and asked for my help. And no, I didn't go in. Not after I made you a promise last night."

"But you want to," she says quietly, catching my gaze as it flicks to the door. "You need to hurt someone. Hurt me, Jack. Let me try to give you what you need."

I cup her face between my hands, studying her intently, trying to figure out what's going on behind her overly bright eyes. "I told you last night, you're enough for me the way you are. This is not something you have to do."

She closes her eyes, takes a breath. When she looks up again, the fervor has gone from her face. "I want to do it. And before you say anything, I'll tell you I'm not being totally altruistic. When you hurt me, I don't need to hurt myself. Maybe it's unconventional and not something a therapist would approve, but it works for me. I want to be with you the way you need me. You can embrace your darkness, and I can embrace mine."

I can refuse her nothing.

"If you're free tonight, we could go in now."

"No." She gives an almost violent shake of her head. "Not here. It's…um…unnerving. Especially since there are women there who you…you know."

"You're jealous?"

"Yes! I'm jealous." She sounds almost relieved to reveal this fact to me, so much that her admission doesn't ring true. But she is offering so much, I can't ask for more.

"Wednesday. After the charity fight." I kiss her softly. "I'll set something up outside the club. And I will give you pain."

20 I suffer. You suffer.

WEDNESDAY NIGHT, TEAM REDEMPTION IS OUT IN FORCE FOR Jack's charity match at the Kezar Pavilion. As with most of the fights I've attended, the crowd is crazy loud. Every punch, every kick, and every submission throws them into a frenzy. Although the match isn't being broadcast, the organizers have set up giant screens, and with Torment on my left, Blade Saw on my right, and a grinning Cora beside him, there is no chance I'll miss a single detail.

"Christ," Torment mutters. "What the hell kind of fighters is Duke's Promotions pulling in these days? Did you see all that flailing around? If Rampage fights like that when it's his turn in the cage, I'm gonna go in there and shake things up."

Blade Saw barks a laugh and points at the cage. "Fuck. Lookit that dude. I think he's going for a gogoplata, but all he's doing is spinning his opponent."

"Aren't they just starting out in the pros?" Cora asks. "Maybe they're just nervous."

Blade Saw whispers in her ear, and she blushes. I'm happy things worked out after the bar brawl, although I would have been happier if Cora hadn't texted me details of just how good Blade Saw is in bed while I had to endure two days of abstinence. Jack needed to focus while he prepared for his fight, and that meant I had to sleep alone.

"Who has a fight card?"

Doctor Death leans across Torment and taps my arm. "He's up next."

Bam. Torment knocks Doctor Death's hand away. "There was a reason I switched seats with you," Torment says. "And that reason is to make sure you stay out of touching distance of Rampage's girl."

"He didn't do the walk-around." Doctor Death lifts an eyebrow. "Until he does the walk-around, introducing her as his girl at Redemption, she's free game."

"Game?" I narrow my eyes. "I'm not a wild animal."

"Oh, you're wild. I've seen the wildness in you. It's why I can't stay away." Doctor Death leans behind Torment and pets my hair.

"Break his arm," Torment mutters to Blade Saw. "Or I'm going to rip it off."

Doctor Death's arm is saved by the timely arrival of Jack, a.k.a. Rampage, and his opponent, Razzor. I remember the tall, blond Swede from Redemption. He and Shilla used to train together but he moved to another gym last year. Physically, he doesn't appear to be any match for Jack, who is broader and more muscular despite being about two inches shorter.

They enter the cage, and I jump on my seat and scream.

Doctor Death looks up and grins. "Wild. Just like I said."

The referee blows his whistle, and Razzor shoots in and scores a quick takedown. He positions himself on top of Jack and plants big shots and elbows. Jack throws his own vertical elbows to the top of Razzor's head.

"He's keeping his guard closed." Blade Saw gives me a nudge. "That's good. He's still in control."

Razzor moves to pass, and Jack gets in a butterfly half guard and uses it to elevate Razzor and get up, despite being four minutes on the mat. Once up, he blasts Razzor with straight punches against the cage. He is mesmerizingly powerful, fiercely beautiful. My knees go weak at the thought of those muscles bunching beneath my hands, those hips driving into me, his cock thrusting inside me…

"He was playing with him," Torment says. "Pretending he was stuck on the mat."

Razzor shoots again, but his aim is off, and he eats more shots from a powerful, ruthless Jack. Muscles straining, abs rippling, Jack pummels Razzor, landing one last straight left hand to the chin before Razzor drops. He follows Razzor down, and the fight is stopped with three seconds left in the round.

"Jump and scream, Pen." Torment helps me up on my chair. "That's why you're here. Nothing a fighter likes more than to see his girl cheering for him."

I jump.

I scream.

Jack looks over and smiles.

Half an hour later, Jack walks out of the changing room and into my arms in the hallway outside the pavilion.

"You were awesome, except for the four minutes where you toyed with him." I kiss him lightly. "Didn't anyone ever tell you not to play with your food?"

"I'm glad no one did." He pulls me into his chest and deepens the kiss. "I'm in the mood to play right now. Nothing winds me up more than a good fight, especially after I had to go two days without you while I was prepping for the fight."

"Here?" I glance around. "Now?"

He nuzzles my neck and nips so hard I gasp. "Do you want to play, darlin'?"

"Yes." A flush of heat sweeps over my skin. "I want to play. But I want to play hard. I don't want you to hold back. I want to be what you need me to be."

"Come." He leads me down the hallway to a supply closet. I pull the string on the light above us as he closes the door.

"I promised you pain," he continues. "And I'm gonna give it to you."

For a moment I wonder if I really know what I've gotten myself into, but before I can protest, Jack's lips are on mine, and his hands are pushing down my jeans.

"Take off your panties." His eyes take on the gleam I know so well, and I shimmy my jeans and knickers down and step out of them.

"Spread your legs."

Heart thudding, I part my legs. Jack reaches into his duffel bag and pulls out a soft black velvet bag.

"Have you ever used Ben Wa balls, Pen?" He shows me two bright pink balls attached by a string and covered in what appear to be little rounded plastic spikes.

I hesitate, look up, and meet his gaze. "No. But the ones I've read about or seen are smooth. The spikes look…like they might hurt."

"They will, but in a good way."

My pussy clenches, and I swallow hard. "Hurt, not harm?"

"I will never harm you, and I'll never push you farther than I think you can go. The spikes will make you more sensitive after we remove them."

"Okay." I lick my lips in anticipation.

"Lift for me. One leg over my shoulder." He drops to his knees in front of me, and I lean against a shelf, one leg over his shoulder, leaving me exposed and open to him.

"Very nice." He slicks a thick finger along my slit. "You're already soaked. I think you're going to enjoy your present." He leans in to me and flicks his tongue over my clit. I moan and tilt my hips, encouraging, but Jack holds me in position and pushes two fingers inside me.

"Stay still. I need to get you ready."

His words seem to have a direct effect on my pussy, and I clench around his finger. "I think you could make me ready just by the things you say."

"You like to hear about how I'm going to hurt you?" He drives his fingers deep inside me, taking what he wants but not giving me what I need. "Do you like to hear how it will hurt but it will be good for you because the pleasure I give you after will make up for the pain?"

"Yes." I grip his head, my fingers threading through the softness of his hair. "And if you're going to talk dirty in that sexy accent, then you'd better make me come."

His lips quirk in a smile, his steely gaze softening. "This isn't about what you want." He reaches for the velvet bag. "It's about what I want. And right now, what I want is to hear you tell me you are ready to take the pain I'm going to give you."

"I'm ready."

Jack gently presses one of the balls against my opening, rolling it over my labia. I am relieved that the spiky nodules aren't sharp, although they are fairly rigid. Still, when he pushes the first ball inside me, I can feel every bump and ridge on my inner walls, and the friction the spikes create makes me tense up inside.

"I can't, Jack. Two would be too much."

"You can take it." He frowns, that single shift in expression telling me he's not backing down. "They're going in, so you need to relax." He leans forward and flicks his tongue over my clit, sending a rush of wetness through my pussy. I tilt my hips forward for more, and he pushes the second ball inside.

"Oh God." I feel full, overly stretched. The balls must have little weights on them because when Jack lowers my leg to the ground, they shift inside me, kicking my arousal up another notch.

"How do they feel?" He helps me into my knickers and jeans, and I slide them over my hips.

"Uncomfortable." I take a few steps, try to adjust to the small weights shifting inside me. "They feel too big, and the spiky things give me a sensation that is halfway between pleasure and pain, and the way they move is driving me crazy, like when you lick my clit and then stop." I lift an admonishing eyebrow, and Jack laughs.

"There's a string for removing them, but you can only use it if you've given me your safe word first. Which is…?"

"*Redemption.*"

"I want you to wear a skirt tonight," he says. "We'll stop at your place on the way to the gym so you can change."

"Maybe we can do something at my place while I'm changing since I won't have any clothes on?" I give a suggestive wiggle of my hips, and Jack laughs.

"We're going to the post-fight party. I have a surprise waiting for you there." He cups my face between his hands and kisses me, hard and hungry. I can taste his need, as fierce and deep as mine.

"Haven't you forgotten something?" I point to the bulge in his jeans, his shaft very visibly erect.

Jack lifts his duffel bag, letting it fall discreetly over his front. "We're both going to suffer tonight."

⌇⌇⌇

Team Redemption roars when Jack and I walk into the gym after a quick stop at my place for a change of clothes. Torment has opened Redemption up after hours for a celebration party. Jack is immediately surrounded, thudded on the back, his hand pumped, high-fived, and fist-bumped. Relieved to be out of the limelight, I take a step back and try not to think about the balls shifting inside me, or how badly I need to come.

We head over to the lounge where Obsidian is pouring drinks at a small makeshift wet bar in the corner. It's a small group—just the team and a few close friends and partners. I wave to Makayla and Amanda talking with Shilla on one of the big brown leather couches, and follow Jack to the bar where Blade Saw, Cora, and Homicide Hank have lined up some shots.

"Where's your wife?" I ask. Homicide Hank has so many kids we've lost count, and his wife doesn't come out to the parties as often as she used to.

"Pregnant." He throws back a shot.

"What is that? Five? Six?" Blade Saw toys with the ribbons on Cora's halter top, and I pull off my sweater just in case she needs a quick cover-up.

"You're showing a lot of skin," Jack murmurs in my ear. "Don't like how the guys are checking you out." He wasn't happy with my change of clothes, and especially not the draped gray satin tank that plunges low or the short white skirt that is just long enough to be decent.

"You suffer. I suffer."

"Sweater on," he snaps.

"Toys out," I answer.

He presses his lips together and glares. "It's gonna be a long fucking night."

Obsidian hands me a vodka shooter, and I take a sip, savoring the sweet liquid as it slides over my tongue. Maybe the naughty toy experience will be easier to manage if I've had a few drinks.

I finish my shot in one gulp and wave to the bartender for another. Jack looks over and frowns.

Torment gives a toast to Jack's awesomeness in the ring. We drink. He toasts Redemption. We drink. He toasts Redemption's amazing coaches that have produced some professional fighters. We drink. He waxes eloquent about Redemption's history and the days when it was only he, Renegade, and Rampage fighting each other on some old, worn mats in a big empty warehouse. We drink. He mumbles something about the women behind the men. I take a sip for every Redemption woman I know. I wave to the bartender for another. Jack snatches it away.

"Enough."

I stand on my toes and kiss him. "It's helping me deal with the fact that my knickers are so wet they are now redundant," I whisper in his ear.

Jack's eyes darken almost to black. "Then we'll take them off." The deep rumble of his voice stirs naughty thoughts that tempt me to disobey him just to see what he'll do.

"You wouldn't dare."

He gives me a scorching, sensual look that tells me he would dare indeed and I might be asking for more trouble than I can handle.

After an hour of drinking and chatting, the party moves into the gym, where Homicide Hank challenges Shilla to a fight in the cage. Although Shilla is no match for the heavier fighters, she can hold her own against a featherweight like Homicide Hank. The consummate sadist, Jack takes me the long way, step by agonizing step through every hallway in the building, followed by a slow walk through the crowd until I am unable to think of anything but my desperate, almost-painful need to come.

Shilla wins the fight in ten seconds flat. While Jack is congratulating her on a job well done, I slip out of the gym, intending to find some secret relief in the ladies' restroom.

"Wait up. I'm heading your way." Doctor Death catches up with me in the hallway. "I guess congratulations are in order."

"What's that supposed to mean?"

"You just got the walk-around."

We stop near the restrooms, and he runs a hand through his golden hair. "It's a tradition at Redemption. When a fighter finds his girl, he parades her around Redemption to warn everyone else away."

And I thought Jack was just being his sadistic self. "That sounds very…primitive."

Doctor Death laughs. "It is. But Redemption fighters are very territorial. Once you've been claimed—"

"Claimed?"

"There's no going back." He sighs and brushes a kiss over my cheek. "Another good one gone. One day it's going to be me in there, staking my claim with a bevy of buxom beauties."

"Death!" Jack's angry voice echoes down the corridor. "Get your fucking paws off her. Were you fucking unclear about the message I sent tonight?"

"Claimed," Doctor Death whispers before he hurries away.

Jack backs me up against the wall, one hand beside my head, his face creased in a scowl. "You going somewhere without me?"

"Freshening up?" I press my lips together and try for a wide-eyed innocent "I wasn't about to get myself off in the restroom" look, but there's no fooling Jack.

"Naughty girl." His voice drops, husky and low. "I know what you were going to do. And I'm going to punish you for it."

"How about we go back to the party?" I slide under his arm and take a few quick steps down the hallway, but Jack is fast. He catches me around the waist and pulls me back against his chest.

"Party's over," he whispers in my ear. "Now you get your pain."

My breath leaves me in a rush. "I thought that's what the toys were all about."

His dark, sensual laugh sends a delicious chill down my spine. "That wasn't even a warm-up."

He leads me out of the gym and into the new wing of Redemption. We pass Torment's new office and Sia's tattoo shop, and then he yanks me around a corner and into the spa that is still under construction.

"It's dark." I look around as Jack closes and locks the door, my heart thudding in my chest. "And it smells like sawdust. I think we should go back to the party. I've gotten kinda fond of these naughty toys. I think I'll just keep them."

Jack leans against the door, licking his lips like a predator about to feast. "We're not going anywhere. They've finished off the rooms in the back, and there's a massage table in one of them and enough space to have some fun without anyone hearing us. I've got it all ready for us."

"Fun? I think we might have different ideas about what constitutes fun. What if someone comes in and sees me in my knickers?"

"We'll have to make sure you're not screaming when they do."

A thrill of fear shoots through me. I back away and bump into the curved reception counter. "I'm not really in a screaming mood. I'm more in a 'get these damn toys out of me and fuck me hard' mood. How about we put that massage table to a good, happy, and nonscreaming use?"

A wicked smile spreads across his face. "How about you come over here and I'll show you the real meaning of the word *sadist*?" He moves toward me, and I turn and run.

Jack gives a shout and comes after me, moving at what seems to be incredible speed for a man his size. Laughing, I race down the corridor, checking for an exit. Bathroom. Office. Treatment room. Treatment room. Treatment room. Closet. One door left. I run in and slam it behind me.

Chest heaving, I stare at the bed in front of me. Of all the rooms I could have picked, it was the one he wanted.

His footsteps echo in the hallway, slow and sure. Doors open and close. My little room has no windows, no closets, nowhere to hide except behind the massage table. I shiver, knowing he's coming for me, and my insides twist with a mixture of excitement and arousal.

I slide down behind the bed, press myself against the cold metal base. Everything smells fresh and new, from the sharp smell of paint to the almost-overpowering scent of vinyl.

The door squeaks open, and a thin beam of light floods the small room. My heart pounds so hard I'm sure he can hear it, but I hold my breath and squeeze my eyes shut, trying not to laugh.

"Pen?"

After what seems like an eternity, the door closes. I count off three seconds and peek around the corner.

"Ah. That was a mistake." He grabs my wrist and pulls me up and into his arms.

I struggle, trying to push his hands away, but he walks forward, forcing me back until I hit the wall with a soft thud.

"Open for me, Pen." He doesn't wait for my compliance. Instead, he shoves a thick thigh between my legs and rocks me over the top.

"Torment is outside in the hallway," he murmurs. "He's talking to Renegade about what they're going to do with the spa. Don't make a sound."

Holding my arms over my head, with one hand clasped firmly around my wrists, he kisses me hard, taking my mouth slowly, surely, so thoroughly he leaves no inch untouched. His fingers dive into my shirt, play with my nipples beneath my bra until my arousal threatens to overwhelm me.

"You are not going to make me come with Torment right outside the door," I warn.

"Try me." He rocks me again, harder, grinding my clit against the rough fabric of his jeans. The balls roll inside me, and the ache of unfulfilled desire becomes a throbbing pain as I hover on the excruciating edge of climax.

"Oh God, Jack." Just as I shatter, he pulls me against him, burying my head in his neck. I let out a low, guttural moan as my lower half throbs and pulses with the most intense orgasm of my life, every ripple of my pussy against the balls sending a new wave of sensation through my body. Jack keeps rocking me, dragging my climax out until I can't tell where one sensation ends and another begins.

"That was so fucking hot," he murmurs. "Good thing Torment and Renegade didn't stick around."

Before I have a chance to come down, he pulls away and spins me around to face the massage table. "Down, darlin'." He pushes me over the cool, smooth padded surface and slides my knickers down so I can step out of them.

"Christ," he mutters as he slicks his finger through my labia. "I knew the toys would make you wet, but I never imagined this."

"How about you imagine taking them out and putting something else in?"

"Be careful what you wish for." With a firm hand on my lower back, holding me still, he tugs on the string, pulling out the Ben Wa balls with excruciating slowness. With my hips pressed to the table, I feel every bump and ridge as they stroke against my sweet spot. Just when I think I can't take any more, Jack yanks on the string, pulling the balls out, and I climax hard and fast, a bolt of white lightning shooting through my body.

"Oh God, Jack." I moan as he helps me stand. "Fuck me. Please. I need you."

"Now you're ready." With one hand around my waist, holding me against him, he pulls down a set of cuffs, draped over an exposed beam. "Let's get you undressed."

I tremble when he unbuttons my skirt and drops it to the floor. "I don't know about this."

"You've been cuffed like this in my playroom. You know

how it feels. And the endorphin rush you just had will help you deal with the pain." He helps me pull my top over my head.

"Pain from what?"

He undoes the clasp of my bra, and I slide it down over my arms, dropping it on the floor with the rest of my clothes.

"From my flogger." He reaches up again and pulls down the flogger he has hidden on top of the beam.

My throat tightens when I look at the black leather handle and all the leather strips attached. "That looks…not very nice."

Jack chuckles. "This is the nice one."

My trembles become a violent shudder as Jack secures my wrists in the cuffs overhead. He adjusts the chain on the beam until I'm stretched up with my toes on the ground. Vulnerable. Exposed. Hanging—like a piñata. Except when he hits me, I'm pretty sure sweet things won't be coming out of my mouth.

Jack smooths his warm hand up and down my body, but his touch does little to alleviate my fear.

"We're going to use the traffic light system so I can assess how you're doing during the scene. Green is go. Yellow is slow down. Red is stop. Or you can you use your safe word to end the scene. What is it?"

"*Redemption.*" Although after this, I won't think of Redemption as my safe place anymore.

He trails the flogger over my skin, the little tails tickling their way across my back and over my bottom. Surely something so soft can't cause too much pain. I take a deep breath, and my tension eases the tiniest bit.

"Are you ready?" He flicks the flogger, and the little tails pitter-patter over my skin like soft little raindrops. Not bad at all.

"Yes."

He continues with the soft, light strokes, first on my back and buttocks, then on my front. My skin warms, but every time I start to relax, he ups the intensity. Thuddy blows hit my ass, my upper back, and the tops of my thighs in a slow, steady rhythm, then faster. I try to get to the place in my head where I go when I cut myself, a little oasis of calm, but I am not in control. I don't know when or where he will strike me. I don't know how hard it will be. After a few more strokes, my skin starts to burn. And then the burn turns to pain.

Bloody hell, that hurts. I hold my breath, tense, waiting for the next blow.

"Where are you on the traffic light system?" he asks.

Yellow. Definitely yellow. Close to red. "Green," I lie.

The flogger tails thud against my skin so hard they steal my breath away.

"Breathe." He changes his strokes so only the very ends of the flogger touch my skin. The thudding turns to stinging. I reach for my safe place, but I am lost in the pain.

"Open your eyes, Pen." Only when he commands me do I realize my eyes are squeezed shut. I look up at him, and his brow creases in a frown. "Stay here with me. Where are you now on the safety scale?"

Red. But he looks so expectant…maybe hopeful? I can't let him down. "Green."

His muscles ripple as he raises the flogger, and I whimper in anticipation of the pain where I am most vulnerable, but the blows he delivers to my stomach, breasts, and thighs are lighter, softer, just enough to make me rock toward him, seeking more of the sensation that is at once pleasure and pain. My tension eases, muscles slack, and I lean in to the gentle blows.

"Good girl." He drops the flogger, and I sag in the restraints. All over. I did it. It hurt. It was bad, but not as bad as I imagined.

"Let's see if you're warmed up."

Warmed up?

He pinches my nipple so hard I gasp. With his other hand he cups my mound, pressing his palm over my clit as he pushes two thick fingers inside me.

"You're very wet. Are you ready for more?"

More?

"We can stop if you need to stop," he says softly as if he knows what I'm thinking.

I want to stop. God, I want to stop. But I won't. For me and for him. For once in my life, I want to be worthy, wanted. No matter how hard I tried, no matter what I did, I couldn't please my father or Adam. Nothing I did was enough. I don't want to fail again. He needs this, and I want to give it to him.

"No. I want to keep going." I stiffen my spine, meet his gaze with all the determination I can muster, even though I hurt all over and ache inside.

"Are you sure?" His studies me intently, as if he's trying to see into my soul.

"Yes."

"Use your safe word if you need it." He walks behind me.

A second later I hear a whoosh, and then the sting of a dozen bees sheets across my skin. My breath hitches, and I scramble to find a way to process the pain, but before I can get there, he lands another fierce blow that rips a scream from my throat. My ears ring. My brain fuzzes. There is no pleasure for me in this pain. No fun in this encounter. No release at hand. I just bloody hurt all over, and I can't even imagine how it will end.

"Safety? Red, yellow, or green?" His voice sounds far away, or maybe it's strained.

Redredredredredred. "Green."

He strikes again, and I bite through my lip to hold back my scream. Tears streak down my face. My body is slick with sweat. I am on fire. Scorching, burning, searing in the very pit of hell. Caught between determination and despair, I let my head fall against my arm, squeeze my eyes shut, and try to give myself over to the pain.

Silence.

Stillness.

Redemption.

A gentle hand on my head makes me shudder, my muscles tighten in anticipation of what is to come.

"Shh."

Seconds pass. I open my eyes. Jack is front of me, reaching for the cuffs. His shirt is stained with sweat, hair mussed, jaw clenched. My pulse kicks up as he tugs on the Velcro. Is he going to tighten them? Raise me higher? Can it possibly get worse than this? A whimper escapes my lips, and pain flickers across

Jack's face. Pain. Not satisfaction. Not pleasure. Not release. If anything, he looks tenser than he did before we started.

"We're done, darlin'."

"Done?" My heart sinks to my stomach. "No. Not done. I can take more."

"You can't." He gently wipes my tears away. "Even that was too much. I thought it would be, but you were so determined to try. And then you weren't honest with me."

He pulls on the cuff, growls in frustration when the Velcro doesn't loosen. "Fuck."

Whirling around, he thuds his fist against the wall. "Fuck."

Overwhelmed by the realization that I am not enough for Jack, I bite back a sob.

Jack turns back, his face stricken and strained. "Damn cuffs. Just give me a sec. I'll get you down."

"It's not…that." My throat tightens, and words fail me.

He gives the offending cuff a vicious yank, and it finally loosens. He unfastens the other cuff and lowers my arms slowly, rubbing my hands and wrists with his thumbs to restore my circulation. I can see the tension in the lines around his eyes, and I want desperately to give him the kind of release he craves. "Is there something else?" My voice drops to a pleading whisper. "Something I can do? I know you need…"

"You." He spins me around and bends me over the massage table. "All I need is you." His palm slides down my back over my burning, sensitive skin. I whimper and try to squirm away.

"Don't even think about it." His voice turns cold. Distant. "This pain you can take, and I like to look at your beautiful ass, all red from my flogger." He slaps me hard, but in this position, vulnerable and yet in control, his hand on me at once firm and soothing, the pain slides into pleasure, and I moan.

"That's the sound I like to hear." He smacks me again, his hand on my nape, holding me still.

"Where else should I smack you?" He kicks my legs apart and shoves a rough hand between my thighs. "You think that needy clit of yours needs a little discipline?"

"No." I gasp, buck against him, try to wiggle away, but his heavy hand presses me down on the bed, and he delivers a stinging slap to my pussy.

I groan into the bed as molten heat surges from my clit, spreading through my body, tightening every muscle in its wake. My hands clench the edge of the table, and I moan softly. Wet. Hot. Needy. Desperate to come.

Jack curses and groans, a low, guttural, entirely sensual sound. I hear the rustle of clothes, the crinkle of a wrapper, the soft slide of latex, and then the head of his cock presses against my opening.

"You're gonna be real sensitive." He slaps my bottom again, and he pushes his thick cock inside me with one hard thrust. "Scream for me."

This time, I can't muffle all the sound. I am so sensitive inside, that each slide of his cock is an exquisitely painful pleasure.

Jack is merciless, his cock huge and thick. He hammers into me, letting loose a stream of filthy words, about what he was thinking when I was in the gym, the things he wanted to do to me, how he'd never been so hard. Another orgasm builds deep inside me. My legs tremble. My hands fist the edge of the table. My heart pounds. I am caught in a maelstrom of sensation—pain, pleasure, need, and desire. I spiral up and up and out of control.

"There she is." Jack reaches around my hip and gives my clit a cruel pinch. My climax hits in a tidal wave of white heat that surges through my body, leaving ripples of pleasure in its wake.

Jack pounds into me, his fingers tight around my hips. He comes with a low, guttural groan, holding me still as he pumps his release inside me.

"Thank you," he whispers, leaning over me, his fingers threaded through mine.

"For what?"

Jack presses a kiss to my nape. "For trying."

In other words, I failed.

21

I am worth loving

RAMPAGE

Sylvia is standing at the back door to Club Sin when I arrive after giving Penny the aftercare she needed and tending to her injuries at home. She is wearing her blond hair up tonight, loose tendrils framing her delicately shaped face and gray-blue eyes.

"What are you doing out here?" I pull out my security pass. "It isn't safe." Although the discreet alleyway entrance is well lit, some of our high-profile female members have had unpleasant encounters, and most usually call ahead for an escort before they arrive.

"Master Greg was supposed to meet me around the corner and walk me in, but he just texted to say he's been held up. I didn't want to wait for someone else and didn't see anyone around, so I decided to go in. I was just looking for my pass."

She gives me an assessing look. "Are you looking for a sub tonight, Master Jack? You look all wound up."

So tempting. *Wound up* doesn't begin to describe the turmoil raging inside me. I trusted Penny to tell me when she reached her limit, and she let me go too far. Or did I lose control? Regret and remorse coil in my gut. Only a good, hard session at the club can relieve me, and it is not something I can do with Penny.

"Master Jack? I'm here for you."

The need to inflict pain—real pain—hums beneath my skin. I just need one night in my playroom with a willing masochist. One night to relieve the tension so I can be fully in control. Sylvia is one of the few women who can give me what I need. I can let go with Sylvia. Be the man I hate to be.

As if sensing my hesitation, she looks up, her blue eyes liquid. "You haven't been coming to the club, and I know you can't go anywhere else. I can help. You know I can. I won't take it out of the club. We'll just do a scene. I promise."

Craving takes hold of me, deep and dark. Even if the club scene didn't turn Penny off, as I assume it does, I'm a sadist. And after tonight, I'm damn sure she's not a masochist. She needs pain for the release the endorphin rush gives her, but she doesn't enjoy it the way Sylvia does. We could never make it work, and I'm selfish for pursuing her, selfish for pushing her, selfish for not wanting to let her go.

Sylvia twines her arms around my neck and presses herself against me. She is nothing if not persistent. "Please, Master Jack."

It all hits me in a rush—the craving, the restraint I have to exercise with Penny, my longing and desire to have her the way a normal man would, and the burning, seething need to hear her scream with pain before she screams with pleasure. I don't want to be this man, but I am. I don't want to hurt her, but I will. And the best thing for her would be for me to stay away.

"Fuck." I swipe my card and pull open the door, holding it for Sylvia to pass through.

"Yes. Anything you want." Sylvia brushes her lips over mine as she walks inside. "I'll be waiting in your playroom."

Before I can say anything more, she hurries down the hallway, her heels tapping on the tile floor.

Disgusted with myself and what I'm about to do, I follow her in.

Club Sin is heaving tonight, with all the equipment in use, from the cage in one corner to the St. Andrew's Cross in the other. Doms hold subs on the aftercare couches or pet submissives kneeling at their feet. Music pounds through the speakers, punctuated by the occasional scream.

I spot Damien walking the floor and catch up to him by the water station. "Are we at capacity tonight?"

Damien gives me a conspiratorial grin. "Over capacity. We've become so popular we could add another level and still have a wait list. If the landlord wasn't so determined to get us out of here in a hurry, I would have considered some renovations."

"Any fallout from Gerry's attempt to send in the contractors the other day?" I step to the side as a Domme leads a male sub past on a leash.

"Nothing. My lawyer is trying to drag things out while I find somewhere to relocate. I've seen a few interesting properties.

You'll have to come and check them out." He gives me a searching look. "And where is our newest member? I thought we'd
be seeing a lot more of her. Don't tell me you scared her away."

"Story of my life."

"I'm surprised," he says. "She didn't seem the type to be
easily put off. After all, she came back here and sat in the waiting room for almost two full nights before I let her in. And she
jumped at the chance to play with me—"

"Don't go there." I don't want to remember seeing Penny
on Damien's bench and the amount of effort it took not to pick
him up and toss him out of the room.

Damien laughs. "So it's not over."

"It is, or I wouldn't be here with Sylvia waiting in my playroom." I run my hand through my hair. "I told Pen I could cope
without the club, but she was worried she wasn't enough for
me. She agreed to do a scene, and it went all fucking wrong."

"So now she feels like a failure."

What the fuck is he talking about? "*I'm* the failure. It was my
scene. I was in control. I'm the monster Avery always thought
I was."

Damien's gaze lingers on a threesome over by the St.
Andrew's Cross. I recognize Master Daniel and the male sub
chained to the cross, but the woman is new and not wearing
the usual club fetish attire. Master Daniel has restrained her in a
bondage chair and positioned her so she can watch him, but at
a safe distance away. When Penny first showed up at the club, I
imagined her chained to the cross, trembling under the bite of
my whip. But not now. Not ever.

"I had to rearrange some furniture to accommodate them," Damien says. "The alcove was booked up tonight. Master Daniel's wife has never been to the club before, and I suggested he bring her sooner rather than later because the future of the club is so uncertain."

"Fucking Gerry," I mutter. "Would it really have been so hard to just give us the proper notice? I can't even imagine what he's paid in legal fees."

"I can," Damien says dryly. "The lawyers are the only real winners in this dispute."

We walk the length of the main floor and turn down the hallway to the private rooms. Damien stops beside the door to my playroom. "You're still hung up on being the man your family expects you to be instead of embracing who you are. Give yourself permission to enjoy your scenes instead of just enduring them. If you do, you might discover you don't need the intensity you think you do, and you might open yourself up to being with a woman who can offer you something more. You're fighting this harder than you fight in the ring, and I don't know why."

"I wanted to give her normal."

"Normal?" Damien laughs. "There is no normal. There are only degrees of kink. You need to free yourself from expectations and judgments and decide who you really are and what you really want. And if that means meeting Sylvia in your playroom, then accept it and embrace it. Be the sadist. Enjoy her pain. But if it means taking a risk with a woman who sees the man behind the monster you think you are and who needs what you have to give, then that's the wrong fucking door."

I already know it's the wrong door. There's only one place I want to be. One woman I want to be with. But after tonight, will she want me?

"She wants some pain, but she can't take too much." I scrub my hand over my face. "But she wasn't happy when I told her I could give up the club. She thought she wouldn't be enough for me."

"She's a people pleaser," Damien says. "I saw that when she walked in, and I saw a lot of strength. She was very accepting of what goes on here, which means you have options. I know a sadist whose vanilla wife gets off watching him dish out pain. She sits in on his scenes—play only, no sex—and then they go home and burn up the sheets." Damien chuckles. "Your sexual preferences don't have to inform your entire life. I know you got burned in the past, but Penny isn't Avery. She saw to the heart of you, and she came back for more."

My gaze flicks to the room where Sylvia is waiting. "I can't go back. Not to who I am at the club. Not to who I was in Tennessee. I'll need to find a way to be both the sadist and the man."

"Life isn't about moving back. It's about moving on," Damien says. "But it takes courage. The kind of courage that brings a young English legal assistant into a kinky sex club looking for normal."

—⁓—

PENNY

Cut. Don't cut. Cut. Don't cut.

I stare at the green plastic case on my bed. Everything is ready—bandages, disinfectant, blades. My legs are bare. My heart is pounding, and the familiar thrill of fear slides through my veins. All I have to do is pick up the case; close my fingers around the cold, unforgiving steel; press it against my flesh and release the demons. My mouth waters in anticipation of the pain followed by the rush. Release.

We didn't want you.

Worthless, no good…

No one would want a broken girl like you.

I pick up the case and pop the lid. Six razor blades glint in the light.

Promise me. Promise you'll call if you think about hurting your-self again.

Jack's voice wars with the voices of my past. But how can I call him now? I wasn't enough. Would it really have been so wrong to tell him the truth? Broken people make broken decisions. And I'm too broken to be fixed.

My phone buzzes on the kitchen counter, but I tune it out. Once I let the darkness take me, I need to be alone.

Taking a deep breath, I pull out a blade. Adrenaline surges through my body, and my senses sharpen. I feel the scratchy dark towel beneath me. I hear the steady ticking of the clock, the hum of traffic outside, the rasp of my breaths. I taste Jack on my lips, the lingering sweetness of vodka. I inhale and I smell him, the faint fragrance of soap and sex and a hint of vinyl from the massage table at Redemption.

Was it only a few hours ago I was in Redemption, laughing

as he chased me? Moaning as he made me come? His touch lingers on my skin, the rush of our evening together still warms me deep inside.

"Jack." His name is as soft on my lips as his flogger was hard on my skin. I could have taken more. Should have taken more. If I had, I wouldn't need this blade. And yet the craving is not as fierce as it usually is, the monsters not as loud, the need not as strong.

Not as strong as me.

I want you to see what I see. I want you to know that you are worth so much more than you got from the people in your life. You are strong. You are brave. You are worth loving, Penny. You are the kind of woman who deserves to have a man on his knees.

Do I really need this tonight? Do I want it?

I may not have been enough for Jack, but he showed me there are other ways to deal with the darkness. He has opened my eyes for me.

With curiously steady hands, I put the blade back into the box. I don't need this crutch tonight.

But I do need to find out who is on the goddamn phone.

———

An hour later, Cora and I are drinking coffee at a small all-night diner that serves breakfast twenty-four hours a day. Despite the fact that it is well past midnight, she had no problem meeting me to talk. Although she knew a few things about my past, she didn't know everything.

Now she does. The only thing I haven't told her about is Jack's kink, and why I don't feel the need to self-harm when I'm with him.

"I don't know what to say." Cora toys with the croissant on her plate after I tell her the long story about my father, Adam, Vetch, and the self-harm that has plagued me for so long. Until I met Jack, I had never shared my secrets with anyone except my therapist. But it gets a little easier each time.

"I knew you'd been through a lot, but I never imagined it was so bad." She lifts her eyes and meets my gaze. "I admire the hell out of you. You're a very strong person to be as together as you are after all that. And the cutting thing…if that's the only fallout from all those abusive relationships, you've done better than people I know who have suffered far less."

"Can I get you anything else?" The waitress refills our cups, and the aroma of sizzling bacon, fried eggs, and freshly brewed coffee tempts me to order a midnight breakfast. But I'm already on my second piece of chocolate cake, and I know I would be sorry for the feast in the morning. "Just the coffee. Thanks."

I turn back to Cora. "You don't think I'm disgusting or sick or broken?" I didn't know how Cora would feel after I told her all my secrets, but admiration wasn't anywhere near the top of the list.

"No. I knew something was wrong when you'd get all quiet and shut me out. Drove me crazy because I wanted to help you. Now I know, and I'll be there for you whenever you need me." She gives up toying with the croissant and takes a big bite.

Emotion wells up in my throat. "That means a lot to me. Adam twisted everything up in my head. He'd hit me and tell me he was doing it because I clearly liked the pain, and he was giving me what I wanted. He told me I was sick and broken and no one would ever want someone like me."

"Except him." Her lips tighten. "I can't believe you even spoke to him on the phone. If that bastard ever shows up when I'm around, I won't be responsible for my actions." She mocks a few punches in the air. "I've learned a lot in jiu-jitsu already. I'll bet I could take him down."

"You might have to stand in line." I take another bite of the chocolaty goodness in front of me—my go-to indulgence when I'm feeling down. "Ray was there when I took the call from Adam. He must have seen something in my face because he followed me around the office demanding I tell him who it was and where he lived. I finally gave in and told him it was my ex and it was a bad situation that was now over. Of course, he wouldn't let it go. I'm almost dreading going to work tomorrow."

"I can't imagine what Jack would do." Cora washes down her croissant with a sip of coffee. "He's the reason I called you tonight. He was worried about you after he dropped you off. He didn't want you to be alone. He tracked down Jimmy to get my number. I'd say he cares about you something fierce."

Her words make me feel warm inside, beating away the chill that settled over me when Jack suggested it would be better if we spent the night apart.

I look out the window and spot a familiar face. "Is that Blade Saw…er…Jimmy sitting out there in that SUV?"

Cora's cheeks heat, and she bites back a smile. "Yeah. I call him by his real name because the whole ring name thing you Redemption people have going on is kinda weird outside the gym. I was with him when Jack called. He came to my place after the party. When I told him we were going for coffee, he insisted on driving. He said he didn't want us to go out unprotected, and he was happy to sit outside until we were done."

"That sounds pretty serious."

Cora shrugs. "It's casual."

"Jimmy doesn't do casual. I thought you might have picked that up at Score when he got the whole team thrown out."

Cora shifts in her seat and toys with her hair. "Yeah, but he understands I'm not looking for a commitment right now."

Something else is going on. Cora is not a casual hook-up kind of woman. She's been desperate to find a non-geek to date, and now she has one…or is it two? "You slept with Doctor Death, didn't you?"

Her lips quiver with a guilty smile. "It was before Jimmy and I really hooked up. Except now, Don—that's his real name, Doctor Donald Drake—keeps calling me. I've never had any men interested in me, and now I have two. It's kind of hard to get my head around it all."

"If it was anyone else, I'd be dancing on the table for you," I say. "But I told you about Jimmy. He's a big-hearted guy, but a heart can only take so many breaks. He's the most loyal guy I know. If he's with you, he's with you 100 percent. If Don is with you, he's there and then he's gone. He likes to share himself around. He is pretty much Jimmy's opposite. You need to decide what you want."

"What about you? You haven't told me what happened tonight and why I'm here instead of Jack. Did you have a fight?

Did he find out that you hurt yourself and that's why he was worried about you tonight?"

My last bite of cake is one too many, and I push away the plate. "I think we both realized I can't give him what he needs, and it was just sad and awkward when he left. I'm tired of feeling like a failure. I think I'm going to break it off with him and he can go back to being who he is and I can go back to being who I am."

"Are you crazy?" Cora thunks her coffee cup on the table. "I thought you said you didn't need to hurt yourself after you've been with him. Doesn't that mean he's the right guy for you?"

My stomach twists as I look out at Jimmy alone in his car. Sometimes it's better to be alone. When you're alone, you can't get hurt.

"Yes. He's the right guy for me. But I'm not the right woman for him."

Are you trying to turn me on?

PENNY

MY EYES SNAP OPEN, A CREEPING SENSE OF DANGER WASHING OVER me, as I blink into the icy blue glare of Ray's eyes. Damn. Mind wandering. Again. After leaving Jack a cowardly phone message this morning, I haven't been able to focus. And now I've been caught out in the middle of our Thursday staff meeting.

I glance around the boardroom table to see if anyone else noticed my lapse. Jill's smirk and Dana's raised eyebrow answer my unspoken question.

"Amanda just asked if you've got the PI reports on those three new road accident cases." Ray's tone says he's going to be all over my ass the minute we leave the meeting, but he's holding back because Amanda is the only person in the room who didn't catch me having a mid-meeting snooze.

"Um…yes." I sift through the files in front of me, mentally congratulating myself for preparing them in advance so I didn't have to worry about coming in late after my early morning chat with Cora. "I have them here."

Amanda takes the reports and sighs as she flips through them. "I don't think we can take any more of these smaller contingency cases. We need paying clients who can provide a steady income stream or I won't be able to pay the bills or even continue our pro bono work. I don't know what's happened over the last year. We're doing everything we did before, but we're not bringing in the big-dollar clients."

"World is full of deadbeats," Ray offers. "Get rid of the deadweight. Start again."

"Thank you for that." Amanda catches my gaze and rolls her eyes. "I'll just call up all the clients I don't like and tell them to get lost."

"Thought you just did that with Gerry." Ray leans back in his chair, and I just know he is tempted to put his feet on the table.

I am suddenly and very acutely awake. "Gerry's not a client anymore?"

"No." Amanda's lips thin. "Yesterday evening, I had a meeting with him. I told him if he wanted to handle things legally, then I would continue to represent him, but if he was going to continue harassing Damien Stone the way he did when he hired those contractors or by threatening to blackmail Stone's clients, we were through. I'm desperate for work, but I'm not willing to compromise my standards or have my reputation tarnished. He didn't like what I said, so we parted ways."

Ray gives an approving nod. "You don't need clients like him. The guy's a fucking piece of shit. Word on the street is that he's involved in some nasty stuff."

Amanda lifts an eyebrow. "Language, Ray. This is a professional office."

"Pardon me." His voice drips with amused sarcasm. "He's a fucking piece of scum."

"Can we…" I shuffle the papers in front of me. "Can we tell people at the club now…warn them that he might have cameras?"

"I'm sorry, but no." Amanda's face creases in sympathy. "What he said to us in confidence remains in confidence even after our client agreement is terminated and even if the client is…" She looks over at Ray and laughs. "Not the kind of client we want to have. We just need to focus now on finding some good, honest, paying clients."

I stare down at my notepad where I've doodled variations of Amanda's law firm name, some modern, some retro, some traditional, and a few eclectic to match her taste for country chic. She's a great lawyer, and she should she be attracting top-notch clients to balance out all the pro bono work she does. All these years I've kept quiet, just gone with the flow, afraid to step out of my comfort zone in case something tipped me back into darkness. But I've stepped out of my comfort zone again and again since the night I went to Club Sin. I've tried new things. I've been brave. I've been strong. I opened myself up to new possibilities. I even found someone who accepted me for who I was, even if I wasn't enough for him. My heart aches for Jack, but he's helped me see a future where I don't need to self-harm anymore, where I can find another way to ease my pain, where I don't have to hide who I am.

"You could rebrand," I suggest. "Something more appealing to the kind of clientele you are targeting. Then we could do a big marketing campaign to get the brand out there—ads, flyers, and sponsorships. That kind of thing."

Everyone stares at me like I've grown a second head, and I instantly regret speaking up. "Or not," I say quietly. "It was just a suggestion."

"It's a great suggestion." Amanda smiles. "Do you have any ideas?"

"I have a few design ideas." I push the pad across the table. "I was trying out different things. I know you're interested in doing more work with charities and the arts community, so I thought something a bit more artsy and fitting more with your love of country chic."

"I'm not giving up my couch for some pink chintz shit," Ray says. "Men don't like pink."

"Good to know you're in touch with your inner caveman," I quip.

Ray raises an eyebrow, but his fierce expression makes me laugh. I know he's just a pussycat inside.

"I love these." Amanda taps two of my designs. "They're perfect. Why didn't I know you were a marketing genius?"

"It's just something I do for fun. My mom was big into PR and marketing. She ran her own design company, and on the rare occasion she was home she used to let me sit in her office and tell me all about what she was doing and why." I lived for those moments because it was the only way I could spend time with her, the only attention I got.

Amanda pushes my paper across the table to Jill. "Look at the ones I've circled. They're perfect for the firm. Why don't we set up a marketing strategy meeting later this week and Penny can tell us some more about her ideas?"

We chat about the designs for a few more minutes. Jill and Dana head back to their offices, and I hand Amanda a few documents for signatures.

"Don't I get to see the designs?" Ray folds his arms and huffs.

"Technically, you're not part of the firm," Amanda says. "You're an independent contractor. Also, since you don't like pink chintz shit, I hardly think you'll be able to give us an honest opinion."

"Sia doesn't let him swear at home," I say helpfully. "You shouldn't let him indulge at the office. Maybe he should stand outside for five minutes and think about his behavior."

"Good idea." Amanda smiles. "He can get it all out before he goes home to babysit. Shayla, Sia, and I are taking Makayla to Death's Dungeon for some pre-baby fun. Penny, you and Cora are invited since you're connected to the Redemption team."

"What the fuck?" Ray shoots out of his seat. "Sia's not going to Death's fucking Dungeon. That's a death metal bar. It's almost all men. Lowlifes who can't get their own women."

"I think she has a different view on that matter," Amanda says, her lips quivering with a smile. "And you get to spend some quality time at home with Sam. She gets a girls' night out and you get a guys' night in."

"Christ," Ray mutters. "A man can't even relax in his own place of work, and now I won't be able to relax at home 'cause Sia's gonna be out with no protection." His eyes narrow. "Does Renegade know about this? How about Torment? Or Rampage? Or Blade Saw?"

He must be agitated since he's using ring names and we're not even in the gym, but Amanda just laughs. "Of course not. And you're not going to tell them, or you'll find yourself out of a job."

"Isn't that illegal?" Ray's frown becomes a scowl. "I should report you for threats and violations of employment standards."

"People in glass houses…" She lifts an eyebrow, and Ray's lips press together. Amanda knows what Ray did to Vetch Retch, not that she would ever tell anyone, but sometimes she likes to pull that little nugget out to keep him in line.

"Can I tell one person?" He gives me a pointed stare. "Jack would want to know where his girl's at."

"No one," Amanda snaps, saving me from telling them I'm not Jack's girl. Not anymore.

—◊◊◊—

RAMPAGE

"We need to talk." James, my manager, stops me in Redemption's hallway. If not for my distillery, I would be hard-pressed to pay all the people on my team. The big money doesn't roll in for professional fighters until you start getting the big fights and the really big sponsorships.

Four inches shorter than me, lean, and ropy, James wears his blond hair in a crew cut. I hired him because he has a reputation as a pit bull and has worked for several newbie fighters who made it to the top level.

"I just knocked Fuzzy flat in less than sixty seconds. What is there to talk about?" Still reeling from Penny's voice message telling me she was breaking it off because she wasn't enough for me, I need to burn off the extra energy, not sit around having a chat. James is a four-time world lightweight champion and he knows his stuff, but five years out of the game, he's become a corporate lapdog, and sometimes I wonder if he remembers what it feels like to be in that cage.

"Your image." We walk through the crowded corridor to the changing room. As always, the hallways are packed with people talking and waiting for classes, and, now that Torment has added Saturday family classes, there are also lots of energetic kids.

"You're good in the ring," he says. "Fierce, ruthless, relentless. You live up to your cage name. But out of the ring, you're too nice, and the fans are getting confused. They see you talking to your opponents, laughing with reporters, posing for selfies, and patting kids' heads. At Redemption, you're everybody's friend." He pulls out his phone and shows me a news website with a picture of me having a laugh with one of the workers who was outside Club Sin.

"Yeah. About that…"

"This is not the image you need to project when you're first starting out in the pros," James says. "You need to be Rampage in and out of the ring. You need to be storming up to the cage, knocking people out of the way like Juice Can did, going after your opponents at the weigh-ins. If you want to attract the big sponsors and make your way to the top tier, you need to build a reputation that will scare your opponents even if they're a thousand miles away."

"I just want to fight a good fight." I pull open the door to the changing room, and James follows me in, checking to make sure we're alone.

"That's good. That's what we want. But we also need you to fight a good fight out of the ring. Psych your opponents like you did when you beat up Juice Can after the fight a few weeks ago. Make them think Rampage goes through to your core, that you're the kid who picked fights in school—"

"I did," I say, cutting him off.

"That you were the badass who was kicked out of class."

"I was." Now that I think about it, I was always a disappointment to my parents, my violent streak showing through even at an early age, when I was supposed to be the perfect son, the up-and-coming next CEO of the family business. Fighting is in my blood. But maybe that's not such a surprise. My great-grandfather immigrated from Ireland and made his money in street fights and boxing rings.

"So what happened?" James sits on the bench as I pull open my locker. "And I don't mean that in a bad way."

"I had to bury that side of myself for reasons that are none of your business, and I only let it out in the ring." And at the club, but that's just about the last thing I would ever share with James.

"Let it out, or learn how to act. That's my advice." He tugs at the red-and-blue tie around his neck, his attempt at looking professional. "I want to see you rise to the top, but a big part of it is showmanship. You can earn six figures from sponsorships alone if you give them something to work with."

Christ. When I signed the pro contract, I naively thought I was signing up for the chance to fight some of the best fighters in the world. Instead, I've signed up to be a trick pony, not just a fighter but also a circus freak.

"Fine. I'll go growl at a few babies, make some kids cry, knock over a few chairs on my way out."

"That's the spirit." His phone buzzes, and he excuses himself to take a call. I pull out my phone and check my messages, although there is only one person I want to hear from—the woman for whom I turned down Sylvia and left Club Sin last night.

"I've got an opportunity for you right now." James covers the mouthpiece on his phone. "The CEO of Swish Athletics is in town. I was talking to him yesterday about sponsorship. He wants to take the brand in a new direction—give it a dangerous edge. His daughter is with him and she wants to meet you. Maybe we can set up a dinner and you can put on a bit of a show. Get into a fight in the restaurant, knock over a few chairs. Women love that kind of stuff. You could get even get lucky, and if she tells her daddy just how big and bad you are…"

My phone buzzes with a message from Ray telling me that Penny, Sia, Makayla, and Amanda are going out to a death metal bar with a few of the female Redemption fighters tonight. He wants to know if I knew about this. How the hell is he supposed to watch his woman when he has a baby at home? And how fast can I get my ass down to the bar? I notice he has sent the message to Torment and Renegade to warn them that their women are in danger. Ray takes overprotectiveness to a whole new level.

There is only one place I want to be. One thing I want to do. And it doesn't involve fucking my way to greatness.

"Sorry, James." I grab my gym bag and tuck away my phone. "Tell her big, bad Rampage is on his way to kiss some sense into his girl tonight."

PENNY

Death's Dungeon, San Francisco's premier death metal bar, is hopping tonight. The last time I was here, Amanda had just started her new firm and I had just started seeing Vetch Retch. Little did I know he was reeling me in, bit by bit, waiting until I was so emotionally involved I wouldn't run the first time he hit me.

Shirtless male bartenders mix cocktails behind the counter, and metalheads fill almost every seat. Death metal band posters are plastered over the walls, and the air is thick with the yeasty scent of beer. We make our way through the crowd to a red vinyl booth near the back where Makayla, Sia, and Shilla a.k.a. Shayla are waiting.

It's been a long time since I was in a death metal bar, and the loud, heavy beat pulls me out of my funk. I haven't stopped worrying about Jack ever since Amanda told us Gerry was no longer a client. Now that Amanda isn't around to rein Gerry in, there is no one to stop him from carrying out his blackmail threat. Just how desperate is he to evict Club Sin? And how can I keep Jack safe?

Except for a slight roundness of her cheeks, Sia doesn't look like she just had a baby. Slim and pretty with long, dark hair, she is an incredible artist and her work is in high demand. I walk past her tattoo parlor every time I'm in Redemption, trying to work up the nerve to go inside. She thanks Amanda for sending Ray home and cracks us up with an impression of him complaining about women bossing him around while he lovingly cradles Sam in his arms.

Shayla slides her cut, muscular body over to accommodate us, and Cora and I slide in beside her.

"Help yourself." She gestures to a tray of drinks on the table. "We started without you because we wanted to be all warmed up for the Redemption fighter bash fest."

Amanda laughs. "Sometimes the overbearing, protective, possessive alpha male thing gets a little too much, and we need to blow off some steam before we go home and cut our men down to size."

"Sex Bomb," Shayla says, pointing to my drink as I take a sip. "Not that you need it."

Savoring the combined sweet-and-sour taste, I lean back in my seat and chat with Cora. After our talk at the coffee shop, she decided to be honest with Blade Saw. I'm not sure what she was thinking might happen, but, of course, he broke it off with her. Blade Saw, like most of the Redemption fighters, is not the kind of man who shares.

"I don't know how to get him back," she moans. "That weekend we spent together was awesome. He actually likes sci-fi stuff, and he loved my robot shirts. He made me wear them when we had sex on the balcony, and that's all he wanted me to wear all weekend. I can't believe I have the longest dry spell on earth, and then I get and lose a perfect man in less than a month."

"He still wants you," Shayla says, joining our conversation. "I almost knocked him out when we were training together the other night because he couldn't take his eyes off you."

I sip my drink, considering. "Why don't you get a robot shirt made with his name on it? Put his ring name on the back like you're on his team. If he's always watching you and he sees you in that shirt…"

Amanda stirs her Maggot Brain, a nauseatingly green concoction that is foamy on top. "You're good at the marketing and branding stuff. Really good. You should seriously consider doing something with that talent, maybe take some courses with a view to doing it professionally."

My cheeks burn, but in a good way. "I'd like to do that. I just never thought I was good enough."

"You are," she says. "Never think you aren't good enough. For anything or anyone."

The waitress stops by, and I order a round of whiskey from Jack's distillery. At first I don't tell them that Jack and Blade Saw own the distillery, but it turns out to be the worst-kept secret at Redemption, and everybody knows.

"Hey, this is from Rampage's and Blade Saw's distillery."

Shayla gulps down her shot and orders another one. "Where is Rampage tonight? I'm surprised he let Penny out of his sight. The Redemption men fall hard for their women, but I never thought he would fall the hardest of all."

"I assume he's at the gym." I sip my whiskey, and the smooth, smoky taste reminds me of the night Jack poured whiskey on me and licked it off. "We kinda broke it off, so I guess he'll be there tonight."

Everyone laughs.

"Not a chance," Sia says.

Makayla grins. "He'll come looking for you."

"He's probably already on his way." Amanda looks out over the dance floor. "No way could Ray keep that secret. He was probably texting everyone before we even left the office."

"They tend to travel in packs." Shayla flexes her biceps. "Sometimes I go with them if they think things are gonna get really rough."

Over the next few hours, I drown my sorrows in too many drinks. Shayla tries to cheer me up by doing impressions of the fighters at Redemption, and Sia tells us stories about Ray and their new baby. Who would have imagined Ray would be such a good dad? Or that he would be a total pushover, picking Sam up and singing to him every time he cries? Amanda hints that she and Jake might have finally set a wedding date. And Makayla tells us all the different ways she has escaped from under Torment's overprotective thumb.

"Does he know you're here?" Sia asks.

"I bought a wig and caught a ride with the cleaner," Makayla says. "I texted after I was safely away to tell him I was going out with friends. Otherwise he'd call the police and report me missing after an hour. I always turn off my phone because if I don't he uses an app to try and track me and fills up my mailbox with 'where are you' messages."

"I collect them." Amanda pulls out her phone. "I have a separate mailbox to store Jake's 'where are you' messages. I read them when I need a laugh."

Now that I've got an alcohol-induced buzz going, I hit the dance floor with Cora and Shayla in tow, and we dance to Cannibal Corpse's "Hammer Smashed Face," with some hot biology majors from Berkeley. From the way they keep trying to feel us up, I figure they're still learning about human anatomy, but Shayla isn't in a teaching mood and abandons us to our octopus friends.

A murmur ripples through the bar, and I sense a disturbance at the door. I work my way to the edge of the dance floor just as the crowd parts to reveal Torment stalking through the bar.

"Uh-oh." I give Cora a nudge. "He found her. I can't decide if I want to keep dancing or go back to the table for the show."

Cora looks over, and her smile fades. "Jimmy is with him." Her breath hitches. "And Renegade…"

My personal octopus slithers his hands down my curves, and I wiggle against him. "There's an advantage to being single again."

"And Jack," Cora says in a rush of breath.

Jack's gaze locks on me. Suddenly, I don't feel single anymore.

"Save yourself." I turn and push my new friend away. "Quickly. Go."

Moments later, I feel Jack's heated presence behind me. He hooks one arm around my waist, the other across my ribs, and plasters me against the heat of his hard body. "Clearly, I was too soft with you," he murmurs in my ear.

"What do you mean?" I tremble at his touch, the harsh rasp of his voice, the strong arms holding me fast.

"Too much pleasure. Not enough pain." He nips my earlobe and I gasp.

"Enjoy your dance. Because when it's done, you're coming with me to learn a lesson about jumping to conclusions and not talking things through." He slides his hand around my throat and gently tips my head back so I look into his cold, hard eyes. "And if I see any mark on you other than the ones I put there, you are going to be one very sorry girl."

My body flames at his touch, the subtle threat in his voice, and the pressure of his hand on my throat. "Are you trying to turn me on?"

He tightens his grip, giving me just enough air to breathe. "I don't have to try."

"I can't give you what you need, Jack. You should be with someone like that woman you were with when I saw you the very first time."

"I tried. I went to Club Sin last night and met up with one of my old play partners, Sylvia. She was waiting for me in my playroom."

Oh God. He went to the club. Of course he went to the club. I wasn't enough, and now his career is at risk and he's back with Sylvia. I sag in his arms, and he releases me and turns me to face him.

"I left," he says.

I stare at the dance floor. Does he expect me to be happy that he played with her but didn't take her home? Not even Bloodbath's "Soul Evisceration" could lift my mood now.

Jack threads his hand through my hair, tips my head back, and studies me intently. "I left, Penny." For some reason his soft Tennessee twang seems more pronounced and *Penny* sounds like *PINny*. He never calls me Penny. Always Pen or darlin'. Why is he being so formal now? My mother was only ever formal when I was in trouble or she had something important to say, and wanted my full attention. *Listen to me, Penny Grace Worthington.*

"You're not listening to me." His chin dips down so his face is close to mine. "I left. I didn't play with Sylvia or anyone at the club."

"But you will. You need it. I understand that. Really, I do."

He moves closer, and his eyes grow intense. "I've thought of something that will work for both of us. But first we're gonna go for a drive, sober you up, and talk this through."

I give an indignant sniff. "I'm not hammered."

"Yeah, you are. You're fucking cute when you're drunk— all smiley and happy, dancing around—and so goddamn sexy I couldn't drive fast enough to the bar, 'cause I knew the guys would be all over you. But that's the last time."

I give him a puzzled look. "Last time?"

"You don't go drinking without me again." Jack scowls and his hand drops to my waist, fingers digging into my hip. "You don't dance with anyone except me, and you don't let anyone touch you except me."

"That would be unacceptable even if we were together."

"We are together, and that's how it is when you get involved with a Redemption fighter." He tips his chin toward our booth where a cohort of angry Redemption males is engaged in a battle with their equally angry women. Torment, in particular, looks like he's about to explode because it's clear Makayla isn't in any hurry to leave.

"That didn't help your case." I laugh softly. "I'm not about to be the only woman who does what she's told."

"You're the only one who doesn't get a choice," he snaps. "Because you're the one who left a message on my phone telling me it was over. You're the one who didn't return my calls so we could talk things out. You didn't text me. You didn't come to me. And you went out alone without me." He sweeps me up in his arms and carries me off the dance floor, knocking dancers aside with reckless abandon.

Mortified, I struggle against him. "Put me down right now."

"We're going for a drive, and you're gonna hear me out."

"Jack, this isn't funny." I slap at his chest, and he huffs his annoyance.

"You're right. It wasn't funny to be cut off without any explanation." He weaves through the crowd, and I pull in my legs and arms, trying to not hit anyone. "It wasn't funny to get your message and hear the hurt in your voice. So after we've sobered you up and talked it out, we're going to Club Sin because there's only one way I know how to get through to you. I'm gonna break down your walls, show you who I am and how strong you are, and how perfect we are for each other. Then maybe you'll understand exactly how I feel about you."

I look up at him, so intense, determined, hopeful. I want this. I want him. But I don't want him to risk his career and reputation. If he managed to avoid Gerry's cameras last night, I don't want to be the reason he's caught tonight. "Okay." I lean up, press a kiss to his neck. "I'll go with you. But only if you wear a hat."

23

I can take your pain

RAMPAGE

Damien is waiting when we arrive at Club Sin a few hours later.

"What's with the ballcap?" He snorts a laugh as I make my way down the hallway to the private members' play space. Penny is waiting in my room. I haven't asked her to remove any clothing because she's never played in public before. And even if she had, I would make her wear her dress. Only Penny would wear a soft, white lace dress to a death metal bar.

I pull the cap off my head and run my hand through my hair, now damp with sweat. "Pen asked me to wear it. She said she was worried I would be recognized going into the club. I told her we've never had an issue, but she wouldn't let it go, and frankly I wasn't about to start a fight about a cap when we've got bigger things to work out."

"I got your text," Damien says. "Everything's ready for you.

Peter is going to be your sub tonight. He's waiting for you in the alcove. He wasn't happy about the shorts-on rule, but he says he'll make an exception for the opportunity to scene with you."

I nod, approving Damien's choice. Peter is a hard-core masochist and one of the most experienced subs in the club. Although I prefer women, I scene with men when I really want to let go. I can push them harder, take them higher, and in this case, I can avoid any suggestion of intimacy that might make Penny uncomfortable because I have no sexual interest in men.

After meeting with Peter to discuss the scene and go over his limits, I call for Damien to bring Penny to the alcove while Peter gets ready. I haven't discussed what we're going to do, but when she sees a chair and the St. Andrew's Cross, she clues in pretty fast.

"You want me to watch?"

I nod and point to the chair Damien has placed in the corner. "I'm going to restrain you right there, and you're going to listen to Peter scream and think about the pain I'm going to give you when I'm done. Not pain like that and not more than you can take, but I will push you so we can find out just how much you need from me and how far I can go. Are you good with that?"

Her eyes sparkle and she answers without hesitation. "Yes."

I shove my hand between her legs, spread my fingers so she is forced to part her thighs. Her breath catches, and her cheeks bloom. My girl is so damn responsive.

Pushing aside her panties, I slick my finger through her folds and shove it deep inside her. "Already wet. You like the idea of watching."

She grips my shoulder to steady herself. "I thought it was so incredibly hot when I saw you in the alcove the first time. So hot, I…" Her blush deepens, and I frown.

"From now on, if you have needs of any kind, you come to me." I push a small bullet vibe inside her and show her the remote. "I'm gonna enjoy watching you squirm."

"You wouldn't." Her face pales. "Peter will be here. The alcove is open."

"You got a problem with that, tell me now. You've got your safe word. I expect you to use it when you need to. No lies." I flick the remote switch, and her eyes widen as the vibrator comes to life.

"I'm good." She hisses out a breath. "I can take it."

I brush a kiss over her cheek. "I know you can."

Peter arrives after I've secured Penny to the chair, her wrists cuffed to the arms and her ankles to the legs. I introduce her to Peter, and we talk about the scene and their experience in the club. Although Penny is just watching, she will be as much a part of the scene as Peter, and I want them to feel comfortable with each other. Finally, I take Peter over to the cross and fasten cuffs around his wrists and ankles. He's a welder, in his mid-forties, his skin bronzed by the sun, his muscles thick and hard. I won't have to hold back anything tonight. I can let it all go so I can be with Penny the way she needs me—fully, completely, and totally in control.

"You okay?" I turn up the vibrator with one hand and grab a flogger with the other. Penny makes a noise that sounds halfway between a grunt and a whimper, and I turn the speed back down. I don't want to get her too worked up too fast. I have plans for her tonight.

———~~~———

PENNY

Breathe. Breathe. Breathe. I watch Jack's muscles ripple as he cracks the whip over Peter's back, already red from his earlier flogging. Peter screams, his back bowing inward to get away from the sting of the lash, but there is nowhere to go.

Jack raises his arm again, and I tremble in anticipation. I have only ever seen him this focused and intense in the cage, his muscles taut, jaw clenched, body vibrating ever so slightly before he unleashes his power with each brutal strike. His skin is slick with sweat, and his black T-shirt clings to every ridge of his muscular torso. His is breathtaking and terrifying, fierce and furious, and yet every time he stops to allow Peter to catch his breath, his gaze is warm on mine.

Deceptive. Because beneath those icy-blue depths lies the heart of a true sadist.

The vibrator kicks up a notch, and I glance over to see him watching me, one hand in his pocket, the other dangling the whip on the floor. He knows how close I am, how much I ache, how desperate I am to come. And yet he keeps me on edge, brings me up and takes me down, making me whimper for his sadistic pleasure.

His biceps flex and strain, and then he releases his next strike with such incredible force the crack of the whip explodes through the alcove. Peter howls in anguish, yanks against the restraints, thick muscles straining with the effort to get free. Energy pulses between us, binding us all together. Jack is clearly in his element—his face is dark with power, alive with pleasure. I think of all that intensity focused on me, and I feel my knickers dampen.

I could never take that much pain. There is a freedom in knowing that no matter how I tried, I would never be able to give Jack this. I am limited by biology and not by the lack of strength or courage or fortitude. Maybe this is what he wanted me to see.

Jack works Peter up to the point his screams turn to moans and his muscles unclench as he floats on an endorphin high. Master Damien arrives to help lift Peter down from the cross, and together they help him walk to the couch in the corner and wrap a blanket around his shoulders.

"How are you doing?" Jack squats down beside me and gives me a look that says he knows exactly how I'm doing after spending more than an hour watching his powerful body in action while tied to a chair with a vibrator buzzing inside me.

"Good, thanks. And you?" Regardless of the situation, it never hurts to be polite.

Jack chuckles. "I feel physically sated but not satisfied." He traces a finger around and around my nipple, taut beneath my clothing, until I squirm in the chair.

"I know that feeling. It's lovely for a little while, but it doesn't last."

"Oh, this is going to last." He crouches down in front of me and draws lazy circles along my inner thigh, pushing up my dress as he goes. "You're so hot, you were burning up the room. You liked watching me hurt someone."

"Yes," I whisper so Master Damien and Peter don't hear. "But only because it was you. If I had to watch someone else do what you did, it wouldn't turn me on."

"Glad to hear it." He pushes my knickers aside, and rubs his fingers along my slit. "You're so wet, I would have known if you were lying to me."

I gasp when he pushes a finger inside me. "I would never lie to you, Jack."

"Good. Because it is the one thing I cannot stand. Avery lied. She told me she loved me when she was fucking Beau behind my back. She told me she would keep my secret, and the next day she shared it to the world." He pulls the tiny vibrator out of my pussy, and I moan as it slides over my sweet spot.

"Poor baby." He wraps his hand around my hair, pulls it tight. "So wet. So needy. So desperate to come. I've only just warmed you up. It's going to be a long time before you get your release. You wait here. I'll be back in a minute."

As if I could move with my hands and ankles bound. But now I have something to keep me company. Fear.

After Jack finishes tending to Peter and cleaning up the play space, he unlocks my restraints and rubs my ankles and wrists to bring back the circulation. With one strong arm around my waist, he helps me from the chair and steers me out of the alcove.

"Where are we going?"

He gives me an evil smile. "I'm taking you to the dungeon. It's your turn for pain."

—◦◦◦—

A door slams, making me jump. My hands fly to the blindfold around my head, but before I can touch it, someone slaps my hands away. Trembling, I try to orient myself in the darkness.

After the scene with Peter, Jack had me change out of my dress and into his oversized club T-shirt with my bra and knickers on underneath. Then he brought me down to this dark, dank room under the club, blindfolded me, and left me sitting on the hard bed with instructions not to move.

"What's going on? Jack?"

"Why are you here?" The voice above me is low, rough, and unfamiliar.

"What?" My heart thuds in my chest. "I came here with Jack…er, Master Jack. Who are you?"

"Security." He pulls off the blindfold and shines a flashlight on his chest. Blinking as my eyes adjust to the light, I see the familiar black security vest the bouncers and monitors wear at Club Sin.

"What are you hiding?"

"Nothing. I…" My words trail off when he grabs my hair and pulls me off the bed. I let out a scream as I fall to my knees on the floor.

"Stop. Wait. Where's Jack?"

Laughter echoes in the room, but in the flicker of the flashlight I catch a glimpse of a familiar profile.

"No one is coming for you. It's just you and me and the secret you don't want to share."

"Secret?" I try to turn my head to confirm it was Jack I just saw, but he forces me back.

"Everyone who comes here has a secret. You will tell me yours." He yanks my hair, pulling me up, and marches me over to a chair in the corner. "Sit."

"Jack?" I sit on the curious wooden chair that has a cutout in the middle of the seat.

"What is your safe word?" he growls as he sets the flashlight on the floor.

Safe word. It is Jack. And we're playing, just like we talked about in the car on the way to the club. Role-playing. A thrill of excitement runs through me. I've been caught by security, and now he wants to know my secret. Well, it's not a secret I will ever divulge.

"*Redemption.*" I struggle in his grip, let him know I want to play. "And you'll never get the secret out of me."

"Hands behind your back."

I've never heard Jack so abrupt, his voice so clipped. If I hadn't caught that quick glimpse of him in the shadows, heard his voice soften the tiniest bit when he mentioned my safe word, I might worry about being locked in the dungeon with a sadist I don't know.

Hands trembling, I cross my wrists behind the chair. Jack kneels behind me and cuffs them together. The snap of the handcuffs makes me jump, and I tug on the unforgiving steel. Ray will have a fit tomorrow when he sees the bruises on my wrists.

Jack pulls a long bar from his bag and attaches the cuff on

one end to my ankle. With a yank, he spreads my legs apart and repeats the process on the other side. My legs are spread wide, unable to close because of the thick bar between them. Wearing only his big T-shirt and my underwear, I feel open and vulnerable. Adrenaline shoots through me in a panicked wave.

"Breathe." His voice echoes in the semi-dark room, his commanding tone ringing around me.

I take a deep breath and another, focusing on the rise and fall of my chest and not the man in the dungeon and what he is going to do.

"Anything too tight?" He clicks on a spotlight above the chair, and my eyes widen at the formidable sight. In his dark shirt and leathers, massive black boots, the heavy security vest, and the cap I made him wear, he looks at once terrifying and breathtaking, like he has let his darkness free.

"No."

He folds his arms over his chest, his massive biceps swelling above his hands. "You are being retained on suspicion of withholding information that should have been disclosed to one Jack Caldwell. What is your name?"

"Penny Grace Worthington."

He scowls as if I've just said the name of a serial killer. "What were you doing in Club Sin at the time of your arrest?"

A smile tugs at my lips. "Sitting in the dark."

Without another word he reaches into his bag and takes out various toys and implements, placing them carefully on a table at the edge of the circle of light.

My mouth goes dry as I look over the array of toys, from

two-pronged vibrators to whips and floggers, and from clamps to things I can't even identify.

Jack picks a pair of scissors and stands in front of me. "You will tell me everything I want to know."

"What if I don't?" The words drop from my lips before I can catch them, and I am surprised by my own audacity. But with Jack I feel strong, bold, wanted. And worthy.

His lips quiver at the corners, and he runs the edge of the scissors very gently down my neck to the collar of the shirt. With slow, deliberate movements, he snips the collar and cuts a line down to the crescents of my breasts.

"I'm disappointed at your refusal to cooperate." He places the scissors on the table.

Shocked that he would cut my T-shirt, I can only stare when he grasps either side of the cut and violently tears the shirt in two.

Oh. My. God.

Before I can speak, he slides the scissors between my breasts and cuts my bra away.

"Jack." I whisper his name in horror as my shredded clothes fall to the floor. But even as fear slides up my spine, arousal coils deep in my core.

He tosses the scissors aside and squeezes my breasts. "Why are you here?" He tightens his grip, twisting until I'm squirming and panting in my seat.

"You bastard. I can't believe you cut up my clothes. I'm not telling you anything. I liked that T-shirt. I thought it was a gift."

With a grunt of annoyance, he releases me and picks up

two clothespins from the table. "Maybe these will change your mind." He clamps a clothespin on my right nipple, and I yelp in pain.

Jack studies me for a long moment before clamping my other nipple. I yelp again, struggle against my bonds, trying to breathe through the fire. After what seems like forever, the pain turns into a dull ache, which turns into an erotic burn that shoots down to my clit. I moan, and Jack gives a bitter laugh.

"Now she's talking."

"Piss off." I glare, torn between anger and arousal, fear and disbelief.

Jack shakes his head. "Tsk, tsk, tsk." He slides the cold metal scissors over my hip and inside my knickers. With a snip on each side and a vicious tug, he tears them free.

Bared, exquisitely vulnerable, I whimper.

Jack stares down at me, his face taut and hard, barely recognizable. "You are totally open to me. There is nowhere you can run. Nowhere you can hide. No part of your body I can't access. This is your last chance to tell me what you're hiding."

I don't know where I get the courage to defy him or why I want to do it. With my nipples clamped and my breasts sore and aching, my pussy engorged and throbbing, my body desperate to come, part of me wants to end this now, tell him what he wants to know so we can get on with the fucking and I can get the climax that is hovering just out of reach. "No."

He raises an eyebrow, and that controlled, limited response carries with it a heavier threat than any implement ever could. "You are forcing me to take drastic measures," he says as he pulls on a pair of latex gloves. The impersonal snap of latex does strange things to my stomach, and heat surges through my veins. "I will break you, Penny Worthington. I will make you talk."

With his eyes on me, he crouches down and shoves two fingers deep inside me through the cut-out in the seat.

"Oh God." I am drenched with need, my pussy hot and pulsing around his fingers. I stare at him, silently begging. In this moment, his face is severely handsome, half hidden in the shadows, his eyes dark and glittering, his hair mussed, his mouth both sensual and cruel. I want to touch him, kiss him. I want his mouth on my burning nipples, his tongue licking between my thighs.

"You will crack. It's just a matter of time." He adds a third finger, stretching me. I try to relax to accommodate the intrusion, but before I can soften my inner muscles, he curls his fingers and rubs them over and over against my G-spot, pumping his hand so hard, I jerk on the bench. I feel pressure building low in my womb, my body tightening. Without warning, liquid gushes from me, not urine but something else. It gives me only momentary respite, not the kind of release that comes from an orgasm, and then he starts again, fucking me hard with his hand, his fingers pounding against the same spot. The pain is excruciating and at the same time intensely pleasurable, and I don't know whether to cry or moan. He pushes hard, and more liquid gushes from me and with it a scream.

"Please," I beg, panting when his fingers push deeper inside me. "Not again."

"Your cunt is swollen and wet," he says, his voice low and

dangerous. "Your clit is engorged, your nipples swollen. I can be cruel, but I can be kind. Tell me what I want to know, and I can give you as much pleasure as I give you pain."

I want to come, need to come, would do anything in this moment for relief, but I do have a secret, a real secret, and some stubborn part of me is not willing to let go, even if this is just a game. I want to go as far as he will take me. Bend but not let him break me.

"I can take your pain," I mutter through clenched teeth. "And I mean it. Green light. Do your worst. I dare you."

His eyebrows fly up. I have surprised him. And I have surprised myself.

Without a word, he pulls a crop from his belt with his free hand and flicks it along the insides of my thighs. I have never felt pain like the sharp sting of the crop, and I immediately regret my foolish words. But for every flick of the crop on my tender skin, he pumps his fingers inside me, blending pleasure and pain. And it feels so good. So right.

"Don't stop," I beg. "Please. Don't. Stop." Drenched in sweat, my clit alive with longing, my arousal a nagging, excruciating weight in my pelvis, my thighs stinging, my breasts sore and swollen, I wait for the release only he can give me.

"Tell me," he whispers. "Why are you here?"

"Because I love you."

Silence. Long seconds tick by. I try to decipher the unfathomable expression on his handsome face, but I come up blank.

Finally, he withdraws his fingers and picks up a tiny flogger, each soft leather strand tipped with a bead. He speaks in a soft, authoritative voice. "You're wound up so tight, the only way to give you pleasure is through pain. Will you take the pain I offer you?"

I wonder if he heard my declaration, understood the secret I let fly from my heart. "Yes."

He slaps the flogger over my pussy, the little beads stinging like tiny needles on my delicate skin. My clit swells to meet each gentle blow, welcomes the pain as pleasure.

"Come for me." He flicks the flogger again, and the orgasm rips through me, a fierce tidal wave of pent-up desire unleashed through my body, crashing through me in a molten wave. My pussy contracts over and over, and I tumble into a vortex of sensation, anchored only by the press of his lips against mine and the whisper of words in my ear.

Dazed, the sensations softening, I watch as he strips off his security vest and pulls off his shirt, baring his beautiful body— the massive toned chest, rippling abs, the biceps thick and strong. With quick, practiced movements, he undoes his belt and drops his jeans to the floor. He is magnificent, his body all lean muscle, his cock thick and hard jutting from its nest of curls. My mouth waters as he kneels before me and sheaths himself. I imagine pressing a kiss to the base of his neck, running my fingers through his soft, dark hair, taking his cock in my mouth and driving him wild.

He unclips the spreader bar and undoes the cuffs. "Brace yourself. This is going to hurt." He removes one of the clothespins, and I let out a strangled groan as blood rushes to my poor, abused nipple.

"Beautiful." Jack leans forward and draws my nipple between his teeth, swirling it with his tongue, soothing it with the heat of his mouth. He repeats the process with my other nipple, gently squeezing my breast, rocking me with sensation. When my breathing steadies, he helps me up and lays me gently on the bed.

"Penny."

PINny. My name is a reverent whisper of soft Tennessee twang on his lips as he pushes his cock inside me, bracing his body with his strong, powerful arms.

"Legs around my hips." He presses me down against the mattress. His teeth close on the sensitive skin of my neck, nibbling and biting, and I wrap my arms around his shoulders and hold on for the ride.

"I was going to fuck the secret out of you," he murmurs. "I wanted to fuck you so hard you would remember me every day until I took you again. But now…" He reaches between us, slides his fingers along the sides of my swollen clit.

I moan and arch against him, almost as desperate to come again as I was only five minutes ago. We fit together, as if we were one body, not two, as if all that I am and all I was meant to be is the other half of him.

He slides one hand under my back, pulls me close, and drives in so deep I gasp. His gaze flies to mine, and I see only softness and desire. I see love. But I don't hear the words.

My heart thuds, and I rock my hips, taking him that tiny bit deeper, holding him that little bit closer. "Jack."

As if his name frees him, his forceful thighs spread my legs, and he pounds into me, his cock sliding over my sweet spot, stroking it to pleasure all over again. His body moves over me with sinuous grace, muscles taut and straining as he rubs my clit until I reach a wrenching peak.

"God, Jack. Now."

"Fuck, yes." He growls as his cock thickens inside me, and he climaxes in long, hot jerks, his release sending me over the edge in an orgasm that ripples through me, spreading out to my fingers and toes.

When we have both come down, he gathers me up and presses his rough cheek to my forehead. "You humble me with your trust," he says quietly.

"I was scared at first," I admit, cupping his cheek in my palm. "But when you asked about my safe word, your face softened, and I knew you cared and you wouldn't push me farther than I could go, although you did get pretty close." I bite my lip, considering. "I couldn't do that every time…"

"I wouldn't ask it every time." He rolls to his back, pulling me with him so I am tucked against his side, my head on his shoulder, watching the light cast shadows on the walls.

"I can handle it as long as I feel you care. I lost it in that scene because I needed a connection—a kiss, a touch, even a word to let me know we were still together on an emotional level."

"So," he says. "You and me."

"I broke us," I say. "And you put us back together."

"Always." He presses a kiss to my forehead. "I'm here for you. Whatever you need, however you need it, I'll give it to you. If you're sad, I'll comfort you. If you're scared, I'll chase your fears away. If you're drowning, I'll save you."

God. My beautiful, perfect man. But if Gerry makes good his threats, who's going to save him?

24

Sadist in pain

PENNY

"DON'T SAY ANYTHING." I WALK PAST RAY AND POUR MY COFFEE, angling my body so he doesn't see the bruises around my wrists. Although I'm wearing long sleeves, and I've tried to cover them with makeup, I'm not foolish enough to think Ray's sharp eyes will give them a miss. I've also worn a longer skirt than usual today. Even I was a bit shocked at the bruises and welts on my inner thighs.

"That's like asking me not to breathe." He follows me into my office and slams the door.

With a sigh, I turn to face him, fortifying myself with liquid caffeine. Next time I'll tell Jack to keep the bruising to where people can't see—especially Ray.

"Motherfu—"

"Calm down." I hold up my free hand. "Not that it is any of your business, but it was consensual. I'm good."

His hands clench into fists. "Have you forgotten about Vetch Retch? You know how easy it is to fall into the cycle. It starts with one fucking blow. He apologizes. You forgive him, and he does it again. There's something about you that attracts that kind of guy. You've been there. I don't want to see you there again."

I sip my coffee, considering. I've never tied it all together, but Ray is right. First my dad, then Adam, and then Vetch. But it's not that I attract abusive men. Instead, I tolerated the abuse because I never felt I deserved better. But I'm not the same woman anymore. I have discovered other ways of dealing with my pain. I am strong, not weak; courageous, not a coward; cared for, not alone. I have found someone who accepts me, who takes what I give and returns it ten times over. And his kinky side just makes me feel free to express my kinky side, too.

"You won't see me there again. I'm different now, Ray. I'm going to leave the past in the past and move into the future."

"The past has a way of coming back to haunt you. Trust me. I know."

"Don't go there, and if you say anything to Jack or if you hurt him in any way, I will make your life a living hell, starting with the coffee and finishing with beating your sorry ass around Redemption."

Ray's lips twitch at the corners, and he pulls the door open. "Might be worth picking that fight to see you try." And then his face softens. "You know I'm here for you, Pen. No matter what. Don't feel like you can't tell me if something's going wrong. I'm your safety net."

His words make me feel warm and fuzzy inside. "Thanks, Ray. That means a lot to me."

"Good morning," Amanda calls out from reception.

I follow Ray out of the office and feel a stab of jealousy when I see Amanda in a charcoal-gray suit and a cream blouse that have been perfectly tailored to her figure. When I got my acceptance letter to law school, the first thing I did was run out and buy a suit almost exactly the same. I never got a chance to wear it, and it's been hanging in my closet for all these years with the tags still on.

We exchange good mornings and Ray jerks his chin to her door. "I got that information you asked me to get. You want to talk in your office?"

"You can talk in front of Penny," Amanda says. "I'm not hiding anything from her."

Ray twists his lips to the side, considering. "So you asked me to find out if that bastard set up cameras at Club Sin. The answer is, yeah, he did."

My heart sinks into my stomach. Oh God. Jack.

"He was using old technology. No streaming. He had a digital recorder on site instead. But sometimes old technology doesn't work so well. Wires fray. Cameras disappear. Digital files get erased…"

I steel myself not to react. We've been through this before. When someone beat Vetch Retch almost to death, Ray somehow knew about it before anyone else. But when I asked directly if he was involved, he just shrugged and looked away. Even Sia doesn't know all the roads Ray travels.

They share a look, and Amanda nods. "I hope it failed in time."

So do I.

We spend the rest of the day changing out the office stationery and briefing our web designer about the new branding. We put up new signs and flip through catalogs looking for some art pieces that reflect Amanda's style. At closing time, after the rest of the staff have gone, Jake stops by to check out the new look and asks if I would be interested in helping a few of his Redemption friends rebrand their small businesses, too.

"You should charge for your work," Ray says from the couch that Amanda now wants to replace.

"The whole 'you should charge for something you love to do for fun' thing is getting old."

He grunts from behind his newspaper. "Just sayin'."

Our front doorbell tinkles. A cold breeze gusts through the room. The office shakes when the door slams and Jack stalks into the reception area, his handsome face a mask of furious anger.

"What the fuck?" he shouts, filling the room with his rage.

My skin prickles, and I take a step back. Ray puts down his paper and slowly, carefully stands, positioning his body in front of me. Jake puts out one arm, pushing Amanda behind him.

"What's up?" Ray's voice is calm and even.

"Did you see the fucking news?" Jack pulls out his phone and punches his finger over the screen, holding it up for Ray to see.

Ray takes the phone, and his back stiffens. He shows it to Amanda and then to me.

My stomach sinks. Right under the headline "MMA Star

Outed as Sadist" is a picture of Jack. We were too late. Gerry
made good on his threat.

"We thought it was a joke," Jack snaps. "He called me up last
week and threatened to publish a picture. Damien and I went
over the entire building and couldn't find the cameras, so when
he called Damien and threatened to go to the papers if he didn't
vacate the premises in twenty-four hours, Damien told him to
fuck the hell off."

"I took the cameras," Ray mutters. "And erased the digital
recorder. He must have taken a copy of the tape."

"You represent him." Jack glares at Amanda, and then he
turns his cold, hard gaze on me. "You knew about the cameras.
You knew there was a risk. That's why you wanted me to wear
a hat. You fucking knew, and you didn't tell me. I built up a
new life here, a life where no one knew about me, a life out
of the ashes of the one I destroyed. And now I'm going to lose
this one, too."

"I'm sorry." My voice comes out in a croak and I wring
my hands. "I'm so sorry. I didn't have a choice, Jack. It was an
impossible situation. I did the best I could to keep you away."

"Like hell you did."

"Don't take it out on her," Amanda snaps. "She couldn't tell
you because I wouldn't let her. We were given that information
under attorney–client privilege, and that privilege extends to my
staff. We did what damage control we could do, but in the end,
you knew there was always a risk that someone would talk."

"Jesus Christ." He takes a step toward her, but Jake blocks
his way.

"That's as far as you go. I know you're upset, but—"

"Upset?" Jack turns and smashes his fist into the wall, leaving a huge dent beside the window. "It's the end of my career. And once this gets out on social media, my family will be destroyed. I thought you were my friends. My team…" His gaze bores into me, making me flinch. "And you." His lips curl in a snarl. "I trusted you, and you betrayed me. Just like Avery did. You took what I had to offer knowing how it would end. That's not love, Pen. Love means trust and sacrifice. You wanted to be worthy, but the one thing that makes you worthy is the choices you make, and you made the wrong fucking choice."

His words slice through my heart and coalesce into one. *Worthless.*

The story of my life.

—⁓—

"Are you gonna be okay?" Ray holds my door as I step into my car outside Amanda's office. Raindrops slide down his face, patter on his leather jacket, but he doesn't seem to mind.

"Yes. I'm fine."

"I'm worried about you." His hand clenches around the top of the door. "Why don't you come to my place? Sia's making lasagna tonight…"

"I don't think I would be good company. I just want to go home." My voice cracks, my emotions so raw I am afraid they will spill out all over the street. Ray is a good friend, but not the kind of person you want around when you're having an emotional breakdown.

"I'll call you later," he says, reluctantly. "Make sure you're okay."

"I'm a big girl, Ray. I've been through breakups before. In fact, I've been through worse and survived."

For the first few miles, after I drive away, I manage to keep it together. But then Adele's "Someone Like You" plays over the radio, and I am utterly destroyed.

Pulling into a gas station, I give myself over to emotion. Why did I think this relationship would be any different? Why did I think *I* would be different? I'm the same person. No matter how hard I try, I always screw up. I couldn't please my father. I couldn't make Adam happy. And now, I've betrayed the one person I wanted more than anything. All it would have taken was a few damn words…words I couldn't say because I was trying to do the right thing.

I start the car and drive through the rain. My normally cheery house is gray in the fading light, water streaming off the roof, trickling down the windows like tears.

Inside, I toss my wet jacket in the hallway and make my way to the bedroom. Clarice follows me, silent on her little cat feet. It has been so long since I cut, I am halfway to the night table before I remember the ritual. Cat out. Clothes off. Towels, bandages, antiseptic. But what's the point of going through all the motions? Why waste time?

Clarice watches from the hallway as I strip down to my underwear and inspect my thighs. What a mess. Jack's marks are everywhere, obliterating the scars on my legs, leaving no inch untouched. I look for my pain, and I see only him.

"Fuck." I turn from side to side, but he was thorough with his punishment. Finally, I find a small section of unmarked skin near my inner thigh. I trail my fingers over it, remembering the softness of Jack's lips when he kissed me there, the rasp of his five-o'clock shadow, and the determination in his eyes when he made me promise that before I did this again, I would come to him.

Promise me.

Yes, I promised him. But curiously I don't feel the urge to cut myself. The monsters are silent in my head. The darkness has given way to the light of the love he showed me when he marked my skin. I may have hurt him, but I had no other choice. It was a lose-lose situation from the start. At least I had a chance to tell him I loved him before I lost him and to feel his love returned to me.

Ten minutes later I am in my vehicle driving through the night. The rain has stopped. Lights flash. Horns blare. Meghan Trainor's "Like I'm Gonna Lose You" plays on the radio, and a curious calm settles over me. I know what I have to do.

I pull my vehicle to a stop in the parking lot of the Twin Peaks lookout. High above the city, with an incredible view of the Golden Gate and Bay bridges, beneath the stars, I am utterly and blissfully alone.

Pushing open my door, I am greeted with the scent of pine and a cool mountain breeze. Gravel crunches under my feet as I make my way to the low stone wall that separates the parking lot from the formidable drop into the valley below. Lights twinkle in the distance, lining the freeways, illuminating buildings and signs.

I breathe in deep, place my hands on the cold stone wall, and ground myself in the darkness.

Yes, the darkness is still with me. And I am at rock bottom all over again. It was bad with my father, worse with Adam, but now that I know what love really is, losing it is the worst of all.

But the difference is that this time I had it. I gave it. And I believe in it. But more than that, I believe in myself.

"Worthy," I say into the stillness. "Not worthless."

I pull the little green plastic case from my pocket and throw it over the cliff. After I hear the soft thud, I pull Adam's ring off my neck and throw it and the chain away, too. Adrenaline surges through my body, giving me the same rush I got the night I slit my wrist. I feel release and freedom. I feel no pain. It's not over, but I've taken a step in the right direction. And now I will take another.

I pull out my phone and call Cora. "It's Penny," I say. "Do you fancy a trip to LA?"

—〰—

RAMPAGE

2:30 a.m. I text Penny for the tenth time.

2:35 a.m. I throw a few bills on the table and walk out of the all-night diner.

2:45 a.m. I drive to Penny's house.

3:10 a.m. I arrive and park outside. Her lights are off. Her car is gone. I knock on the door, ring the bell, and peer into the window. Is she inside? Hurt? Bleeding? Will she ever forgive me for being such an ass? For the first time ever, I miss Clarice.

3:15 a.m. I jog around the back of her house and check out

her bedroom window. The curtains are open, and her bed is made. Where the fuck is she? Now that I've cooled down, I regret my overreaction. Yes, I wish she had told me, but I understand why she did what she did and how she tried her best to warn me without compromising her ethical responsibilities. My Penny has honor, which is more than I can say for most of the people I know, including me.

3:25 a.m. I sit on the front steps to await her return.

3:45 a.m. I mentally prepare to grovel and beg forgiveness. Rehearse a few lines out loud.

4:00 a.m. I flip through the news on my phone, just in case something has happened.

4:15 a.m. I check all the doors and windows for a way inside in case she is unconscious.

4:30 a.m. I call the police to find out how long a person has to be missing before I can file a missing persons report.

5:00 a.m. I call the local hospitals and ask if a woman matching Penny's appearance has been brought in.

5:30 a.m. I drive around the neighborhood looking for Penny's car. My stomach is twisted in a knot. If she doesn't show up at work, I don't know what I will do. But when I find her, I will put her over my knee and spank the shit out of her for making me worry like this…right after I grovel for being an asshole and kiss her senseless.

6:30 a.m. I arrive at Redemption. The gym is already packed. Torment is in his office. He has read the news article about my extracurricular activities. I brief him on my stupidity vis-à-vis Penny. He suggests I burn off some energy at the gym until eight o'clock when Penny starts work. I tell him to fuck off. He drags me out for a long run.

8:00 a.m. I call Penny from Torment's office. No answer.

8:05 a.m. Ray, a.k.a. the Predator, storms into Torment's office. Torment throws him out and suggests he try again with manners. Suitably chastised, the Predator knocks on the door. Torment beckons him in. The Predator crosses the room in two strides, pulls me out of the chair, and punches me in the face.

8:06 a.m. Full-on fight in Torment's office. Excellent way to relieve stress.

8:16 a.m. Renegade arrives to help Torment pull us apart. Blade Saw, Homicide Hank, Fuzzy, and Obsidian gather outside to enjoy the show. Torment says we are an embarrassment to the club.

8:30 a.m. Torment's phone rings. Amanda is worried. She wants to know if the Predator knows where Penny is. She got a text from Penny saying she wouldn't be coming to work for a couple of days. Penny is not answering calls.

8:32 a.m. Breakdown.

"Are you finished?" Torment glowers at me from behind the safety of his desk as I pause for breath after a full-on rampage around his office.

"I have to find her."

The Predator snorts a laugh from the doorway. "Find her? She's probably hiding from you, you fucking bastard. After what you pulled at the office, she's probably gone and she won't come back. She did what she had to do, and I can tell you it was killing her to keep that secret. And what do you do? You fucking give her grief for doing her job. You drag her through the mud because she chose to follow the rules. You broke her, and the minute we're out of this office, I'm gonna make sure you pay for every hurt you dished out before I go get her."

It takes my brain a few seconds to process what he has just said. "You know where she is?"

He gives me a smug look. "I can find anyone. And I'm gonna keep her far away from you."

There have been rumors floating around Redemption that the Predator was in the CIA. Of course, he has never admitted it, but now I am ready to believe, and if he can find Penny, he won't be keeping that information from me.

"Fucking bastard." I grab the Predator around the neck and shove him against the wall. But the Predator is no lightweight, and he doesn't fight by the rules. He knees me in the groin and head-butts me when I double over, replacing my emotional misery with excruciating physical pain.

"You have other problems to deal with," Torment says as I take a little breather on the floor and wonder if I'll ever be able to stand up again. "We've got a team meeting tomorrow—your team—to do some damage control. Fierce fighters are good. Kinky fighters who whip women, not so much, especially in the South and Midwest. MEFC might even break your contract, and you'll definitely lose sponsors…"

"I don't care." I stagger to my feet. "I'll deal with it after I find her."

The Predator folds his arms across his chest. "After *I* find her."

There is only one way to solve this dispute. I smack my fist into my palm and glare at the Predator. "Five minutes in the cage. If I win, I'm coming with you."

—◦◦◦—

PENNY

Ricky's Café in the University Hills district of Los Angeles is a typical college hangout. Cheap food, watered-down beer, a dodgy house band, and a youthful clientele—too youthful, from the number of underage students who have been turned away since Cora and I first sat down.

"Adam is on his way." I put down my phone and pick at the tortilla chips on the table. I am at once excited for and dreading our reunion. But after talking to Cora, I decided I need closure, and I need to understand what Adam and I had together so I can make sense of what I have lost with Jack and figure out a way to get him back.

A group of students walks through the door, laughing about one of their professors. I feel a pang of nostalgia remembering my few short university days and the promise of a future that never came to be. I don't know if I would have made a good lawyer. Over the years I have worked with Amanda, I have watched her struggle with some moral and ethical issues that I would never have wanted to face—the whole Gerry fiasco being one of them. And certainly I've never felt the kind of pride in my work as I did when I helped her rebrand her business. Maybe that's where my heart lies and I've been chasing the wrong dream.

"Can I throw a beer in his face?" Cora nurses her drink. She's been stalking a sandy-haired doctor since we arrived, and she bet me twenty dollars she can get him out of his scrubs before we leave the city.

"I think you've been hanging around Redemption too much. You never used to be violent." I follow her gaze to the bar, where the object of her affection is toying with the stethoscope around his neck. It all seems a little too forced for me. Why couldn't he change before he left the hospital? Why does he need his stethoscope in the bar?

"I never had a bestie ask me to go with her to LA to confront her bastard of an ex." She reaches across the table and gives my hand a squeeze. "I wish you'd told me all about him a long time ago, or at least when I was with Blade Saw. I would have snuck down here with a couple of the Redemption fighters and arranged for him to meet up with them in a dark alley."

"Now I know you've spent too long at Redemption."

She grins. "Maybe one day it will be me going all vigilante on some dude's sorry ass."

"You don't have to stick around when he comes in," I say. "I mean, I'm sure there are other things you'd rather be doing…" I glance over at the doctor, who has been joined by a drop-dead-gorgeous friend.

"Are you kidding me?" She stares at me, aghast. "I came on this road trip for you, babe. You shouldn't have to face your ex alone, especially after what he did to you. You're gonna get your closure, and then I'm going to help you forget Jack and start your new life with tequila shots and a couple of hot men."

"I don't want to forget Jack. I want him back. He's hurting, and I want to save him."

"Then that's what we'll do. But after you rip your ex to shreds, we'll have a couple of celebratory drinks, and spend the night getting to know the resident doctor and his friend in a very intimate way."

"What about Blade Saw?"

Her smile fades. "I messed that one up in a pretty bad way. I wish I could turn back the clock and undo that conversation I had with him. He's just so intense and protective, it kinda scared me away. I've never been with anyone like him. He gets my jokes. He likes my geek side. And he's probably the first truly decent guy I've ever met…" Her voice trails off, and she gives me a nudge. "Is that Adam?"

I look up as Adam walks toward us. Although he's thinner than he was before and a goatee slightly darker than his sandy hair now covers his weak chin, he hasn't changed much since I last saw him. Same rounded shoulders and awkward gait, same dark eyes, same lean frame, same charisma that has already drawn the attention of a few women in the bar.

"Yes, that's him." I feel nothing as I watch him. No longing, no regret, none of the thrill I used to feel whenever I saw him. Too small, too weak, too pale. My taste now seems to run to big, muscular fighters with blond hair who know how to crack a whip.

"Do we get to punch him now or later?" Cora curls her tiny hand into a fist, and I laugh, breaking the tension.

"Never. We stick with the plan. I'll introduce you, and then you make yourself scarce while I talk to him. I'll text you if I need an out."

"I'll apologize now in case I lose control of my fist." She squeezes my leg as Adam stops at the table and smiles.

"Penny." He leans down and kisses my cheeks, British style. "I was so happy you called."

I introduce him to Cora, and she glares as she slides out of the seat beside me. "Don't try that kissing thing with me," she snaps as he leans forward to do just that. "I know about you, and I'm just waiting for an excuse to give it back."

I snort a laugh. Although no longer my type, Adam is a good-looking guy, and he's not used to women brushing him off. With a puzzled glance for Cora, he slides into the seat across from me and reaches for my hand.

"I'm not here to start anything, not even a friendship." I pull my hand away, not wanting to waste any time. "I just wanted to talk."

Adam smirks, clearly not believing I could possibly want anything less than what we had before. After all, I almost killed myself over him, which would have done wonders for his already-huge ego.

"Right, love. You drove all the way down here to talk. So, let's talk. I can tell you about my field study about broken girls like you, and then we can go back to mine and—"

"Did you love me at all?"

His brow creases in a frown, and he shrugs. "Dunno. Maybe at first, although you were fucked in the head with all the cutting shit." His mouth tightens in a thin line. "Why the fuck does it matter?"

I slide my fingers over the scar on my wrist, remembering how utterly overwhelmed I was with grief. Lacking the ability to handle intense emotion, I did the only thing I knew how to do to relieve the pain. "I thought I loved you. I would have done anything for you. But I don't think you ever really loved me. You don't hurt the people you love. You don't hit them. You don't put them down. You don't tell them they're worthless."

His face hardens, his tight, angry expression so familiar a shiver runs down my spine. "What the fuck?" His hands ball into fists on the table. "Did you come here for a shag or to waste my fucking time? You want to hear the truth? Fine. The truth is no, I didn't love you. But I put up with your fucked-up shit because you were a good lay and I needed someone to cook and clean for me. And then you got into law school and started thinking you were better than me, so I had to keep reminding you of your fucking place. You didn't seem to understand that you were so broken no one else would have you. But were you grateful I took pity on you? No. You gave me attitude, and I gave it right back."

His words and his demeanor don't surprise me, but my reaction does. I imagined this moment countless times over the years. I imagined shouting at him, throwing a drink in his face, punching him the way he punched me. But now that the moment is here, I feel nothing. No sadness. No fear. No anger. No burning need for vindication or revenge. He has confirmed what I always knew. I said what I had to say. And I know now what we felt for each other wasn't love. Because I've felt love, and it takes my breath away.

"Thank you for still being a right bastard." I wrap my hand around my glass, contemplate tossing the drink in his face just to make Cora smile. "Because if you'd had even a shred of decency, I would never have come to America. I would never have changed my life. And I would never have fallen in love."

"What the fuck are you talking about?" he mutters.

"She's talking about me."

I look up, and there is Jack, his face lit up with a breathtaking smile. With a huff, I turn away. He may have tracked me down and is gearing up to punch my ex, but there's something I need to hear him say.

"You wish," I mutter.

"You love me," Jack says. "I know you do. You said it."

"Maybe I changed my mind after you were such an ass." I look over at the biggest ass in the world sitting across from me at the table and smile. "You two have a lot in common."

Jack growls, deep in his chest. "He's your ex, isn't he? Well, I'm nothing like that piece of shit."

"Fucking wanker." Adam moves to stand, and Ray appears out of nowhere and pushes him back down.

"I know who you are, and that means we're not done with you," Ray warns.

Jack gets down on one knee. He clasps my hand, presses his lips to my knuckles. "I fucked up. I said stuff I shouldn't have said and stuff I didn't mean. I know you tried. I know you couldn't say anything. And even if you had told me about the cameras, I wouldn't have stopped going to the club. I'm not the

kind of man who bows to threats. I meet my enemies head-on."
He glances over at Adam and then back to me. "Like you."

Ray barks a laugh. "You grovel good. It's not a skill I picked
up easily. I can't even count the number of times I had to sleep
on the couch until I learned how to say sorry."

I press my lips together, fight back a smile. "It's the accent.
Everything sounds sexy with that soft Tennessee twang."

"So I'm forgiven?" He gives my hand a squeeze, and I shake
my head.

"Not yet. I'm going to make you suffer first. I have a little bit
of sadist in me."

Jack leans in and whispers in my ear. "You're gonna have a
lot of sadist in you as soon as we deal with this tosser."

"Tosser?"

"I learned a few British words on the drive to find you."
He kisses my cheek, and warmth spreads through my body. "I
thought I should learn all the insults so I would understand what
you said when I found you."

Adam rolls his eyes. "What the fuck is this? Why the fuck
did you call me? Did you think I was going to feel jealous that
someone else picked up my broken piece of trash? I never
thought about you from the day I kicked you out until I started
my psych course and realized you would make a perfect case
study 'cause you're the most twisted, broken bitch I know."

Ray's face smooths into an expressionless mask. "Just con-
firming. This is the ex?"

I came here for closure, not revenge, but maybe I do want
some payback after all.

"Yes." I briefly consider listing out all the abuse I suffered at Adam's hands—emotional and physical—but it
doesn't really matter. For men like Ray and Jack, he crossed
a line with the very first punch, and his punishment will be
the same.

"The one who hurt you?" Jack's voice is deceptively mild,
but I can feel the anger rolling off his body in waves.

"Yes."

Ray turns to Cora, who has just returned to the table, an
apologetic look on her face. "We're gonna need a clear path to
the back door. Blade Saw is out there. He'll give you a hand."

Her eyes go wide. "Jimmy?"

"You think he was gonna get left behind when his woman
was on the road in a potentially dangerous situation?"

A smile tugs at her lips, and she leans in to whisper. "His
woman." And then louder she says, "Got it. I think we can
manage a distraction."

"You got two choices," Jack says to Adam after Cora slips
away. "You can walk with us out the back door, or we'll drag
you by your fucking hair."

Clearly unaware of the danger, Adam snorts a laugh. "This
has nothing to do with you. And if you think I'm going anywhere…" His voice trails off when Jack grabs his shirt and yanks
him out of his seat.

"Looks like he picked curtain number two," Jack says to Ray.

Ray gives him an evil grin. "I always like curtain number
two. Gets them warmed up for the big event."

I hear a scream and then a shout and breaking glass. The

bouncers race over to the bar, and Ray pulls Adam up and shoves him toward the back door.

"Out of the way," Jack shouts, grabbing Adam's other arm with one hand and covering his mouth with the other. "He's had too much to drink. He's gonna puke."

People scramble out of the way as Ray and Jack half-drag, half-shove a struggling Adam out the back door.

"Wait." I run up to them, my glass in my hand. "He forgot his drink." I dump the glass of beer on Adam's head, and he splutters and curses as they take him away.

"We'll meet you at your hotel," Jack shouts over his shoulder.

"How do you know where we're staying?"

"Ray."

A breathless Cora runs up to the table. "Let's go. Distraction in progress, but it's best if I'm not around for the fallout."

"What did you do?"

"The handsome doctor at the bar got the impression I was going home with him. Jimmy wasn't pleased. Punches got thrown. I don't want to be around when the best man wins." She looks to the rapidly disappearing trio in the back hallway. "You got a lot of love happening there."

My heart gives a little squeeze. I hope I can find some for-giveness, too.

Oh Jack, my lord and master

PENNY

WAKING UP WITH JACK'S MOUTH ON MY PUSSY, HIS TONGUE licking me hard, is not a bad way to greet the dawn. Throw in his naked body and the throb in my clit that means I'm about to peak, and it's damn near perfect. Lucky for me I got a hotel room with a super-king-size bed. Even luckier Jack insisted on staying with me last night.

He cups my ass with his broad hands, and I whimper. He was wound up tight after his drive with Ray, and doling out a little Redemption justice to Adam pushed him to the edge. So I let him release a little tension, sadist style. And now I'm paying the price.

"Shh." His gentle caress soothes my abused skin. "I'm not going to hurt you this morning. I'm going to love you slow and gentle."

"Do sadists do slow and gentle?" I fall back on the pillow as his tongue glides up the side of my clit.

"They do after they've acted like an ass."

His hair is soft and thick in my hands, and I tug his head back so I can stare into his eyes. "Is that your way of saying sorry?"

"Best you're gonna get." He spreads me apart, massaging my labia with his thumbs as he plunges his tongue inside me.

"Oh God." I arch my back, moving against his mouth, wanting more.

"*Oh Jack* is what you should say." He lifts me, squeezing my sore flesh as his tongue delves deep. "'Oh Jack, my lord and master, love of my life, man who is going to make me come so hard I'll beg for his cock.'"

I spread my legs wider to accommodate his broad shoulders, offer him more, everything. "How about 'Oh Jack, if you don't make me come right now, you'll be sleeping in the hallway'?"

He laughs softly, the sound vibrating against my slit. "I want to taste you while you come."

I tug on his hair, pulling him closer. "I want to come while you're tasting me."

He traces his tongue over my clit and drives his fingers inside me. So deep I can barely breathe. So hard I'm afraid to move. With measured strokes, he moves his mouth and fingers together, nudging me closer and closer to climax but always drawing back before I fall over the edge.

"Please." I rock against him, hovering on the brink of pleasure, so desperate to come I am panting.

"The sadist in me is tempted to keep you on the edge," he murmurs. "But I can't wait to taste you when you come in my mouth." He thrusts his fingers deeper, licks me harder, moves faster. Finally, I shatter, throbbing against his mouth as he draws out my orgasm with little pulses of his fingers and gentle licks of his tongue. I come for what seems to be forever, trembling, groaning, and praying Cora and Jimmy in the room next to us aren't awake.

Jack rubs his fingers over my wet pussy, and my muscles tighten. How can I want more when I've just come so hard I can barely see?

"I like this sexed-up look." He sheaths himself and then stretches out on top of me, taking his weight on his elbows. His erection is thick and heavy against my stomach, but he seems in no hurry to find his release. "I'm gonna fuck you every day so you always look all soft and sexy."

"You don't even know if I've accepted your many apologies," I tease. "Maybe I'm still pissed at the way you treated me."

He gives me a warning look. "Maybe I should spank some sense into you."

"Actually, I'm glad you reacted like you did. It gave me a chance to see my cutting was as much a habit as it was a true emotional release. I was upset, but now I know other ways to deal with the emotional pain. I even threw the box of blades away, along with Adam's ring. It felt good. Liberating."

"I'm proud of you, darlin'." He shifts his weight and slides his shaft between my thighs, pressing the head against my entrance.

"That's how you show me you're proud?" I give an indignant sniff. "You give me your cock?"

"That's how I show you I'm horny." He crushes my lips in a passionate kiss. His mouth softens, grazes against mine. "That's how I show you I'm proud."

I run my tongue over the seam of his lips. "How do you show me I'm yours?"

"I beat the shit out of anyone who hurts you or gets the fuck in my way. Then I convince you to get my name tattooed on your ass so you can be returned to me when you're lost."

I brace myself, waiting to feel his cock inside me, but he is in a rare talking mood, and all I get is the barest taste of what is to come.

"Why get a tattoo when you have Ray? How did he find me?"

"He has a friend who was able to track your license plate and credit card." He nips my earlobe, grinning when I suck in a sharp breath. "At first, he didn't want to share his information. Obviously that was unacceptable."

"Obviously." I run my hands down his back, feeling his muscles bunch and flex when he glides his cock along my slit. Teasing. Tantalizing. But not giving me what I want.

His smug expression leads me to make a wild guess that's not so wild. "How long was the fight?"

"Three and a half minutes."

"From all those bruises on your face, it looks like you took quite a few hits." I lean up and press a kiss to his bruised cheek.

"Fuck yeah. He's an underground fighter. Means he fights dirty. But I was an underground fighter too, back when Redemption was just an empty warehouse." He kisses me softly on the lips. "And I needed a win to find my girl."

"So you won?"

He twists his lips to the side. "Not exactly. I got him in a bulldog choke, but he wouldn't tap out. Torment had to end it. Ray wants a rematch when we get back."

"Ray doesn't take defeat lightly. Actually, I don't think he has ever been defeated."

His expression becomes thoughtful. "It wasn't until I was in the vehicle coming down here, listening to him curse up a storm, that I realized no one at Redemption treated me any differently when I showed up at the gym. I'd hidden that side of myself, carried the shame for so long, I didn't know how I would cope. But they accepted me just like you did. So now everyone knows I'm a sadist. Maybe it will deal with the problem my manager had with me being perceived as a nice guy."

An idea takes root at the back of my mind, but before I can tell him, he sits back on the covers and flips me over, positioning me on all fours, my chest down on the covers and my ass in the air.

"Don't waste any time asking if I want to be sexed up in this position." I look back over my shoulder and glare. "See a woman you want to fuck. Flip her over and do the deed."

"Is that supposed to be a joke?" He shoves my legs apart with his thick thigh and leans over me to press his lips to my shoulder.

"We'll see who's laughing when I run off with another man who doesn't treat me like a toy."

Jack laughs. "Not gonna happen."

"No?"

He feathers kisses across my shoulder to my nape and then down my spine, making me shiver in delight. "You'll always choose me," he continues.

"How do you know?" Tightness builds inside me, heat pooling

in my stomach. I slide my hand between my legs and slick a finger over my clit, seeking the release I so desperately need.

Jack gives a low growl and presses me down, cheek to the bed. He grabs my hands and yanks them back, securing them at the base of my spine. "No one can give you what I can give you. No one can hurt you the way I hurt you. Do you know why?"

I swallow hard. Tremble. "Why?"

"Because no one can love you the way I love you."

Hope flares bright in my heart. "You love me?"

"Yeah, darlin'. I love you, and now I'm going to show you by making you scream my name so Blade Saw and Cora next door know it, too." His hand cracks across my ass, sending fire skittering across my skin. Before I can catch my breath, he fills me roughly, slamming his pelvis against my ass. Pleasure ripples through me, and I lose the last threads of that thought to focus on the feel of him inside me, filling me with his heat. He alternates thrusts with slaps, pulling me against him as he pumps into me hard and fast.

Pain and pleasure become one. He slides his hand over my hip and pinches my clit. With a low, guttural groan, I clench around him. My climax hits me like an explosion, and I cry out, lost in a pleasure so intense I am dizzy with the rush.

"Fuck. I'm going to come." Jack releases my hands and plunges deeper, thrusts harder, digs his fingers into my tender ass. He stiffens and chokes back a shout as he throbs his release inside me.

He collapses over me, kisses my back, my shoulder, nuzzles my neck, threads his fingers through mine on the bed.

"I have an idea," I whisper.

Jack gives a satisfied rumble. "I have lots of ideas when it comes to you."

"I mean I have an idea to save you."

He drops to his side, turning me so I am cradled against him. "You already saved me."

"Well, now I'm going to save you again."

26

Sadist! Sadist! Sadist!

RAMPAGE

"Where is she?" I stare at the door to the Redemption meeting room, willing Penny to appear. I've been dragged over the coals for the last half hour in the team meeting, as everyone from my agent to my manager to the MEFC crisis team fights about the best way to salvage my career.

"Don't worry." Torment pats me on the back. "She'll be here. Penny isn't the kind of person who would let you down."

She's also not the kind of person to give a secret away, so I have no idea what she has planned for today that she promises will save my career.

Finally, the door opens, and Penny walks in. She's wearing a fitted gray suit and a cream blouse, her hair in a neat ponytail. Damn, my girl looks good. Sexy and professional and walking with all the confidence in the world.

After I make the introductions, she hooks her computer up to the projection screen, faces the table, and smiles.

"Meet Sadist." She turns on the computer, and there I am, in the middle of a fight, my face twisted in a snarl as I bend my opponent's arm into an impossible angle. "Is he a true sadist? Are the rumors true? Does his nice guy exterior hide a monster inside?" She flips between images of me drinking beer at Score with the team, talking with the seniors in one of what have now become our weekly visits to Ambleside, and holding up a victory fist with an unconscious opponent at my feet.

Now she flashes some logos on the screen. The word *Sadist* written in red, dripping blood on a black background. Fucking awesome.

"Now that Jack has gone pro, he needs a new image. Rampage was good for the amateurs, but moving into the top ranks of the pros takes more than talent. We need to build up his reputation. People need to be scared just hearing his name. So, to get a feel for the market, we spread a few rumors that he might be a true sadist, positioned him in places where suggestive pictures might be taken. And, as you saw, the media ate it up. Now we need to run with it. We rebrand him as Sadist. We keep people guessing. We build up a cult of fear. Maybe it's true and he enjoys making his opponents bleed. Maybe he feeds off their pain. Maybe he spends his weekends whipping people in underground sex clubs. Maybe it's part of the act. They'll never know."

She outlines a detailed marketing and branding plan. More pictures. Logos—some with whips and chains, me crushing a skull in my hand, fierce faces and lots of blood.

Torment leans over and whispers, "Fucking genius. If I wasn't with Makayla, I might steal her away."

"Friend or no friend," I growl, "I'd break your fucking neck."

My manager, James, claps at the end of Penny's presentation and pronounces it a kick-ass plan. More claps follow. The MEFC crisis team has a brief discussion and gives her proposal the thumbs-up.

"So, is it true?" one of them asks.

"The fact you had to ask that question just shows how effective the campaign can be." Penny smiles through her evasive answer, never losing her cool. That's my girl up there. Rocking the entire room. Saving my ass. She is magnificent.

"What agency are you with?" James asks her.

For the first time since she walked into the room, Penny stumbles. "I…"

"Worthington Communications," I say. "They are a boutique agency based in the Lower Haight." I grab my phone and send a quick text to Renegade, letting him know I'll be renting out the top floor of the building that houses Amanda's office.

"We'll put them on file," he says. "Very impressive work."

"She's an impressive woman." I swallow past the lump in my throat.

And she's mine.

—◠◠◠—

PENNY

"Sadist!"

"Sadist!"

"Sadist!"

All heads turn as Jack enters the Kezar Pavilion for his first professional MMA fight as Sadist. Through the shouts and cheers of the near-capacity crowd, I can hear the voices of the Redemption fighters, come to cheer on the most popular member of the team. But no one is cheering louder than me.

"You did an amazing job," Amanda says, holding up her phone to snap a picture. "The logo, the shirt, the cape… Everyone is talking about him. They all want to know…is he a sadist for real?"

"His family kept asking him that when we went down to Tennessee," I shout over the cheers. "I think they hoped his old girlfriend had been wrong and it was all made up." I sigh, remembering our trip and how impressed his family was at his success in the MMA world. How they couldn't know what their son did for a living was beyond me, but I made it my mission to make sure they understood just how hard he had worked and exactly what he had achieved.

Convincing them that his kink didn't make him a different person was a harder sell than rebranding him at the team meeting—especially when that Avery bitch kept insisting he was sick—but we won them over in the end. Not only because they missed him and just wanted an excuse to get their family back together, but also because they saw us together in what appeared to be a normal loving relationship. Of course, after the lights went out and we went to bed, "normal" went out the window.

"He's loving this." Cora says, nestled in the crook of Blade Saw's arm. "Look at that scowl. He's really putting on a good show."

"He's probably imagining how I'm going to be spending my nights taking marketing courses instead of jumping into bed with him," I say. "And the weekends fixing up my new office."

Amanda looks over and frowns. "Don't mention the new office. I'll never be able to replace you."

"At least you're going to get rid of Ray's blue couch." I offered to take the couch, and Ray with it, so Amanda could buy new furniture consistent with her new look. "I'll just be upstairs. And I got you a new client to make up for losing Gerry. Damien's the bomb. You're going to love him."

Poor Gerry had it rough after the article about Jack hit the stands. What was meant to be a warning to the rest of the people he planned to blackmail almost became a death sentence. His office was ransacked, surveillance equipment destroyed, and he was found badly beaten in an alley not far from Club Sin. Witnesses saw six men and a woman in the vicinity, but no identities were confirmed. However, after the beating, Gerry had a change of heart. As a gesture of "goodwill," he signed the title of the building over to Damien and then retired to Barbados. I had a strong suspicion his gesture of goodwill was made under duress and an even stronger suspicion about who led the attack. But I knew better than to ask.

Jack stops and poses for the cameras. A shiver runs down my spine as I drink in all six feet two inches of my gorgeous sadist who has been killing it in training for the last three months. His opponent, Scorpion, is in for some pain tonight. And I would know. I'm standing on my chair for a reason—and it isn't just to cheer my man on or because I am wearing his family ring around my neck.

"She's back on the chair." Amanda sighs. "Pen, don't you remember what happened last time?"

Yes, I do. And that first moment when I saw Jack as more than a friend is one of my fondest memories. "You think anyone is going to knock Sadist's woman off a chair? The other fighters are terrified of him. At the weigh-in he took a step toward Scorpion, and the dude almost wet his shorts."

My voice trails off when Jack makes an unexpected detour that will take him right past our seats. Heart pounding, I scream his name and pump my fist in the air.

Adrenaline shoots through me, and I get the rush I've been craving all day. My heart beats a little faster, my vision becomes a little clearer, my smile grows a little wider, and all my stress fades away.

Jack stops in front of us. His gaze lingers on me. His dark eyes warm, and his scowl fades. He is Redemption's gossip king, everyone's best friend, all-around nice guy, fighter, sadist, and the other half of my soul. He is darkness, and he is light. His mask is gone, and the real Jack is free.

My breath catches in my throat as he stares at me. I know that darkness. Understand it. Because beneath my pearls, pastels, and pretty clothes, I share that darkness, too.

He reaches up and kisses me, his hand behind my neck, his lips soft on mine. Cameras swing toward us, showing close-ups on the big screens. Lights flash, the crowd cheers. He loves me. And he's not afraid to let the world know.

"You got the present I left for you?" he whispers.

"Yes, I did."

"You wearing them?"

"Yes. And they hurt so good."

"Are we gonna have some fun tonight?" He steps back and licks his lips, a predator about to feast. Or a sadist about to inflict a whole lot of pain.

"Only if you win."

"I already won, darlin'. There is no better prize than you."

Acknowledgments

Thanks to my amazing editor, Cat Clyne, and the Sourcebooks Casablanca team for whipping Rampage's story into shape (ha-ha). Thanks to my agent, Laura Bradford, for all her support; my beta reader, Casey Britton; and the awesome Danielle Gorman, without whom I would have no time to write. And thanks to my Redemption fans who love my sexy fighters and begged for Rampage's story. You guys rock! And, John, you definitely don't want to read this one. Or maybe you do…

About the Author

After graduating from law school, *New York Times* and *USA Today* bestselling author Sarah Castille practiced law on the West Coast, and then with one of the world's largest law firms in London, England, for many years. She obtained a master's degree in law and traveled extensively before returning to Canada, where she began writing novels about alpha males and the women who tame them. After her first book, *Legal Heat*, won prizes in nine Romance Writers of America chapter contests, Sarah decided to take a break from the practice of law to pursue a writing career. She is the author of the Redemption series and writes contemporary and erotic romance and romantic suspense.

Sarah's books have been listed as *Publishers Weekly*'s Top Ten Picks and Best Summer Reads, Amazon's Best Romance Books of the Year, and have appeared at number one on Amazon's Erotic Romance bestseller lists, as well as winning the Holt Medallion and being selected as "Must Read Erotic Romance of the Year."

Sarah lives with her husband and three children on Vancouver Island, where she is currently working on her next novel.

AGAINST THE ROPES

First in the smokin' hot Redemption series from *New York Times* and *USA Today* bestselling author Sarah Castille

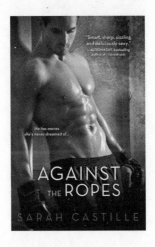

He scared me. He thrilled me. And after one touch, all I could think about was getting more…

Makayla never thought she'd set foot in an elite mixed martial arts club. But if anyone needs a medic on hand, it's these guys. Then again, at her first sight of the club's owner, she's the one feeling breathless.

The man they call Torment is all sleek muscle and restrained power. Whether it's in the ring or in the bedroom, he knows exactly when a soft touch is required and when to launch a full-on assault. He always knows just how far he can push. And he's about to tempt Makayla in ways she never imagined…

"Fifty Shades of Grey meets Fight Club."

—RT Book Reviews

For more Sarah Castille, visit:
www.sourcebooks.com

IN YOUR CORNER

New York Times and USA Today bestselling author
Sarah Castille's sizzling Redemption series continues

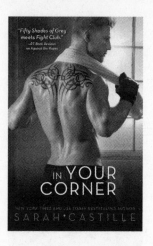

*Primitive. Primal. His need speaks to me. I tighten my grip on his neck
and rock up to kiss him. He takes over. His kiss is hard and demanding.
"Mine." His voice is raw, savage and for a moment I truly believe he may
lose control.*

Two years ago, Jake and Amanda were going hot and heavy.
But when Jake wanted more, Amanda walked away. Jake
immersed himself in mixed martial arts, living life on the edge.
But that didn't dull the pain of Amanda's rejection–until a chance
encounter throws them together.

Jake is darker, sexier, and impossible to resist. As their chemistry
builds, Amanda's not sure if she can stay in control, or if she's
finally willing to let him claim her body and soul.

> *"Castille's follow-up to the excellent* Against
> the Ropes *doesn't pull its punches."*
>
> **—Publishers Weekly, STARRED Review**

For more Sarah Castille, visit:
www.sourcebooks.com

FULL CONTACT

Winner of the 2016 HOLT MEDALLION
Award for outstanding literary fiction

Third in the Redemption series from *New York Times*
and *USA Today* bestselling author Sarah Castille

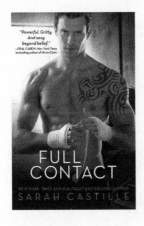

Ray wraps his arms around me and holds me tight as if something terrible has happened and he doesn't want to let me go.

Full Contact. This is how Ray speaks when his emotions overwhelm him. I melt into his stillness. His body is hot and hard, his breath warm on my neck. He smells of leather and sweat, sex and sin. Nothing can tear me away.

Sia O'Donnell can't help but push the limits. She secretly attends every underground MMA fight featuring the Predator, the undisputed champion. When he stalks his prey in the ring, Sia is mesmerized. He is dominant and dangerous and every instinct tells her to run.

Every beautiful thing Ray "The Predator" touches he knows he'll eventually destroy. Soft, sweet, and innocent, Sia is the light to Ray's darkness and completely irresistible. From the moment he lays eyes on her, he knows he's going to have to put his dark past behind him to win her body and soul…

"Powerful. Gritty. And sexy beyond belief. Sarah is a true master!"

**——Opal Carew, *New York Times* bestselling author
of the Mastered By series**

For more Sarah Castille, visit:
www.sourcebooks.com

UNDER HER SKIN

First in an exciting dark contemporary series from debut author Adriana Anders

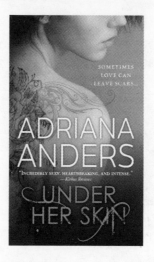

A dark relationship left Uma alone and on the run. Beneath her clothing, she hides a terrible secret—proof of her abuse, tattooed on her skin in a lurid reminder of everything she's survived.

Caught between a brutal past and an uncertain future, Uma is reluctant to bare herself to anyone, much less a rough ex-con whose rage drives him in ways she doesn't understand. But beneath his frightening exterior, Ivan is gentle. Warm. Compassionate. And just as determined to heal Uma's broken heart as he is to destroy the monster who left his mark scrawled across her delicate skin.

RECKLESS HEARTS

It's three alpha men and a baby in this steamy contemporary romance series

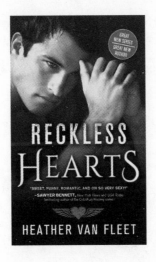

Addison Booker needs a job desperately. She shows up to interview for a nanny position only to find the sexy, cocky man she can't get out of her head. Collin Montgomery knows hiring her is a bad idea—she's the hottest, smartest woman he's ever met and they disagree about almost everything—but Addison is so good with little Chloe. And there's no substitute for chemistry, right?

"An emotional, heartfelt, and absolutely beautiful story. I wanted each character to be my best friend."

—Jennifer Blackwood, *USA Today* bestselling author

For more Heather Van Fleet, visit:
www.sourcebooks.com

BODY SHOP BAD BOYS

These rough-and-tumble mechanics live fast
and love hard.

**By Marie Harte, *New York Times* and
USA Today Bestselling Author**

Test Drive
Johnny Devlin's a charmer with a checkered
past. He's had his eye on bartender Lara
Valley for ages, but she's rejected him more
than once. That doesn't mean he won't come
to her aid when some dirtbag mauls her.

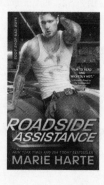

Roadside Assistance
Foley might look like a bad idea, but
underneath, he's all gentleman. Too bad Cyn
Nichols isn't buying it. What's a bad boy to
do when the goddess of his dreams won't give
him the time of day?

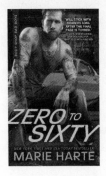

Zero to Sixty
Hot-headed Sam finds a sense of purpose in rescuing strays. When the puppy who's stolen his heart runs into blond, beautiful Ivy, Sam can't help hoping she'll take in one more stray—him—for good.

"*Readers will swoon at the romantic gestures and fan themselves during the steamy love scenes.*"

—RT Book Reviews for *Roadside Assistance*

ROCK-N-INK

A steamy contemporary romance series where ambitious, conservative suits and inked-up, edgy rockers fall in love.

By Kasey Lane

Beautiful Crazy

When businesswoman Kevan fights Mason, the smoldering CEO of a mega PR corporation, to sign a hot new rock group, temperatures scorch in a battle for the band and the bedroom.

Beautiful Mess

When attorney Jami Dillon strides into the conference room to meet her new client, she's shocked by an all-too-familiar figure. Jackson Paige was, in fact, Jax Pain, the drummer of Manix Curse. The tall, tattooed, sexy-as-hell hookup from law school—who also broke her heart.

"Get ready for your new auto-buy author! Kasey Lane's debut hits all the high notes."

—**Megan Crane, *USA Today* bestselling author**